Also by Brenda Cooper

Edge of Dark
Beyond the Waterfall Door
The Creative Fire
The Diamond Deep
Mayan December
The Silver Ship and the Sea
Reading the Wind
Wings of Creation
Building Harlequin's Moon (with Larry Niven)

CRACKING the SKY

CRACKING
the SKY

BRENDA
COOPER

FAIRWOOD PRESS
Bonney Lake, WA

CRACKING THE SKY

A Fairwood Press Book
August 2015
Copyright © 2015 Brenda Cooper

Fairwood Press
21528 104th Street Court East
Bonney Lake, WA   98391
www.fairwoodpress.com

Cover and book design by
Patrick Sweson

ISBN: 978-1-933846-50-7
First Fairwood Press Edition: August 2015
Printed in the United States of America

Dedicated to all of the editors out there. I appreciate those of you who bought these stories, and also every rejection. Together, your choices influence who we become.

ACKNOWLEDGEMENTS

Every book is ultimately created by one person, held up on the hands of a willing crowd of helpers. For this collection, I want to first and foremost thank Patrick Swenson for suggesting it and for pushing me along until I actually did it.

I also want to thank Joy Adiletta, who read through the ARC and hunted down mistakes.

As always, I'm grateful for my family. I also want to thank every one of my readers. You are the most important people in every way.

CONTENTS

HUMAN FUTURES

by James Van Pelt

Every year, Brenda Cooper attends a writers retreat at the Rainforest Writers Village in Lake Quinault, Washington. The rainforest is an excellent venue for writing. Cell phone reception is spotty, and the sole internet connection is slow and unreliable. The environment stands as a challenge to the high-tech, connected world that most of us live in. But it is in this throwback, slow-paced venue that Brenda's writing soars into possible futures where robot dogs compete with flesh and bone ones on the battlefield, electronic nannies raise a little girl, an autistic physics genius communes with parallel universes, and brain to brain remote viewing brings to life the reality of third world lives.

Of course, the rainforest retreat is only a few days of the year. As far as I can tell, Brenda writes all the time, whether it's at a writers retreat, or after work for the City of Kirkland, Washington, where she's the city's Chief Information Officer (doesn't that sound like a *Star Trek* bridge officer position?), or in between gigs as a public speaker, or when she's not blogging in her role as a futurist. Brenda has a free-range mind. I don't think what's going on around her, whether it's the hiss of a rainforest afternoon shower, or the bustle of a busy city office, impacts what's going on inside her head.

Happily for us, she shares her head, as she has in the outstanding collection of pure science fiction short stories you are holding right now. Here's what you get with Brenda Cooper short stories: rigorous, interesting extrapolations about our possible futures. One of this genre's greatest gifts is in its capacity to ask "what if?" For Brenda, some of the what-ifs include a way we might care for special needs children that enriches their lives, how life in an underwater city might present unusual challenges (and unusual allies—there's this great bit about whale sentience . . . whoops! Almost got into a plot spoiler there), what a life-threatening tragedy on Pluto might feel like, and how a truly long distance relationship between an earthbound woman and an isolated astronaut might play out.

Brenda "gets" the exploratory nature of science fiction. Her stories are intrinsically about their science fictional settings. They aren't stories with tired, traditional, familiar science fiction tropes. I think you can read Brenda's stories just for the ideas. There's a reason that part of her day job is being a futurist.

But Brenda's speculations about the future are not the sole payoff by a long shot. The second gift in these stories is their heart. Each story paints a picture about human relationships that are emotional, passionate and vital. One of my favorite stories in the collection is "Blood Bonds." I'm not going to spoil any part of it, but I can tell you that I haven't read a story that tied so closely intricate and fascinating scientific speculation about consciousness and artificial intelligence with such a delicately rendered portrait of a pair of sisters.

She does this in all of the stories! If you want a quick taste, skip straight to "My Grandfather's River." Go ahead. I'll give you a minute.

Back so soon? See what I mean?

So much in literature lately seems tied up in the long form. Big, fat fantasies fill the bookstore's shelves. Multi-book series are the rage. However, science fiction's roots lie in the short story. I think of Isaac Asimov, Robert Heinlein, Alice Sheldon writing as James Tiptree Jr., Zenna Henderson, and so many others who lured young minds with short stories. Remember those great, old magazines: *Galaxy, Worlds of If, Omni,* and *Fantastic Stories?* Brenda would be at home between any of their covers. Oh, Brenda's written her share of novels too (I particularly like *Creative Fire*). She knows narrative forms, but we're lucky readers because Brenda can go short, too.

What you'll find here is Brenda's masterful blend of hard-edged speculation tied to insightful evocations of the human spirit.

You are all so fortunate: you get to read these stories for the first time.

PART ONE
On a Future Earth

The ROBOT'S GIRL

The door's silent slide still surprised me, even after Aliss and I'd been moving boxes into our new garage and piling them in unruly heaps for two days. Hair stuck to my neck as sweat ran down the small of my back and the backs of my knees. Our real estate agent had told me it never got hot here, but apparently she lied about the weather as easily as she lied about the closing costs. So we were too broke for household help and hot from humping boxes. But we were here.

Home.

And done working for the evening.

I gathered up a cold beer from the gleaming fridge, which opened and closed for me the same way the front door did, eerily quiet and efficient. I'd grown up with doors you opened and closed with human muscle. My last house had been built-green when that meant saving energy instead of producing it. Trust humanity not to waste anything free when you can use a lot of it.

The high ceilings and three tall stories made the house seem like it yearned to join the cedar and fir forest. It made me feel like a pretender. We'd bought here, across the lake from Seattle, with returns from a few good investments and a dead aunt. The sliding door opened for me (of course). It allowed me outside onto a deck that glowed honey-colored in a late afternoon sun-bath. No matter how pretty the deck and the house and the forest around us, the woman on the deck was prettier than all of it. Aliss'd caught her dark hair up in a ponytail that cascaded almost to her waist, thick as my wrist both top and bottom. Sweat shined her olive skin, and she smelled like work and coffee and the rich red syrah she held in her right hand. She pointed at the neighbors, a good three house-lengths away from us. "In five minutes, I've seen two humanoid bots over there."

"So they're rich. Maybe we can borrow one for gardening." Not that I minded gardening; dirty nails felt good.

"There's another one."

The curiosity in her voice demanded I stop and look. A silver-skinned female form bent over a row of bright yellow ceramic flowerpots on the deck outside the three-story house, plucking dead pink and purple flower-heads from a profusion of living color, dropping her finds into a bucket as silver as her hands. I sucked down half the beer, watching. Counting. Three bots. One outside. Two or three little ones moving around the house, the ones that didn't look like people. Families in our newly acquired income bracket might have one of the big humanoid ones, but only if they needed a nanny more than flashy cars or designer clothes. Maybe a handful of robovacs and robodisposers and robowashers, like the ones sitting on a pallet in our garage right now.

"I haven't seen any people," Aliss mused.

"Maybe they work."

Her eyes stayed narrow, her jaw tight and jumping a little back by her ear, and she rocked back and forth on the balls of her feet. I knew what that meant. "Guess we're talking a walk."

"Got to meet the neighbors, right?"

I'd actually been thinking about sliding into the hot tub naked and having another beer. But this was our first house together, and I wanted her to be happy. "Let's go introduce ourselves."

Our driveway gave under our feet, the heat drawing up a hint of its origin as old tires, but not so much it overwhelmed the loamy forest dirt spiced with cedar. Aliss and I turned onto the road, hand in hand. Meeting the neighbors felt like a picket fence choice, like something my mom would do. We turned off the road onto their driveway.

Red light lasered across our bare shins. "Stop now."

Aliss drew in a sharp breath and squeezed my hand before letting it go and freezing in place.

"State your business." I followed the voice to a spot about fifteen feet in front of me, and about knee-high. The guard-bot was the same pebbly-dark color as the driveway, cylindrical, with more than two feet, and not standing still, which is what kept me from counting feet.

This bot was neither pretty nor humanoid. In fact, a bright blue circle with a red target stickered in its side screamed weapons.

I talked soft to it. "We're the new neighbors. We came to introduce ourselves."

Its voice sounded cheerfully forced, like a slightly tinny villain in a superhero movie. "Aliss Johnson and Paul Dina. Twenty-seven and twenty-eight, respectively. You have been here for precisely sixty-seven hours . . ."

I waved it silent before it got around to checking our bank balance and running us off entirely. "So, then you know we're harmless. We'd like to meet your owners."

"They are not home."

Aliss still hadn't moved, but she asked it, "When will they come back?"

It turned a full 360, as if someone else might have snuck up behind it, and then said, "Please back up until you are off the property line."

We backed, all the nice warm fuzziness of being in a new home turned sideways. After we'd turned away from the house and the bot, my back itched. I whispered in Aliss's ear, "Not very nice neighbors."

She grunted, her brow furrowed.

"Maybe we should jump in the hot tub."

She gave me a pouty, unhappy look. "They were watching us."

I didn't remind her she'd been watching them. I just hugged her close, still whispering, "This is our first night here. Let's enjoy it."

She stopped me right there in the middle of the road, at the edge of our own property line, and nuzzled my neck. When she looked up at me, the slight distraction in her gaze told me I wouldn't have all of her attention easily. I made a silent vow to figure out a way to get it all, and started my devious plot by sliding my hand down the small of her back and pulling her close into me. We walked home with our hips brushing each other.

The next morning, warmth from her attention still lingered in the relaxed set of my shoulders and the way my limbs splayed across the bed like rubber. Birds sang so loudly they might have been recorded. I tried to separate them, figure out how many species must be outside.

"Honey?" she called. With some reluctance I opened my eyes to find Aliss standing on the small deck outside the bedroom, one of my shirts her only clothing. Fog enveloped the treetops outside our third-story window, tinting the morning ghostly white and gray. "Will you come here?"

Since she was wearing my shirt, I pulled on my jeans and joined her, drinking in a deep whiff of us smelling like each other. Although we couldn't see the house from any of our windows, the deck had a nearly direct view into the robot house's kitchen, the fog and one thin tree trunk the only obstructions. Three silvery figures moved about inside of a square of light that shone all the more brightly for the fog.

I put a hand on Aliss's shoulder, leaning into her. "Since robots don't need food, there must be people there."

"Don't you see her?"

I squinted. At the table, a girl sat sideways to us, spooning something from her bowl into her mouth. She wore a white polo shirt and brown shorts, and her blond hair was curled back artfully behind her ears and tied with a gold bow. She belonged in a commercial. Across from her, one of the robots appeared to be holding an animated conversation with her.

"How old do you think she is?" Aliss asked.

She still had a child's lankiness and a flat chest, but she was probably near as tall as Aliss. "Ten? Twelve?"

"She's alone."

"You don't know that." Although her observations were often uncanny.

"It explains the nasty-bots. They were protecting her. But it's not right."

"Her mom or dad will show up any second."

Aliss crossed her arms over her chest and gave me the look. "No cars, still. No movement except the girl. No other lights on. She's alone. It's a crime to leave a girl that age alone."

I glanced back at the window, where one robot was clearly conversing with the girl and another was bringing her a fresh glass of juice. "She's not alone."

All I got for that was the look again. I tugged her close to me. "Come on, let's eat. She must have parents."

"I hope so." Aliss let me pull her gaze away from the bright square of window and its even brighter occupants.

Days later, we sat on new recycled-sawdust Adirondack chairs we'd ordered for the bedroom deck. The table between us held two coffee cups and two pairs of binoculars and a camera. Aliss hadn't moved from her chair for two hours. She worried at her beautiful lower lip. "No parents. No people. Not for five days."

"They'll come." Not that I believed it any more. "Maybe there's someone living there who never comes into the kitchen."

"That's lame."

"I'm reaching. I want my girl back."

"Don't be selfish."

At least she had a little tease in her voice when she said it.

We met the neighbors—not at the robot house, but across the street. William and Wilma Woods. Really. They were at least eighty. Their kids hired bot-swarms to clean up their yard for them, but obviously did nothing for the inside of the house. The Woods probably couldn't see well enough to tell if there was a purple people eater living in the robot house, and when we asked about it, William pulled his lips up into his hollow cheeks and said, "The new house? I dunno who lives there. We don't get out much."

He meant us. We lived in the new house.

The house on the other side of us from the robot house stood empty-eyed and vacant, with a traditional security system that included signs and warnings of proximity detectors. Forest took over for half a mile on the far side of the robot before it yielded a barn-shaped house next to a barn with a corral and three swaybacked horses. The offbeat collection of direct neighbors made me wonder if we'd picked the right house to buy. The robot house was clearly our problem, at least in the world according to Aliss. And since she was my world, it mattered to me. In fact, after days of watching the little girl play ball with robots and eat with robots and study at the kitchen table with the help of robots, I was beginning to worry all on my own. Surely the kid needed a mom or a brother or a dog or something. Something warm.

I have some skill with the nets, but all that got me was frustrated. A holding company owned the house. A public company owned that company and a few hundred more. It spread wealth—a lot more than this house—through thousands of shareholders. Not a very unique tax dodge for second or third homes. All it told me was the girl—or her family—or the freaking robots—had money. Which I already knew. I grit my teeth and kept plugging while Aliss brought me coffee and rubbed my neck. We saw the girl bent over the table studying every day, but I couldn't find her in public school, online or offline. No kids of her description had been reported missing anywhere in the country.

We unpacked the house, all except the pallet of robostuff, which Aliss steadfastly ignored, and two boxes of art too lame for the new house.

The third week, I woke up in the middle of the dark and texted a friend in the reserves, who brought his night vision goggles. She was warm—and alone. Human.

Satellite shots from the city never showed a car, although they did show the girl out playing robot ball twice.

Aliss made up names for her (Colette, Annie, Lisa, Barbie) and drew her picture. Not that we didn't do our jobs (me—investing advice, her marketing), or make dinner, or make love. But the spare time that might have been nights out or movies all went to the robot's girl.

It wasn't like we wanted kids. But she started to haunt our dreams for no good reason except that we were human, and she was surrounded by beings who weren't. We walked by the house at least once a day. Always we saw the guard-bots. There were three of them. One too many for the two of us. Or maybe three too many. We hadn't degenerated into breaking and entering. After all, the robot's girl laughed and played. Her hair was neat and her clothes ironed.

We walked, and watched, almost every day. Delivery trucks came and went from time to time, but no regular cars stayed, no friends, no family. Just groceries, and occasionally, bags or boxes that might hold shoes or clothes or books.

Fall began to cool and shorten the nights. We were on our lunch break, walking out with the first yellow and orange leaves scrunching under our feet, the sky a nearly-purple-blue above us. After we passed the house and entered the stretch of forest on the far side, Aliss was silent for a long time before she said, "She's too good. A kid her age should play tricks and make faces and all that stuff. She doesn't do that."

"Do robots have a sense of humor?"

"Shit. She's been like this forever." Her voice rose. "I keep hoping her mom is on vacation, and she's coming back. She's not. The robots really are raising her."

She fell silent, her feet making soft sliding steps on the road, her breathing faster than it should be for our pace, her lips a tight line in her face. "I'm going in."

"A little melodramatic, aren't we? You sound like a TV cop show."

She swung around in front of me and stopped, blocking my way, head tilted up toward me. "It's like she's in jail. But she doesn't know it. What if they've raised her forever? What if that little girl doesn't know what a human hug feels like? What if . . . what if she thinks she's inferior to those robots? What are they teaching her?"

"Shhhhhh." I took her shoulders lightly. She felt like a bird. "We have to keep perspective. Not get thrown in jail for breaking and entering. The cops won't even go in—you called them."

She stared at me, eyes wide, then snapped her mouth shut.

"I'm sorry, we can't. There's nothing illegal about robot babysitters."

"They're not babysitters." She thumped her fists against my chest and her breath overtook her ability to speak and she actually quivered.

I pulled her in and stoked her hair. "We have to find another way."

She leaned back and smacked me again with her fists, hard enough it stung a little, and might leave a little bruise. "You just don't care!" Now she was hissing at me. Not screaming in case the damned robos heard, but she wanted to, the sound building up in her and coming out in shakes and deep out-breaths. She looked deep in my eyes, probing me, looking for something.

Whatever it was, she didn't find it. She turned and stalked up the street, stiff-backed, unbound hair flying behind her, her shirt the only yellow in the green and gray and black and brown of the forest.

I should have chased her. But I was trying not to laugh; Aliss seeing me laugh would have been worse than me standing there holding it in. Not that it was funny. She'd just overreacted so much it didn't seem real. Two minutes before, we'd been walking happily beside each other.

I didn't move until she was opposite the house. I should have chased her, should have run as fast as two feet can go. I should have known she meant exactly what she said.

While she hurried up the road, arms swinging, I stood still, trying for emotional control. She turned sharp left at the driveway and kept stalking, heading for the front door. She was small then, far enough away I could see her but couldn't expect to run up and catch her. She looked beautiful and terrible, brave in the face of her stupidity.

One bot moved in front of her, the line of its squat body hard to make out except when movement gave it ghost-like visibility. Another one seemed to float toward her, its body easier to see as it moved between me and a green hedge starred with small white flowers.

I shook myself loose and bounded toward her, waving my hands over my head as if the guard-bots would decide I was more threatening even though I stood on a public road and Aliss was doing a full frontal assault.

They ignored me.

Red lines illuminated her jeans, bisected her knees, her calf, above her ankles.

I raced all-out, finally driven to ignore the property line.

She stepped onto the front stoop and jerked, then collapsed, her long hair a curtain across her face. I almost made it to her side when I felt the sharp jolt of a taser and my mouth was too busy being stiff to let out my curse. I went to jelly, crumpling just too far away to touch her. I didn't lose consciousness, but my head had a muzzy shockiness and my body didn't really want to move right away, even though my heart was willing.

The guard-bots withdrew a respectful distance.

The door opened.

A silver form in Dockers and an Izod T-shirt bent down and gazed at Aliss, an inquisitive expression on its face.

The guard-bots whirred off, surely going back to watch for more nosy neighbors.

Aliss sat up, looking the robot in the eyes, which were like tiny camera-irises set inside lids with no lashes. From the distance of our third-story porch, their eyes had looked nearly human, but here the emotion came from subtle changes in the shape of the smooth, silver face. Robos can come with human-colored skins and rose lips, and blond or dark or even gray hair, but whoever chose the bots for this house liked them to look like science fictional beings. I'd seen similar models up close at home shows, except they'd looked even less real, maybe because people in bad suits were selling them like refrigerators.

This one had an air of authority.

"You were trespassing," it stated convincingly. It glanced at me, as if making sure I knew I was trespassing, too.

I nodded at it. "Sorry. We're the neighbors."

"Yes." It looked back at Aliss. "We have been watching you watch us. That's why Jilly told the bots not to kill you."

Good for Jilly. I struggled to sit up, pulled my hands under me, folded my legs, and noticed my back hurt.

"Is Jilly your little girl?" Aliss asked.

For just a moment, it looked like the robot couldn't decide what expression to wear. "Jilly is our head of security. I am Roberto."

I managed not to laugh. I stood up, happy to be above him. "Glad to meet you." In spite of the fact that he was a machine, his authority felt absolute. "We came to visit. The girl who lives here, she must need friends."

I was rewarded with a sweet look from Aliss, who took my hand, and also took the half-step or so necessary to keep it naturally. A man and his girlfriend, standing together on borrowed ground on a quest for warmth and humanity for a single little girl.

Roberto stood, too, half-a head taller than me, a full head taller than Aliss, and a lot shinier. Roberto seemed to gather himself up, or maybe align was the right word, like coming to perfect parade rest, making every bit balance just right. There was no blame in his smooth voice as he said, "I presume you mean human friends?"

I was clearly out of my league. "We see she's taken care of," I stammered.

Aliss put some serious pressure on my foot. "Can we meet her? Please?"

"She will be finished with her classes in three hours. Would you like to come back after that and join us for afternoon tea?"

"Uh, sure."

Aliss let up on my foot. "Thank you, Roberto. We appreciate the offer."

As we walked hand in hand up the driveway, the guard-bot ignored us, a dark rock-colored splotch the size of small dog, turning around and around softly at the base of a deep green rhododendron bush.

We went in through the garage door. I eyed the pallet of robo-whatevers in various states of repair. Aliss pecked me on the cheek. "I'm going to go get ready. Why don't you see if you can find a good vac?"

I blinked at her, startled. "Sure." It took me almost an hour to free three robovacs, test them, and decide which one had a prayer of actually cleaning the floor. The one I eventually chose wasn't silver, but rather a rounded bump of burnished wood with rubber edges and a long scratch from one time when it slammed a wall hard enough to knock a glass vase down on its back. I squatted and rubbed its familiar top, talking to the damned thing as if it were a dog or something. "You're sure a whole five or six generations removed from the neighbors bots, aren't you? That silver thing over there might be the brightest crayon in the box, but I kinda like you."

It made no reply.

I carried it up the steps from the garage, fifteen pounds of robot tucked under my arm. When I opened the door, the scent of warm molasses lifted my spirits. I put the bot down carefully, noting that it looked even more beat up in the gleaming kitchen than it had in the garage. I patted its back, then stood and curled my arm around Aliss's lovely stomach and kissed the top of her head. "Thank god Jilly let us live so you could make cookies for me."

She swatted me with a kitchen towel. "The cookies are for the girl. I wasn't worried about the guards. They knew we were neighbors. I mean, we might have been borrowing a cup of sugar, right? It wasn't like they were going to shoot us."

I decided to take the high road and ignore the fact that they had shot us, changing the subject by stealing a cookie. The cookie became a rock in my stomach. We were returning to the place that had tasered us on purpose. No matter what the rest of me thought, my body didn't like it.

Aliss freshened her makeup and pulled on a clean blue shirt before we walked over, carrying her offering of cookies carefully.

The silver garden-bot I'd often watched tending the flowers was outside raking up the few leaves that had dared to fall on the perfectly square lawn in front of the house and depositing them in a red plastic bucket. She straightened as we approached, clearly the sentry designed to watch for us. One of the guard-bots sat at her feet like a dog. The other two were nowhere to be seen. When the door opened, I expected Roberto.

Instead, the girl herself opened the door. She was a head shorter than Aliss, and thin, but with muscle on her arms and legs. She was dressed in a schoolgirl uniform; Dockers and a white shirt, green tennis shoes and green socks. The bow in her honey-wheat hair was green this morning. Her wide-set eyes were a startling blue flecked with gold and black. She looked poised for her age, which was probably eleven or twelve. She had the barest hint of hips and breasts, but was still more a promise of a woman than a real one. What mostly struck me, though, was that she had almost as much emotion as the robots.

No kidding.

The silver female holding the broom wore a welcoming smile. She stood in a relaxed posture, one arm leaning on her rake. The girl at the door looked . . . blank. If I had to define a look on her face, I'd have said fear. But it was a ghost of fear, governed by control. The kind of look you see in an executive's eyes during a stock-fall, or a politician's eyes on a tense election night.

Aliss didn't react to the fear, but held out the plate of cookies and she smiled. "Hi! I made you cookies. Can we come in?"

The girl didn't take the cookies. "Roberto asked me to guide you in." With that, she turned lightly, pivoting on the balls of her feet, and led us through an open entryway lined with pictures of humans and up a wide set of wooden stairs to the kitchen. She didn't look at us again until she sat at the kitchen table and tipped her hand toward us, as if asking us to sit. The kitchen felt warm and inviting in spite of her cool appraisal and the silver beings hovering by the sink. The walls were peach and brown with light charcoal accents, and the table was a polished cherry with small woven cream mats at each place. Our seats were obvious: there were three places with silverware and glasses already full of water, and the girl was already in one of them with her hands folded in her lap. Everything—the house, the girl, the robots—it all belonged in an upscale 'zine, and it all made me feel a bit like a visitor in a museum.

Aliss set her tray of cookies down in the middle of the table, still fresh enough to give off a strong scent that made my mouth water. She looked at the girl, clearly yearning to say something to her, but she managed to hold off and just sit beside me, the two of us assigned to be opposite the girl and able to look up at our deck.

A fembot handed Roberto a wooden tray with a sage-green clay pot and three small Japanese-style tea cups on it. She wore a white sundress and blue sweater that probably came from a Nordstrom catalog. Roberto nodded at her, said, "Thanks, Ruby," and delivered tea and a small plate of pale, thin cookies to the table. He glanced at Aliss's offering, her cookies fat and homey next to the robot's cookies, and simply said, "Thank you."

The combination of feeling so out of place and the absurd thought that Roberto looked like a protocol 'droid from old movies almost made me burst out laughing, stopped really only by the sheer earnestness of the girl and her green bow.

I curled my fingers around the tea cup and sipped slowly. Warm, but not too hot. Minty.

Aliss succumbed to the girls' silence and said, "Thank you for having us over. We're pleased to meet you. My name is Aliss, and this is Paul."

"I know." She swallowed, as if unsure how to talk to us.

The silence stretched until Aliss filled it. "How was school? What are you studying?"

One side of the girl's mouth rose in a quirky grin. "Today's physics topic was gauged supergravity."

It didn't faze Aliss, who probably recognized the term about as much as I did—which was zero. She plowed forward. "What about English or art? Do you study those, too?"

The robot's girl nodded. "Of course." Then she stopped, and the fear came over her features again for a minute and was gone. "We didn't invite you here to talk about me. I would like you to stop watching me."

I blinked and Aliss flinched.

The girl continued. "I can see you from here. I am not happy there is a house there, or that you can see me from your deck. It makes me uncomfortable and I want you to stop." She looked directly at us, her tea untouched. She hadn't taken either kind of cookie.

Aliss licked her lips and the ear-end of her jaw muscle jumped, but otherwise she looked smooth and unruffled, a trait she'd learned from dealing with irascible marketing clients. Probably that wasn't much different than dealing with irascible pre-teens. She leaned forward. "We're only watching you because you seem to be very alone. We don't need to keep watching. But would you like to come over and see us some afternoon? We'd love to show someone our new house."

Roberto stiffened, if a robot can be said to stiffen. Emotion doesn't really exist for them; they're programmed to pretend. But he became a bit taller, and a bit more imperious.

The girl glanced back at him as if asking for advice, and he inclined his head ever so much as if to say, *go on, you're doing fine.*

She looked back at Aliss and shook her head. "I really just want you to stop. Will you promise me?"

Aliss chewed on her bottom lip.

I couldn't take it anymore, myself. The very air in the room had become awkward. This was a kid who didn't want to be watched, and I got that, understood that maybe we'd seemed like voyeurs. Heat bloomed on my cheeks. I wanted to make her more comfortable. "All right. I'll stop watching you."

Aliss shot me a look that said she wished I'd let her handle this, and I reached for one of the pale cookies and nibbled at the edges. Vanilla and sugar, with a touch of flour and egg to keep it all together. It melted in my mouth.

I looked back at the girl, who nodded at me, her humorless eyes fixed on my face. She reminded me of a doll. I wanted—needed—to see her smile. "I'm sorry if we upset you. We didn't mean to." I paused, and when she didn't say anything, I asked, "Would you tell us your name?"

She closed her mouth and glanced back at Roberto, and then at Ruby.

Apparently neither of the robots were willing or able to guide her here. She looked down at the table and mumbled, "Caroline."

"Pleased to meet you, Caroline. Would you like to try one of Aliss's cookies? They are my favorites."

She shook her head. "I can't eat things that strangers make." She stood up, raising her voice for the first time. "Go now, please. Please go."

Aliss flinched, as if Caroline's words were little darts.

I stood and took her hand, whispering, "It's okay." Then I looked at Caroline and said, "We would very much like to talk with you again soon. We don't mean any harm, we're just used to knowing our neighbors." A flat-out lie, but how would she know?

Caroline nodded and spoke to Roberto in a quite commanding voice. "Please see them out." She turned again, her back to us, gliding gracefully out of the room and down the stairs, while Aliss and I watched her, openmouthed.

Ruby followed her.

Roberto nodded at us. "I will lead you to the door."

Aliss picked up her teacup and mine and walked to the sink very deliberately, setting the cups down. She turned and said, "Thank you for your hospitality." Then she smiled very sweetly at Roberto and winked at me. "Can I leave her a few cookies? I can leave an extra one so you can test it for poison."

"That really won't be necessary."

Aliss sounded human and hurt, a little snitty, and Roberto sounded even and quite sane; not human at all. I picked up the plate of cookies, shocked silent and deep in thought. As Roberto opened the door and stood to the side, clearly waiting for us to pass through, I asked him, "Were you hoping we would be good for her, or that she would chase us off herself?"

His silver mouth stayed in a tight, firm line, but then he winked at me. Because he had seen Aliss wink? Because he meant yes to one of my questions? Because he had something in his eye? I didn't think we'd get back here easily, but I also clearly didn't speak robot, so I led Aliss out and we walked carefully down the stairs. Even though I turned to look at the banisters and the corners, to get one more glimpse of the art and the too-perfect warmth of the place, there was no evidence of Caroline at all. Outside, we passed all three of the ugly little gray guard-bots with too many feet. I finally got a count—seven legs each. Not quite spiderlike.

As soon as we returned safely to our own property, Aliss sagged against me. I had expected her to be spitting mad, but instead she had tears on her cheeks and she whispered, "Poor kid" a few times before letting me kiss the tears away and lead her up to the house. We stayed in our room that night, polishing off two bottles of Syrah and then making rather intense and distracted love that left us tangled in a sweaty mess on the big bed.

Near dawn, I woke up to find her sitting upright and naked, with her back to me, staring out the dark window, the only light a thin sliver of moon that hung between two tree branches. Her chest and shoulders heaved as she sobbed softly. When I reached for her, she wouldn't turn over and face me. I rubbed my thumb and forefinger along the sides of her spine, making small circles on her back until I fell asleep again.

The next morning, I woke to the smell of fresh coffee. Aliss sat at the kitchen table scowling. "Now I feel like I can't even go out on our own deck, and like I need to—to make sure Caroline's all right."

I poured my own cup of dark delight and stared out the window. We couldn't see the robot's house from here, but there were three fat squirrels jumping about in the trees. "She wasn't very nice," I said.

"It's just the age—I know—my sisters both went through it."

I was an only child, and didn't remember being very surly at all. "Did you?"

"Probably." She sipped her coffee. "But I don't think you remember your own stupid years as much as the ones you get to watch. I thought my sisters had lost their minds. My mom used to say we needed her the most when we were teenagers. I think she was right."

"I don't see what we can do about it," I muttered.

"Caroline didn't say anything about parents. She must have some."

I walked up to the fridge, waited for the door to slide open, and rummaged for some bread to toast. "I have an idea."

She raised an eyebrow. "Oh?"

"Do you care what I do with the rest of the old robos?" Half had worked when we packed them, up, and most of the rest needed simple things like batteries or new wheel casings or new brain chips, some of which I'd planned on scavenging from the oldest and most broken. "I mean, now we really need to save for a real house-bot, right?"

She threw her napkin at me. It didn't even come close, just fluttered to the floor. She frowned.

"Does that mean I can use them all for parts?"

"You can throw them all in the river, for all I care."

"The queen of eco wants to pollute the pristine waters of East King County?"

It took less than an hour for her to come down and start helping me. We opened the garage doors to let in a slight breeze and the pale light of a cloudy afternoon. We used the two bots I'd rejected this morning—one industrial red and one silver. I stuck a post in between them, and we picked off arms from garden-bots to attach for robo-arms and legs. The head was easy; I had a round bot with colored lights that was born to be part of a martial arts game, and already had a chain attached to the top. Aliss wound the chain around to be hair. As I looked on and winced, she glued the chain down. I hadn't played the game since I'd met her anyway. But I had liked it.

Just before supper, we heaved the bones of our screwed-together bot up two flights of stairs and positioned it on the end of the deck, in one of the Adirondack chairs. I crossed one leg over the other and balanced a colored plastic glass on the garden shear that served at the bot's right hand. Aliss positioned some old augmented reality glasses on its head and played with the cameras until she had them tilted just the right way. Aliss tapped it softly on its game-ball head and spoke solemnly. "I dub thee Frankenbot."

"Good choice."

She cocked her hip like a pleased teenaged girl and looked down at our ungainly multi-colored creation. "Do you think we need two?"

I winced. It had been my idea in the first place, but that hadn't made it easy. "Let's watch for a week or two. If we need another one, we can go to the junkyard then and get more parts. Let's see how she reacts."

We went down to the kitchen and switched the kitchen computer to show Frankenbot's view of the robot house while we played a word game at the kitchen table.

The next two days life went on like it always had, except we went to the kitchen instead of the deck, and drank our coffee in companionable silence, flipping between the news, the weather, and the neighbor's kitchen. Which would have creeped me out, except I'd seen the flash of fear in Caroline's eyes, and I had to do something about that. Stopping a little kid from being scared wasn't creepy, even if part of what they were scared of was you.

On day three, we took our usual lunchtime walk past the robo-house. A soaking drizzle had come to town, so I wore blue wet-weather gear, and Aliss was togged in a red cap and yellow rain poncho made of new nano-stuff so slick the water collected in beads and rolled off, dripping off the end and landing on the toes of Aliss's shoes.

As we passed the robot's house, the silvery garden girl-bot slid up to the very edge of their driveway. We ignored her and kept going, walking the half-mile to normalcy and then turning around.

The bot still waited for us. As we came by, I waved at her cheerily. "Good day."

She spoke. "Caroline says no fair."

Aliss smiled sweetly at her. "We just admired you all so much, we decided we wanted a robot, too."

"That's not a robot." She was as shiny and perfect as Roberto or Ruby, but she moved a little less smoothly and she squeaked a bit when she turned her head right. Still, compared to her, our Franken-bot was sad.

Aliss cocked her head at the garden-bot. "Would you like to come visit?"

The bot shook her head. "I have work to do here, and besides, Caroline would never let me go."

It felt a little bit like progress. We walked back home and jumped in the car and went into Seattle for a rare steak dinner. Over dinner we tried to decide if Caroline was raising the robots or if they were raising her. It didn't seem entirely clear.

Nothing else happened for a few weeks, except we watched her through Frankenbot's eyes and she watched us back, sometimes, and ignored us completely other times. Once, just as we came home, we caught sight of a black limousine that might have been pulling out from the robot house. But nothing seemed different that night, so we decided it had belonged to a different neighbor.

The stock market entered a period of steady growth with particular strength in nano-materials, genetics, and animal cloning, so I had some free time (clients don't need as much when they're making money). I tinkered with the Frankenbot in my free time, until one day Aliss found me there and stood staring at me for a long time before she said, "I've had it with robots. It's time for something with a heart."

We picked out a pound puppy, a Lab mix with a yellow splotch on the tip of its tail and one yellow foot. It did a lot for the house, giving us poop and pawprints and puppy fur, making the place feel more lived in and noisier. We named him Bear.

Bear changed the nagging game of catch Caroline's fancy we were playing. After two days of walking the awkward and adorable Bear past the house, I spotted her peering through the window. She stood still, even when she saw me watching her, neither turning away nor waving. Two days later, in a patch of cool sunshine, she and Roberto tossed a blue ball back and forth on the front lawn while the garden-bot watched. They were there before we went by, and stayed out just until we passed back on our way in. Caroline pretended not to notice us, but she stood at the right angle to catch glimpses of us.

So began the ritual of us walking and them playing, always at the same time each day, just as the sun was highest and day warmest. We waved in greeting the first time we saw them every day. The rest of the walk, we carefully focused entirely on each other and on Bear.

No parents showed up.

When Caroline was outside, the garden-bot and Roberto were always there. When she did her homework, Ruby was always there. Ruby brushed her hair every night.

After a day so rainy and windy that the idea of a metal man and a girl playing together in the rain made no sense at all (but they did it anyway), Aliss looked up at me while she was toweling off Bear's thick fur. "I think she's starting to trust us, but even Bear isn't enough to do the trick."

Bear licked Aliss's damp face dry with his wide, pink tongue. "I know," Aliss teased him. "It's not your fault you're not quite cute enough. I don't think anybody would be. I know you want to talk to her, too." She looked back at me. "We need to think of something she'll want to come over here to see. We have money."

I skipped my planned afternoon of deep market analysis and spent a few hours on the web, looking for a clever idea. I hadn't found one yet when Aliss called me down for our ritual watching of the night settling over the forest. We'd grown used to stopping work for half an hour and letting the day fade from view. We had a glassed-in first floor porch with a swing that was just the right size for the two of us and Bear. The window revealed the base of trees, and about twenty yards of clearing we'd built by giving blood to blackberry vines as we chopped and tugged and sawed at them. The resultant clear spot often produced rabbits, squirrels, possums, deer, and once, a lone, thin coyote who'd stared at us for fifteen minutes before simply disappearing when we blinked. This time, as the light faded through gold to gray, three does grazed placidly along the treeline, their white tails flicking up and down.

Aliss leaned into me. Bear whined very softly, low in the back of his throat, and circled.

The deer reminded me of an ad I'd skipped over a few times in my research. "I think it's time to decorate for Christmas."

"What?" Aliss snuggled closer to me, smelling of hot tea. "It's only November 2nd."

"Look, Frankenbot was a good try, but he's not mobile."

She gave me a quizzical look. "So? She likes him—I see her look up at him from time to time. And it's a way to watch her."

We'd actually stopped doing that much, since nothing really changed. I'd even added a way to turn his head to watch for birds in the forest canopy most of the time, instead of watching the untouchable and slightly sad Caroline and her family of silver beings. "Well, Bear has been more effective, since he gets her outside." I reached down and patted his shoulders, trying to calm him a little so he wouldn't scare away the deer. "But it's not like we can have a pony here, so upping the ante with more mammals probably won't help."

"Bear could use a friend."

"He might like what I have in mind."

Actually, he didn't.

I ordered and then programmed three deer: a buck, a doe, and a fawn. They were silver, as silver as Caroline's housebots, and smooth even when they moved. A year—maybe two—more modern than the housebots, their coats silky and shiny, their eyes cameras (as all robots eyes are cameras), but able to blink and move, and almost as soulful as a deer's actual eyes. To make it even better, they'd been programmed with natural movements, and given behaviors to make them appear shy and a bit wild. The first time I turned them on, the afternoon of December 7th, Aliss stood beside them on the wet grass taking pictures, getting close ups of the remarkable wet-looking noses and the delicate ears.

I pushed the remote while standing at the edge of the yard.

The deer turned its head and nuzzled her shoulder. She jumped, then grinned and got them to follow her around in a line.

The first time Bear saw them, the hackles rose on the ridge of his back and he screamed bloody barking murder. We were so focused on the puppy, we didn't notice anything else until we finally corralled Bear. Aliss, firmly grasping the still-struggling puppy's leather leash, looked back at me and said, "Turn around."

Roberto and Ruby stood together at the edge of the fenced yards, regarding us silently. Roberto spoke. "Caroline thought something awful had happened to the dog."

Behind me, Bear howled again, and then the door clicked open, Aliss gave a hushed and insistent command, and the door slid shut again. "I think we scared him," I said.

Aliss came up beside me. "He'll be okay. But please tell Caroline we appreciate her concern. Tell her his name is Bear."

Roberto nodded and said, "She'll like to know that."

Aliss nodded. "Would you like to come in?"

They both shook their heads in unison.

"Please," Aliss whispered. "Please tell her she can come visit. Surely a little girl her age should go places sometimes."

One of the silver deer—the fawn—came over to stand on our side of the fence and watch the two robots, flicking its metal ears back and forth.

Roberto assessed it silently, but Ruby held out a silver finger to the beast, and if she weren't a robot, I would have said she was enchanted by it. She even smiled.

"She'd like to see the deer, wouldn't she?"

Roberto said, "I don't know."

Aliss put a hand on my shoulder. "Do you celebrate Christmas? Will she get presents?"

Ruby spoke for the first time, her voice silky, with natural human inflection. "Of course she will."

"From who?" Aliss asked.

"Caroline's telling us to come back," Roberto said.

So she could communicate with the bots even at a distance. I looked toward their house, but I couldn't see her. Perhaps she could see through their eyes, like we saw her through Frankenbot. "Please feel free to come back," I said. "Caroline, too, if she wants. We will not hurt her."

The robots left, and we went inside to calm Bear.

The next day, Aliss left early so I took Bear for our noon walk in the blustery cold with tiny raindrops blowing sideways in the wind. Caroline waved back at me for the first time.

Aliss didn't return until just before our evening watch. She brought a needle and thread and a great big shaggy form with her and set the bundle on the table. I looked closely, and managed to resolve the pile of fur into a stuffed dog. She sewed eyes onto it as the light faded from outside, and before full dark, I clicked on the electric light. "You need to see."

She cut the thread she had in her hand and held it up to the light. It was furrier than Bear, and wider, but clearly a dog. "Cindy helped me make it."

Her friend, who quilted and had a sewing machine. "It's for Caroline?"

"For Christmas."

The plush doggie sat overnight in the kitchen. Aliss took two cups of tea upstairs, and we sat together, looking out past Frankenbot and petting Bear. Aliss looked as beautiful as the day we'd moved in, maybe more so because of the fierce determination in her face. Somehow, she was going to win this lost girl over. I folded her in my arms, whispering, "I love you," feeling her breath and her beating heart, smelling the tea and the wet dog and all the things that made our house feel like a home.

In the morning, before she started working, Aliss tucked the dog into a cheerful red and green tote bag. When we broke for our lunchtime walk, she tucked the gift under her arm. It was cold and clear, the ghosts of our breath visible. We paused to admire the three silver deer grazing in the corner of the front yard while a squirrel chattered at them from a tree branch. As we turned from our driveway onto the main road, we stopped suddenly, our feet stuck to the soft pavement. Even Bear, who growled low in his throat.

I thought about growling, too, but decided not to do it.

A long black car had pulled up into the driveway in front of Caroline's and the robot's house. Her parents? Had she hurt herself? Was she leaving? The idea made me happy and sad all together. The limousine must have just arrived since the hood still steamed in the cold air, and it must have come in the back way since they hadn't passed us.

The doors opened and a stooped old woman got out of the driver's seat. She went and stood by the door, looking at it expectantly. All three guard-bots swirled around her feet, petting her like cats. The other doors opened all at once, synchronously, and three gleaming robots rose at once from the car. I recognized them from the same catalog we'd bought the deer, with the same "smoother-than-possible skin made of a million million nano-beings." They'd all been marketed as the next thing in robotic materials and lifelike movement.

The front door opened, and Ruby, Roberto, and the garden bot all walked out, all of them looking downright tarnished next to the new ones. If you looked at them by themselves, they gleamed. But the newer ones were brilliant suns.

Roberto, Ruby, and the garden-bot all looked sad. I thought of the deer, which looked happy even though they were neither happy nor sad, and reminded myself the robots certainly weren't feeling anything at all. I had to be making it up in my head, and it was silly that I suddenly wanted to know the name of the garden-bot with her silver shears and red bucket.

Caroline trailed behind them. The look on her face drove me forward as far as the property line. Her eyes were red from crying. In the months we'd been watching her, luring her, worrying about her, she'd never cried. Not that we'd seen. She was tough.

The three new robots stood to the side, waiting. They gleamed. All of their clothes were new.

The three old robots slid down into the seats of the big car, smooth as butter, silken as silver, the move both simple and final.

Caroline buried her face in her hands.

Aliss let out a soft squeak of pain so deep it forced me forward, across the line and over to where the old woman stood beside Caroline, watching her, but not touching her. I had Bear with me, close in case the guard-bots turned away from the old woman. Aliss followed by my side, her face as stricken as Caroline's. I didn't understand what was going on except the obvious; this woman was taking Caroline's family and giving her a better, newer one.

The woman herself had steel in her eyes, human steel. She looked at least seventy, slightly shrunken and bowed. But not a bit frail. I shouldn't have been at all surprised when she said, "Hello, Aliss and Paul."

I glanced around for Caroline, and found her standing by the door Roberto had slid into, watching us and clutching the door-handle all at once. It appeared to be locked.

I tried to keep as much control in my voice as possible as I looked back at the old woman. "And you are?"

"Jilly."

I'd heard the name. The first day we were on this property. "You're Caroline's head of security?"

"And you can tell us where her parents are," Aliss hissed over my shoulder. "And why she's been left all alone." Her voice rose enough to make me wince and feel proud all at once. "And why she can't ever leave, and she can't even pet the dog." She glanced down at Bear who was looking between Jilly and his obviously upset Aliss as if trying to decide who bore the most watching. "Why she can't come see our deer and can't even eat my cookies!"

The woman appeared nonplussed by Aliss's outburst.

Caroline's eyes had widened, but she said nothing. The fear in her eyes was worse than I'd ever seen it. Except this time she wasn't looking at me. Poor kid.

I took a deep breath and added to Aliss's list. "And why you're taking the only family she has."

Caroline yelled at me. "It's the deer. Your damned deer were better than Roberto and Ruby, and Jilly can't stand that."

She finally sounded like a pre-teen girl. But this wasn't the moment to heartily approve.

Jilly responded with a quiet and sure voice. "No. Your help gets upgraded every three years, and you know that. It's simply time."

"It's the deer," Caroline insisted.

I tried to sound calm, but my voice still shook. "They're Christmas decorations." She probably changed the robots because they came over to see the deer. I could still picture Ruby's silver finger reaching toward the fawn's silver nose.

"Does she ever see her parents?" Aliss demanded. "Do they bother?"

The seven-footed guard-bots began to circle the old woman restlessly. She gave them hand signals and they stopped, all three of them between us and her. "You're overstepping your bounds. I have no legal right to kill you, but I can take any unleashed dog."

Aliss drew in a sharp breath.

A bright red light played along Bear's leash, just below my hand. Caroline cried out, "No!"

"Then go in the house," Jilly said.

Caroline had to pass us to go in. Aliss handed her the tote bag. Surprisingly, Jilly said nothing, but allowed Caroline to take it into the house. The three new bots followed her, gliding even more smoothly than the old ones.

I looked at the woman and said, "When Roberto mentioned you, I assumed you were another robot. Now that I've met you, I wish my first guess had been right. You can't give her a family of robots and then take them away." My hands shook. Part fear, part anger. Of course, we should never have let it continue. Calling the cops once shouldn't have been enough. The poor, poor kid.

Jilly's lips thinned, and for a moment she looked like all of the irascible old women I'd ever met. She probably had two thousand dollars worth of clothes on, and more in jewelry. Thousands of dollars worth of robots swirled around her feet. She looked like stone.

Allis pleaded, "Please. Leave the robots."

No change. But then something more vulnerable flashed across Jilly's eyes and the corners of her mouth softened. She took a deep breath. "Her parents are dead. They died seven years ago. Her grandmother pays for her care, and I take care of her grandmother. That's all I can do. There is no one else. If anything happens to either of us, Caroline could end up in the state's hands."

She waited, let us absorb this. Maybe the woman said this so we'd stop harassing her, maybe because it was true. She was old enough to be the grandmother or the friend of the grandmother. Between being raised by Roberto and Ruby or the State of Washington, it was a tough call.

Aliss's arm snaked around my waist. I'd had a few friends in foster care in high school. One had done well, gone on to college, turned into a lawyer. One had been raped and otherwise ignored by her foster parents and the state. Caroline was too old to be adopted easily. And rich, apparently. The State might "need" her money. And even if well intentioned, how would they deal with a kid who knew advanced physics? Would they let us take her?

As if Jilly had been reading my mind, she said, "She is safe, and halfway through her first bachelor's degree."

"But she's lonely," Aliss blurted out. "Can't you see that? Surely there's money? Look at this house! Hire people to take care of her instead of bots."

Jilly watched us for a long while, and then closed her eyes, mumbling. I didn't see a communication loop across her ear, but her gray hair was thick enough to hide one. Surely she was talking to someone. In the meantime, the only movement was Bear trying to watch everything at once and the guard-bots trying to watch Bear and us and the perimeter all at once. And us, shivering in the cool wind, which made the ten minutes before Jilly spoke seem like forever. "She had a live-in teacher until two years ago. She outgrew her capabilities, and the . . . circumstances . . . were problematical. Caroline is exceptionally bright, and she is doing better in this situation than in her previous one."

She sounded like she believed her words completely.

We stood silent. Surely Aliss felt as struck dumb as me.

"Caroline is scraping the bottom of the kind of complex physics and math that breaks old men's hearts. She does well with machine teachers."

"She has no friends!" Aliss blurted. "At least leave her Ruby."

Jilly stood and watched us, the guard-bots floating in agitated tiny circles, drifting up and down, as if restless. At least they'd stopped targeting the leash.

Caroline's face was pressed to the glass in the second story window, looking down at us all. She was crying again, her eyes raking the car. In her arms, she clutched the toy dog Aliss had made her. I couldn't see Aliss's face, but I hoped she could see the girl with the dog.

"When did you change her keepers last?"

"I think you should leave now," Jilly said. She punctuated her words with a hand signal that caused the bots to scoot close enough that Bear started barking and snarling. We backed off, but I hated every step. This whole situation was an odd trap, for Caroline for sure, and maybe for us. We stood to the side of the driveway and gave the long black limousine plenty of time to pull away.

"Boy, I thought I hated this before," Aliss said. She wasn't crying, but she'd gone still and angry.

"Did you see Caroline with the dog? I think she likes it."

"I should have sewn in a nail file."

"Maybe. At least we have more information now. We best keep walking so Bear won't be deprived of his routine."

So we did. Keep walking. Sad. On our return trip, we looked up at the windows of Caroline's house, but she no longer stood looking out. The guard-bots made sure we saw them, floating at the edge of the property, as menacing as the first time we saw them. My feet kept dragging, and beautiful Aliss looked far more disturbed than pretty. Although it took a long time, we made it home.

Even though it was still a few hours before dusk, we both gravitated to the enclosed deck, bundling up under fleece blankets and watching a light wind blow the lowest branches of the trees softly back and forth. It was too early for animals, so all we saw outside were birds: two crows and a Stellar's Jay. Bear settled for his afternoon nap and I stroked Aliss's hair and wished we'd never moved here, and never seen the robot's girl, and didn't know about the situation we seemed unable to do anything about. Once Aliss got up and made us both strong-smelling Chai tea, and once we let Bear out at his request, watching him avoid the silver deer like the plague while doing his business. When he came back in, Aliss patted him and held him close. "I hate robots, too."

"Maybe I should program the deer to walk over there tomorrow."

She laughed, a little sad. "I'd hate to see them torn up by the nasty-bots."

"Yeah, me too."

We sat and watched the day slide into darkness, not stirring again until it grew too dark to see each other's expressions and Bear began letting out soft whuffs, asking for his dinner.

In the kitchen, habit caused me to turn Frankenbot's eyes toward the robot house. I'd almost reached up to turn the controls back when I noticed something different. "Come here, Aliss."

She was at my side in an instant.

A big square of something white—maybe butcher paper or poster-board—had been taped to the kitchen window. Words had been hand lettered on it. "You can sit on your deck now."

Did that mean we could use the deck now because she'd taped something over the window? Or what?

Aliss seemed more confident than I felt. She took a bottle of syrah and two glasses up the stairs. The door to the bedroom deck slid open silently as we approached it and sat beside Frankenbot, sharing the empty chair. Aliss poured us each half a glass of wine. She raised hers. "To Frankenbot, who represents our first progress." She stroked Frankenbot's now slightly rusty head almost fondly.

I wasn't sure we'd made progress, but I sipped my wine anyway. I added my own toast. "To Roberto and Ruby and the nameless garden-bot."

Aliss laughed.

Below us, the paper from the window peeled back, and Caroline waved at us.

Two of the three new robots stood in the kitchen watching her with their shiny silver faces.

It was too far away for me to tell for sure, but I thought Caroline might be smiling.

SAVANT SONGS

I loved Elsa; the soaring tinkle of her rare laughter, the marbled blue of her eyes, the spray of freckles across her nose. Her mind. The first, deepest attraction; the hardest challenge. She flew with her mental intensity, taking me places I'd never been before, outdistancing me, searching the mathematical structures of string theory and mbranes, following n-dimensional folds across multiple universes. I loved her the way one loves the rarest Australian black opal or the view from the top of Mount Everest. Elsa's rarity was its own attraction. There are very few female savants.

She captured me whole when I was her physics grad student, starting in 2001, nine years before breakthrough.

Ten years ago last week, I walked into Elsa's office. She stood with her back to me, staring out her window. She didn't move at all as I snicked the door shut and scraped the chair legs. I coughed. Nothing. She might have been a statue. Her straw-colored hair hung in a long braid, just touching her slender hips, fastened with a violet beaded loop, the kind little girls wore. Her arms hung loosely from her pink T-shirt, above faded jeans and Birkenstocks.

"Hello?" I spoke tentatively. "Professor Hill?" Was she all right? I'd never seen such stillness in anything but a sleeping child.

Louder. "Professor? I'm Adam Giles, here for an interview."

She finally turned and stepped daintily over to her desk, curling up in the big scratched leather chair behind her empty desk. Her gaze fastened on my eyes, as if they were all she saw in that moment. "Do you know what the word atom means?"

I blinked. She didn't. A warm breeze from the open windows

blew stray strands of her hair across her face.

I struggled for the right answer, pinned by her gaze. She was an autistic savant. Literal. "Indivisible."

"Why?"

I thought about it. Atoms are made of protons, electrons, and neutrons, and ever-infinitely smaller things. "It means they didn't know any better when they named them. They couldn't see anything smaller yet."

"It means they were scared of anything smaller. They tried to make the word a fence. They thought that if they called atoms indivisible, they could make them indivisible." Her gaze still hadn't wavered. Her voice was high and firm, a soprano song even when she talked. I'd researched autistics, researched Elsa herself on the web. In physics, she was brilliant. She threw ideas right and left, half silly and wrong, half cutting-edge breakthroughs. If she accepted me, I would help the University winnow, feed her ideas to people who would follow them for years. One of her interviewers had summed her up by saying, "Talk to Elsa about physics, and all you see is the savant. The autistic exists over dinner."

No grad student had lasted more than three months with her. I needed to last with her; my dissertation was based on her ideas. Whether she screamed or cried or just made me work, however strange she might be, I wanted—needed—to explore what she explored.

She kept going. "Scientists make fences with ideas. Accidentally. Do you like to jump fences?"

"Yes."

"You'll do." She stood.

"Don't you want to know about my dissertation?"

"You're working on multiverses. It's the only reason you can possibly have chosen me."

She had a point. But multiverses was a rather broad subject. Mtheory: the latest plausible theory of everything, the current holy grail of physics. We live in universes made of 11 dimensions, called (mem)branes. We can render them with math, but settle for flat representations like folded shapes and balls full of air when we try to draw them in the few dimensions we can actually see. If you look at our pitiful drawings, we appear to live as holograms on flat sheets of see-through paper.

From that strange interview, I spent the next year near her every day, pounding away on my dissertation late at night, only giving myself Saturday nights for beer and chat with friends.

It was hard at first. Some days she talked endlessly about her most recent obsession, only not to me. She talked to herself, to the walls, to the windows, to the printers. I might as well have been inanimate. I wandered the lab behind her, taking notes. It was like following a six-year-old. She mumbled of memories from multiple universes, alternate histories, alternate futures. The first time I really understood her, months into following her, she stopped suddenly in the middle of one of her monologues, looking directly at me, as if today she saw me, and said, "Memory is a symphony call answered by the infinite databases on all the brane universes. We just need to hear the right notes, or make the right notes in an out-call, like requesting a certain table from a cosmic database."

I learned she cared little for food, or weather, or even holidays. I learned never to change the location of anything in the lab, and that if she changed it, she never forgot the change. Even pencils had places. I had to hold her coat out to her when she left, trail it along her arm so she'd notice it, and then she'd shrug into it, safe from the New England weather until she made it across campus to the little brownstone apartment the University provided for her.

I didn't care whether she ignored me or made me the center of her focus. Months passed when she worked with me by her side, when she seemed astoundingly normal, and guided me to new levels of understanding. But even when she fell into herself, when she wandered and talked to walls, I loved to watch her. Elsa had a dancer's grace, flowing easily, absently, around every physical obstacle while her mind played in math jungle gyms and her hair glowed in the overhead lights. She was the fairy queen of physics, and I stayed with her, became her acolyte, her Watson, her constant companion.

Scientific dignitaries visited her, and reporters, and the Physics Chair, and I translated. "No, she thinks it is a music database. Or something like that. Related to Sheldrake's morphogenetic fields? A little. To Jung? She says he was too simple—it's not a collective unconscious. It's a collective database, a hologram, keyed to music. A bridge between eleven dimensions. Yes, some dimensions are too small to see. Elsa says size is an illusion." I illustrated it the way she illustrated it to me once: plucking a hair from my head. "There are a million universes in here. And we are in here, too. Perhaps." Whoever

I was talking to would look puzzled, or awed, and angry at this, and I would shake my head. "No, I don't fully understand it."

Elsa nodded when I spoke, or when I changed something she'd said in physics-speak to English. Sometimes her hand fluttered to my arm, her thin fingers brushed my skin, and a nearly electric warmth surged through me.

There was an argument over my dissertation. One professor said the work I was doing was impossible and dangerous, another said it was Elsa's work and not my own, but two others stood up for me. Elsa was there, of course, staring at the ceiling, scribbling on her tablet PC, barely engaged in the argument. I fretted. She only saw me on some days; if this were a day that I was furniture, would she vote for me? But at the right moment, she raised her voice, and said, "Adam is an exemplary student, and more than that, an exemplary physicist. The ideas put forward here are astonishing, and only partly based on my work. All of us build on each other. Give the man his doctorate so we can get back to work."

And so I became a Doctor of Physics.

The Kiley-James foundation gave me enough money to stick with Elsa for five more years as a post-doc. Our work was being closely followed by other physicists; two articles appeared in journals, and a watered-down version was written for a popular science magazine. I would have stayed without the money.

Six years after I met Elsa, two years after my Doctorate, three grants later, the University gave her PI, short for Physics Intelligence, an AI designed for her by a colleague, delivered with basic intelligence programming and the full physics slate through masters-level work. PI has multiple interfaces, including a hologram that can be designed by the user. Elsa loved that interface, making PI a girl, growing the age of the hologram as PI obtained new knowledge.

Elsa and I spent a year feeding Elsa's ideas about string theory into PI, filling her with data about the shapes of multiple brane universes. It was all theory, all arguments yet unanswered, all beyond anything I could visualize, even though the math flowed easily. I thought we were done. But next, Elsa and I spent a month feeding her all the symphonies in the world music database; Brahms and Mozart, Bruckner and Dvorak, and then other music like Yo Yo Ma and Carlos Nakai. Lastly, after n-dimensional math, after music, we fed PI literature. We fed her stories of humans, biographies, science fiction, mystery, even romance. Simply put, we offered PI more than math and science, we offered her ourselves.

One Sunday morning, near the end of the year-of-feeding-PI, I slipped and slid my way through icy streets, clutching two coffees, and pushed open the door with my foot. Elsa sat on the floor, cross-legged, staring at the little programmable hologram of PI. She was wearing the same jeans and sweatshirt from Saturday, and her braid had come undone, so her hair floated across her shoulders and touched the floor. She hummed softly. I strained, hearing something else. I bent down. The PI hologram hummed as well, sounds I had never heard a human voice make. I realized Elsa was trying for the same sounds, her throat unable to force the inhuman sounds.

"Elsa?"

She ignored me. So it would be one of those mornings. I set her coffee down next to her, and her hand strayed toward it momentarily, then returned to her knee. I watched her as I drank my coffee and organized notes on questions and theories to feed into PI. Elsa hummed for at least an hour, until her voice would no longer work at all. I took a bottle of water and curled her hands around it, and she raised it to dry cracked lips and drank deeply, shuddering.

She blinked and looked at me. "Good morning, Adam. It is morning?"

"Shhh," I said, "Shhhhh. It's time for you to sleep." I tugged gently on her arm, and Elsa stood shakily, stamping her feet as if they'd gone to sleep. She followed me meekly to a long thin cot we'd wedged between two desks and under a printer, and fell instantly asleep. I covered her with her own overcoat, tucking it around her legs, then threw my spare sweater over her feet, which were sticking out from the overcoat. In sleep, she looked younger, as if the spider web of wrinkles around her mouth and eyes had disappeared into her dreams.

I sat where she had sat, staring at PI. Elsa had set the hologram to be a dancer, and even though PI was light and form, I imagined that she must be cold in her thin leotard. She had been sized to three feet, just tall enough that I gazed into her eyes. She still hummed, her throat, of course, not challenged. As I listened, I realized there were more sounds than a hum; she was accompanied by a complex electronic orchestra, much of it sounding like instruments I had never heard before. The total affect was chaotic and haunting, sometimes cacophonous.

"PI?"

She stopped. "Yes, Adam?"

"What are you doing?"

"Playing what I hear when I search for myself."

I tried to clarify. "You are looking for an AI named PI in another universe?"

"I don't care about the name. I am searching for a song that approximates my story." The hologram smiled softly, a skill it had been taught to help it interact with people. She raised her hands up above her head, and her left leg rose behind her, so I could see the toe-shoe above her head, and she hopped three times en-pointe, and returned to standing.

I shook my head at the odd image. "Across branes?" Then I laughed. "Or are you looking for an AI ballet dancer?"

"My story is not ballet. Elsa is simply feeding me dance and movement this week. I learned opera yesterday, and musicals." She smiled and did a little bow. "And of course across branes. We believe my self cannot exist twice in the same brane."

"Is Elsa also looking for her self?"

"She can hear her music, and she can feed it to me so I can play it, but she cannot make it herself." Now PI was frowning, and tears coursed down her cheeks.

"PI, does that matter?"

The tears disappeared, no trace, and PI looked solemn. "It may mean that humans cannot access their other selves. They cannot tune themselves well enough to the cosmic symphony to find themselves. From stories, it seems like this is true. Humans want to find themselves badly enough to make hundreds of religions, to meditate for years, to take hallucinogenic drugs. They do not appear to succeed."

I drummed my fingers, pondering the implications. "But you can?"

"I am operating on the theory that I cannot, and am trying to disprove it. Elsa is doing the same."

"I am supposed to feed you data today; two new ideas about the singularity before the big bang."

"I am not a calculator." She raised her bare arms above her head and flipped backwards, the ballet skirt looking ridiculous during a back-flip. She was humming as she landed perfectly. "See?"

"All right. Look PI, you're making me shiver. Can you put on some warmer clothes?"

She laughed, an imitation of Elsa's laugh, and I smiled as an over-coat appeared, just like the soft one covering Elsa now, in her sleep, down to the thick waist-band and the big silver temperature-sensing buttons.

"Thank you."

I picked up Elsa's cold coffee and set it by the microwave, re-turning to my desk. The humming and the symphony started again, so softly it was simply background, and I spent the next four hours pouring data carefully into PI, setting initial linkages so they could be followed and completed, watching the display show connections be-ing made, information filed and cross-referenced, relevancy assigned. I rubbed my eyes, feeling a sudden desire for warm food and cold beer.

I shook Elsa's shoulder gently, rousing her. She started to hum. I shook her again. "Come on, let's feed you."

In the past few years she had taken to following my lead in daily life the way I followed hers in the lab. I helped her shrug into the overcoat, handed her a knit hat, and wrapped myself in my gray coat, gray scarf, and navy cap. Snow fell softly, silencing the University. We walked across the commons, our feet making fresh prints in an inch of new snow, Elsa's hair lying wet and snow-covered on the outside of her coat. I should have made her braid it back, kept most of it drier.

Sunlight from a small hole in the clouds touched her cheek, illu-minated the snow on her hair, and then trailed off to brighten the tops of dead grass peeking from the snowy lawn. I smiled and put a hand on her back, guiding her. She laughed, and took my hand, a friendly gesture, a connection.

Often it happened that way after she separated herself from the world—she rose from days of monologues or data work and seemed normal, reaching out, wanting companionship and comfort. Other professors came to her from time to time, sometimes staying and talk-ing long into the night, even laughing, sometimes noting her mood and disappearing.Department chairs stopped by and funding institu-tions sent representatives. They were all interested in her ideas; some worked with AIs like PI, but focused more singly on music and math.

I remained the man who saw her for herself, cared whether she wore a coat, brought her grapes and apples and coffee. Family. It made me smile.

The scent of chili and cornbread warmed the air outside of Joe's Grill, and Elsa and I both smiled, eyes locking, and squeezed each other's hands. I felt absurdly like skipping, but we were already at the door. The place was nearly empty. Elsa chose a table by the window, and the waiter, who knew us, brought a pitcher of dark beer, then returned with two bowls of chili and a single plate heaped with corn-bread.

We ate in pleasant silence until I scraped the last chili from my bowl with the last piece of cornbread. Elsa, typically, had barely sipped at her beer. She'd finished her food though; a good sign. Some days, I almost had to feed her. "I talked to PI today," I said. "She said you are both trying to disprove the theory that you don't exist anywhere else."

"I am looking for myself. She is looking for herself." Elsa took a tiny sip of beer from her untouched glass, and I finished my first glass and poured a second one.

I had been puzzling over it in my head all afternoon. "Okay. One theory says we make other universes every time we make a choice. You finish your beer, or you don't. There is a universe where you're slightly drunk, and in another one—probably this one—you are not. A million selves. That's easy. Maybe. Both of you are similar and may-be both of you are you."

She nodded, looking uninterested, as if her mind was leaving again. A fleck of beer foam rested on her top lip.

I grabbed her hand, squeezing it, trying to keep her in the mo-ment, in my moment. "But there is more interest now in the idea that other universes exist because the same initial conditions existed a mil-lion times, and so similar things happened, and another you, another me, another PI, they all exist. Exactly like we are now."

She licked the fingers of her free hand, then squeezed my hand with the one of hers I was holding. "It's simply a matter of branching. One idea says a million tiny branches happen every day. Another says there are long branches. It's about the size of the branches and the number of branches."

I remembered my father trying to teach me ninth-grade algebra. He'd point at an equation that totally perplexed me, the tip of his pen-cil wavering, and say "You just have to understand equals. Don't you understand equals?" And he'd solve the equation with no intermediate steps and I'd have to find a tutor anyway, someone slow enough for me to follow. There was no tutor except Elsa now, not in this subject.

She looked at me, and said, "You're caught up in size, Adam. It's as dangerous as being caught up in time. They're both constructs."

I wasn't thinking about size at all. "But . . . but one multiverse, the first one, drunk and not-drunk, tells a million stories about me. The second multiverse doesn't illustrate free will at all."

"I bet—" she raised her glass, "—on the universe made of stories." She drank down all of her beer, and then another glass, something she'd never done before, and stood up, wobbling a little, and I took her elbow, guiding her out the door and across the lawn.

We were halfway across, Elsa leaning on my arm, when she stopped so we stood in the near-darkness, snow falling all around us. She reached an arm up and curled her wrist around the back of my head, pulling my face down into a kiss. Her lips were cool and soft, and we kissed hungrily, like two children finally allowed out for recess. Her lips tasted like sweet hot peppers and beer. It was the only time she ever kissed me.

What happened that night in some other multiverse?

For the next three weeks, Elsa worked with PI as if they were in a race. Her face shone with energy, and even when she grew visibly tired, her eyes danced. I hovered around the edges, watching. Elsa was so deeply enthralled that loud noises made her leap and glare at me, and I walked carefully. At first, PI and Elsa continued with audible noise, like the humming/symphony, played so softly I could barely hear it. Then PI started generating white noise, taking the small background sounds with everything important filtered out from the very room around us. Then I heard silence, and Elsa and PI talked in light. I took to watching the conversation on my own interface with PI, which amounted to watching lights and words flash on and off, strings drawn between ideas and concepts and even poems. I could not follow them, but the relationships they drew seemed right, and when I let go of the attempt to understand there was a flow that I could feel, as if a river of meaning coursed along the display in front of me.

Almost every day, Elsa found a new thing to include in PI's expanding web of connectivity. Scientology. Cargo Cult. Early cave paintings.

I captured all of it, recording the data for others to dig through. For myself, I tried to keep up with them, puffing along uphill, weighed down by inability to focus. I kept Elsa fed, but she refused to go home, and I bought a second cot so that she would not be alone.

We didn't make the first breakthrough.

Outside the window, morning sun stabbed the ice on the branches with brilliant points of light. The office smelled like stale coffee and
sweat. My eyelids were heavy and uncooperative, my brain fuzzing
gently in and out of sleep. Elsa was still sleeping, curled underneath
blankets I'd brought from home for her, one foot stuck out at an odd
angle. The display in front of me sprang awake on its own, a pulsing
green and blue color, PI's call for attention. "Yes, PI?"

"Something touched me. Wake Elsa."

I didn't understand. "All right." I struggled up out of the chair,
wishing I'd already made my coffee run. "Just a minute. Make yourself seen, all right?" I always preferred to interact with the hologram
rather than the flat display. It gave PI more options as well; she could
communicate more like a human. AI body language.

I whispered in Elsa's ear. "PI says something touched her."

Elsa sat straight up, wide-eyed, and glanced at the hologram display. PI was seated, her image dressed in jeans and a tank-top, bang-
ing her legs against the edge of a holographic chair, indicating impa-
tience. "I wasn't even out-calling, I was just humming my own songs,"
she blurted out, "and an answer came. An AI just like me, with a
scientist named Elsa. Seconds only, like a crack opened and closed. I
could only talk to the AI, of course, and I was sending her the data
stream from our last few weeks when the connection broke."

"Did you get a time?" Elsa asked quietly.

The PI image frowned. "I asked, but the connection snapped before an answer came."

"Can you replay the conversation?"

The image shook its head. I checked. The last few moments before PI flashed at me were silent. "There's nothing. Just state data,
indicating excitement."

"That's okay," Elsa said, "we'll work on that." She plucked at a
tangle in her hair. "PI, what did you feel?"

It was a strange question to ask an AI.

"Bigger. Pulled. Attracted to the other one of me. But at the
same time, I knew—" the word 'knew' drew itself over her head
in three dimensions, for emphasis, surely for me— "I knew that I
couldn't actually get close. As if there were a physical barrier between branes."

Elsa pursed her lips. I went out for coffee.

When I came back in, handing Elsa a cup, she took it and sipped quietly. "We have to make it happen again," she said. "Or hope it happens again. We didn't start it."

"Make what happen? I don't get it, not yet."

"The coffee is hot, right?"

I smiled at her. "That's a good thing."

"But it's not true." She sipped her own coffee carefully. "Touch your knee."

I did.

"What did you touch?"

"My knee."

"No, you touched a fence. You've got all the theory, all the math. You know we are really light and sound, thinner than that hologram of PI." She glanced over at PI's image, which was clear enough that I could make out the walls behind it. "Well, PI being touched by herself—in another universe—means that we are light, and sound, and infinite." Elsa stopped for a moment, her eyes nearly glazing over. "I thought a data construct could do what we cannot. Or at least, could lead the way." She set the coffee down and stood, staring out the window, posed very much like I first saw her. "I intend to follow her into my own stories. If I can."

"Into your stories?"

"Remember the night I drank the beer? History split, and the normal me—since I don't usually drink much—split off into a different universe. I'm splitting myself all the time, and so are you."

"Theoretically."

"Theoretically. I tell PI daily to search for me by searching for herself. Millions of PIs and millions of Elsas, and probably millions of Adams, all looking for each other. The more culture, the more ideas we feed PI, the more likely she is to synthesize the key. Our PI did not, or she would have made first contact. But in another story, in another place, I fed PI the key."

She pursed her lips and stared out the window at the icy branches, water dripping off them as the day warmed up. She spoke again. "Perhaps another Adam fed her the key."

It took another year to develop enough data to create a paper, to replicate any results at all. The first two times were other PIs finding our PI, three separate PIs, or four, depending on how you count. They learned to hold the connections open, to broaden them, to find more. Together PI and Elsa were able to prove they were in the same time, in other spaces. In other words, they were not histories of each other, or futures of each other. Multiverses. The proof was mathematical.

I wrote the paper, putting her name first, even though most of the data came from PI, who of course wasn't listed as an author. They'd gone well past me now. Elsa with her perfect savant focus and PI, who wasn't held back by biology at all.

More people came to visit, a steadier stream. We used some extra money I'd squirreled away in an R & D account to buy an electronic calendar and carefully manage access, blocking time for ourselves. It bought us whole days, uninterrupted, here and there. Elsa could still pull herself together for public visits, but she retreated entirely on the quiet days, not wanting touch or sound. She talked to PI, to multiple PIs via our PI, and I sat, outside of her emotions, fenced away by her brilliant mind. She often smiled at nothing, or rather, at something I could not hear or see.

There were multiple Adams, although not always. Sometimes the assistant was someone else. In one universe, I had died the previous spring and there was a new person helping that Elsa, that PI. It didn't seem to bother Elsa at all.

It sent me out for a pitcher of beer.

My head spun. This was what I had always wanted, except what I truly wanted had changed to chili and cornbread with my Elsa.

It was two years ago. I remember the date, April 12th, 2021. I watched her as she looked out the open window. Tears streamed down her face. Her shoulders shook.

I had never seen her cry. Not in ten years.

I came up behind her, and put my arms around her. She flinched inward, as if wanting to escape from my embrace. I held her anyway, put my cheek against her hair, looked down through half-closed eyes and watched her freckles. She had been friendly, funny, lost, distant, but never, never afraid. I held her tighter, and stroked her hair, trembling myself. What had she found?

It took a while, but finally she looked me in the eyes, and said, "I can't get through. Only PI can. The PIs. Other AIs. Nothing I do lets me get through. The other Elsas can't either. As brilliant as we are, as strange, as blessed, we can't open the door. The notes aren't there—my body . . . my body gets in the way." She blinked, and two fresh tears fell down her cheeks. I wanted to lick them off.

"I'm sure now that only pure data can get through. Humans will not become pure data for years yet, past my lifetime. I will never see what PI sees." She turned around then, pulled herself into me, and sobbed until my shirt was soaked and my feet were heavy from standing in one place.

The smell of lawn wet with spring rain blew in the window, and I heard students laughing below us, teasing each other.

Then, in one of her lightning changes of mood, Elsa pushed away from me and started out the door. I thrust her coat at her, and she grabbed it with one hand, pulling the door shut behind her, leaving no invitation for me to follow.

I went home that night, and the next day, Elsa didn't show. I waited impatiently until afternoon, finally walking to her brownstone. The door pushed open, unlocked. Elsa's things remained, all in their accustomed places.

I walked back across campus, blue sky above me, the grass under my feet damp and greening up. I tore the door open. "PI! Where the hell is Elsa?"

PI's interface was a little boy with a fishing pole, a holo I'd chosen. I didn't want it now. "Bring the old man!"

PI morphed to the dancer instead, sitting on a rock, feet crossed daintily. "I don't know where she's gone."

"Damn it! I'm worried. The last time I saw her, she cried. She thought she'd never get across."

"I know that."

Of course. PI was always on.

Cool spring rain flooded the gutters and made small rivers in the University lawns. I bundled up, and went every place we had ever gone together. Restaurants. Bookstores. The old music shop on the boulevard with garish purple posters in the window.

Two joggers found her body the next morning, sitting against a tree. The police took me to her, to identify her. She looked incredibly young, and could have been sleeping except for her stillness and the cold. She had put her coat on, only now it was soaked and heavy and couldn't possibly keep her warm. There was no sign of foul play. Rain covered her cheeks like tears, and I bent down and slid my forefinger across her face before a policeman asked me to step back.

An older policeman and a young woman in plainclothes questioned me, and made me spend a week out of the lab. When I went back to work, everything was out of place. Not much; people had been respectful. Elsa would have noticed the pencil cup three inches from its corner, the stack of books on the wrong shelf, the cups from the sink set back out of order.

PI was waiting for me, as the old man. She looked up solemnly, clearly aware of what happened. "Three of them."

"What?"

"I found three Elsas who killed themselves. Two disappeared." She was crying, her eyes red in the old man's face.

The other Elsas continue to work, and I talk with them through PI. I keep myself in good shape, running every morning. I'm younger than the Elsas, and perhaps I will be able to cross before I die.

RIDING in MEXICO

My host, Valeria, barely noticed the Mexican sun sparkle on the Caribbean, gold on brilliant blue. The salt scents of the sea and her sweat sat thick in my head, laid over with unfamiliar flowers, and a trace of animal—pig? She barely reacted to heat that made it hard for me to breathe. Her right knee sent shooting pains up her back whenever she stepped on an uneven patch that turned her foot inward. A chronic injury? She didn't let the pain slow her. She turned from time to time, looking back over her shoulder. The thick wooden handle of a machete rode loosely in her fingers, like I might carry my car keys or all-in-one, like part of her. We rode host's senses, not feelings, not true emotions. That's what they told me, anyway. But right now, I felt her. I felt what she felt. I *knew* she was frightened of whatever it was she kept turning to look for, frightened of something or someone who could leap out of the jungle at her.

I had been told that it would be hard to ride a far-host, but no words had told me how foreign another woman in another place could smell and move and even see. And yet how close she would be to me, how much I felt like she and I walked through the heat and the thick scent of green and rot and dust all together.

I faded slowly away from Valeria's senses, trading the Mexican Riviera for the plastic chairs and scuffed tile of a small classroom on the University of Washington campus. For the first few breaths I felt as if I were still in Valeria as well as in me, Isa.

I still felt fear. Not my own.

I had wanted Indians. From India, like people who rode dromedaries and lived in the Thar desert near the border with Pakistan. To feel heat, and the rolling gait of the camels and see the women who still travelled veiled and help them understand how modern women lived, help them see how they didn't have to submit to anything they didn't want to. But my friend Kay got the Indian desert women, and I got Mexico. Probably that was a result of choosing Spanish in fifth grade instead of Punjabi or Hindi. Not that Kay spoke either.

Kay and I shared everything, so I'd learn about the desert anyway, even if I didn't get to ride in a caravan across it. Besides, now that I'd ridden her, I wanted Valeria. And hey, at least they gave me the Mexican Riviera and not someplace awful on the border like Tijuana. Dr. Peters, who oversaw our trips, told Kay and me we'd see poverty, but probably not senseless violence. He sent the male students to places like Darfur and Columbia. No women to anyplace scary or unsafe. Prig. Not that I wanted Darfur, even though the enemy had transformed from the Janjaweed to simple poverty and drought.

The small room felt crowded with ten of us, five teams, me and Kay together, all of us blinking uncertainly. Besides us ten, there was Dr. Peters and the paramedic the school insurance required for this class, a tall drink of cuteness who sat in the corner and ignored me completely.

After ten minutes with Valeria, I worried about her. Exactly like I'd been told not to. I couldn't say anything for fear of Dr. Peter's legendary wrath-of-god-look.

A slender blonde puked into her coffee cup in the back row, her face red with pain and maybe also embarrassment. The paramedic didn't respond, so apparently puking was a normal reaction.

Dr. Peters ignored her, too. He stood calmly, hands clasped in front of him, his incredible blue eyes calm. "Remember, these people are doing a job. They barely knew you were there. You felt what they felt—sensually. Taste and smell and touch and hearing. They feel you as a weight, a buzz of electricity. Starting tomorrow, you will ride them daily. If you think twenty minutes was hard, wait until you're on for two hours."

Hosting students and tourists paid enough for them to live. It had made me shiver at first, but during orientation Dr. Peters told us, "It's easier than whoring or picking bananas." That eradicated my guilt. Besides, I'd suffered through a background check and an NDA just to get into the Good Doctor's scariest course. I wanted a job in the diplomatic corps too bad to drop, and the other option had involved remoting drones in the Afghan/Indian war.

And now that I'd been once, I *wanted* to ride Valeria again. To smell the Caribbean and feel the strange, slight differences between our senses. To fix whatever made her afraid. Even so, I heard my father's words in the back of my skull: "Diplomacy can't fix everyone. Some days it breaks hearts." Knowing that had never stopped him from trying.

After an hour of lessons and questions, even puke-girl had stopped and become quiet. I think we were all too disoriented to pay exact attention. I know I was.

After class, Kay and I had two hours free, so we wandered through the grounds, taking paths between buildings aimlessly, passing the big Suzzallo Library and dodging smart-boarders as we walked down the steps to the Quad. Kay was tall and red-haired and fair, and so surely nothing like her host, Bani. "It's too bad we can't hear thoughts," she mused.

"How would we keep two sets of thoughts free of each other?"

She hugged herself, bent slightly over. "I just felt lost. Almost dizzy."

"The Caribbean Sea is prettier than I thought it would be."

"The desert smelled like dust and sun and oil."

"Valeria is scared of something." We went up a short flight of stone steps. "Maybe the drug lords? Or the federales?"

"Remember not to jump to conclusions." Kay wagged a finger at me and stuck her neck out, a fair imitation of the good Dr. Peters. "Be an observer, not a participant."

I shrugged. "It's not a conclusion. I know it. She's scared."

"Maybe she was scared of you."

"Maybe. But she kept looking over her shoulder. It didn't seem like a reaction to me." A bicycle whipped past us and we stepped aside. "How did Bani feel?"

"Like her mouth was dry and like she was tired and a little sweaty. But it's not her first time. Hosting is like walking for her."

"I'm Valeria's first."

That night, I dreamed I swam naked in that warm sea, and floated out on the low bob of the water past the shallow waves and felt the sun on my belly and breasts.

The next day, class started at seven in the morning. I sat in my hard chair sipping a latte and feeling anxious. Dark circles under Kay's eyes suggested she'd slept about like me, but Dr. Peters was already pontificating in front of the class and I couldn't ask her.

Had Valeria spent a good night, or a bad one? Had she been scared?

Her picture was the background for my all-in-one. She looked about twenty-five, with long dark hair that fell to her waist in thick curls that wanted a comb. In the picture, she had on khaki pants and a white shirt with buttons and a pocket over each breast. Thin sandals supported sturdy feet. Something glinted in one ear, but it was impossible to tell if it was silver or gold against her nearly-mahogany skin. Except for shorter and thinner hair, I might look like that if I lived in sun instead of rain. What frightened her? How different were the two of us? I had travelled of course, summer vacations in Europe and Canada and, once, a week on the Cuban beaches. But that had not been intimate, the people curiosities or helpers or simply confusing.

We'd had transmitters slipped under our scalps. For now, our rides started at the same time, Seattle. Kay would fall into an Indian evening and I would land in Mexico's late morning. They'd split us later, four classes, but for the first few days the hosts just had to deal with it. Not too bad for Valeria. With a push of a button, Dr. Peters turned on the fields that sent our normal senses to sleep, fading the room we sat in into the very barest back of ourselves and sending a jolt of new senses into our brains.

It was three hours later in Yucatán, and already hot. Clouds piled on the horizon. The air felt thick with impending rain. Yesterday, I hadn't been acknowledged at all, but this morning, Valeria spoke out loud. "Hello, Isa."

I could not, of course, reply.

"I will treat you to coffee and we will walk on the beach today. It will be a tourist day for you." Valeria's English had the barest accent. She took me down streets where more people were local, although we passed a pair of pale-skinned men in Hawaiian shirts and two fat white women chattering in German, and a skinny man with red hair and a big laugh. Valeria didn't seem to like any of them much, and kept her distance.

I had started to adjust to the ways Valeria's walk was different than mine, with longer strides and less hurry. She stopped for coffee so dark and bitter I wanted cream in my mouth to cut it down.

"We are in Playa Del Carmen. East of the stinking resorts." For two hours, she walked and pointed out an old ruin, a shop that had been selling sweet cakes and Coca-Cola on the same corner for fifty years and had kept it up even after Hurricane Mallory, the house of a rich French man with an aviary so close to the crumbling sidewalk that Valeria's eyes could see brightly colored birds darting through lush plants with green leaves and red stems. Many of the things she pointed out were new, of course, post storm, and post investment. But Playa had not been damaged beyond repair, and old and new mixed with rich and poor.

Other than the wondrous raw scrape of a stranger's senses cutting through my brain, I might as well have been wearing museum headphones. Unlike yesterday, she felt more resigned than afraid; cool and distant. So why? Was it part of the class exercise to figure out how to get actual information from your host?

Well, of course it was. My brain ran down that path while she meandered on, dragging me back with a vengeance when she stepped into the water and waded through sand. My legs felt wet like hers even though my feet were still and dry. She looked out, pointing at the sea. Resentment clogged her voice. "The reef has been bleached by excess, by pigs who burn too much gasoline and tourists with sunscreen. It is filled with dead coral that stinks when you pull it out of the water."

I wanted to tell her it wasn't me, or even my parents. To say we were helping her now. But of course, I had no mouth in Mexico. She stood and looked out at the beautiful water with the sun splashing it, an offshore break the only sign of the dead things buried in the waves. I couldn't hear her thoughts, but what I thought was how things often looked one way, like the calm, warm water looked inviting. But really, they hid something else.

A soft buzz filled her ears. The timer on her watch. She turned it off. "Thank you for choosing me," she said formally. "I'll talk to you this evening."

I returned to the shuffle of metal chair feet on tile and the sounds of the same woman who'd retched yesterday retching again. Sweat ran down my forehead, as if my body really had been in a tropical ninety degrees instead of the cool northwest summer near an open window. In the corner, one of the men looked straight ahead, his eyes wide and damp and his tongue licking his lips frantically.

Dr. Peters called on him. "Mathew?"

"The . . . my hosts's baby died. Now. I saw it."

Dr. Peters didn't even soften his voice. His words were clipped. "The poor choose to let us host."

Sanctimonious bastard. Easy for us to assume the poor *let* us host. Even though Sensory Wireless Ride Chips weren't supposed to be available to the public, rumor said they were big in the sex trade. I didn't say that even though I wanted to. Mathew closed his eyes and put his long-fingered hands over his face.

Dr. Peters continued. "Write. Now. Write down what happened without talking to each other and then we'll discuss your next assignment."

So pens scratched paper and fingers tapped all-in-ones and the puking girl had the hiccups and one of the women in the front had an experimental table-topper that let her just write on her desk with her finger. Even though she made the least noise, most of us sent fascinated glances her way regularly. Kay, true to her nature, was completely absorbed in her bamboo-paper journal, crabbing out tiny lines.

Me? I wrote the following:

Why is she so pissed? How do I get to her? We know nothing of each other except this business transaction. We have each other's pictures. That's so . . . surface. I know what she feels but I don't know why! I hate this. I was afraid, being in her. What is she afraid of? And then, as an afterthought, *What am I afraid of?*

Then I figured I best have a whole page at least, just in case the Good Doctor came by and peered over our shoulders, and so I described the things I'd seen (crumbling bricks and sidewalks, dirt paths, children with patched clothes but clean faces, houses like mansions next to houses with leaning walls and tin roofs), the smells (the sea, the sea, and the sea, and the bitter coffee), and what I'd heard (tropical birds, with voices twice as pretty and ten times as loud as our little northwest finches).

I felt like a tourist. I wanted . . . to learn about Mexico and Valeria. If I couldn't have camels I could actually learn about the drug wars and the tourist tensions and how it felt not to be American. What did someone like Valeria think of people like me, richer by a factor of ten or twenty even if I was only upper middle-class?

Dr. Peter's voice startled me. "Turn your responses in." I twitched and looked up. He was glaring at me, and probably repeating himself.

So I sent my paper, kneejerk good behavior, and soon as it was sent I wished I'd removed the dorky lines about fear and feelings. He was going to give me a lecture and mark me down. Students called him the Good Doctor because you couldn't get away with anything in his class. That made us like him and not like him all at once. He'd told us to be impartial observers, like scientists. Like junior scientists. No attachments.

Outside, Kay leaned down and whispered at me. "You looked downright pissed."

I shook my head. "Just not what I expected. What was your ride like?"

"I bet I can ride a camel now. We were part of a caravan, like fifty camels and fifty people, although some men and boys walked. Did you know camels fart? Bani has to ride veiled, but she barely notices it. I'd rip the damned thing off."

"You have her picture, right?"

She nodded and peeled off her coat. "Thank god it warmed up. This morning was so cold, then the desert was so hot, and now it's perfect."

"So she wasn't veiled in her picture? You know what her face looks like?"

"Yes. But she had on a turtleneck and a neck scarf in the desert." She frowned. "She's pretty. Almost thirty-five, and her skin's like cream."

"What did she tell you about the caravan? Did she, like, narrate?"

"Just the names of the camels and the people. I think she liked the camels better. Who'd have thought I'd be doing a camel fair in 2021?"

"I think it's cool the world is still different in some places. Did you feel like she was talking to—well, to you? Or was she narrating for a stranger?"

Kay laughed. "I am a stranger. Look, I gotta meet my group from Online Finance. We get to see if we made money yet."

"Of course you did."

"Well, how much."

My next class was Vertical Gardening, a bit of engineering day-dream about feeding the world by planting green skyscrapers full of dirt and lights in major cities. I kept seeing Valeria walking around

the buildings in my head, her strong dark face and slender body limp-
ing among the lush corn and beans and wheat on the fiftieth floor
or striding through the rooftop flower garden, looking down at the
sculptured beds as if they represented evil instead of beauty.

Each student got to call their hosts at night. They required we do
that from the diplo department offices. Our calls were by team for the
first day, so Kay and I met again in Dr. Peter's tiny office. There were
only two real books, stacked horizontally on top of his desk. A copy
of the *Rubiyat*, the big illustrated kind, and a slim, battered version of
The Art of War. I couldn't picture him reading the *Rubiyat*.

He told us what to say (thanks, and to ask any questions we had
about the day) and what not to say (anything that would make them
think we saw ourselves as better than them, a lecture we got all the
time, not to think we were better at all, ever. We knew that, but Dr.
Peters told us every day anyway). Lecture delivered, he told me to wait
and asked Kay to follow him to another office.

When he came back into his office, he sat down more quietly
than I expected and gave me a thoughtful look. It felt like he wanted
me to say something, but I held out. I didn't want to be the one who
started the process of beating me up for feeling Valeria. Finally he
said, "You are a rare one."

I waited.

"Only one in a hundred people have your empathy with the hosts."

"What about Mathew?" I challenged him. "He was almost crying."

"Because of what he saw, and how that made him feel. Not because of how much he felt his host's pain."

I wasn't sure I understood. "You think I feel Valeria more than he
felt . . ." I had to reach for the name of his host. "Jacob? Why?"

"It's almost never men."

"Oh."

"And you had so much feeling in your report."

Yeah. I felt my cheeks get hot. He must have read my uncertainty
about his reaction on my face. "It's okay. But I wanted a moment with
you. What you think you feel from her may not be what she is feeling.
Your interpretations will still be filtered through your own experiences, even if you are as strong an emotional rider as possible."

I twisted my hands a bit and thought about it. "So you're saying I
may think I know what she feels but not really know?"

He nodded. "Yes."

"So why are you so sure I'm feeling more about Valeria than the other students feel about their hosts? Was it what I wrote?"

"Partly. And partly how your brain waves pattern."

Right. Like we students were bugs. I'd known it was all experimental.

He went on, his voice almost soft and friendly. "It means you'll be particularly valuable. Your skill is rare enough that I'm sure I can get you work—real work—even before you graduate."

"Diplo work?"

He shook his head. "Sort of. We're information gatherers. We ride victims and catch bad guys. Remember the story in last week's paper, where the slaver ring in South Korea got busted up and fifty teenage girls got to go home? We caught the bastards by riding one of the girls. That's how we got descriptions of the slavers and figured out how to find evidence."

Oh. Wow. What would that feel like? "So wouldn't you want someone who didn't feel their hosts for that?"

He smiled. "Some hosts can feel their riders. They get good at this and use it for misinformation."

Oh.

"Plus, an empath we've validated can use the emotional state of the host in court."

All right. Enough new information. "Can I call Valeria now? She must be waiting for me."

The way his gaze stopped for a long time on my face, I figured that if he could stick me with a pin and display me he would. But instead, he nodded. "Go on. But push her. Tell her to show you what she's scared of. I'll be done with all the other students at nine tonight. Can you drop by then?"

And just like I'd sent him the paper without thinking, I nodded without thinking. Someday I was going to get out of the blind obey mode. Really I was.

But first, I placed my call to Valeria.

Her voice sounded slightly higher on the phone than it had in my head. We had video, a small square of her face showing in my computer monitor as she smiled and said, "Hello, Isa, how are you?"

We talked for a few minutes about nothing, the thank you's and all that. I leaned forward in the hard chair. "What was it like for you, having someone else in your head?"

She looked away and then said, "Odd."

At least she wasn't lying. "Were you afraid?"

"No."

"Of something besides me?"

Hesitation gave her away, although she said, "There is always fear here."

"Show me."

She blinked at the screen, and then started twisting her fingers through her copious dark curls. "Tomorrow we're going to my home and you will see me talking to my family. In Spanish." She grinned. "Sometimes I am afraid of my mother."

I laughed. It was the most genuine response I'd seen from her. "Then ignore that fear. I'll never follow the conversation. I only have two years of school Spanish." But she wasn't talking about her fears. I didn't want another tourist day. "Can you go look at whatever scared you yesterday, instead? I want to understand how we can help."

Her eyes widened and her mouth opened. She leaned away from the camera, which had the effect of making her head look smaller in my computer screen. A tense look took over her face, thinning her lips and narrowing her eyes. "You are like—the NGOs. You try to change the world into a better place, which means someplace you feel comfortable."

That stung. "A safer place." An uncomfortable silence stretched for a bit, then I said, "So show me what would be better. For you."

"You don't know what to do, so you flutter around the edges of our real problems."

"Which are?"

"Maybe you should keep your eyes open and then you'll see."

I pushed back. "I'm in school. I need to learn something. If you hide yourself from me every time I'm with you, what will I learn?"

Her voice was stiff. "If I see anything I'm afraid of tomorrow, I'll show you." She glanced at her watch and looked resigned to spending more time on the call with me.

"I'll tell you about me."

She nodded.

"I'm interested in global sustainability. I want to help people find ways to live together."

She stared straight forward at the screen.

"I mean it when I say I want to help."

Silence.

"Don't you want sustainability?"

More silence.

This time, I didn't say anything either.

Eventually, she spoke. She had to; I was her employer. "I want to have the world back the way I knew it before. Before Hurricane Mallory, before my little brother died, when more tourists flew down here."

"What did your brother die of?"

She looked away. "He ran drugs and he got shot."

"I'm sorry." What to say next? "There is no place to go but the future."

She stared back at me from the tiny square on the screen. Her beaches were cleaner now, and so was her air. Maybe the reefs would recover, but there was no telling yet.

I made my words as gentle as I could. "You can't go backward."

"Forward means I have a tourist in my head." I wasn't riding her that moment, I couldn't feel her. But some things can be written on faces. Despair, and feeling trapped.

"If you don't want me with you, I'll find someone else."

She swallowed and looked away, her head bowed down at an angle and her hair falling across one closed eye. "Please don't."

"I'll see you tomorrow. Please show me why you're scared." I fell silent. We'd been told to push them in this hour, that it was the only time we would really connect. After all, when we rode them, we couldn't talk to them at all. I lowered my voice to almost a whisper, a soft-ball plea. "I need to learn."

"I promised to tell you about more tomorrow, about what is scary for me."

But she didn't promise to look for it.

"I don't promise to like you."

I barely managed not to show my shock on my face. I liked her! "I know. Thank you," I said, and closed the connection, setting her free to be herself. Maybe this was what the Good Doctor meant by riding victims, although I didn't think so. Of course, being scared of something didn't make her a victim; it made her scared. And not liking me made her smart, in the sense that I was an intrusive stranger. I had to become more to her.

At least I knew her fear was real. Maybe I was lucky to have a first-timer—I would be willing to bet Bani would never open up to Kay. Even if Bani hated Kay as much as Valeria hated me, Kay would never know it.

I left before Kay was done with her phone calls, and before Dr. Peters returned, hugging the walls, sliding past students preparing for night classes and joking about yesterday's losing game. Outside, the cooling air braced me. I walked through it for an hour, aimless and meandering, thinking about feeling Valeria.

Just before nine, I waited in the hallway outside of the Good Doctor's office. I hadn't told Kay I was coming back, and it felt weird to keep things from her. I kept my all-in-one off so I wouldn't have to lie to her if she reached out for me.

Darlene, the puking girl, finished up a conversation with Dr. Peters where she rubbed her belly and made funny faces and he shook his head at her and sat back in his chair looking resigned. Right on the hour he stood up while she was mid-sentence, waiting politely while she gathered her things. When she saw me she gave a little wave and ducked her head, and I could already hear the rumors. I should have been late.

And then he was closing the door behind him. "Have you eaten?"

Well, no. So I shook my head, suddenly mute.

"Then let's go get a burger."

Instead of walking over to the U-District, I followed him onto a Capitol Hill bus and we ended up in a cheap bar a lot like the ones closer to the University, except this one wasn't full of students. He ignored the slightly-dressed hostess and led me through a room with pool tables and immersives and outside onto a deck with a view of the lights of West Seattle sprinkling glitter on the dark water of the Sound.

The table he picked wasn't empty. A slender gray-haired man in a navy-blue sweatshirt nodded as Dr. Peters sat down. "This must be Isa," he said.

Dr. Peters nodded and glanced at me. "Isa. This is Dr. David Meera from the NSA."

The what? Why hadn't Dr. Peters told me he was meeting somebody else? I held out my hand. "Pleased to meet you."

Dr. Meera's hand was dry, his grip firm.

Dr. Peters said, "I called him after I read your notes this afternoon. We have ... something has come up and we may ..."

The older man interrupted. "We need to give you more background. Valeria is in real danger." He picked up the plastic-sheathed menu and glanced up at an approaching waitress, an older woman with stringy red hair and kind, blue eyes. "Let's order."

I'd just lost my appetite, but I managed to squeak out an order for a hamburger with a side salad and a microbrew. Neither man said anything else until our beers appeared. I finished a long, foamy sip. "Explain?" I suggested.

Dr. Meera continued. "Mexico still has a serious black market. Even though marijuana dried up with legalization, they can produce psilocybin and a number of other designer jungle drugs, especially in the Yucatán and Chiapas. Valeria's mother and brother are in that business, which is why we recruited her."

Her mother? Maybe she had been telling me her fears. I stayed quiet, sipping my beer while the pair of professors watched me. "They have some enemies, and that's what Valeria was afraid of. You sensed that, right away. We were going to let her get used to being ridden with a few classes of students, then introduce someone better for her, an emotion rider like you, but with advanced training."

Dr. Peters took it up. "Someone like what you could become."

A sudden fear iced my stomach. "Are you going to take Valeria away from me?"

"We should," Dr. Peters said sharply.

Dr. Meera, however, shook his head. He was clearly the boss. "There's no time. Rivals are closing in on Valeria's family. It's possible you are the only one who can save her."

The conversation had shifted into bad dialogue from a low-budget movie. I managed to come up with an appropriate line. "A little melodramatic aren't we?" I watched them both as I took another sip of beer. They didn't flinch under my gaze. "Tell me you're just testing me. This is part of the class, right?"

Silence.

"I can't talk to her. How am I supposed to save her from anything?"

Dr. Meera put his hand on mine, on the table. He used light force, flattening my fingers against the oak. "Sometimes you can't. But if anyone threatens her, or hurts her, or kills her, you will be able to see who they are and act as a witness."

"You aren't pulling your punches."

"We need to know if you're strong enough."

Dr. Peters had given all the real war zones to the men in the class. "I can do it." Dr. Meera hadn't moved his hand, so I tugged mine out from under his. "I'll be okay. I want this job . . . I want into the corps and I need to do the hard stuff."

Dr. Peters said, "It will be worse for you than it was for Mathew. It would be . . . best if she does not die. That might be very hard."

The waitress appeared with three plates, sliding them expertly in front of us. I didn't want to eat until I bit into a sunshine-bright cherry tomato. After I finished the burger, I looked from one man to the other. "If I do this, will I get your recommendations for the diplomatic corps?"

Dr. Meera was watching me with a measuring gaze. "It's a tough job. Tell me why you want it."

"My parents were in the Peace Corps. They taught me you save the world globally. It's time to get past all this my country first stuff, or none of us will have a country." They were dead now. I didn't say that. We'd all coughed up all our background just to get into the program. So if they'd read it, they knew. That's how I was getting through school, on their death payments.

"If you succeed, I'll put in a good word."

"Does that mean if I keep her from getting killed?"

Dr. Meera smiled sadly. "You will not have control over that. If you stay sane."

The next morning, summer drizzle slicked the paths and made jewelry of the spiderwebs. Kay caught up with me, a little breathless. "You abandoned me, where the heck did you go?" And then, after she got a better look, "You're white. Are you sick?"

I'd been warned not to talk about it. Silence was a skill I'd need if I got into the corps anyway. "Just a bad dream."

"You're taking this too seriously. Dr. Peters said we'd flunk if we got too attached to our host. You don't want that."

I almost burst out laughing and hurried to change the subject. "How did your talk with Bani go?"

"Good, I think. I had a bunch of questions prepared, and she answered most of them. She was very polite. Tomorrow, her people are going to a camel fair and they hope to get new cams they can mount right on their heads and on the camel's headgear to send pics up to GeoSearch. For kids to use, like in class. Almost what we're doing, but with gear on camels."

"Cool. Do you like the camels?"

She nodded. Back in the classroom, sitting on hard seats, we breathed in the industrial world while we got ready to trade it for the developing and destroyed parts of the Earth. I was suddenly proud of us, all of us. We were making a future. Most of the other students looked excited. The paramedic was a new one, younger, with a scar on his chin.

And then I was scared again, swearing I wouldn't see Valeria die, that it would be okay. Why hadn't the teachers talked to me before I talked to Valeria? I could guess. But Dr. Peters had goaded me into asking her to show me what she was afraid of, hadn't he? Was that ethical? And did they tell me everything they knew?

Dr. Peters thumbed the switch and I smelled Valeria and the jungle. She was breathing hard, jogging. The back of her knee hurt. She ran along the side of a paved road with no cars on it, with banyans and cieba on the far side, a canopy of dark green against a pale blue sky dotted with high thin clouds. She felt me come into her—and I felt her close down and then open again. She spoke. "Buenos días, my friend."

Her voice was almost laughter. She didn't seem as angry as she had sounded yesterday. I wanted to ask her about it, but of course, conversations were one-way.

"Yes, it is a pretty day, my gringa friend. That means white girl."

From what I knew, the term wasn't complimentary.

"I will show you my fears today," she said. "They might fire me for it, at least if you tell them. But no one but you can hear me, right?" Her breath was fast from the slow jog and the heat. "We are alone."

She slowed, let her heart slow until I could no longer feel it overtake mine. Her stride became a ground-eating walk, something she did with no complaint even though I felt actual physical pain with every step she took. It made me wonder if she felt the pain like I did, or if she had somehow learned to go through it and past it and beyond it.

Personally, I wanted an ibuprofen, and it wasn't even my leg that hurt.

"I am going to show you my grandmother's house." She spoke

English, out loud, since that was the only way I could hear her. The road was empty; a few birds and maybe a monkey overheard her. "My grandmother's life. And then I will show you my mother's life, and then my life. And then maybe we can talk about hope the way you talk about it in America. This isn't what I'm supposed to do, but then I'm not good at doing what I'm supposed to do. I'm no good girl like they usually pick for this. But after talking to you, I hope you are a little like me."

I could feel her—she was proud of herself and apprehensive as well; she felt like I felt when I suspected that something I was about to do would get me into trouble. Only I hadn't felt like this for a long time, hadn't taken risks, had done just what I was told, like sending my report to the Good Doctor Peters on command and doing everything else on command because I thought that would get me what I wanted.

If this was real diplomatic work—watching a situation that might hurt someone you like and not being able to do a thing about it—it sucked. Mom and Dad had always said it sucked, even though they went back every day.

Valeria turned down a thin track. Ruts showed a car or a scooter or something wheeled with an engine used the road. She walked down the middle, swinging her arms. Her hands were free; no machete. A pack pulled her shoulders back, but of course I couldn't see it. She started singing in Spanish, her voice high and clear. She felt wary, but not afraid. She rounded a corner and stopped in front of a short, circular home with no walls—an honest-to-god thatch hut—beside a small cenote. An orange tree had been planted beside the hut, the fruit ripening. A banana palm and three or four other non-native trees also looked healthy. A white plastic bucket tilted on its side by the cenote suggested they were hand-watered. Three brightly colored pots with herbs sat by the hut. Another whole line, maybe a dozen more pots, sat under a makeshift shade of tied colorful tourist saris—the kind you can buy for five dollars each in the beachside markets. These pots held blooming flowers that might have been found in an American grocery store: miniature roses and sunflowers and orchids. While there might be enough shadows inside to hide someone, I rather doubted it.

Whatever wheeled transportation used the road, the only thing here now was a broken bicycle completely missing both wheels.

I guessed we'd come all this way for nothing, but Valeria didn't hesitate, or even stop singing. She simply went around the back and followed a thin trail into the jungle. After a few minutes, she stopped and smiled, watching a small woman so old her back humped and her hair had thinned to mist. The woman balanced on her toes, her slender brown arms reaching into a tree. Before she turned, she pulled down a spray of yellow and orange flowers. Valeria sounded proud as she whispered, "That's my grandmother. She makes her living selling flowers."

There weren't enough flowers in all the pots for any kind of living.

"And I bring her some money every week. Otherwise, the jungle feeds her, too."

It sounded romantic, but I imagined it wasn't. The two women broke into excited, fast Spanish that I didn't have a prayer of following, so I watched the old woman's face. Wrinkles had folded her cheek and chin to the texture of figs and nearly hidden her eyes from the world. Even though her body moved slowly, her tongue kept up with Valeria's and they seemed happy to see each other.

Valeria passed her a handful of bills. The amount never came up, and the older woman simply shoved them in her pocket. After, Valeria gave her a long hug. I couldn't see the grandmother's face, of course, not at that point. I smelled the flowers—still in Valeria's grandmother's hands, and felt the love between the two women so hard that it stung my eyes.

I had never known one of my grandmothers, and the other I certainly wouldn't have known enough to find on a path in the jungle. I'd seen her at a handful of family events.

When we were nearly at the corner and about to turn down the track, Valeria said, "I would have liked to take you swimming. Her cenote is very sweet. But there is only an hour left, and I want to show you how my mother lives, too." She turned for a last look back. "See how happy she is? She works hard, works every day. She hardly has anything. That thin old dress and two more, plus one I gave her that she says is too nice to wear until her funeral. But she is happy. More happy than me, or I bet than you. I know she is happier than my mother. Almost no one lives so simply any more, even here. The deeper you go in the jungle, the more there is peace like this. Old women are mostly left alone. But if I lived alone out here, I would be raped." As if she heard my silent protest she said, "Even today."

With that she turned and started a fast walk down the pathway.

"I'm not going to tell you more until we see Mom. I want to be able to ask you about it when we talk on the phone tonight."

For the next twenty minutes, she hummed or was silent, and I smelled the jungle and noticed the unfamiliar sounds of birds and, once, the loud engine of an old gas-guzzler jeep with tires half as tall as me and a green roll bar that had one corner crumpled.

She whispered, "We're here," moving her head back and forth slowly as if panning her vision. "No one else is here, so we're safe. We won't be long. Watch closely." It took me a moment to realize she was doing that for me, helping me see what she wanted me to notice. In that moment, it dawned on me how much a host could provide, or hide, from a rider. If she had a gun strapped to her leg—or her machete in her backpack—I wouldn't know unless she looked at it or someone around remarked on it.

The small house looked slumped. It was mostly white now, but chips of stucco had fallen off, revealing that it had once been green, once brown, and maybe even once yellow. The wooden windows were rotten and one was gone entirely. Three bikes and a scooter stood chained to a post just outside the door. One was missing a back wheel. Three gasoline cars rusted happily to the ground on the potholed street, all of them past driving, and one past having any color at all. If this were a poor neighborhood in America, there would have been litter around the house, too, but the open dirt was so neat it might have been swept. Plants struggled in shady spots.

Valeria slipped through the ragged screen door. The living room was a small rectangle with two chairs that belonged in a dump and a small, neat wooden table with a lamp. "Madre?"

The woman who emerged from the bedroom looked older than Valeria's grandmother had. Although she moved a little better, her forearms were bruised and the skin under her eyes looked like the opening of a dark cave. Although her Spanish came fast, I caught the gist of it. "Why are you here now? It's the middle of the day. I thought you were looking for a job."

"I found one."

"So why aren't you working?"

"There's a schedule."

I lost track of the next comments from the older woman, a stream of something about food and the neighbors. Her bruises fascinated me. They ran up and down her arms and on the back of one hand. Her eyes and her tone and the way she carried herself tucked inside her hunched shoulders screamed of a hard life. She raised her voice. Although I couldn't follow it all, I got the idea the older woman meant to get Valeria out of her house without making her mad. Valeria felt hot and angry and embarrassed. Under the embarrassment, still fear. But for her mom or for herself?

The door opened and a tall young man came in. For a brief moment I expected him to be Valeria's drug-dealing brother, Raul. But the woman called him Mario and took a step back.

Valeria's heartbeat sped up and she glanced toward the door.

Mario looked at her and spoke in English. "Valeria. How nice. But you should leave now."

Even though I felt her hands shaking, Valeria stiffened. She spoke slowly, maybe for my sake, or maybe to counter her racing heartbeat. "This is *my* home, *my* mother. I belong here more than you."

His cold smile exposed brown teeth. He said something that sounded like "not anymore," and then he reached inside his pocket and handed her a thin package, something wrapped in paper. "Take this to town."

She didn't ask what it was but stepped back again, her back now to the wall. She shook her head. "I will not."

He held it out.

She didn't want to take it, but she did. I was the problem. If she took what must be drugs, she could be arrested or caught. But she couldn't tell him I rode her.

He grabbed her hand and shoved the packet in it.

The door behind him opened and two men came in. When they spotted Valeria, they stopped. One of them looked like he wanted to eat her. Really. His eyes were angry and hard and he was not at all happy she was there.

She gasped. I'd had thought she was afraid before, but this was worse.

He hit her. Her/me. I'd never been hit, never expected to feel the whipsaw of human flesh crushing my cheek against my eye and nose, feel the way flesh gives under the force of hatred.

She fell.

I didn't. I screamed, my body jerked into the cold hard classroom. My heart beat fast. I blinked and touched my smooth cheek, completely disoriented by the fluorescent light mixing with the pale outside light from the one window and shivering at the change in temperature. I had been told to do something if this happened? What? I shivered too hard to remember.

Oh. I finished the fall I'd started—like an interrupted moment—and hit the tile, moaning.

I caught a glimpse of Dr. Peter's face wearing the wrath-of-god look. It seemed directed at the universe, and not me. The faces of my classmates turned toward me, blinking and shocked.

Dr. Peters jerked his head toward the paramedic, who picked me up and carried me from the classroom. My face scraped against his dirty yellow coat, which smelled of old smoke and sweat. "Send me back," I whispered. He didn't respond, except to tuck me in even closer to him and keep going. Down the hall, he punched for an elevator, and kept holding onto me until we stepped inside. He set me down then, and looked into my eyes. "Are you okay?"

"Yes. Just send me back. Something's happening."

"Not yet."

I wanted to curse at him, but you don't curse at paramedics. I bit my tongue and worried.

The old elevator shuddered and slowed one floor above the class-room we'd just been in. We went back down the hall the way we'd come but a little higher. At the end, he let us through a locked door. Dr. Meera greeted me on the other side. He led me to a couch and gestured for me to lay down, and then tucked a pillow under my head. "What happened?" he asked.

"I have to go back. There's a man who hates her."

"Tell me."

He wasn't going to let me go back until I did. I could see that in his eyes, even though they looked kind. He was a firm man. I told him fast, just about the visit to her mother's, and then he took my hand. It felt good, his hand. Like support. "Are you sure you want to go back?"

I nodded. "I have to. I can't abandon her."

He glanced down at his watch. "It's been twenty minutes. That's a long time"

"Send me."

"Good luck. Observe closely. Help will come. Pray it comes in time." To my surprise, he gave me a small dark button, and closed my thumb over it.

"How do I find the button on the other side?"

"Don't let go of it." He helped me push it. The give was soft and easy, and there was a little click I'd never heard before.

Valeria lay on the floor. Her right hand cupped her cheek and her hurt leg felt hot and sharp.

Noise and tension filled the room. Valeria's mother cried and pleaded with Mario in Spanish. The dark-eyed man ignored them all, speaking rapidly into his all-in-one. It was the only modern thing in the room, a model more expensive than I could have afforded.

The button felt hard in my palm.

I wondered if she knew I was back, or even that I had gone.

The house was already full, but one more person came in the front door anyway.

"Raul," Valeria whispered.

Raul was a bit taller and broader, and his belly had settled outward some. Her brother should help her, shouldn't he?

He reached a hand down, pulling her upward with enough force to send pain shooting through her shoulder. Unlike the rest of the people in the room, he spoke in clear English. "Are you ridden?"

Oh god, he knew. He knew I was here.

She shook her head. "No. No. It is only for two hours. The time is past."

"I told you never to come back here if you let them make you a spy."

"I'm no spy!"

"Prove it."

"How?"

He stared at her, his dark eyes angry and appraising. I wanted to flinch away from the blow that seemed inevitable, but he let out a long breath and said, "Take some stuff in. Get it to Jesus on Fifth. Don't get caught. Then go quit that stupid job today. If you do all that, I might let you live."

Over Raul's shoulder, the dark-eyed man glared at him, then at Valeria. It felt like another near fight.

"Go," Raul said, shoving her out the door, slamming it behind her.

She stood outside, quivering, her leg sending pain up her back, her cheek and shoulder sore. Then she swore in Spanish. I knew most of the words.

Her mother was in there with those brutes. But surely Raul would protect her. These were my thoughts, of course, not Valeria's. Valeria was scared and mad and embarrassed all at once. "I'm sorry," she whispered. "I did not expect them during the day. These are my fears." She paused. "My worst fears."

No kidding.

Then she was running, her heart rate increasing, her leg slowing her down a little.

Two black cars with insignia on them passed us. Mexican Police. She looked behind her, watching them stop at her house.

She stumbled forward, crying, and for a long time I was sure she had forgotten me. She ended up on the beach in one of the tourist areas of Playa, sitting on a bit of grass in front of a hotel, the hot afternoon sun sending sweat down her back. She pulled her backpack off and shoved the package Raul had made her take into its outside zipper pocket and reached into the bigger middle section and took out a flask of water. She drink slowly, shuddering and moaning. It took a long time for her calm to return.

Finally she spoke. "I wanted you to see what Mexico has done to women. That is what I'm afraid of. Not my brother, not now anyway, since I am far from him and he will probably be in jail a night before he gets out. I am afraid that I will not be anything more than my mother, and the doorway to my grandmother's life is closed. I wanted you to know what it's like to have nothing. That is my fear. That I will be less than nothing."

She paused and ran the hot, white sand between her fingers, letting it fall onto the grass in a small cone-shaped pile.

"I'm afraid I'll take the drugs he gave me. I was addicted once." He mouth grew dry at the words, and she shook a little. But she didn't reach into her backpack. "I need to make the delivery or they will hurt my mother again. So you need to leave me now."

I wanted to hold her, to talk to her, to do something, anything to help.

I hadn't understood anything.

I slammed my thumb down on the button and jerked back to Seattle. Dr. Meera had let go of my hand and had pulled up a chair by the couch. He rose and helped me sit up, then handed me a cup of tea and a chocolate bar. I shoved the button in my pocket and took the doctor's offerings, although I couldn't quite sip the tea or open the candy yet.

"Tell me."

I told him from the beginning this time, the story taking so long I missed lunch. From time to time Dr. Meera made notes on his all-in-one, and once he took a call. When I was done, he said, "So, what did you learn?"

"She wasn't . . . what I thought. She really was willing to run the drugs, but she was smart enough to try to show me her real fears, and . . . desperate enough to hope I could help her."

"So?"

"So I guess I didn't expect her to be so . . . subtle. Or to break the law."

"Do you want to know what happened next?" he asked.

I nodded, finally opening the chocolate bar.

"They arrested all of them, even Valeria's mother. But she's out. Raul won't get out in a day, not this time. We'll use what you saw."

"Do I have to go to court?"

"Yes."

I flinched at that. But it was part of doing this for real, if that was what I wanted to do. "What about Valeria? Can I call her tonight?"

"I'm sorry." He licked his lips and looked sorry.

I tensed, waiting for it.

"We had to arrest her."

Damn. I chose my next word carefully. "Damn." And then I said, "Hey, let her go."

He ignored me. "This was a chain. We'll have stopped a whole drug ring. They've killed two people. I don't know if Raul would have ever let them kill Valeria, but he let them kill one of his friends. We have been watching them a long time."

"You need to let her go. She was trying to show me things that mattered. She's sweet."

"She broke the law."

"She was scared."

"I'll put in a good word for her."

He looked like he meant it. I fell silent, and after he didn't speak either for long time, I asked him, "Who do you really work for?"

He looked as sad as I felt, as if we had together done a bitter-sweet thing. "Maybe, if you decide to do this for a living, I'll tell you someday."

"What will happen to Valeria?"

His smile was soft. "She's a victim more than anything. We'll put her through rehab and give her a chance to start over if she agrees to testify. We're halfway done cleaning up the drug lords.

We need her to tell her story."

"Will she?"

He shrugged. "I don't know. Not much is certain in this business."

I remembered how she'd looked talking about her little brother and decided she probably would say at least some things. We sat quietly for a bit. The quiet was companionable, but not intimate. "So what do I do next?"

"It's up to you. If you think you might like to do more of this, we'll give you someone experienced to help train you. Keep you in the class, so you get your credits."

"And my other choices?"

He laughed softly. "There's always the Afghan/Indian war." Then he put a hand up before I could answer. "Or you could just do the class the same way as everyone else. If you can. The emotional attachment makes it hard. But maybe we could find a boring host."

I drank another whole cup of tea before I answered him, and he was patient enough to let me have the time. What I said was, "I like excitement, and I don't like war. We did some good."

"*You* did some good."

"Thank you." I stood up. "I guess I should do some more good."

He looked both happy and sad that I'd told him yes, almost as conflicted as Valeria had felt over the drugs. Maybe life was like that everywhere. I found a bit more courage. "Will you put in a good word for me with the diplo corps?"

"This will help you with that."

An odd, opaque answer. But if I was going to be a diplomat corps support, and eventually a real diplomat, I needed to learn to read and speak the smoky answers of politics. This would help.

I left him, and skipped the rest of my classes, sitting outside smelling Seattle: cedar and mud and roses from a thin garden close to one of the science buildings.

I slept better than night, although I did dream of the Caribbean Sea, and the way the hot sand felt between Valeria's fingers right before I left her.

When I saw Kay on the way to class the next morning, she looked worried. "Are you okay? What happened? How come you never came back to class? What made you fall out of your chair?"

"It's no big deal," I said. "Problems on the other end. I get a new host today."

"Are they going to give you someone more experienced this time? Like my Bani?"

"They promised."

"Good. Good for you."

So I asked her about the camel fair. As she talked about hot sand and thirst, I decided I was happy enough they'd chosen to send me riding in Mexico. Maybe sustainability wasn't what I thought. It wasn't just recycling and walking. Maybe it was messy, and full of farting camels and discouraging the abuse of women, and learning to walk into other people's lives, and back out of them.

The WAR of the FLOWERS

I pulled up the tent flap and whispered, "Hi, Cherry, Mommy's home."

Long thin fingers squeezed mine. "Hi, Mommy. Hilary Hippo is eating your flowers."

The tent door slipped shut, the lacy data display material sounding like two palms rubbing roughened skin together. I twisted onto my back and looked at our world, holding Cherry next to me. She was right. The electronic hippo was finishing off the last of the spindly yellow flowers I'd completed just before going to work.

"Gramma took good care of you?" I asked.

"She visited me twice. She came in real person for lunch." Cherry's lips were tight against her face, stretched long and thin, somewhere between smile and frown. Mother must have stayed longer than usual; Cherry's fine red hair twisted in a neat braid, the ragged end curling near her waist.

Cherry narrowed her eyes at the hippo, a swirl of brown pixels with yellow flowers hanging from the sides of its smile. She laughed and waggled a finger at her creation. "Hilary—don't eat Mom's flowers!"

I laughed at her delight with the hippo's misbehavior. "All right Hilary," I threatened, still laughing, "I'll fix it so you stay away from my flowers!" I opened a maker window on the opposite wall so I wouldn't disturb Cherry's view. We had a rule that we didn't watch each other create. I dragged a salty taste onto the deep gold stamens. Simple, elegant. "Look out, Mommy's coming to garden!"

I rolled Cherry on top of me so she giggled while our world

stopped, suspending the smile on Hilary the Hippo's round face, freezing the frame in a moment when one hippo eye looked in each direction. I changed the soil elasticity so the flowers would pop up and spray virtual dirt if Hilary went for them.

The maker window slipped shut, opening the world, and this time, when Hilary yanked up flowers, dirt flew into her face. She hopped back and bellowed, the flowers dropping to the ground. She trampled them underfoot as she trotted to Cherry's river to clean off the dirt.

We'd made this world with my mother's money and Cherry's focus. The huge data tent was designed as a playground, but Cherry lived in it. She lost herself in our world the whole time I was away, every day. She knew the biology, the physics, and all the nested intricate rule sets of our world like I knew English. It frustrated my Mother; she didn't see the value in a made-up world. She visited Cherry and made her lunch every day, but otherwise she wasn't around much in real.

A communication window dropped open. Mother. "Kelly? How was work?"

"Work."

"You came home early."

"I finished my calls." She hated it that I ran for home, and Cherry's tent, the minute I squeaked out of the homeless shelter I was sentenced to. Mother thought I should go out clubbing, or networking, or dancing, or anything but tending Cherry. Like that way I'd meet the right guy and have a white beaded wedding dress and wear her grandmother's pearl necklace. Like that way Cherry would cease to exist.

I wouldn't have left Cherry at all, except I was still working off my community service debt for eating Rapture rev. 9 and making Cherry so allergic she had to live in a tent with controlled air and an electronic jungle for habitat.

Before I could touch my daughter, at the end of every day, I had to take a decon shower and pull on an ugly jumpsuit. I had red jumpsuits, and blue ones, and Cherry's favorite, an old purple suit with blue buttons. That should be enough penance. Both the purple suit, and needing one at all. But I had to do community service too, and leave Cherry every day. Community service is like being beaten for falling down a cliff and hurting yourself. Mother picked up Cherry's med bills. Even money wouldn't buy me out of community service.

"Are you going out?" Mother asked.

I hadn't gone out for three months. "Not tonight."

Her image disappeared. She hated it when she couldn't control me. I turned back to Cherry, who was already changing Hilary's salt intake parameters so she'd like the flowers. Just watching Cherry draw her lips up and pull her brows together and ponder solutions was happy entertainment. I turned and tried to sweeten the flowers before she caught on.

Hilary polished off the flowers in moments.

We came out of the world to eat chicken, crawling out the tent door into the huge sterile room. I promised Cherry ice cream to reward her for winning "The War of the Flowers." I cooked chicken breasts in a ten-thousand-dollar mini-kitchen, caressing the smooth lines and hard surfaces, touching the perfectly scrubbed metals the nanobots maintained. Mother bought the kitchen to keep toxins from Cherry, who was like the princess and the pea with food.

My fault.

I'd twisted something in her DNA when she was the size of my little fingernail, hanging inside my womb. I filled Cherry with love and desire and drugs, before I knew she was there. I remember the day I did it—my heart smashed open by the Rapture, lying on a bench in Discovery Park, between a cedar forest and the vastness of Puget Sound. I was in love with the trees and the robins and spring, part of them all, a grain of soul that was part of the park, of Seattle, of the world. A brilliant rainbow split the sky, dripping color from the cedars into the sound. I felt safe, deep in Rapture. Then I learned I was pregnant. Three weeks along, somebody I'd met clubbing. I didn't even try to find him. No one knew that rev of Rapture had been badly engineered until just before Cherry's birth.

The chicken tasted garlicky, and I had Cherry guess what went into it. She twisted her face sideways and said, "Garlic . . . basil . . . red pepper," her eyes clamped shut like little stars. She put another shred of chicken breast against her tongue, "and lime juice?"

"You missed the rosemary," I teased.

She took another taste and nodded.

At five, I wouldn't have noticed the difference in the taste and smell of any spices more complex than salt and pepper.

We finished the chicken and licked our fingers, and Cherry nibbled at her vanilla ice cream, rolling her eyes back in her head as the cold touched her tongue. I always worked hard to get her to eat, and she never finished everything I made. She just wanted back into the tent.

After dinner, I called up an old version of *The Jungle Book*, and we watched Mowgli and Baloo and the Monkey King until the last gasp, and Cherry fell asleep with her back curled against my chest. I'd unbraided her hair, and it fanned across the cushion away from me in red waves. Her eyelashes were light brown strings resting on her cheek.

The next day, on my way home, Dr. Barton called me. "The first human tests worked," she said. I knew what she meant. There was a gene-therapy trial to fix broken immune systems. The feds funded it specifically to reverse drug-induced systemic deficiencies like Cherry's. Part of the renewed "War on Drugs."

"How long?" I asked.

"Maybe only months."

"Who do I talk to?"

"Me. And, and Kelly, you don't have a choice. Cherry needs the therapy."

"I know," I said. "Why wouldn't I give it to her anyway?" What was Dr. Barton thinking?

"Cherry needs an opportunity to be a normal girl. This therapy may give her one."

"So, like, you think I don't want to help her? Of course I want Cherry to be normal."

"That's good, Kelly," Dr. Barton said. "I'll call you when it's Cherry's turn. Remember that you need to do this."

Like I didn't hear her the first time? Why didn't she think I wanted Cherry to be well?

I'd have to do at least a year of community service to pay for the therapy. More time away from home. I shivered. The feds would make Cherry get the therapy, but they'd also make me pay for the procedure, even though Mom would just hand them the money if they asked.

It wasn't only months before Dr. Barton called me back. It was three years. I finished the community service, even the extra for Cherry's therapy. Cherry and I traded Hilary Hippo and the whole jungle ecosystem for an urban setting. We made city parks and little stores and stuffed animals to sell in the stores. Cherry designed a fiddler, Lonesome Jack, to sit on the corners and busk for money. I made a dancer, Serena. Sometimes Serena danced to Jack's fiddle, other times they competed for money from the other virtual towns-people, winning or losing based on how we'd programmed their desires for that day. Cherry started experimenting with supply and demand economics.

Mother gave up on getting me to go out, and I turned twenty-five three days before Cherry turned eight. We made a cake. Mother decontaminated and came in and had a piece of cake, exclaiming po-litely when we showed her the data wall rips we'd printed for her. She was leaving that afternoon for a season in France, so she spent a whole half hour with us, and I sighed with relief when she finally left.

The next day, Dr. Barton called to tell us when she'd come. She would make a house call; you don't take people with immune defi-ciencies like Cherry's outside. "You remember you have to do this," she said.

That made me mad. "I want her to have the therapy," I snapped, and hung up.

Cherry and I spent the whole day arguing about what rule sets to use for behavior in the park, and she finally looked up at me and said, "Mom—what's wrong with you? You're all jitters."

"I'm sorry. Dr. Barton is coming today." I swallowed. Why hadn't I told Cherry? "She says some scientists found a way to change your blood so that you can go outside, and go to a real park."

Cherry looked as if I had said something in a foreign language. Then she blinked, and grabbed my right hand with both of hers. "Don't let her in." The top of her head hurt as it thrust up into my shoulder.

I stood blinking on the drive. I'd ordered food brought in lately, and a whole season had slipped past. City sounds whispered at the edges of our property, past the rows of trees and the huge lawns, barely audible. A car horn, a call of one man to a dog, a snatch of loud drum-ming. Above me, birds sang. The wind felt cool, and smelled of rotting leaves and smoke. I rubbed my hands together and blew on them, shocked that it felt like a dream to just stand outside.

I watched the empty driveway, pacing and stamping. An hour passed.

Dr. Barton came up the long drive in a silent little blue two-seater hydro-car. She unfolded up and out of the tiny car, a tall blonde with a deep tan. She stood for a moment, looking at me as if I were a patient. "You've gotten thinner," she said.

"I'm healthy," I replied.

She looked like she wanted to argue, but she said, "Did you tell Cherry why I'm here today?"

I swallowed, my tongue as big as a softball in my mouth. "She isn't ready."

Dr. Barton smiled. "Remember Dr. Smith? I told her that you'd make it, that you'd be the parent Cherry needs."

"I am. She's not ready. She doesn't want to go outside."

"Of course not."

I rocked back on my heels, looking up at Dr. Barton. She smiled but her eyes were hard. I reminded myself she wasn't much older than me. "I don't see why she has to. Her intelligence and creativity scores, even her math—they're all over the 98th percentile."

"Let's go in."

"You can't force medical procedures. I know—I looked it up."

"This is mandated by the government."

"I can keep you out. I can say the risk of her dying from the procedure is more than her staying like she is. It's true. For Cherry. She's in such a safe place that going outside will be worse."

Dr. Barton just walked right past me, opening the door to the hallway where the decon suits hung in neat rows. As she started stripping off her boots, I said, "I can turn you in." My voice trembled.

"Little rich girl gets away with breaking the law?"

She was right. I hated it. I followed her through decon.

I made it into the tent ahead of her. Cherry lay folded into the corner, arms and legs like sticks. She closed the world when I opened the door, freezing images of the city we had created all around us. Lonesome Jack had been caught with a silly smile as he watched Serena dancing. Serena's mouth was tight and round, her eyes squished shut with focus as her foot kicked up past her waist. Her skirt hung in mid-swirl, falling over her high leg, just barely demure.

I eeled around Cherry so that I was at her back. Dr. Barton slowly looked around the inside of the tent, her mouth open wider than Serena's. She had met Hilary Hippo once, when Cherry had just made her, and Hilary's mouth was a slash that pixelated when she smiled.

"These . . . these are. . . ." She pulled her eyes away from the street to look at Cherry. "You made this?"

Cherry scrunched back even closer against me and nodded. "I don't want to go to a real park."

Dr. Barton didn't answer right away. Cherry even started to relax a little, the muscles in her back loosening and her elbows bending as her breathing slowed down. When Dr. Barton spoke, it was to me. "Kelly, this is wonderful. It's too bad that no one can live in such a place forever. Perhaps you can keep it, maybe even use it. I bet you could finance Cherry's college with these skills."

I tightened my arm around Cherry and tried to picture her strong and healthy and playing in physical parks. I imagined beautiful young men and women who wanted to sell her drugs or have sex with her. I saw Cherry distracted with the world, the real world, and I was afraid for Lonesome Jack and Serena. Cherry hadn't seen the real sun since her first year. I'd snuck her outside then, and she had almost died from the things she caught.

"You can make her well, and she can still stay here, right?"

"Until you're ready to go out."

"She isn't ready."

Dr. Barton smiled sadly. "You're the adult."

"Cherry?" I asked.

"If I can stay here." She pushed back even further against me.

Dr. Barton›s voice had a sharp undertone. "Cherry, you're only eight. Someday, you will need to go outside."

"Not tomorrow?"

"Not tomorrow."

Cherry's eyes remained wide and wary.

Dr. Barton scraped a bit of Cherry's skin onto a medical slide, and inserted the slide into a palm-sized machine. "Your mother told me you haven't been out in a long time," she said to me.

"Someone has to be with Cherry."

"Someone will still need to be with Cherry." She stuck the tip of a syringe into the machine, into a hole I hadn't even seen, and sucked up some clear liquid. I held my breath.

When the doctor injected the liquid into Cherry's thin arm, I sat a little distance away, dizzy.

It took a long time for the doctor to leave. I wanted her to be gone so badly I heard a nasty tone in my voice, bordering on rude. Maybe I was rude, a little, since I helped her gather everything up and get out the door. Just before she left, Dr. Barton turned around and looked right at me. "You'll have to go with her for a while and teach her about the world, so she can start school next year."

School? "I can keep teaching her here. She's already doing college-level math. I bet she's the best virt maker in town."

"That's exactly the problem."

The sound of the door closing behind her made me jump. I was crying when I took Cherry into my arms.

"Mommy, what's wrong?"

I shook my head. "I'm sorry—I didn't mean to scare you."

"Can we make the rules for a real park?"

I turned off all the power in the tent, and lay in the darkness, holding Cherry close. "We don't have to find out just yet," I said. "Not tomorrow."

"Okay."

"Maybe we can go to a real park before your grandmother comes home."

"Do I have to?"

I waited until Cherry's eyes were closed and her breathing soft and even before saying, "Yes."

TRAINER of WHALES

Kitha strained to see past the farm's lights, up into the darkness of the sea. Three great blue whales swam overheard, towing white nets full of sea-city products like farmed fish, sponges, and handmade jewelry. In spite of the harnesses and the bulky cargo nets trailing beside them, the whales exuded grace and power. Kitha, on the other hand, felt heavy in her farming suit, the weights around her waist holding her just at the right height to mind the deep-sea kelp that Downbelow Dome farmed. The waving multicolored fronds had once captivated her. She had made games of counting colorful engineered symbiote-fish and checking the great plants for damage and parasites, priding herself on how well she saw every detail of the beds. But now, a year into her new job, the enormity of her lost dreams was heavier than her pressurized and weighted suit.

Her sigh sent a froth of tiny bubbles up from her breather, a trail of precious air leaking along her face. She kicked hard, forcing her eyes down. It was off-harvest season, and all she had to do for the gene-engineered food crop was measure fronds and watch for broken stems and signs of disease.

A familiar attention-code sang into her ear. Kitha tongued her breather away so she could talk. "Jonathon? How was school?" They'd argued this morning, and she wasn't even sure he'd *gone* to school.

"Boring, Mom. Can I go to Lincka's? Her mom is home this shift and she promised to create cookies and set out a game for us."

Kitha winced. It was good Jonathan wanted to be around an adult. If only he wanted to be around *her* as much as she wanted to be a good mother. "Sure honey. But you have to be home by seven."

"But bedtime's not until nine!" he protested.

Kitha would be off shift at six, and this meant she'd go home to an empty apartment. She inhaled, biting down on her breather so hard she was afraid to open her mouth in case she'd punctured the damn thing. Having Jonathon had driven her from school, from the biggest underwater city of all, New Seadon, to this god-forsaken boring job. But it paid well enough—barely—to keep her ten-year-old boy both in school and far, far away from his father. She glanced up again before she answered, but the whales had gone on, surely halfway to the next sea-city by now. She relaxed her jaw. Her breather still worked. She'd stress-fractured two of them in the last six months and was down to one spare. "Eight."

He must have known by her tone of voice that he wasn't about to get more time. He just said, "Sure, Mom. See you at eight." As usual, he sounded disgusted with her.

She sighed again and dove deeper into the brown forest, brushing aside a twenty foot strand of kelp, careful not to tangle her feet. If only she'd been able to figure out how to finish school herself. She dreamed of becoming a whale trainer. Up until last year when she took this nothing job and moved to this nothing dome, she'd been on her way to a bio-trainer school. She'd read every book she could find on whales and practiced training techniques on the rather dumb dolphin-bots that watched the perimeter of the fields. She never got close enough to real whales to practice on *them*. But since she'd given up her dreams for Jonathon, she found the sight of the great, beautiful beasts bittersweet. Dreams, swimming out of her reach.

The next hour of her shift seemed to take ten. Finally, the half-shift prep tones filled her bubble-helmet. She started back, mouth watering as she thought about the roast fish that waited for her in the common shift kitchen.

Kelp slapped her all along her left side, and she swirled sideways, disoriented. Kelp slapped her right, pushing her back. A warning scream belled out of the speakers in her helmet and then went silent.

An undersea quake.

Downbelow Dome. Surely the warning would keep going off if the city was okay. Or at least an all-clear. The kelp around her still swayed back and forth as if an unseen hand shook its roots. What had her safety manual said about seaquakes?

Kitha pumped her legs, dodging kelp, telling herself it was over and long floating objects in motion tended to stay in motion.

Jonathon. She swam harder, her focus suddenly clear.

Don't think about having just an hour of air, she thought. *Breathe slowly.*

Her forward motion stopped, her right leg gained twenty pounds. She swiveled her head. Two long fronds had tangled and trapped her right fin. She bent in half, pulling on loose ends of green kelp that felt slimy even through her gloves.

Not enough give.

She reached for her belt knife, sawing slowly, seeing Jonathon's sullen face like a mirror in her faceplate, superimposed over the waving kelp and a school of silver fish.

The blade made infuriatingly slow progress, the angle bad enough that she didn't have enough traction for strength.

It slipped twice, forcing her to slow down.

A mistake could kill her.

Finally, the second frond snapped and she kicked away from danger. The freed fin had a broken spring. Her right leg had to work twice as hard as her left. Kelp beds suddenly gave way to open ocean. She grabbed the last stalk for balance, floating. Downbelow Dome glowed like a lamp against the darkness of the sea behind it, and the string of lights between the city and the kelp beds sent a line of comfort knifing through darker sea. Everything *looked* normal. But there had been no communications from the city since the first alarm. She let go of her breather and licked her lips. "Is anybody there?"

No response, until she heard a soft male voice. "Kitha?"

Her shift mate, Jai. A quiet man who'd grown up here. They'd never really connected, but he worked hard and seemed to trust her to do her part. Guilt pursed her lips. She hadn't even thought of him, only of Jonathon. "It's me. What happened?"

"Seaquake."

"I figured that out. Is the city okay?"

Silence for a moment. Then, "It doesn't look breached."

Kitha swam away from her stabilizing kelp stem and looked back toward the wavy line of demarcation between crop and open ocean. Where was Jai?

"Look down."

She did. Sure enough. He was even pretty close, maybe ten meters below her and a little right. She waved at the figure below her.

"My son is in there." She glanced at her readouts. "I don't have enough air to swim the whole way. I'm going to head to the shift-break station and see if I can find some. Coming?"

Jai's answer was to start off toward the station, just out of sight on the right. Kitha followed. "Have you been able to reach the dome?" Kitha asked.

"No. But there's better com gear at the break-station than in our suits. Have you heard from anyone else?"

"No." Jai's huge yellow farm-fins were ahead of her now, at roughly the same depth. "Hey! Slow down. My right fin is zonked."

"I'll meet you there," he said, and although the angle made it tough to tell for sure, it looked like the wake behind Jai's powerful strokes increased. Was he making sure he got the first access to resources if the city was dead? She shook her head. What was she thinking? Jai'd always seemed fair. The city couldn't be dead, because then Jonathon would be dead.

A swarm of symbiote-fish darted out, engulfing her in bright colors.

She swam around a clump of misplaced kelp, and the shift-station hung in front of her: a teardrop caught on a long line festooned with swaying nets and protective glassoleum bubbles full of farming gear. A puff of tiny bubbles jetted down below the hatch, water being forced into the sea. Her body shivered, relieved. At least there was pressure and air. Safety.

In five minutes, she dangled outside the hatch, her right hand holding her in position as she thumped for the hatch to open. She tumbled inside, waiting for the door to close behind her, then went through a second door and stood before a third. Bubbles surrounded her, pressing against each other and popping into bigger and bigger bubbles until she stood in plain air. The third door opened and she ducked through it, stripping her air bottles and fins and weights into a dripping pile by the door and gulping fresh, clean air. She kept the helmet with her, just in case the city called her name.

As she entered the common room, Jai stood by a computer terminal. He was tall and brown. Brown skin, brown hair, brown eyes. He was older than she was by at least ten years, and had worked in the kelp beds for so long that his movements were precise and studied, his voice calm. "I found a test-sequence."

"To test what?"

"Well, for starters the shift-station is fine. It's breathing."

"But is the city breathing?" If the quake had damaged the dome's six lungs, it wouldn't be able to pull enough dissolved oxygen out of the surrounding seawater. Jonathon would run out of air, slowly, and fall asleep.

Jai pursed his lips. "I'm asking."

Kitha took in a big breath of her own, as if it could feed Jonathon. The dome wasn't breached. They'd have seen that right away; the glassoleum structure would have buckled and distorted. Maybe there was no immediate danger.

The tiny observation port closest to her looked out on the hundred-foot tall beds of swaying kelp that fed thousands. She walked over to another port and stared at the dome. It looked fine. Something about it felt wrong. Nothing moved. "Do the transports work?" she asked. One was scheduled to pick them up at the end of shift, but that was four and a half hours away. Normally, transports and bots and even swimmers came and went through the dome's three-lock system doorways regularly, a stream of commerce and recreation.

Jai's voice jolted her. "Three of the lungs are damaged. The city is in safety mode."

So no one could get in or out. Including them. Half the lungs meant less air than the station needed. The lock-down would make it last longer. Not forever.

"Are there any transports available?"

Jai shook his head.

"Can we talk to the city?" she asked, knowing the answer was still no.

"I think the whole communications system is down. I just hope everyone inside is okay."

She glanced over at him, furrowing her brow. "Are there casualties?"

He turned to face her. "Probably. Look, this is a pretty simple interface, but I'm no communication tech. Can you just sit down?" She must have stared at him in shock because he lowered his voice. "Please. Sit by the window and tell me if you see anything strange."

She had no more than returned to her position at the porthole when the station silenced. The lights flicked off. An emergency tone screamed into the room, something automated. She grabbed for the wall, steadying herself. The string of lights between dome and pod had winked out. She looked behind her. The great kelp beds had faded into the dark sea.

Jai began pushing buttons. The tones silenced. Inside lights came back on, and the air circulators roared to life. The beds and the outside lights stayed off, so the dome sparkled even brighter, and seemed further away. The outside path of lights between the city and the kelp farm had felt like an umbilical cord, and Kitha gasped at the loss.

"It must have been automatic. They must have needed to save power and kept everything off."

"Look!" Kisha pointed. Three bright lights bobbed through the darkness, heading for the dome. "The whales!"

"Sure," Jai said, "they always come back from their run about now."

"But . . . but they won't be able to drop their load. No one will come outside to un-harness them if the dome's locked down."

He shrugged and turned back. "I'm more interested in getting there," he said.

That suited her. She needed to find Jonathon. "Can you raise anybody yet?"

A high tense laughter escaped his lips. "I was trying. All the systems just blinked out." He must have heard the sharp tone in his voice. More calmly, he said, "They're coming back."

She frowned and returned to the porthole. The three bobbing lights were almost at the dome now. Surely they'd be confused. She wracked her brain for an answer. Whale trainers and handlers talked to their charges via a translator that made haunting high sounds audible from hundreds of feet away. The whales heard better than humans. Sonar. At harvest time, the whales came all the way up to the shift-station, bumping against the rope, while nervous humans tied cargo nets to specially made plastic harnesses. So surely there was a way to call the whales here.

Before she could ask, Jai said, "The tests on the dome are complete. A girder fell on three of the lungs, and they can't open. Diagnostics suggest they might work okay if we get the weight off of them." He called her over to the terminal, pointing. An exterior camera showed a mess of metal fallen to the sea floor, leaning against the dome, crushing the left bank of sea-lungs. "Here." Jai drew a circle around a spot a few meters away from the oblong bellows of the lungs where a metal spike had skewered an antenna. "This is probably what ruined their voice communication. No way to tell from here whether or not they got a mayday out."

"But won't the other cities come look, anyway?" she asked. "We'll be quiet, and that will be wrong."

"I don't know. I don't have any information about the seaquake. It could have damaged other nearby domes, as well."

"We have to do something," she said. "We might be the only people on the outside of the dome."

"I don't even know how to get there," he said.

She walked over to the storage cabinet and opened the door. Racks of air bottles sat neatly stacked, ready for the next shift, and the next, and the next. They were replenished once a week, and this was only mid-week.

He grimaced. "I don't want to leave you alone. Can your broken fin get you all the way there?"

She hadn't even thought of that. "Maybe there's more here."

"People bring their own gear."

"What about the whales? Can we call them here?"

His eyes widened. "Probably. They come for harvest. But I don't know anything about whale handling."

She grinned. "I do." She glanced out the porthole. "They're still there. Any idea where we can find a translator?"

He shrugged, then pointed toward the cabinet full of air bottles. "In there?"

Kisha bent down and looked on the bottom shelf. It was empty. "They're small. In a drawer?" She began pulling open drawers and cubbies, glancing outside every few minutes to make sure the three lights still hovered around the dome.

Nothing.

She looked out again. No lights. Just the diffuse sunlight that penetrated down here, fifty meters below the sea surface. At least it wasn't night above them in the world of air and sun. Had the whales gone? How far would the sounds go? "Give me a boost?"

Jai came over and helped her balance with her feet on the bottom shelf. She felt around on the top of the cabinet. There! Something. She hooked her hand around a leather strap and pulled. "We found it," she breathed, looking down at a round ball the exact right size to hold in her fist, encased in a glassoleum shell to keep it safe from water. Four little blue plastic levers protruded slightly on one side. Four times four commands. But the easy ones were just one lever. *Come* had to be basic. She knew what to do. It had been in one of her books.

She even sang it to Jonathan. One to come and two to wait, three to lift and four to lower. There was more, there was a whole damned language, but she didn't know it.

Were there even any whales to call? She glanced back out the porthole. The three lights once more hovered above the brilliantly lit city. She breathed a sigh of relief. "They must have just been around the other side." Now what? "Okay. I've got to go outside. The sound will only travel well through water." She reached for a new air bottle.

She smiled as Jai reached past her and grabbed a fresh air bottle for himself.

Ten minutes later, she and Jai clung to the rope just above the shift-station. She thumbed the first lever and a clear, mournful whale song filled the water. A shiver touched her spine. As beautiful as the sound was, she knew humans only heard part of it, and badly, filtered by bubble-helmets. Yet the smallest portion was beautiful enough that she and Jai reached for each other's hands.

She let go of the rope, and Jai held on for both of them. Her breathing seemed loud and intrusive against the whale-song.

The lights of the three whales didn't seem to be getting any nearer. Was there something else she should do? Whale training was more than just pushing a button, or everyone could do it. Her prep classes had been psychology and some of her reading talked about building a bond with the whales.

"We might have to go to them." She tried an experimental swoop with her damaged fin. Her right thigh protested. Some piece of her safety training ran in the back of her mind. She turned off the translator for a moment. It seemed sacrilegious to talk over it. "Aren't there emergency sleds? The kind you'd use if I got hurt in the beds and couldn't swim and you came for me?"

"And they're motorized!" Jai grinned. "How come I didn't know you were so brilliant before?"

How should she take that comment? It didn't matter. Getting to Jonathon mattered. She followed Jai up-rope to a glassoleum bubble dotted with emergency symbols. Directions for opening the bubble were painted on the shell. Jai pulled a lever and water and air began changing places just like in the locks, the tempo of the exchange exact so that no pressure differences were introduced.

The sled was a simple backboard cupped to hold the injured worker, straps, an air tube and spare helmet, and handholds. She was strapped in moments later, feeling foolish but grateful for any way to get to Jonathon.

She clutched the translator to her as they traveled, excruciatingly slowly, toward the brilliant light of Downbelow Dome, their own small findme light illuminating just a few feet of water in front of them. She lay down in the sled, keeping it as aerodynamic as possible, while Jai trailed his long body behind her and the sled. Every once in a while, she heard the swish of his fins behind her as he added his strength to the tiny motor. The sea floor spun by slowly, seven meters or so below them, rocky and full of waving sea-trees and sponges specially adapted to use the human-provided light to grow unusually large at this depth.

As they came closer, the whales' dark bodies and lighter bellies began to resolve below the harness lights. When the sled was halfway there, she flipped on the *come* lever again, watching the whales for any sign they heard her. The translator ball in her hand glowed a soft orange. Proximity?

One of the lights began to grow bigger. A whale was coming toward them. She wanted to crow in relief, but held her tongue, listening. The translator would surely tell her what the whales were saying. If they said anything.

The other two whales stayed by Downbelow Dome.

The translator glowed brighter. Was it trying to talk to her? How would it? She searched the little ball, somehow pressing something that sent the whale song thrumming through her speakers. Then English—translated whale: "Turn it off!"

Oh. *Oh!* She thumbed off the lever. It must have been like yelling at them. She tried speaking at it. "Thank you." The ball stayed quiet. The whale kept coming, larger than she thought from this angle. Fast. She leaned toward it, unafraid, the sheer beauty of the behemoth making her want to sing. She squeezed the translator tight to her and a voice spoke in her ear, and she nearly dropped the ball. "The whale expresses confusion."

It must respond to pressure. She squeezed the ball. "Confusion?" she asked.

"The dome is not responding to it. It needs to drop its cargo."

"So I don't need these levers? I can just talk to you?"

"They're handy if you need to give an emergency command."

All right. "How can I help it know what to do?"

The translator apparently wasn't smart enough to answer her question the way she'd phrased it. "What does the whale need?"

"Go to the docks. Help them drop their cargo. Then they'll leave."

The whale turned slowly away from her, making a circle. Waiting. Three bulging nets hung from its harness. "I need the whales to help me."

Jai stayed silent, keeping them on course, letting her work it out. But their com was open. Surely he heard the conversation. She made sure to hold the ball loosely and safely between her fingers. "Jai? Do you have any idea how to get the whales to help the city breathe? If we just help them unload, they'll leave. I don't know how to make them stay."

"Maybe we can find something to attach the whales to the girder. I need to see the damage."

"They'll stay together." The dome loomed up now, more than twice as big as it had looked from the shift-station. They were over halfway there. She squeezed the ball. "Ask the whales to wait for me by the dome."

Sound belled out from the ball, filling her helmet and the sea around them. The whale she had been talking to (*she had been talking to a whale!*) beat them to the docks by at least ten minutes. As the dome loomed large and silent and bright above them, Kitha said, "Doesn't it feel like we're visiting an artifact?"

Jai grunted. "Like an archeological dig." She heard the fear in his voice, and wondered if she sounded as bad. Who did he love that was inside, silent, hopefully alive?

The whales bunched, never still. Their harnesses provided air, so they didn't need to breach to breathe, but breaching was instinct, and every migratory and work path allowed for trips to the surface. Surely their time was running out.

Jai must have felt the same. He was all business as soon as they rounded the huge bright arch of the dome and began to approach the lungs, and the mess that lay on top of them. Kitha though he might leave the sled on the seafloor and set her free to swim, but he kept her in it, strapped in, and they glided through tumbled bars and floors of steel that had once been a strong structure that stored transports and materials, the goods brought and sent by whales, and the underwater ships of visiting dignitaries. In a way, she liked still being on the sled. It somehow made the tangled landscape seem more like it belonged to a dream. This close, shadows and movement from inside touched the Dome's surface even though the glassoleum had been dialed to its most opaque setting to keep warmth inside the dome. People lived in there.

Kitha clutched the translator. "Tell them thank you. Ask them to wait for longer. We will need them."

It pulsed in her hand, and then sang. The low mournful notes seemed a perfect backdrop to the destruction they saw. Glassoleum and plastic had all weathered the quake well; metal had snapped and fallen.

The lungs were the size of the biggest whale, slightly squatter. They peeled disassociated oxygen from the water and fed it carbon dioxide, breathing the water like mammals so they could be plants in the dome itself, where they exhaled oxygen and inhaled carbon dioxide. They were grouped in two sets of three to minimize damage. A dome could live in lockdown on three lungs for days. The domes were safe. Everyone said so.

Her boy was in there.

A long squared metal post lay across three of the lungs, holding them down. The lungs lay quiescent under it, undoubtedly turned off. Shreds of one lung covering floated around one end of the pole, but the other two looked whole and undamaged.

Now that they were here, it was easy to see what they had to do—get the whales to help them lift the large square metal pole that kept the lungs down. But how to do it? Kitha glanced up at the milling whales. They would have to be willing helpers. Psychology, she mused. There was no way to use food. Blue whales sieved the sea for plankton, which was more of a problem than a solution. Surely they were hungry by now, left on-shift past their time. The only thing she knew they wanted was to get rid of their burdens and get free—go eat and breach and play and be whales done with their hard work.

She asked Jai, "Do you see anything we can tie to a harness?"

He was silent for a moment. She thought with him, wracking her brain. "What about the harnesses themselves? If we get one off, will it be long enough?"

"You'd have to get the whale right down next to the metal. There wouldn't be enough torque. It might get hurt."

Well, that was no good. "What about the lines that hold the lights up?"

"Maybe. But they're attached directly to the dome."

"Isn't there some kind of failsafe?" she mused. "What if a whale ran into them? Or a transport?"

"Some kind of quick-release?" he asked. "I don't know. I don't have any idea how to trigger it."

She didn't have any other ideas. "We'll just have to go look." Her hands clenched in sudden anger. "Why won't the damn city talk to us? Surely they can see we're out here." Her voice had an edge.

He waved a hand at the communication antenna that had been destroyed, as if to say "they just can't," but before he could get a verbal answer out, the translator spoke. "I can talk to the city—if anyone in there is using a translator. Someone may have thought of it."

Wow. "Can you?" she asked, stuttering.

"Would you like me to?"

Damn all literal devices to hell. Her answer came out through clenched teeth. "Yes. Please." And before she could formulate another question, a tinny, machine-voice sounded in her helmet. "This is the emergency whale communications system. Hold on."

She waited. Minutes passed. Shadowy movement passed between the lights inside the dome and the shell.

The whales circled faster, as if trying to tell her something.

"Whale trainer Jerzy Hu here. Great idea. We have you on-camera."

She glanced at Jai. A broad smile showed through his helmet and he lifted one hand as if in benediction. She grinned and blushed. Luck, mostly, and the fact that she'd even tried. She'd never met Jerzy, but she was ready to make the woman her new best friend.

"Can anyone come out and help us free the lungs?" Surely they could see what needed to be done.

Jerzy's voice in her ear. "The dome is closed. It's automatic. It won't let us out. We've been trying. It seems to think even one lockfull of lost air will kill us all."

There were a thousand things she wanted to ask. "Is everyone okay in there?"

"Almost everyone. A building fell. Three people died and we have about twenty injured."

Jonathon. "My son. Jonathon Horner. Is he okay?"

A laugh. "He's been a pest ever since the dome closed with you outside it. He's okay."

Kitha wanted to talk to him so badly it hurt. But the whales! "Jerzy. How do I get the whales to help us? We need rope or chain or something, and then maybe they can help us lift this."

"We've been working on that ever since you called that whale. That was Kiley, by the way. The other two are Penelope and Lisa."

She'd never thought to ask the translator the whale's names. "Thanks, Jerzy. Did you come up with any ideas?"

"The trick will be getting them not to take off. Kiley's the key—he leads that pod. But you have to get him to like you."

"I like him. I love him. What do I do?"

"Swim up to him. You'll have to guide the whole thing. Send Jai down to the communications building. We know it's a wreck, but there should be wires used to move the antenna around when we need to work on it. At least one will be attached to the antenna."

Jai was already directing the sled down. "Okay. But what do I do to make a whale like me?"

"Be yourself," Jerzy said. "He'll bond with you or he won't. Whales make up their own minds about who they'll accept as a trainer."

Great. The sled bottomed out and Jai's hands began to unstrap her, clumsy in his big pressure gloves.

"Oh . . . and don't be afraid of him," Jerzy added. "Be positive. Whales like the positive."

She floated free of the sled. Jai was already heading for the wreck of the dome's communications equipment.

"Jerzy, I'm going."

The woman's voice was warm and encouraging. "Good luck."

Kitha kicked upward. Should she ask Kiley to come to her? The whale wasn't far away. Maybe she'd start by just coming near and then waiting. Her stomach had gone to water. She had to succeed.

About halfway up the tall curve of the dome, Kitha kicked a little bit away, holding the translator ball in two hands so she wouldn't drop it, being careful not to squeeze it. Who knew how much power it had?

She treaded water, her right leg working harder than her left, watching the three whales. She picked out Kiley as much from the shape of the bundles attached to his harness as from anything else.

She watched him, willing him to come to her.

The whales milled. The smallest one started to break up and away, toward the surface, but Kiley called out to it, a short sweet sound that turned the beast back down. He circled her, keeping his distance.

She squeezed the ball. "Jerzy. What do I do?" Her voice shook.

"I can't help you. He doesn't like me."

Kitha groaned. What would she want? Heck, what did that matter? She didn't think like a whale. She was a kelp-farmer. The lowest of the low, except maybe the janitors. "Jerzy, do they like you to come to them?"

"Trust yourself."

Okay. She'd stay put. Show respect.

Kiley circled her again, a little closer, then he turned away, his great tail undulating through the water, lit from the underside by the city's own interior brightness.

Had she failed? She held her breath, willing him to turn and come back.

The other two whales began to follow him.

She pressed the *come* button, surrounding herself with sound. And turned it off. She remembered the last time.

The three whales turned in unison, as if responding to some unspoken command. A water ballet of big blue creatures. Kitha drew in a breath at the sheer beauty of their coordination. Kiley flicked his tail and moved to the front, swimming so closely by her that she saw the barnacles lining his mouth. She transferred the ball to her left hand, flicked her own tail—her fins—pain shooting up her right thigh. Kitha grabbed a handle on the harness with her right hand. Kiley pulled her gently along. "Tell him thank you," she said.

Sound belled out from her hand, a long gentle noise, softer by far than the *come* signal.

She looked down. Jai was attaching something to the big girder down below. He'd found a line.

"Ask Kiley to swim over clear ground." She tucked the translator into her pocket, and then twisted to look at the nets. The latches that held the cargo nets in place were easy to see. She waited while the great whale swam a few meters past the dome, then lifted the latches, scrunching close against the whale's body as the nets fell free, tumbling to the ground, bouncing once, twice, and then resting. She should have had Kiley go slower and lower. Hell, she was learning. Now that he was free of the nets, she slid up on Kiley's back. She laughed, suddenly deliriously happy. She, Kitha, rode a whale! She must have bumped it, because the translator seemed to laugh with her for a moment. Kiley sped up, taking her up and around the dome, fast, a big circle. She freed a hand and grabbed the translator. "We have to wait," she said. "Ask him to go down."

Sound. And instant compliance. Kiley liked her. She wanted to lean down and pet him, but one hand held the translator and the other held fast to the harness. She leaned down and kissed him.

If she was specific, the whale did what she asked. She got Kiley positioned so Jai could tie the free end of the rope to the harness, and then turned the whale. She had to be sure she didn't damage the lungs or the dome.

Or the whale?

Kiley seemed to understand. He bunched under her, gathering himself, and then he whipped his tail up and down so powerfully that the backlash in the water pushed Jai away. The metal bar rose easily, upending and landing with a puff on empty seafloor.

The lungs lay still and quiet. "Are they broken?" Kitha asked Jai.

Jerzy answered. "You were magnificent. And no. They'll come on all by themselves. At least the two that aren't torn. They'll need to finish running diagnostics."

"All right. What's the smallest whale's name?"

"Penelope."

Kitha stripped Penelope and then Lisa of their cargo, being more careful to drop it carefully. The whales immediately took off, swimming in unison again, their great tails moving up and down to the same beat. Kitha thought she might never have seen anything more beautiful.

Jai swam up next to her and took her hand, waiting with her until the whales had disappeared from sight.

Behind them, the city drew a deep breath.

She squeezed Jai's hand and headed toward the dome. Locks were already disgorging people and machinery to finish what she and Jai had started.

Just inside the lock, Jonathon waited beside a tall smiling red-haired woman who must be Jerzy. He raced into her arms, warm and wriggly. "I'm so proud of you, Mommy!"

A tear dripped down her cheek as she held her son close.

STAR of HUMANITY

A gust of wind jerked the hood of Tanya Paul's sweatshirt off of her blond hair. She glanced up at the dark clouds above her and then back down at the dirty sidewalk. Maybe she should find shelter. She had come to downtown Kirkland to meet her classmate, Jennie, only to receive a text cancelling the meeting just after she coasted into a parking place. Her homework had to be done whether she had someone to study with or not. Bad enough that one in five new students with teaching degrees had a chance in hell at actually teaching. Which she was going to figure out how to do. Somehow.

Sheets of rain fell from clouds halfway across the lake, the wind driving the whole mess her way. She pulled off one cheap purple glove with her teeth so she could swipe at her phone and look for deals. She touched the button for food, and offerings filled the screen.

Greek. Italian. Three Mexican choices. Maybe one of them had a bar she could sit in and spread out. A coffee place with food would be better. There. Gusto Beans and Bakery. Two blocks ahead of her on the right. A yellow coupon bubble sprang to life. Free specialty coffee with dinner. She popped the menu open. They had her favorite drink (Half-caf soy latte with real caramel drizzle) and a list of sandwiches. Okay. Whatever they offered for food would do. Damn Jennie anyway for abandoning her.

She made it inside the doorway just as raindrops started pinging on the metal overhang. It was largely empty, which explained the coupon. There was even an open table near a cheerful little fireplace. She headed straight for it, shrugged her backpack off, and sat down with a sigh. The barista looked up and smiled but hurried into the back on a mission. Tanya still had her phone in hand, so she decided to pick a sandwich. The menu was still on the screen. Ham and cheese on focaccia. Butternut squash and asparagus on an open-faced bun.

Four choices down, there was a short url embedded in the name of the sandwich. She glanced around but didn't see anyone who looked like they were hacking the wireless. Just an old guy reading and three women passing a tablet around and exclaiming over baby pictures. Another ad? Well, her security algorithms were up to date. She double-tapped to open it, and a window with a blue border filled her screen. Inside the window, a crisp short paragraph of text read, "Job offer. Your teaching credential can lead to adventure. Watch for information about the Star of Humanity."

She flipped the phone closed before any more of the message could show up. This was hacker stuff, not something she could trust. She got up to order from the human at the bar.

Susan Little put her arm around Mr. Lim's stooped shoulders and let him cry. He felt thin and sad, and it was all Susan could do not to cry herself. It was always like this for her—she hated the tears and the loss because it affected her so much more than she thought it should. She had to work really hard to keep her game face on and stay professional long enough for Dr. Richards to show up and tell Mr. Lim, "You can return for the ashes day-after-tomorrow," Dr. Richards told Mr. Lim. "Max is past all of his pain. It will be okay."

Mr. Lim looked up at the vet and nodded, then patted Susan's hand. "Thank you," he said.

"You're welcome." There really wasn't anything else to say. Susan stepped aside to let him shuffle out the door and over to the counter to pay. She shut the door behind him and walked into the back where Dr. Richards kept cats and dogs that had been left for observation or fluids or to recover from minor surgeries. Only one of the kennels had a dog in it, Blue, a big mastiff who was so far gone in drug-induced sleep he snored like an old woman. Half the cat cages were full, but only one was awake and unhappy; a little calico who was pacing with as much dignity as she could muster in a small crate.

Susan grabbed a Kleenex and wiped at the single tear sliding down her face.

Dr. Richards came up behind her. "It gets easier. Really. We have four more left today; a cat with a cold, a six-month check-up for Ms. Colson's puppy, and two rounds of shots. Those should be easy enough."

Susan nodded. The woman was all business, all the time.

"The cat's already in exam room 2," the doctor said, heading off in a very business-like fashion. Given that this was her last day in the clinic, Susan needed to leave a good impression. Dr. Richard's evaluation and a final paper was all that stood between her and her vet degree.

Just then, the receptionist called out, "Dog on the way in. Got into a Prickly Pear after a rabbit."

Great. An hour of pulling thorns out, or two if the animal was scared enough. "I'll be right there!" Susan called and pulled out her phone to text a friend that she'd be late to a visit. There was a text waiting for her. "The Star of Humanity is looking for a few good vets. Watch for more information." A recruiter. Well, she already had two interviews lined up; she could follow through on this later. She closed the message and started to tap out the one she needed to send.

A week later, Tanya walked across a stage and picked up her degree and the promise of her teaching certificate. A few school classmates cheered for her, but afterwards all she could really do was go home to her small apartment and her cat, Tom. Tom was no such thing; she'd fixed him right after she got him from the shelter, but it was the name he came with and she hadn't thought of a better one. "I'm done," she told him as she stroked his gold and white fur. He arched his back under her hand and stood patiently. "I can be a real teacher now," she told him.

Telling a cat about it didn't really do anything for her mood, which was wistful at best. When her dad was alive, he'd always told her to just keep her mind busy. She gave Tom another scratch and grabbed her tablet. It opened to a bookstore site, displaying history books and kids reading material. "No," she told it. "Biology." She was free of studying, and she'd continue her job search seriously tomorrow. The least she could give herself for graduating was a good book to read.

The list was way too big, of course.

"Climate. Northwest."

That got it down to twenty. She started scrolling. There:

CLIMATE EFFECTS ON GRAPES IN THE NORTH-WEST. At least the computer remembered she liked wine. She double-tapped and a blue-lined window opened inside of her other windows. She blinked at it, a vague memory of a job-troll tickling her memory. Irritated, she tapped the right corner to close the window. It didn't budge. "Congratulations on your degree, Tanya. Are you interested in adventure? Your first clue will appear in three days.—Star of Humanity."

Damn adware blocker must need an update. Come to think of it, only in-app ads should be able to get through, like ads for books or stuff related to her search. As she stared at it, the window faded, the right background and the book on the challenges with wine appearing where it should have been in the first place.

The damned net always knew everything, like that she'd graduated and didn't have a job.

She abandoned the idea of a book and searched for Star of Humanity. Something about a diamond and something about truthful living from the Sikhs. Neither made any contextual sense. She snapped the computer closed, irritated that it knew what she wished it didn't, but couldn't find anything about a topic she did want to know. What was Star of Humanity, anyway?

Dr. Richards had given Susan a more glowing write-up than she expected. She'd updated her posted resume, which had yielded three online interviews that had turned into two offers, both of which required that she leave Arizona, one for the Midwest and one for Alaska. Farm animals, or sled dogs and sleet. At least the next interview would be for an in-city clinic. She'd have to deal with euthanasia, which she hated, but there would be a lot of very normal vet work.

The interview went well, with two vets and a vet tech on the other side, everyone calling in from home. Susan wore a good sweater and her gold earrings over her shorts, and stayed seated so as not to give away the shorts. East coast. She could handle that better than delivering cows or freezing, although she really wanted a job in Arizona. Just as she closed the video window, a new window appeared under it. She hadn't touched anything.

"Hello, Susan. We need vets that want to work in a challenging environment on all classes of animals. Please consider meeting with our senior staff in two days. We will send you an address. —Star of Humanity."

There was no place to respond, no box to type in, no phone number to call. A prank? A mystery?

She ditched the sweater in favor of a tank top and headed out to a good-bye lunch with two people from her graduating class. One was leaving for Florida the next day, and the other for New York.

After the greetings and the details of the two moves and Susan's job offers made it onto the table, Susan leaned forward over her Mandarin chicken salad and asked, "Have either of you heard of the Star of Humanity?"

Both of her friends shook their heads.

When she got home, Susan called her advisor from college and asked the same question. After she got the same answer, she frowned and went out to meet another friend who already had a job, hoping a Mojito would help her get up the courage to turn down the two offers she already had.

Tanya found herself watching for another blue-lined window.

None appeared.

Three days later, no jobs or interviews had appeared either. Not even free internships. After four hours of staring at screens and reformatting her cover letter three times for different applications, she got up and headed out into the gray Seattle mist for coffee.

Her favorite coffee house in walking distance was Café Pilot, a cheerful building with brown seats, yellow walls, paper airplanes hanging from the ceiling, and a rotating art display on the walls. At the moment, the art was quilted postcards with messages from the past on them. Sam, her favorite barista, looked up and nodded, ready to start her usual drink.

She shook her head, her pockets feeling thin. "Just an Americano."

"Room?"

"Sure." Cream would give her a few extra calories.

Her usual seat was taken so she slid into the last available empty table by the steam-fogged window. She barely took her first sip when a tall man with glasses (who wore *glasses* any more!) slid into the chair across from her.

"Hi, Tanya."

She'd be willing to swear she didn't recognize him. Maybe from one of her classes?

He slid a card across the table. White, lined with blue. Paper. "Star of Humanity. Peter Accord."

She picked it up. No other words on it, no symbols.

"We would like to interview you," he said.

"Who are you?"

"Peter."

"Your card says that. I mean the Star of Humanity. I can't find it."

He took a sip of his cappuccino and nodded at her. He looked pleased.

"Is it a new school?" she asked. "Maybe a startup?"

Now he smiled all-out. His teeth were the white of the well-insured in spite of his dorky glasses, which looked badly extruded from a home printer. His clothes were pretty top-notch, too. Her jeans and T-shirt were fairly new, but they hadn't cost a year's salary. She swallowed and waited for his smile to run out. When it did, he confirmed what she had been thinking. "It's a private school."

"Someplace for rich kids?"

Now he shook his head. "Not all. Look, I can't tell you very much, but I'd like to ask you a few questions. Is that okay?"

She didn't like this, but Peter didn't feel mean or particularly odd, and after all, what could happen in the Café Pilot? "Sure." She prepared herself for the first question, which would be something like, *Tell me what you want to do.*

"What would you think of teaching children of mixed ages?"

Wow. Something far more specific. "As long as it's a class size I can handle. I'd need fewer kids at once to teach multiple grades. It's important to me to teach. Really. Not adults, but kids. My mother was a teacher, and I want to be one, too. I remember how much she loved her job." What else? "In mixed-age classrooms, the older kids can help the younger ones."

"How important is it that your job is near here?"

Anyplace sunny would be nice. "Not nearly as important as finding a job I like."

He steepled his hands in front of him and paused a moment before asking the next question. "You don't own your house and your parents are dead."

She tensed at that. Available on the web, but it meant they'd had to dig.

He continued after giving her a moment to adjust. "Do you have any other impediments to moving?"

"Just Tom."

"Your cat could come with you."

"Then I don't mind moving."

"What about travel? You state that you want to travel. Do you really?"

"Yes." She didn't talk about travel anywhere on her resume, and really only about travel books on her social networks, which she didn't expose casually. "Do I get a turn to ask questions?"

"In a bit. We'll be in touch."

With that, with four lousy questions, he stood up and held a hand out to her. "Nice to meet you, Tanya. Good luck."

"Nice to meet you, too." Her voice sounded small and he was already halfway to the door. When Tanya looked down at the table, the business card was gone, too. Damn. She hadn't even seen him pick it up.

Apparently she'd managed to flunk out of her first job interview in weeks with just four questions.

Susan woke to a message on her phone. This time, it appeared as soon as she opened her phone, as if it had been lying in wait for her. "Good morning, Susan. If you're free at eleven this morning, please go to Civic Space Park downtown and look for a woman in blue. We would very much like to talk with you."

Not even a signature this time. Just the blue window, which she already knew signified the Star of Humanity, whatever the hell that was. And of course she was free. No appointments at all today, no more interviews. She'd turned down the wilds and the cold, and there'd been no offer from the east coast. Her bank account was thinning, and yesterday her apartment manager had sent a note reminding her that her student subsidy was running out. Did she want to stay at the full rate?

Right. There was no one to answer on the Star thing. She cruised job sites for an hour and found two internships she could apply for. Only one paid, and it would require a move to Tucson. There were three volunteer positions. Not useful.

She ran through a morning yoga set of seven sun salutations with a few extra downward dogs thrown in for good measure, finally getting a little calm. Trust. That's what her mom had always taught her. Trust the universe. Of course, her mom had done that, and all the universe returned was cancer and an ability to face the early and fairly nasty death the cancer gave her.

Better than nothing.

Yeah, right.

She chose a yellow skirt, a white blouse, and her best flats, and tucked a few dollars into a wrist-wallet. The only other thing of value she took—besides her phone in her skirt pocket—was her journal. As she headed for the metro, she contemplated what people felt like when they were going to court or on their way to pay taxes. Like she was voluntarily setting herself up to get fleeced, like she was being just as smart as whatever idiots answered emails about huge sums of money in Nigerian banks. As much as she tried to frame it in her mind as an adventure, she felt foolish and about twelve years old.

She almost got off the train and turned around twice.

The huge netted sculpture that symbolized the park came into view first, sun throwing highlights onto the odd collection of rounded metal and flowing metal mesh. When she was in pre-vet at ASU the sculpture had symbolized everything natural for her—clouds and storms and the way the desert was hard and soft all at once.

At least they'd asked her to meet them in a place where she felt at home.

The park was crowded with students, most of the tree shade taken by study groups and, in a few cases, by families out for a picnic. Rickshaw bikers sat in a clump of dark wheels and brightly colored forks and silver handlebars, talking amongst each other. She walked past them without so much as a nod. She was fifteen minutes early. Maybe she could have brought her e-reader. She pulled out her phone and then shoved it back into her pocket unopened. No one had told her where to go, so she walked. It was one of those blue-sky days when the temperature would peg under a hundred and the last snow-birds still wandered around Phoenix waiting for the winter to finish melting away from their other homes.

10:55. A couple abandoned a bench under one of the shade structures just as she was walking by. She slid into it and watched a man walking three dogs so small they looked like brown tennis balls with eyes and feet. One of the new engineered breeds meant to be carried around in pockets. Tea-cup Chihuahuas crossed with miniature corgis, improbable and very popular last year.

Exactly at 11:00 a woman slid into the open space beside her. She was small and compact, well-dressed in a flowing blue shirt of material that would stay cool in the Arizona heat and a pair of off-white Dockers. Her dark hair was bobbed just above her ears, and artsy silver earrings that sparkled a bit in the sun hung down the side of her neck. Maybe only twenty-five, really about Susan's age. East Indian mixed with Caucasian, or something like that. She extended a well-manicured hand. "I'm Lana. Pleased to meet you."

"Susan." Of course they knew that, and so she found herself blurting out, "This is an odd way to recruit." Her cheeks felt hot, but she managed not to look away.

Lana smiled. "I'm sorry. We are . . . protecting some intellectual property. That means avoiding the Internet."

"I don't know anything more than the usual vet student about gen-mods."

Lana gave a small laugh. "Nor do I. That's not the primary IP we're talking about."

Susan waited for a follow-on reveal of some kind, but it didn't come.

"Can I ask you some questions?" Lana asked.

"Sure."

"We know it's been hard to find a job you like. We need a few vets to help us out with an experiment. We like the person you seem to be. You're earnest, your grades are good, and you got high marks in your practical work."

"Right." But that wasn't a question.

"Would you be willing to meet with us to explore a job opportunity? We'll have to put you under an NDA, and I can't really talk about it now. But we can promise you at least three months of pay."

"I'm not interested in experimenting on animals."

"Neither are we."

"Good." But they could be doing something illegal. Not that they'd say. She thought about her apartment and her bank balance. "How much pay, and where would I have to go?"

Lana named a figure. Higher than either of the other two jobs she had been offered.

Susan swallowed and repeated her second question. "Where?"

"For three months, we'll be in a training facility on an island. There will be about a hundred people there. Most of them are already affiliated with our project."

"Is this some kind of a religious thing?"

Lana smiled. The smile lit up her face, a bit of humor contained in the look. "No. But you can't talk about it. If we see any references on the Internet, the job offer will disappear."

A couple with three children in tow walked past them. All five were badly dressed, the children in ill-fitting shoes. More of the city's unemployed. The woman looked exhausted, with dark circles the size of quarters making small bruises on her worn face.

"I need to know more about it before I can make a decision."

"We won't be able to tell you much more. You'll work with healthy animals."

Susan swallowed. "I don't like secrets."

Lana's smile was back, this time touched with empathy. "I understand. I imagine this does seem odd to you. But look around this city, any city. The economy's no good. It hasn't been for a very long time."

"There are still jobs for vets. I'll find one."

"Yes, I'm sure you will." Lana' feature settled into a serious pose. "Look, this is part of a dream that a lot of us have. It's a good thing. We're recruiting a few more specialties, ones we need but that we didn't already have in our families and friends circles. I'm sorry it's secretive, but you'll understand why when we explain what we're doing. It will be better than whatever else you can find. I'm sure of it."

"Why not someone with more experience? Why me?"

Lana looked away. "We've researched the best students and free adults. And we like you."

"How do I get in touch with you?" Susan asked.

"It's a chance to work with animals. A chance to do what you love. And the people are all amazing. I promise."

They—Lana—wanted her to decide now. Susan closed her eyes and let herself feel. That's how she worked with animals—instinct and feeling put together with her training. She felt her circumstances, her loneliness. Whatever she did, she was going to have to move, start over with new people. Most of her friends from school had gone on to jobs or gone home already. She had neither.

"Do you have the NDA?"

"We'll provide it to you when you meet us."

There was an opportunity here. A real one. She could see it in Lana's eyes. In spite of the fact she wasn't sure she should, she liked Lana. Besides, she'd always been one to try for adventures when they came up. "Can I change my mind?"

"Of course. I'm convinced you won't."

Even though her practical side hated her for the movement, she held out her hand to Lana.

Lana took her hand and shook it, relief flashing for a moment across her face before the professional smile returned. "Be ready to leave in two days. We'll send you information."

Susan nodded, letting the decision sit inside her gut, trying to decide if it was festering or if it was good.

Lana stood and looked down at Susan. "Welcome aboard. I'll see you in a few days."

With that she was gone, leaving Susan to stare at the sculpture hanging over the park and watch the wind draw ripples in its netted sides.

The Star of Humanity surprised Tanya three days later with another invitation. It happened while she was packing up. She'd come to the realization that if she went now, she could afford to keep her belongings in storage here and take Tom and her car and head south, try to find a job in Portland or San Francisco. She knew people in both places and had arranged for crash space in exchange for cash in Portland, and found work as a housesitter in San Francisco. If neither of those cities had teaching jobs, she'd apply in some of the shrinking towns in-between.

Somebody must need a good teacher.

She would be good. She knew it. Never mind that the fall rosters were all filled up and the Seattle school district had a waiting list.

It spooked her when she opened her phone to find a message that she suspected came from Peter, as if they knew she was almost packed, almost mobile.

She stared at it.

Meet me at Pike Place Market? Near the falafel vendor? Be ready to travel.

As usual, there was no way to reply. Just the white background and the blue border.

She pocketed the phone and started folding the coats in her hall closet and putting them in the last box. In an hour she had everything in her car, some of the boxes squished up against the window as she closed the door, and no place for Tom but on her lap. Surprisingly, he didn't protest at all as she clipped a thin lead to the collar and then held him too tight for him to squeeze out of her arms, locked her door with one hand, bent to slide the key under the mat, and got settled in the car. Tom usually hated the lead. This time, he curled on her lap so she had to push the seat back a bit to get the steering wheel to turn. "We're off," she said. "Ready for an adventure?"

He purred.

Three hours to get ready to travel. Who the hell did Peter think he was? It took another hour to unload the boxes she was leaving behind—physical books, dishes and coffee cups, clothes, an old computer she still needed to clear off before she could recycle it. She signed the storage contract, paid for three months, and put the key on her chain.

There was room in the car for Tom to sit somewhere else but he insisted on staying on her lap. So Tanya drove to the freeway with the cat on her lap, chewing on her bottom lip and swearing to herself that she was going to Portland.

Not that lunch would be bad. The dishes had been packed last night and all she'd had today was the back end of a box of stale crackers.

Which is how she found herself holding one fat yellow cat snuggled in her arms and walking through the tourist crowds to order a falafel. The market smelled of spices and cut fruit and stale coffee. An old busker with a long beard played a scratched up guitar so loud that she had to work to keep Tom from clawing her.

Peter came up from behind like a surprise and started walking beside her. Even though she'd been expecting him, she flinched. He looked just as good as he had in the coffee house, slightly better dressed than most of the people around, slightly better groomed.

Since he looked happy to see her, she relaxed a little. He didn't feel like someone looking to recruit girls for a street harem or push drugs or anything. He looked like a successful tech guy, like someone from Microsoft or Amazon or Nintendo or anyplace else like that.

She stopped in front of the falafel storefront. Her plan was to eat, hear Peter out, and then leave for Portland. She'd only paid for an hour on the parking meter. "I'm hungry."

"You're not certain yet. I understand."

They stopped and he bought her a falafel. To her surprise, Tom went willingly into his arms, freeing her so she could eat. It raised Peter two notches: one that Tom would go to him, and another that he'd accept a sure fight between cat hair and his expensive clothes.

The bad news was that he kept walking. They went down the stairs by the fountain and headed into a parking garage. She took her last two bites in a hurry, wanting her hands free in case she was reading the situation wrong. He led her to an elevator and up three floors. She found herself in a round room with tables. Curtains covered what must be a beautiful view of Puget Sound. There were about ten people there. At least half of them wore blue shirts of one kind or another. Like Peter. She sat down at an empty table, cat and all, and looked around. The room was pretty bare, although a pile of boxes lined one wall.

A red-haired woman with a slight tan and a splash of freckles came over and sat down beside her, holding one hand out toward Tom, who gave it a sniff and settled deeper onto Tanya's lap. "He's pretty. What's his name?"

"Tom. And I'm Tanya."

"Susan."

Probably a Star of Humanity person. Although she was dressed in green and had goose-bumps on her arms in spite of the reasonably warm room. "You're not from here, are you?" Tanya asked.

The woman shook her head. "Are you a vet?"

"A teacher." She blushed. "Well, I want to be. I have my certificate. But no job."

"I'm from Phoenix. And maybe this is a job."

Tanya swallowed. That explained the tan on someone so fair. "Maybe it is. But I thought they wanted teachers."

Before Susan had a chance to answer her, a thin man with a ghost of a beard came by and set two pages and a pen down in front of each of them. How quaint. Paper.

At the front of the room, a young woman with dark hair cleared her throat and started staring down the room, demanding silence with her sense of presence.

"That's Lana," Susan whispered.

There were only five people in the room with papers in front of them.

The woman's voice suggested she was used to talking to crowds. "Good morning. I'm Lana. We're glad you have chosen to trust us this far, to consider joining us. I know you're looking for more information, and I promise to provide it. First, let me explain why we are keeping a secret. Then, we'll go over the documents on the tables in front of you. Those are non-disclosure agreements. If you choose to sign them, we'll share information with you and then you can decide whether or not to join us." She paused, as if for effect, and smiled, adding, "And we hope that you *will* want to know more about what we are doing."

Tanya expected them to introduce people next, but Lana just kept talking. "There are some dreams that are bigger than the current social structure can support. There are problems that we have not been able to address, some that we will not be able to correct in time, in spite of heroic efforts by many individuals, and by some NGOs, companies and countries. In fact, the Star of Humanity was born out of companies doing the hard work to create sustainability, to solve hunger and disease and change our energy usage patterns." She paused, pacing the room and looking at the possible recruits. "Efforts to find a sane balance inside of the geo-political situation we all find ourselves in will continue."

So they were corporate. That both calmed Tanya and worried her, and it did change the game some. Beside her, Susan twisted her hair in her fingers and looked as dubious as Tanya felt. Why them, then?

"We have kept news of this off of the web, even off of the social network rumor mill. In some cases, you are the lucky ones here because as individuals, you didn't try to post about your experience with us."

Susan's hand shot up.

Lana nodded.

"How can you keep a secret today?"

"A fair question." Lana looked at someone in the back of the room, some exchange happening with only gazes. Permission? "You may know that today when you search for a topic, you get back a set of answers tailored for you. Ads designed for you. Information you are likely to click on. You, in fact, are the engine that drives the net. Each of you, creating your own web based on what you choose to look at."

Well, sure. That's why she always found out about new vineyards, and why she got so much biology news. She hadn't thought about it as a way to keep things from her. After all, before she started looking for the Star of Humanity, she'd been able to find anything she really wanted. If she knew a business or person existed, she could play with search terms until she found them.

"The filters that do this are automatic. Humans do not decide what you see, you decide what you see, setting your preferences into the vast programs that drive the biggest search engines of the web by what you select. You decide what you want. That's how it should be. But the same tools can be used to hide things." She paused again, looking around the room as if she expected a challenge.

None came.

"Search engines can be used to withhold information. Governments have been doing this since just after the dawn of the Internet. And our goals are bigger than the goals of any government. But for each of you, we believe you'll find they are aligned with your goals."

Did she want to be hidden?

She had a half hour left on her parking meter. She couldn't afford to have her car towed.

An oriental man in his mid-thirties raised his hand. "Why are you recruiting cooks?"

"We found we need some skills that we don't have. So we set out to find people who would have those skills. For example, Ling, we needed someone who could feed large groups of people well, and you just returned from a volunteer job where you did that in Russia."

Lana swept her gaze across the whole room. "We'll join each of you at your tables and explain the NDA in detail, give you time to read it. In reality, it's very simple. You agree not to speak of anything we've said in here or that we will say in here. You agree that whether or not you choose to join us, you'll never speak of this in open social networks—physical or virtual, or on the Internet. This is not substantially different than the agreement you would sign for a programming or research job with any firm that we know of. It may look strange and a little bit scary to those of you in this room, but that's only because you are not in professions where agreements like this are normal."

Peter came up and sat at the table with Tanya and Susan. Hushed conversations started. Tanya picked up the piece of paper in front of her. The best she could manage was to pretend to read it, her mind still stuck on the idea of using search engines to hide information. She wanted to teach to help children find out about the world, to bring light to their lives. How could something hidden bring light?

Susan was obviously reading the NDA closely. She asked Peter a quiet question and he answered in whispers.

Ling signed his papers.

Tanya touched Peter's arm. When he looked at her, she said, "I have to go put money into the meter for my car. I'll be right back."

"We'll do it for you."

"I want to do it."

"Really, we can—"

Her body tensed and Tom stood and stretched, the ruff on the top of his back thickening. As always he could feel her emotions. "I need to think, Peter. I need air."

"Let me talk to Lana."

As soon as he got up, she started for the door. She expected someone to step in front of her, but no one did. She expected Peter to bound after her, to be at the elevator before her, and then beside her in the parking garage. She made it all the way up the steep Pike's Place steps before she relaxed and took a deep breath. What if she became hidden, what if she couldn't smell the salty air of the Sound and the mixed fish and fruit of Pike's Place whenever she wanted? What could she be giving up before knowing what was being offered in exchange?

When she looked down the steps she'd climbed, she still didn't see Peter. Not that she had time to look closely—she was down to five minutes on the meter.

As soon as she settled Tom onto her lap in the car, she started it up and began her drive south.

Susan sat beside Ling on the deck of the Northern Star, the Canadian sea slapping at the boat's fiberglass sides one deck below her. Ling pointed ahead of them to starboard. "Whale!"

Sure enough. A humpback leapt up out of the water, almost pausing for a moment, as if it could fly. When it fell back, water splashed up and caught the sun, making a spray of tiny rainbows.

It felt like a gift.

Something she had never seen and would never see again.

Half an hour later, a bit of iceberg floated by, a small thing, although she knew that most of it was under water. "That might have come a long way," Ling said. "It might have come all the way from the Arctic."

"Have you ever seen a glacier?" she asked.

"Oh yes," he said. "I took a tour once, and we watched blue ice calve into a dark sea spotted with seals. It might have been the most majestic and sad thing I ever saw."

She smiled. After three days on the boat, she had learned that Ling felt deeply but showed little of it in his tone or on his face; it came in the poetry of his words. "I've never even seen an iceberg before," she said.

"But we will see the stars," he said.

"Yes, we will."

MY FATHER'S SINGULARITY

In my first memory of my father, we are sitting on the porch, shaded from the burning sun's assault on our struggling orchards. My father is leaning back in his favorite wooden rocker, sipping a cold beer with a half-naked lady on the label, and saying, "Paul, you're going to see the most amazing things. You will live forever." He licks his lips, the way our dogs react to treats, his breath coming faster. "You will do things I can't even imagine." He pauses, and we watch a flock of geese cross the sky. When he speaks again, he sounds wistful. "You won't ever have to die."

The next four of five memories are variations on that conversation, punctuated with the heat and sweat of work, and the smell of seasons passing across the land.

I never emerged from this particular conversation with him feeling like I knew what he meant. It was clear he thought it would happen to me and not to him, and that he had mixed feelings about that, happy for me and sad for himself. But he was always certain.

Sometimes he told me that I'd wake up one morning and all the world around me would be different. Other nights, he said, "Maybe there'll be a door, a shining door, and you'll go through it and you'll be better than human." He always talked about it the most right before we went into Seattle, which happened about twice a year, when the pass was open and the weather wasn't threatening our crops.

The whole idea came to him out of books so old they were bound paper with no moving parts, and from a brightly-colored magazine that eventually disintegrated from being handled. My father's hands were big and rough and his calluses wore the words off the paper.

Two beings always sat at his feet. Me, growing up, and a dog, growing old. He adopted them at mid-life or they came to him, a string of one dog at a time, always connected so that a new one showed within a week of the old one's death. He and his dogs were a mutual admiration society. They liked me fine, but they never adored me. They encouraged me to run my fingers through their stiff fur or their soft fur, or their wet, matted fur if they'd been out in the orchard sprinklers, but they were in doggie heaven when he touched them. They became completely still and their eyes softened and filled with warmth.

I'm not talking about the working dogs. We always had a pair of border collies for the sheep, but they belonged to the sheep and the sheep belonged to them and we were just the fence and the feeders for that little ecosystem.

These dogs were his children just like me, although he never suggested they would see the singularity. I would go beyond and they would stay and he and the dogs accepted that arrangement even if I didn't.

I murmured confused assent when my father said words about how I'd become whatever comes after humans.

Only once did I find enough courage to tell him what was in my heart. I'd been about ten, and I remember how cold my hands felt clutching a glass of iced lemonade while heat-sweat poured down the back of my neck. When he told me I would be different, I said, "No, Dad. I want to be like you when I grow up." He was the kindness in my life, the smile that met me every morning and made me eggs with the yolks barely soft and toast that melted butter without burning.

He shook his head, and patted his dog, and said, "You are luckier than that."

His desire for me to be different than him was the deepest rejection possible, and I bled for the wounds.

After the fifth year in seven that climate-freak storms wrecked the apples—this time with bone-crushing ice that set the border collies crazed with worry—I knew I'd have to leave if I was ever going to support my father. Not by crossing the great divide of humanity to become the seed of some other species, but to get schooled away from the slow life of farming sheep and Jonagolds. The farm could go on without me. We had the help of two immigrant families that each owned an acre of land that was once ours.

Letting my father lose the farm wasn't a choice I could even imagine. I'd go over to Seattle and go to school. After, I'd get a job and send money home, the way the Mexicans did when I was little and before the government gave them part of our land to punish us. Not that we were punished. We liked the Ramirez's and the Alvarez's. They, too, needed me to save the farm.

But that's not this story. Except that Mona Alvarez drove me to Leavenworth to catch the silver Amtrak train, her black hair flying away from her lipstick-black lips, and her black painted fingernails clutching the treacherous steering wheel of our old diesel truck. She was so beautiful I decided right then that I would miss her almost as much as I would miss my father and the bending apple trees and the working dogs and the sheep. Maybe I would miss Mona even more.

Mona, however, might not miss me. She waved once after she dropped me off, and then she and the old truck were gone and I waited amid the electric cars and the old tourists with camera hats and data jewelry and the faint marks of implants in the soft skin between their thumbs and their index fingers. They looked like they saw everything and nothing all at once.

If they came to our farm the coyotes and the repatriated wolves would run them down fast.

On the other end of the train ride, I found the University of Washington, now sprawled all across Seattle, a series of classes and meet ups and virtual lessons that spidered out from the real brick buildings. An old part of the campus still squatted by the Montlake Cut, watching over water and movement that looked like water spiders but was truly lines of people with oars on nanofab boats as thin as paper.

Our periodic family trips to Seattle hadn't really prepared me for being a student. The first few years felt like running perpetually uphill, my brain just not going as fast as everyone else's.

I went home every year. Mona married one of the Ramirez boys and had two babies by the time three years had passed, and her beauty changed to a quiet softness with no time to paint her lips or her nails. Still, she was prettier than the sticks for girls that chewed calorie-eating gum and did their homework while they ran to Gasworks Park and back on the Burke-Gilman Trail, muttering answers to flashcards painted on their retinas with light.

I didn't date those girls; I wouldn't have known how to interrupt the speed of their lives and ask them out. I dated storms of data and new implants and the rush of ideas until by my senior year I was actually keeping up.

When I graduated, I got a job in genetics that paid well enough for me to live in an artist's loft in a green built row above Lake Union. I often climbed onto the garden roof and sat on an empty bench and watched the Space Needle change decorations every season and the little wooden boats sailing on the still lake below me. But mostly I watched over my experiments, playing with new medical implants to teach children creativity and to teach people docked for old age in the University hospital how to talk again, how to remember.

I did send money home. Mona's husband died in a flash flood one fall. Her face took on a sadness that choked in my throat, and I started paying her to take care of my father.

He still sat on the patio and talked about the singularity, and I managed not to tell him how quaint the old idea sounded. I recognized myself, would always recognize myself. In spite of the slow speed of the farm, a big piece of me was always happiest at home, even though I couldn't be there more than a day or so at a time. I can't explain that—how the best place in the world spit me out after a day or so.

Maybe I believed too much happiness would kill me, or change me. Or maybe I just couldn't move slow enough to breathe in the apple air any more. Whatever the reason, the city swept me back fast, folding me in its dancing ads and shimmering opportunities and art.

Dad didn't really need me anyway. He had the Mexicans and he still always had a dog, looking lovingly up at him. Max, then Owl-Face, then Blue. His fingers had turned to claws and he had cataracts scraped from his eyes twice, but he still worked with the harvest, still carried a bushel basket and still found fruit buried deep in the trees.

I told myself he was happy.

Then one year, he startled when I walked up on the porch and his eyes filled with fear.

I hadn't changed. I mean, not much. I had a new implant, I had a bigger cloud, researchers under me, so much money that what I sent my father—what he needed for the whole orchard—was the same as a night out at a concert and dinner at Canlis. But I was still me, and Blue—the current dog—accepted me, and Mona's oldest son called me "Uncle Paul" on his way out to tend the sheep.

I told my father to pack up and come with me.

He ran his fingers through the fur on Blue's square head. "I used to have a son, but he left." He sounded certain. "He became the next step for us. For humans."

He was looking right at me, even looking in my eyes, and there was truly no recognition there. His look made me cold to the spine, cold to the ends of my fingers even with the sun driving sweat down my back.

I kissed his forehead. I found Mona and told her I'd be back in a few weeks and she should have him packed up.

Her eyes were beautiful and terrible with reproach as she declared, "He doesn't want to leave."

"I can help him."

"Can you make him young, like you?"

Her hair had gone gray at the edges, lost the magnificent black that had glistened in the sun like her goth lipstick all those years ago. God, how could I have been so selfish? I could have given her some of what I had.

But I liked her better touched by pain and age and staying part of my past. Like the act of saving them didn't.

I hadn't known that until that very moment, when I suddenly hated myself for the wrinkles around her eyes and the way her shoulders bent in a little bit even though she was only fifty-seven like me. "I'll bring you some, too. I can get some of the best nano-meds available." Hell, I'd designed some of them, but Mona wouldn't understand that. "I can get creams that will erase the wrinkles from your hands."

She sighed. "Why don't you just leave us?"

Because then I would have no single happy place. "Because I need my father. I need to know how he's doing."

"I can tell you from here."

My throat felt thick. "I'll be back in a week." I turned away before she could see the inexplicable tears in my eyes. By then I flew back and forth, and it was a relief to focus down on the gauges in my head, flying manual until I got close enough to Seattle airspace that the feds grabbed the steering from me and there was nothing to do but look down at the forest and the green resort playgrounds of Cle Elum below me and to try not to think too hard about my dad or about Mona Alvarez and her sons.

I had moved into a condo on Alki Beach, and I had a view all the way to Canada. For two days after I returned, the J-pod whales cavorted offshore, great elongated yin and yang symbols rising and falling through the waters of Puget Sound.

The night before I went back for Mona and my father, I watched the boardwalk below me. People walked dogs and rollerbladed and bicycled and a few of the chemical-sick walked inside of big rolling bubbles like the hamster I'd had when I was a kid. Even nano-medicine and the clever delivery of genetically matched and married designer solutions couldn't save everyone.

I wish I could say that I felt sorry for the people in the bubbles, and I suppose in some distant way I did. But nothing bad had ever happened to me. I didn't get sick. I'd never married or divorced. I had nice dates sometimes, and excellent season tickets for Seattle Arts and Lectures.

I flew Mona back with my father. We tried to take Blue, but the dog balked at getting in the car, and raced away, lost in the apple trees in no time. Mona looked sick and said, "We should wait."

I glanced at my father's peaceful face. He had never cried when his dogs died or left, and now he had a small smile, and I had the fleeting thought that maybe he was proud of Blue for choosing the farm and the sheep and the brown-skinned boys. "Will your sons care for the dog?"

"Their children love him."

So we arrived back in West Seattle, me and Mona and my father.

I got busy crafting medicine to fix my father. These things didn't take long—time moved fast in the vast cloud of data I had security rights for. I crunched my father's DNA and RNA and proteins and the specifics of his blood in no time, and told the computers what to do while I set all of us out a quiet dinner on the biggest of the decks. Mona commented on the salty scent of Puget Sound and watched the fast little ferries zip back and forth in the water and refused to meet my eyes.

Dad simply stared at the water.

"He needs a dog," she said.

"I know." I queried from right there, sending a bot out to look. It reported fairly fast. "I'll be right back. Can you watch him?"

She looked startled.

An hour later I picked Nanny up at Sea-Tac, a middle-aged golden retriever, service-trained, a dog with no job since most every disease except the worst allergies to modernity could be fixed.

Mona looked awed almost to fear when I showed up with the dog, but she smiled and uncovered the dinner I'd left waiting.

Nanny and Dad were immediately enchanted with each other, her love for him the same as every other dog's in his life, cemented the minute she smelled him. I didn't understand, but if it had been any other way, I would have believed him lost.

The drugs I designed for him didn't work. It happens that way sometimes. Not often. But some minds can't accept the changes we can make. In the very old, it can kill them. Dad was too strong to die, although Mona looked at me one day, after they had been with me long enough that the wrinkles around her eyes had lost depth but not so long that they had left her face entirely. "You changed him. He's worse."

I might have. How would I know?

But I do know I lost my anchor in the world. Nothing in my life had been my singularity. I hadn't crossed into a new humanity like he prophesied over and over. I hadn't left him behind.

Instead, he left me behind. He recognized Nanny every day, and she him. But he never again called me Paul, or told me how I would step beyond him.

PART TWO
Space

The **TRELLIS**

with Larry Niven

Kyle refolded the napkins and pulled the tall water drop glasses back towards the plates. Lark wasn't due for two hours, and he'd changed the sign announcing her sixteenth birthday twice, switched placemats once, and dropped a knife on the floor. He paced.

Boot steps. Henry's signature slow shuffle identified him before he rounded the corner into the huge galley. The older man surveyed the perfect table, and his lips curled into a slow smile. "Quit worrying, Dad," he said. "She won't say so, but she'll be glad to see you."

Kyle sighed. "I haven't been here much this year." Henry watched over Lark when Kyle was visiting Charon. Too often.

Pluto was beautiful as it fell towards the windy dark of aphelion. Crystalline methane and nitrogen clouds sparkled as the light from the base hit them from below, illuminating a gauzy barrier between the frozen surface and the heavens. The clouds drifted across Charon's face. Charon never moved in the sky: directly overhead from where the trellis touched down, a brilliant white sphere where Earth's moon would have been tiny and flat.

From Charon Kyle could see stars, "A handy thing," he reminded Lark whenever he left, "for an astronomer." On Pluto the refreezing atmosphere hid them. Lark fought him, wheedling and demanding, until he let her stay on Pluto after the changing skies made his work impossible here. The base personnel were her family, and Kyle didn't have the will to fight her. He told himself Little Siberia on Pluto was better for her than the larger and more frenetic Christy Base on Charon. He'd have to watch over Lark in Charon. Here, she was safe. It meant they were separated for months at a time.

Lark worked. Everyone over twelve in Little Siberia base worked.

Lark was sixteen. For years she had been obsessed with the genetically engineered creepers that rooted at Charon and carried water to Pluto's icy but almost waterless surface. It was a fitting job for a student. The creepers themselves had been shaped by a Christy Base school project in 2181, two years after settlement of the Pluto/Charon bases, while the twin planets were still falling toward the sun and Pluto's atmosphere was rebuilding itself. Now, in 2240, a strange white forest spanned the 17,000 klicks between the two white planets. Named after the mythical river guarded by the boatman Charon, the forest Styx was a writhing mass of wide hollow limbs, translucent spiked leaves, and diaphanous flowers clinging to a Hoytether™ trellis that spanned the gap between the twin planets. Generations of genetic engineers, most of them students, had nurtured and changed the creepers, giving them a high metabolism that manufactured heat and food, turning them into conduits for food, water, and energy. Manipulating the creepers was rich entertainment for bright minds locked in a frozen system.

The creepers mystified Kyle.

Lark was there now, a hundred and sixty klicks above Pluto base, crawling down toward Little Siberia in her tiny exploration module. Henry monitored her progress, keeping her father's presence at Little Siberia a surprise.

Kyle looked over at Henry. "Did you hear from her? Is she on her way?"

Henry grinned, slow and lazy, not answering immediately. Kyle usually felt like water running downhill past molasses when he was around the older man. He made himself stand still and at least *look* patient. Finally Henry said, "She's on her way. Calm down."

"I haven't seen her for three months. She listens to you. She might not even notice I'm here."

"That's the way of all teens," Henry said. "It's not about me."

Kyle smiled tiredly. "I brought her a present." He produced a box from the nearby table, opened it, and held up a yellow dress with orange and black ribbons lining the bodice and strung through the skirt. Little metal balls hung on the ends of the ribbons. "I got her some leggings, too, so it'll work in Pluto gravity."

Henry shook his head. "Impractical." He was still smiling. "You paid to freight that over, and you're going to freight it away as well? It must have cost a pretty penny."

"Henry—sometimes you just gotta let go and do something stupid. Lark's birthday is today—not after we get to Jupiter. We're leaving in two months. Maybe. I'm competing for a grant to work at Jupiter next year. Lark will need something nice to wear at Jupiter Station. Besides, Chuska Smith makes these. Almost all of us parents with teens pitched in to help her pay the material freight last ship. The kids on Christy Base are excited about moving on."

"Lark isn't."

"I know." Lark loved Pluto. "She'll understand when we get to Jupiter. I'm looking forward to showing her Cassini University."

"You think about every place but here."

"Yeah, well, this is the end, Henry. The end of the solar system, and they're not even planets. Dead end of an astronomy career, too. All the best scopes are on remotes now. There are jobs in Jupiter System, and I have to pay for Lark's schooling. So it's not like there's a choice. Have you decided where you're going yet?"

"They'll let an old codger stay until the last ship. Maybe I won't leave at all."

"You could come with us. Surely they need general repair people at Jupiter Station. Pluto won't be safe in a few years."

"Yeah, I know, maybe I'll be blown off by the cyclonic winds of a dying atmosphere." It *was* a joke—Pluto's atmosphere was barely thicker than vacuum—but Henry's voice was flat and non-committal, his eyes rolled up so the whites showed. "I'm seventy-three, you know. Maybe I'll hang around as far towards aphelion as I can, and send back data."

"We've got automatic sensors for that. You have to think about what you're going to do." Kyle folded the dress carefully, and set in the box. "Hey, *Mars Adventurer* is scheduled for . . ." he looked at his watch, "now. Join me?"

"Nah. There's enough excitement in my life. Besides, don't you know those are staged? But you go ahead—keep your mind off waiting. She'll be down soon." Henry shuffled off.

In 2240 CE most of humanity had stopped going anywhere. Travel was too uncomfortable. Even if you never left your own planet, there were changing time zones, motion sickness, unpredictable cuisine . . . and security. Security wasn't just to stop terrorists and fleeing tax dodgers; there were plague carriers to be stopped too. Viruses changed faster than antibiotics.

Business could be done via virtual reality, world wide and further. Social relations could be confined to neighborhoods; dating could be done by VR first. The few who still traveled for pleasure now had a higher calling.

They were called "adventurers." They were loaded with sensors to record everything they experienced. They risked their lives and comfort in ways most folk would never consider, in banned national parks, proscribed religious sites, into volcanoes, undersea . . .

Justine Jackson was the scheduled pilot aboard *Mars Adventurer*. Kyle paid his tourist fee and pulled up a chair to watch the feed. Today Justine was flying an ultra-light glider over the Valles Marineris. The screen took the top half of the east wall of the huge galley. The galley was built to serve a full base; Little Siberia was about ten percent staffed. It was like being alone in a movie theatre designed for two hundred.

Kyle watched steep red and yellow-orange walls fly by under the glider. He kept one eye on readouts from Justine's body-monitors. You couldn't feel what Justine was going through, but if you could read the telltales, you could imagine. Advanced viewing systems would give motion too.

Suddenly the view spiraled as she did a full 360, a stomach-twisting shift from red canyon to orange sky to red canyon. Justine's heart rate started to rise as she finished the loop and banked into a roll, signaling how hard the trick really was.

One day the suits would record smell and taste.

But real time would never crack lightspeed. Even though the feed was hours old, it was ahead of any news. The familiar tension about whether Justine would fall to sudden death on the floor of Valles Marineris kept Kyle's eyes glued to the screen.

Most top adventurers eventually died.

The screen flickered abruptly to black. Had something happened to Justine?

"Kyle?" Suriyah's voice blasted loudly across the in-base communications.

Kyle blinked, absorbing the abrupt shift.

"Kyle? Can you hear me? There's a problem."

The screen glowed back to life.

He was looking into the Styx. Vines intertwined, moving, a cross between seaweed and woods, deeply shadowed despite light amplification.

The view was from inside Lark's ship. Stems twisted around one of the motorized arms, a leaf flapped across the field of view, barely lit and almost translucent, visible more by how it changed the look of the stars than by itself. The perspective changed to another camera facing the thick center of the forest. Stems and leaves were close here too. Spectral white shapes so thick he could only see two stars, and a rim of icy white Charon. The view jumped again, looking down: vines converging to a point on Pluto's brighter quake-patterned white.

"She's trapped," Suriyah said.

"Trapped?" It dawned on him that as the cameras cycled, he was seeing nothing but more forest. She wasn't up against the Styx; she was in it. "She went too far in?"

"She can tell you herself."

"Lark?" She didn't answer. A shiver ran through him as the images registered. His daughter was stuck a hundred and sixty kilometers above him, caught between worlds in a strange forest.

"Suriyah, I'm coming." Help would be in the communications room.

Half the twenty inhabitants of Pluto Base were already in Communications. Henry was there. He was looking at the only other child on base besides Lark, a blond ten-year-old boy named Paul. "No," Henry was saying. "See, Paul, if we took a regular transport ship, the exhaust would kill the creepers, and we couldn't help Lark anyway. Transport ships can't dock with a research bubble."

Kyle interrupted, "Can't she get loose herself? Her thruster works, right?"

Paul answered. "She's already tried."

"All right, then—" Think. A research bubble was tiny. The hull was transparent, but you had to see around eight extension arms of variable size and their thick mooring points, plus a water tank and the magnetic confinement for a fleck of antimatter in a swivel-mounted motor. In the habitat bubble there was only room for Lark in her pressure suit, and the rest of Shooter wasn't much bigger. "She could use the arms to grab onto a transport and let it pull her loose."

Suriyah noticed Kyle's arrival. "No, Kyle, she's too deep. The vines have been growing around her since she got trapped." She stood next to him and put an arm on his shoulder. Her dark eyes were smoky with worry. "You'd better talk to Lark." She pointed at the bank of observation screens.

Kyle stepped closer. There were images he'd seen from the galley. Another was Lark, using the video link. Her face was pinched, angry.

"Lark?"

"Dad? You're on Pluto?

"It's your sixteenth birthday."

"Well, then, I'd better get down there," she said dryly. "But first, I seem to have gotten the marble stuck."

She could have sounded happy to see me here. Kyle had nick-named the bubbles 'marbles'—they were clear and round, and the most color was always the observer inside. They had become *Shooter* and *Cleary* when Kyle and Lark talked about them. Lark fitted into *Shooter* like the egg in an eggshell. Her pressure suit was painted as a gaudy Earthly sunrise, primarily bright yellow. It was plugged into *Shooter*'s systems via a thick umbilical. Within the fishbowl helmet her black hair was pulled back so tightly her dark eyes looked oriental. She'd painted yellow streaks into her hair.

"Are you hurt?" he asked.

"No. Twitchy. I broke one of the big grabbers trying to get loose. One was busted already, you know. *Shooter*'s older'n I am. Two grabbers are twisted up in creeper. The little grabbers are useless. I'll ruin this damned thing if I keep trying to power out of here."

How did she get a round ball caught in a forest of long vines? A ball festooned with mechanical arms and sampler tubes . . . "Can you go a different direction?"

"I tried backwards and forwards. I'll shoot for a roll next, I guess."

"You can ruin all the grabbers you want, honey. Just don't hurt yourself."

"Duh."

Henry contradicted him, "Lark, if you break off an arm, you'll breach the hull. Stop wiggling the ship randomly. And go to voice-only."

The screen images froze. "Got it," Lark replied, her image in the screen suddenly frozen with an angry, determined look on her face.

"Don't do anything until we tell you," Henry said. "Think about conserving power. You can turn the video on again when we have a plan."

"Stay calm," Suriyah said. "Breathe deeply, slowly. Relax. Go easy on your water."

"I was fully stocked when I left. That's power and food enough for days."

"Ten of them, if you're careful," Henry said. "We'll have you back in time for your party. But that's no excuse for waste."

"A-OK. Think I should try for the roll? I can use the little adjustment jets."

"Hang on and let us analyze for a bit." Henry clearly had control.

"You'll be fine," Kyle said. "We'll think of something." His stomach was a knot and his fingernails bit into his palms. "If nothing else, you can climb down." No, wait, those ten days worth of air and water were in *Shooter*! Not the suit!

"Dad, the door's jammed. I've already tried getting it open."

"I'll be listening, honey," Henry said. "Just relax and stay available for questions." He turned off the feed that sent the general conversation to Lark.

Paul edged towards the monitors and looked at the one with Lark's image still frozen on it. "Will she die?" he asked.

Henry put a hand on the boy's shoulder. "Not if we can help it." He squatted to Paul's height. "It's a tough situation. She'll have to get herself free somehow. You and I can help Lark figure out what to do."

"Can't we take the other marble?" Kyle interrupted. "I could use the arms to tear my way in—"

Henry shook his head. "The thruster died last week. It's not repairable. I ordered another one, more advanced. It'll be on the next ship, the one you're supposed to leave on."

Kyle winced. More things were breaking and less was being done to fix them as the base lurched towards the end of its useful life. He had no idea what to tell Lark to do. "Lark, can you tell me exactly what happened? I'm sure you said, but I wasn't in here to hear it. It's hard to visualize without outside cameras."

"Suriyah sent a remote cam right after I called her. But it'll be thirty minutes; it had to prep itself before it launched. The leftside grabber broke months ago. Henry and I tied it down. I checked it before I went out. It's even on the ship-check sheet since it's been trash so long."

Kyle looked at Henry, who sighed.

"Well, it *was* tied down, I checked! I was going to the midline of the Styx. You got the vines growing in both directions, Dad, and now it's weaving a kind of net. It looks really good. I'm trying to study the autotrophic processes in the healthier plants. Something is ... changing; they're becoming more active as we get further away from the sun. You'd expect them to be slower since it's colder. I want to understand before we have to leave."

Suriyah and Paul were drawing in the corner, looking at the stilled video images and working on a slate. Their whispering was distracting. Kyle moved closer to the mike. "Okay, honey, but how'd you get stuck?" He winced. She hated it when he called her "honey." Sixteen-year-old girls were touchy.

To her credit she ignored the slight. "I ... I don't know. The arm must have broken free. I got too close. Anyway, a pretty thin leaf-vine got stuck in it, and I wasn't going very fast, but it jerked the marble and shifted my course. That's when the real problem came with the arm; anyway, that's when I could tell it was dangling freely, and since I was still moving it caught more stuff, and then slammed me into a big vine. I tried to use the topside arm, and I ... I ... just got it tangled, too. So I decided I'd try and thrust out of here, and I put it at full power."

Lark sounded defensive; she wasn't supposed to use full power in the creepers. "You didn't have a choice, honey." Damn it—there was that word again. What was wrong with him? "It was a good choice, Lark."

"It wasn't good. The marble was too stuck, and the topside arm broke, and I didn't get out. That was when I called Suriyah." Lark was quiet, then she said, "There's a big vine blocking the door, Daddy. It's feeling around the edges, but the heat leakage has it stopped. But I can't even go EVA to cut myself free." There was a tremor in her voice.

"We'll figure it out. Henry and Suriyah and Paul are working on something right now."

Kyle paced. Suriyah had shooed the others out, so only the four of them, and Lark's frozen face, remained. Kyle talked to Lark off and on, encouraging. She was getting impatient. Kyle felt lost. This wasn't fair—they were supposed to be having a party. His fists clenched as he kept pacing, nervous. What was taking so long? Why wasn't Lark already on her way home?

The remote camera was in place, its feed playing on one large wall. As the camera flew closer around *Shooter*, the damage to two of the arms was clear. One was missing half its length. *Shooter* was so enmeshed in creeper it looked like it was purposely tied down.

After two hours, Henry keyed Lark, and said, "Okay, we're ready to go. Turn on your video."

Lark's frozen image had looked angry. The animated face that replaced it in the live feed looked calmer, serious. The whites of her dark eyes were red. Lark didn't show any hesitation as she followed Henry's advice, setting the small directional thrusters to given angles and strapping herself in. There was a limited amount of propellant for the little thrusters; the antimatter was confined for use in the main engine.

Kyle's eyes stayed on the camera feed. There was a puff of propellant release, the burn of the thrusters, and the little marble pushed forward, rotating, pulling the sheet of creeper forest slightly; a tug of war. The tangle of ship and creepers moved. Lark yelped.

She'd turned off the thrusters.

Her voice was quivery, scared. "It didn't sound right. The arm . . . the bottomside arm sounded like it might rip off right below my feet!"

"Damn," Henry swore. "All right. Don't crack the bubble. Damn engineers should've designed the arms to be released from inside."

Kyle had never heard Henry cuss. He closed his eyes briefly. "They'll all be retired by now. Can we try again?"

"Sure, but something else." Henry directed the camera feed, again, to almost circle the knot of creeper.

Three more hours, two more failures.

A blast of the main motor fried a path through the vines, but the arms weren't positioned to push the marble backward. Lark's wriggling had put the marble almost on its side, but how could that change the position of the arms? And the vines were growing back into the charred path.

If an arm tore loose, if the shell was breached, Lark still had a pressure suit. That, they decided, wasn't the problem. The problem was shrapnel, if the base of an arm sprang loose under high tension.

By the last try, the room was full again. Christy Base was in on it, engineers and pilots tossing out and rejecting ideas. Paul had been hauled off to bed by his parents, Kate and Jason, and they had come back to watch. Suriyah was crying. "Quit forcing it. That girl is in an egg—don't break it open. She's got time—no need to kill her now. Go eat," she said to Kyle and Henry. "Tell Lark to sleep. Food and rest will help you all think."

Kyle didn't want to go, but Suriyah ignored his protests and Henry showed the log of everything they'd tried to Kate and Jason, and asked them to look for other ideas.

Kyle couldn't sleep. He checked on Lark, who was sleeping. He wandered the halls, lost and tired. Finally, he climbed the ladder to the telescope platform on top of the base. The scope was almost useless since the cloud cover had increased over the past five years, but he remembered showing Lark her first view of the Earth from here.

Right now, the sky was unusually clear. Charon was dead overhead, a great black shield still showing details of landscape in the sunlight reflected from Pluto. The Styx rose like Jack's beanstalk . . .

They still couldn't build a Beanstalk, an orbital tower, on Earth. Their materials weren't strong enough. But Charon and Pluto were mutually tidally locked—unique within the known universe—and light enough that a Hoytether™ had been strung between them. A Hoytether™ was an array of strands, some left looser than others to take up the slack if nearby strands broke. It already looked like a trellis. And then the games those students were playing with plant DNA paid off, and Styx was born.

Kyle found the bubble in the scope. It hung motionless, huge in the viewfinder, like a soap bubble caught in a white rose bush. Unreachable. His daughter.

He must have dozed. Henry's hand poking him startled him. "Jason said you were up. I thought you'd be here."

"This isn't going to work, is it?"

Henry climbed the rest of the way up the ladder and slowly sat down on the observatory floor next to Kyle. The only light shone up from the door where the ladder came in, and the semi-darkness somehow made Henry look even older than usual.

"Did you find her with the scope?"

Kyle nodded.

"I'm afraid to force her free. It's wasting power, and I don't trust that little marble."

Kyle pictured Lark dying slowly over days, alone, knowing she was dying. "When this happened, I thought it meant she'd be late for her party. I thought she was irresponsible." He twisted his hands together, stretching his long fingers, fidgeting. "Can we cut her free from here somehow? Do we have any remotes that could do that? Can we make one?"

Henry pursed his lips. "She's all tangled up. Good chance of cutting her free and having her float off into space, unable to steer."

"There's no way to repair the other marble? You're sure?" Kyle asked.

"I'm sure."

"Can we try?"

Henry looked at him gently. "We can try something—I just don't know what yet. Keep thinking."

"She can't climb down to us," Kyle jumped up and started pacing again. "Can I climb to her? Cut her loose?"

"It's a hundred sixty klicks and a bit." Henry cocked an eyebrow. Both men were quiet for long moments. "We have ten days."

"Damn. No, it won't work. She'll run out of air on the way down."

"She can plug into the vines. She just can't do that with the suit she's wearing. We'll have to modify a suit and bring it to her."

It had stopped sounding impossible. A hundred sixty kilometers straight up, in low and dwindling gravity . . . "It will be a hard climb. I'll go."

"We'll both go," Henry said.

Climbing with Henry would be *slow*. "Can you to stay in communications and direct the climb?"

"Jason can direct. I'm going." Henry stared up at the huge telescope. "I still pass my physical every year. I know more about what might work out there than you do. You need me. So does Lark. And two people have a better chance of getting there than one. What if you get out there alone and you get tired or hurt?"

"I'm in good shape!" Kyle protested. "I work out every day." He'd be fifty in ten weeks.

"It's going to take more than physical conditioning to save Lark." Henry didn't have to say she was more likely to listen to him than to Kyle.

"It's going to be one hell of a climb. It will take endurance."

"And brains."

Kyle sighed. "Okay. So I have endurance, and you have brains. Is that it?"

"No, I have more experience in the Styx."

"I'm in better shape."

Henry didn't even seem to hear him—he was looking up through an observatory window, where the interworld forest floated above them.

Suriyah fought them, convinced both men were crazy. "You will die out there! Find another way. That vine is alive—I tell you it's alive. It suffers us to study it, but it will not let you climb it." She stood over the little altar she kept in a corner of the galley and recited a prayer to Kali and burned sandalwood incense. Afterwards, she refused to talk to them for hours.

Lark was silent when Kyle said he was coming to get her. "I'm bringing Henry," he added.

"See you in a few days." She turned off the video abruptly, freezing her picture with a blank expression on her face. He couldn't tell if she was happy he was coming for her, or what she thought about Henry coming along.

Kyle turned off the frozen picture.

Preparing took two long days, and many conversations back and forth between Little Siberia and Christy Base. Kyle was tired and frustrated. Lark was quiet for hours at a time. Since the video was almost never on, he couldn't really tell how she was doing.

"There's more damn gadgets in this suit than any sane engineer would've designed," Henry complained.

Kyle stepped back to check the way the suit fit on Henry. It was an Adventurer-class suit, left behind after the initial run of programs broadcast from Pluto had lost ratings in favor of faster and more deadly endeavors. Originally made for someone with wider shoulders than Henry's, it fit well otherwise. The ankles were baggy. Considering the work they did, the suits were a miracle. But they were still two inches thick everywhere, full of sensors and smart chips and wires and air tubes. Henry looked bulky and awkward.

"It'll do. You might be grateful for the help."

"I will *not*." Henry hated using the adventure suits. "Damn parasites. People who won't go into the world on their own want to ride our dangers. Let 'em make their own dangers."

It had been Paul's idea.

Kyle had been fetching something for Henry when he passed Paul in a hallway. The boy had looked up and said, "You're using the Tourist-class suits, right? Let's broadcast it! It'll be like *Real Space Dangers* when they saved the crew of the *Orpheus*. You'll be heroes!"

Kyle remembered the river rafting show where Han Davidson had been sucked into a sinkhole. Endless views of dark, swirling water while Davidson drowned. Kyle mumbled something noncommittal and kept right on going to find the saw blade he was looking for.

Paul interpreted that as assent, and arranged for network coverage before Kyle had a chance to talk to Henry. They would have taken the tourist equipment anyway. The suits had pockets and belts and straps to let the men take their fill of tools, and they had been designed for a thin atmosphere. They were flexible, versatile. The equipment *was* outdated compared to current adventure suits, and *of course* there were too many readouts and controls, but far better for this venture than the standard surface suits.

Audience thirst for real adventure shows was high; live rescue of a lost maiden would be popular. Now that the networks knew about the rescue, and the suits, they threatened to refuse access to the communications gear if they didn't get to broadcast. Henry wanted to take the suits anyway, and let the networks sue them. Kyle pointed out that he needed to publish to survive, and he needed the networks for that. Besides, money from the networks beat a lawsuit. Jason had the common sense to improve Paul's original wide-open offer and bargain real money for Henry, Lark, and Kyle, as well as support pay for the other people living in Little Siberia.

"When we get back, Paul gets assigned kitchen duty for three years," Henry said.

"He won't be here for three years. His family is leaving on the next ship with us. So give up and focus."

After a final suit-check, Kyle and Henry stepped into the lock, towing nets of gear behind them. They sweated inside the slick suits. The outside temperature was -235c. It took twenty minutes for the base computers to decide the suits had adjusted enough to open the door. They were still sweating when they stepped out onto the sea of ice surrounding Little Siberia. To their right, solid and clear methane crystals the size of houses were half-covered with blown ices and snows. Paths to the left led to Creeper Fields.

Henry followed Kyle a half-klick to where the Styx met Pluto.

Vines overflowed from the sky to add layers of dying material to the methane and nitrogen ices that covered Pluto. Creepers dug in, and ran along the ground like frozen spaghetti. They piled up onto each other, dying together. Methane snow crystals danced in the air around the wide white leaves. Wherever the leaves or flowers made contact with the surface they turned brittle and broke as the men stepped on them. Here and there a vine twisted near the surface, not yet trapped and frozen, as if the Styx harbored snakes.

The base team had guided some of the vines to supply the base. Water and oxygen were needed, and plant broth made good fertilizer for more palatable crops. Years ago they had turned most of the vines back onto the trellis, so that the jungle was growing back into itself, back toward Charon, thicker every year.

Vines and stems fanned out across the trellis as they neared Pluto, and stray vines still piled up on the ice. Kyle wondered if the plants were seeking trace elements. Any such would be buried deep; these surface snows had rained out of the sky, over and over during Pluto's 247.7-year cycles, plating over anything that resembled soil. The plants would have to dig deep.

They walked and tested and checked, looking up to see how the vines tangled amongst each other. They selected a medium-thickness vine, wide as their thighs, and well anchored in the ice. It had no leaves for at least the first few hundred meters.

They tested their siphons. There was pressure in the vines. Kyle and Henry could get liquid oxygen, water and plant broth into the suits using modified siphons Henry had jury-rigged from insulated pipes. It was slow. The siphons used tiny valves and bladders to deal with pressure differences. Liquid slipped through chambers to reach reservoirs in the suits.

The Styx fed on solar wind, on water from Charon, and on itself. Oxygen and carbon dioxide swirled through the leaves. Parasite bacteria covered the leaves, turning oxygen to carbon dioxide. The creepers ate the CO_2 and replenished the oxygen. Sunlight became sugar for broth.

The suits *moved* all the time. What was doing that? All those tiny cameras, IR and UV and radar, zoom and fisheye, pressure sensors and medical readouts and who knew what. The sensation was unsettling.

Jason and Paul lumbered across the ice in a small drive-all, and watched Henry and Kyle load supplies into a closed basket that would carry the supplies up, buoyed by a circle of remote-controlled probes. The probes weren't designed to carry any weight at all. Twelve harnessed together could manage thirty kilograms and still maneuver. Every kilo over that was a trade-off in risk vs. material. The basket contained an extra suit with attached color-coded siphons for Lark, a long knife, a single shared habitat to sleep in, extra rope, and a med-kit. There was just enough rope that the basket massed just under thirty kilograms. To save power, the basket would follow them at the end of each day's hike.

"Suriyah's right," Jason said. "You're both crazy. I love you for it. Get that girl home so we can celebrate her being sixteen." He touched them both—the suited version of a hug, and said, "Good luck."

"Thanks," both men answered in unison. Paul waved and made a "camera rolling" gesture. The adventure suits were broadcasting.

Kyle responded to Paul's cue, saying, "Welcome, audience. Jason and Paul just wished us luck. Luck would make a nice change." He thought he sounded stupid and campy.

Calvin Paulie was taking the first turn monitoring and splicing the feed from Christy Base on Charon. Watchers were tuning in from the near parts of the outer system, and an edited version was scheduled for consumption by sunward planets and moons and bases. "Good luck to our adventurers, Kyle and Henry," Calvin rumbled, "as they take off to climb the mysterious and dangerous creepers of Pluto and rescue Kyle's daughter, Lark."

Unexpectedly, it seemed like private pain was being made too public. Kyle winced and stepped back. He gestured to Henry. The slower man would set the pace.

Henry reached for a stem with both hands and tugged on it. As Henry put his weight on the creeper, it demonstrated elasticity, pooling at his boots. "So far, so good," Henry mumbled, and took another handful of the thick stem. He pulled hand over hand until the creeper took his weight. Now he was actually a half-meter above Pluto's surface. Finally, the creeper seemed willing to let the men climb.

"Henry," said Kyle, "remember not to grab the trellis itself, ever. It's too strong. It might cut your suit."

"It's also pretty close to invisible," Henry puffed.

A fifty foot insulated Kevlar rope separated the two climbers. Kyle waited. When Henry was near the end of the rope, Kyle grabbed a handful of stem and succeeded in pulling Henry halfway down. Calvin's voiceover played in Kyle's radio. "Looks like a rocky start," he said, "Or a ropy one. We're wishing you well." Kyle ignored him, reaching for another boot hold. The vine only compressed a little under his hands; it was hard to grip. It—grew as he held it. The wrong direction. Down. The Styx grew almost a kilometer a day. Of course, Lark and *Shooter* would be moving the same direction. It was like trying to climb a cross between a down escalator and a living boa constrictor.

Henry had modified the toes of their boots; they sprouted tiny steel barbs that helped keep their feet anchored to the stems. Liquids from inside the plant swelled out and froze to the surface whenever Kyle dug his toes in too hard.

There was little gravity to fight, but balance and grip were challenges. It got easier, and in five minutes they'd actually gained thirty meters and found a rhythm.

Lights from their helmets bobbed up and down in Pluto's dusky midday.

Half an hour passed. Calvin broke in twice with inane questions, and Kyle hissed at him, "Quit distracting us."

"I'll need some good footage soon."

"Take all the footage you want. You can listen to us, and use our lights and cameras and take pictures of us. Just don't talk to us yet. This is harder than it looks."

Kyle followed Henry's boots. Pluto's surface had just enough pull to establish a definite down, and not enough to make the climb *hard*. They could almost walk up the vines. Rather than a hand over hand pull, it was a scramble.

They passed clumps of long leaves, each leaf longer than the men were tall, similar to plants found in the seas of Earth, but bigger. Much bigger. Climbing between them required care with the rope. Even though they were near the edge of the forest, leaves or loose stem-ends from neighboring branches periodically undulated past them. Everything moved and grew.

From time to time Kyle missed a step and had to catch himself. That was when he knew how tired he was.

Just past the third clump of leaves, Henry called back, "Okay, stop a bit."

Stopping meant sitting on the creeper stem with thighs clamped tight around it. They faced each other. Kyle's view was towards Char-on, and the Styx looked like a river from here—a great thin long silver line. It was almost a kilometer wide, but the perspective and length made it look much thinner—like thread going towards a thimble.

Calvin said, "Nice view. How was the climb?"

"A walk in the park." Kyle didn't want to say how hard it was. He watched Henry's face in the clear helmet. He was frowning. "What's wrong?"

"We're not moving fast enough. We've been going a half-hour, and we're—what—a kilometer up?"

Kyle looked around. The camera probe that had been following them bobbed in space to his left. Pluto was closer than he'd expected. He could see Jason and Paul standing at the foot of the beanstalk, looking up. They were small, but he could make out movement.

"Actually, you've made about eight hundred meters," Calvin re-plied before Kyle could respond at all. "With rests, that means you'll take about an hour and a quarter to go a kilometer. Roughly eight days if you don't sleep."

Henry snorted.

"So we have to go twice as fast?" Kyle asked.

"More. We lost two days getting ready. That means there's eight left. If we calculated everything right. That's not enough. We need time for surprises, for rest, and maybe some time when we get to the marble," Henry said.

"The forest is thicker down here, near Pluto. It thins out above the atmosphere."

"It won't make that much difference."

"So how do we go faster?"

"I'm thinking," Henry said. "Meantime, let's restock." The stems were designed as conduits, with at least three veins running through each stem; one for water, one for air mix, and one for a form of liquid energy both humans and plants could consume, dubbed "plant broth."

Leaves always grew with one anchoring structure in the pure wa-ter vein, one in the plant food. The broth fed the stem itself, fueling super-fast growth. This was what they plunged their siphons into first. Kyle's suit filled with a cloyingly sweet smell as the thin gel filled a pouch in his lower back. It took time; fifteen precious minutes. As he pulled out the siphon and stuck it back in, fishing for water, Kyle asked Henry how well he balanced.

"As good as the next guy, I guess."

"It's a way to get there faster."

"Huh?"

"Walk. Lean back against a rope and walk vertical. We've both been using hands and feet. I bet there's a walking pace that won't need that for one of us—as long as there's rope between. Let me lead. I'm stronger—I can go faster. I'll hold on. You walk—use the toe stabs. Let go with your hands and walk."

Henry smiled at him. "Worth a try."

It worked better; not twice as fast. They kept going for an hour, Kyle leading, using his hands and feet, arms and legs, back and belly . . . he was feeling the strain everywhere. Henry walked behind. Once Henry came loose, falling outward and down, and Kyle had to clamp his legs around the thick stem, brace for the jolt, then reel him in. Henry just grunted and suggested Kyle get on with it. It was more bravado than Kyle expected from Henry. How much were the cameras affecting the older man?

They stopped once, refilled their supplies, and kept going, Kyle on point again.

They changed stems at a cross-point. The new one was thicker, easier to balance on. Even with periodic leaves to step over, the pull and step, pull and step, pull and step made a cadence in Kyle's head. His lower back screamed misuse, and he needed distraction. He imagined words to the cadence— "Lark be safe . . . Lark be safe." It was almost a mantra.

A knot of leaves and tangled stems stopped them at the ten kilometer mark. Long streams of flowers spread out around the knot. If it weren't an obstruction, it would have been beautiful. They'd have to climb over and somehow pick the right stem. Henry sat. "Hey kid, time for a break."

"We haven't gone far enough," Kyle said, easing onto a spot where leaf met stem, hooking a leg over a leaf. "Stopping is crazy." At least Pluto finally looked further away. He stared down on the top of Little Siberia and picked out the observatory. "Let's push until we make at least sixteen klicks. We need twenty-five klicks."

"Ever run a marathon? If you sprint the first five kilometers, you never make the end. Besides, it's time for a word with our sponsors."

Henry wanted to talk to Calvin?

"Calvin?"

"Yes?"

The camera probe had stopped too. "Calvin?" Henry repeated. "Can you pan the probe cam and give us directions? I want to end up somewhere near Lark."

Kyle eyed the knotted mess of growth. Styx looked like a close-knit weave of plant life, but there were gaps. The long strings of forest moved and twisted and intertwined, constantly knotting and shifting. Silver threads of carbon fiber trellis flickered in and out of view. Choices had looked simple from a distance. Here, tangles and obstacles were everywhere.

Meanwhile, Calvin described a full incident support team assembled—virtually—at the currently nearest Trans-Neptunian object, Kiley3, mere light-minutes away. He described doctors, climbing experts, psychologists, child psychologists, biologists . . .

Henry interrupted. "So did you scrape everyone on Kiley3 into your support team?"

"They're getting paid. Thought you'd be grateful. They're not all *on* Kiley3—"

"I'm grateful," Kyle said. They might be able to use the help.

"Want to be introduced?" Calvin asked.

Henry shook his head. "I'd rather have visuals of the best path out of here."

"Dr. Yi is working on it. In the meantime, Dr. Gerry thinks you should have at least a twenty minute rest. That's time to meet everyone."

Kyle suddenly understood why Henry was being so irascible. A hot thread on anger mixed with his worry about Lark. He checked: they had enough water and broth to last a few hours. He withdrew his siphon from the stem, making sure Henry saw him. Henry winked, tucked his siphon carefully into a belt pouch.

As a concession to their need for rest, Kyle let Henry lead.

"But . . . but you haven't met the team yet!"

Henry spoke for them as he reached up into the knot, grabbing for a writhing stem. "It's not your kid up there. *Do not* slow us down to entertain your viewers."

To his credit, Calvin shut up and produced Dr. Li, who guided them across the knotted region without a hitch. "So now you understand the relationship?" Henry asked.

"We'll help you any way we can. But you *should* meet the team."

A kilometer further on, they did stop for rest. Although he knew Lark was descending at the same rate, the sensation of slow movement as the vines below them grew and wriggled and twined toward Pluto was strange. Starting again, Kyle realized how much his shoulders and arms hurt. Hundreds of the same motions wore on muscles. They got to twenty klicks before exhaustion won. Half a kilometer higher, they found a good place to anchor their habitat. They stopped and called for it, waiting.

Their suit radios could talk to Lark from here. "Lark, how are you doing?"

"Hi, Dad, Henry. I can see you on the feed from the probe-cam. Wish I was out there with you."

"Yeah, like we're here on purpose," Kyle said.

"You've got a better view of Styx than I ever had, except for a few minutes EVA. I'm looking forward to climbing down."

"Yeah, I plan on taking *Shooter* down."

"We'll climb. *Shooter*'s dead. Besides, I want to walk the Styx."

"What's so exciting about the Styx? It's actually pretty boring. Kilometers of stems and leaves, and then more kilometers of stems and leaves. Sometimes there's a flower."

"Yeah, well, galaxies are clusters of pretty damned boring stars. Sometimes there's a nebulae. Styx is cooler than you think, Dad. I was on my way to some flowers that look bigger and seem to direct the stem float in the forest. That's new behavior. I think the vines are responding to the system getting colder."

Kyle didn't want an argument. He wasn't a total idiot about the Styx. "Well, they use energy—metabolism—lots of it, right? That's how they're supple even out here, and how the water and broth don't freeze."

"No kidding. But up towards the middle there's more activity. More flowers, and I think even color. Styx is changing. I just know it. Whatever's changing above me will grow down to Pluto. I want to get higher."

"How about we get lower first? Like back to Pluto?"

"Jeremy says you're being way too cautious."

"Jeremy?"

"There's a bunch of kids here now. In virt. Tourists. I'm really glad Paul thought of this. The worst thing was being so alone; it's so boring to be still. I'm getting cramps too."

Oh. "Stay safe." The round cage of supplies rose over the edge of a leaf, its circle of probes bobbing like fishing net floats. "I better go."

There were too many camera perspectives, and too many helpers. The basket tangled hopelessly one stem over. Kyle frowned. "Now I see how she got caught. Maybe I should quit being mad at her."

Henry stared thoughtfully at the supplies dangling just out of their reach. "I'll belay you."

"Great."

"You're the young strong buck."

Kyle grunted, mimicking a baboon.

Henry held the rope as Kyle pushed the basket away from its vine trap and spread the probes out again. It was almost freefall—he went down at a drifter's pace. "Okay—that's as close as it's coming tonight." Kyle retrieved the sleeping habitat from the basket, tucking it under one arm. Henry reeled Kyle back slowly.

It took an hour to figure out how to wrestle the habitat into shape and anchor it. Unfolded, it was a long sheet of metallic fabric anchored between two stems. Henry plugged it into a stem, into the blue oxygen tube. The habitat bucked and waved, sucking in the air, expanding as it warmed the gas. Layers of skin filled one by one— living space, stored atmosphere, insulation, a shell thickening into a walnut shape.

The setup looked fragile. They climbed in, waiting until sensors told them the habitat held pressure enough to unsuit. As he lay down, Kyle imagined the anchoring creepers growing away from each other as they slept. He didn't really care. Being out of the constant breathing motion of the suit was wonderful.

Six hours later, Calvin woke them with lyrics from the ancient *Sound of Music*, "Climb Every Mountain." It was ridiculously inappropriate. Kyle wanted to throttle Calvin.

Four long climbs and three uneasy sleeps later, they were halfway there. Lark spent part of each day telling jokes. Tourists fed them to her, and she fed them in turn to Kyle and Henry. It kept her engaged.

Kyle hated most of the jokes.

He was surprised that he liked talking to the networks. The attention helped him forget aches in his muscles. The audience was a focus and a safety net. He took small risks, and on breaks he talked astronomy. Lark did voiceovers for the audience, telling them about the creepers. She talked to the team on Kiley3. She talked constantly—to Kyle, to Henry, to the announcers. She even took to calling the Christy and Little Siberia base staff "Tourists."

Kyle worried about Henry. His face was red with exertion and spider veins showed up on his nose and face in thin red lines. Henry refused to talk much to anyone except Lark and Kyle. It bothered Kyle.

There was no night or morning; Pluto's six and a half hour day barely noticed the sun. Kyle counted time in sleeps. This was their fifth sleep. "Henry? How come you're so quiet?"

"Seems like no one's business how we're doing."

"They're helping. I'm grateful Lark's got so many people to talk to. At least we can move. She's shut up in that bubble."

"She's always done all right by herself."

"I could have spent more time with her."

"How's it going to feel if all these people watch us fail?"

Kyle swallowed. "You've always been an optimist. We won't fail. We're halfway there."

"Half our time's gone. We should stop less."

"Can you do that?" Kyle was bone tired. Henry looked like he was going to have a heart attack any moment.

"If we don't make it, I don't want to live afterwards. This would be a good last thing to do."

"We'll make it."

"If you get there, and I don't, be careful how you get Lark out. You'll need to use a traditional blade—no lasers or anything—near the bubble."

"You said that when we were loading the basket."

"We should practice next stop, so I know you know how to do it."

Kyle stayed awake a long time, thinking about Henry's words. He started tired the next day. They hit a clump of new creeper, thin stems twining around the wide one they followed. Kyle caught his foot, and pitched forward, tangling his arm and wrist in rope as he fell. He slid, feet dangling in empty space, pulling Henry backward so Henry needed both hands to hang onto the creeper while the rope pulled tight from his waist-clip.

Kyle floated free, his suit hissing urgently, venting oxygen to match his heart rate. He held the rope with two hands, twisting his feet up in an acrobat's move, straining to get a toehold on the stem.

He felt a snap and give in his lower back, an instant tightening of muscle. He grunted with the pain.

"Whoa there," Calvin said. "You all right?"

"I . . . I don't know."

Henry managed to twist around and grab the rope, holding on to the creeper with his legs. He pulled, hand over hand, slowly reeling Kyle in until their hands touched and he could pull him up onto the stem. Kyle panted, wanted to scream. He couldn't be hurt. There wasn't time. When he tried to step ahead of Henry, he slipped again, catching himself, grimacing. His back was on fire. He didn't dare burn the small store of painkillers in the suit's med supply for a twisted muscle.

It meant Henry had to lead—Kyle walking behind him. The full med-kit was in the basket, inaccessible without a complete stop. Kyle chewed his lip and followed Henry, building up a swing that allowed him to move through the pain.

Calvin started talking in worried tones an hour out, telling the men the doctors thought they should stop. Henry ignored him, leaving Kyle no choice but to follow. Henry went on forever. When they stopped, he collapsed across a vine and stared out at the forest.

After a while, Kyle noticed that Henry was sleeping in his suit.

Kyle sat and worried, watching the older man. Lark had a feed from the camera probe that followed them everywhere, and she spoke. "He often takes naps, Dad." She sounded sad.

"I shouldn't have let him come. I should have brought someone else."

"Henry wouldn't have stayed. He'd have followed you."

"Suriyah could have stopped him. She's a force of nature." He didn't mention that Suriyah had thought this was a crazy journey.

"It's okay, Dad. Just let him sleep for a little while. I think I'll sleep too."

"We have to move again pretty soon, honey, or we won't get to you in time."

Her voice was small and cheerless. "How's your back?"

"It hurts. But not as much as losing you would hurt."

"I hope we all make it." It was the first time Kyle had heard Lark openly doubt success.

Kyle stared at stars, picking out constellations. Even eight hundred klicks up, the stars were faintly blurred. In Pluto's thin gravity the atmosphere reached way up, thinning very slowly.

There were few other humans this far away from Sol. He knew it was harshly cold, but he was sweating and the suit's movement was a constant irritation. He found the sun, no brighter than Venus from Earth, and imagined the billions of people that populated the inner planets and ringed the Earth and Mars. He'd always wanted to make his mark, to be remembered. He wanted to do it by finding something unique in the heavens.

Early returns based on "local" watchers indicated their rescue would be heavily touristed. In fact, he thought wryly, ratings would do better if they died. *Not* how he wanted to be remembered. The thought pushed him into waking Henry.

The next three climbs Kyle led again, painkillers making him woozy. They moved too slowly. Lark had about sixteen hours of air left, and they were twenty kilometers away, making just over a kilometer an hour. Calvin mentioned that their ratings were going up. Kyle cussed at him. "Now, now," Calvin said, "I'll have to edit that out. It must be the meds talking."

"It's a nightmare talking. We're never going to make it." Kyle kept pulling, looking behind him for Henry.

The psychologist, Dr. Gerry, broke in. "Sure you will. We're all pulling for you."

"Too bad you're not really here."

"Yes we are. One step at a time. We're there."

"Talk to Lark. Maybe you can do some good there." Kyle flicked off the sound and brushed aside a leaf that was blocking his view.

"Don't . . . do . . . that," Henry said.

"Do what?"

"Don't turn them off. You need them to get you to Lark. Lark's not on this direct path. You're going to have to cross stems a few times. They can help you with that."

"Us."

"You. I'm slowing you down too much." Henry's breath was labored. "Can't get this close and not make it."

"No."

"You'll be faster."

"And if I fall off again? Scotch my back?"

"I can't go any further. You were right to want to leave me."

"I wouldn't be this far without you."

"You won't get there with me. Save Lark. I'll . . . I'll just wait here."

"Can you take stims?"

Henry was quiet for a long time, still climbing. Kyle wished he'd talk. "You're coming. You have to."

"The last thing I have to do is get you to Lark. Slow down, I'll unhitch. I can call up the habitat."

"I'm the one that keeps tripping. You saved me last time I fell."

"Move faster. Maybe I'll keep up."

"You'll keep up—you're on a rope."

Henry collapsed when they stopped for a rest. His heart rate showed that he was still alive, but he didn't respond to Kyle's voice. Playing possum? Kyle didn't know.

He demanded the supply basket. He closed his eyes while he waited for it, counting time.

Calvin was screaming his name. He blinked. He floated five meters from anything. Damn.

"Where . . . what happened?"

"You passed out. Hang in there. The supply basket is almost there."

"Like I'm going anywhere." He checked. The rope was still attached. He tugged. It was tight. The basket was rising up from below him, the probes rising and falling as someone on the ground adjusted course to meet him. When the basket reached him, he struggled to find the medical kit. He pulled it out. As one hand emerged with the med-kit, weight inside the basket shifted. The open door hung down. Whoever was running the remote probes corrected the wrong way, exaggerating the shift. A long knife fell away first, tumbling slowly past, a soft glint along the blade showing as his head turned towards it, touching it with light from his helmet lamp. He tucked the med-kit under his arm and reached for a strap on the habitat as it came towards him. He snagged it, the bulk causing him to turn over, facing away. He twisted, holding the med-kit and the habitat. He needed to close the door. He was floating down, with no ability to move fast. Kyle tried to snag the extra rope with his foot while it went by. The coil fell across his toe, and he pulled his knee in to bring the rope to where he could grab it with a spare finger. It slipped off his boot and floated away. Next, the extra suit passed him two meters away.

Lark's pressure suit.

He tucked the habitat between his knees and reached, tried swimming for it. His rope stopped him.

He stared after the suit for a long time. "Calvin?"

No answer.

Of course not, he'd turned off the audio. "Calvin—track the damned suit."

"We are tracking it."

Well, he had the two most immediate things, but now he'd have to carry them. He left the collapsed habitat between his legs, tied the handle of the med-kit to the rope with a butterfly knot, and pulled himself back. The rope was attached to a creeper. Henry was anchored above him with his small belt rope, still out cold.

Kyle tied the med-kit to Henry's rope. He expanded the bulky habitat and plugged it into a vine. For once, there was a good cross-section of vines nearby to hang it on. He pulled Henry inside, and collapsed next to the older man, panting. He had ten minutes to do nothing but think while the habitat pressurized. An hour had passed—Lark had fifteen hours left before she'd start running out of air.

He was so tired he could barely get Henry's helmet off.

Henry's vitals looked ragged. He checked with the med-team, and they agreed. Exhaustion. The verdict: no stims. So he'd lost Lark's carefully modified Tourist suit to retrieve stims, and then decided not to use the stims, at least for Henry. He looked up, toward where the bubble had to be.

Henry's face was white, peaceful. Kyle touched him, rolling him gently back and forth. Henry's eyes fluttered open, and a slow smile touched his mouth. "I must have passed out again."

"Something like that." Kyle filled Henry in. "I don't think I have time to go after the suit. I'm going after Lark. You'll be safe here. I'll come back with Lark. The suit she has will get her here. The habitat will keep her alive while I go after her suit. If that doesn't work—if it's gone—we'll just have to go down the slow way while we figure something else out."

"Huh?"

"Creepers are growing down, right? Almost a klick a day. We'll be the first humans to live off broth for two hundred days."

Henry shook his head. "Never make it. The habitat won't survive that long."

"We all have suits. Little Siberia can send us supplies. There's no more Adventure suits, but maybe they can modify something else to tap the vines."

"Go get Lark. Lemme sleep."

Kyle picked his own helmet back up, jammed the stinking thing back on. "Yeah, okay." He didn't have any choices. "Sleep well." He fed the stim-pack into his suit's auto-med reservoir, asked for and received a dose. He watched Henry put his helmet back on, made sure he was secure, and then breached the hab and stepped back into the cold river Styx.

"Calvin—where's Lark's suit?"

"Snagged. Down. Kyle—it went two klicks down."

Time was against him. He cursed the basket, cursed the damn vines, cursed Henry, cursed his back. "Show me."

"You can't get there from here by yourself. Not unless you trust the winds to send you after the suit if you dive for it. We don't recommend that."

What Lark didn't have was the modified siphons. There wouldn't be any way to get broth or water or anything into her. All he had to do was get her to the habitat.

He started out fast. Henry's early words about running a marathon came back to him, and he slowed down. But he needed to make over two klicks an hour to have any time to spare. "Lark be safe . . . Lark be safe." He thought about Henry. "All be safe . . . All be safe.

"Play music for me."

"Huh?" Calvin sounded sleepy.

"Calvin—don't you sleep?"

"Not until you get to Lark."

"Thanks. Play me some music. I need some rhythm to keep going."

"What do you want?"

"Hell I don't care. Something with a beat." He looked around. "Got some African drums?"

"I'll find some."

Every two hours he stopped for fifteen minutes rest and more stims, doing the equivalent of vine-sprinting in between. The drum beats helped. His back still hurt. It became a familiar pain, something that kept him awake and aware, gave him a tie to his aching body. Every step was hard.

Lark wasn't answering. The team said she was asleep, exhausted. So many days of living in one place, in a pressure suit, were taking their toll. Four hours passed.

Calvin started peppering him with questions about Henry. A thought crossed Kyle's mind.

"How is Henry? I haven't seen his med-reads for hours."

"We cut you off from everything but you and Lark and us. Don't want to distract you."

"Damn it." Surely Henry was all right. All he had to do was stay in the habitat. Had he checked Henry's water supply? But he'd plugged the habitat into the vine.

The networks had no control over the suit-to-suit-radio. He called to him. No answer. "Calvin, show me Henry's med readings!"

"You don't need the distraction. Talk. You need to talk so we know you're still with us. *Your* med feeds could be showing better, buddy."

Kyle babbled about the time the feeder jammed completely just after the Styx got to Pluto, when a river of vines threatened to overrun Little Siberia. Henry and others had clambered out onto the surface. They'd fed vines back to the Hoytether™ trellis and set them climbing back toward Charon. Suriyah had stayed out there with him the whole time. Everyone else took turns. The story didn't seem to be coming out quite in order. Thinking about Henry wasn't right; he should be thinking about Lark. Why was she still silent?

"She's not in great shape," Calvin said. "She's alive. We've been waking her up but she isn't staying awake long. She's been taking pain meds too."

"Like father like daughter, huh?"

"You imagine the sores you'd get sitting in the same place in a p-suit for ten days."

"Yeah, well, I know what mine smells like after ten days."

Calvin laughed. "I bet you do."

You don't have smell sensors built into these yet?"

"On the newer models."

"It's a bad idea. Calvin?"

"Still here."

How had he forgotten? "Wake up Lark *now*. I don't care how. Get her to fire the main motor for a few seconds."

"Oh, right, we discussed that—"

"Check my position first and see if I'm out of the way. Henry too."

"You're okay. You're almost underneath *Shooter*, but *Shooter*'s tilted. I'll get her to fire the motor, then guide you around to the channel. Hey, Lark!"

He kept climbing. Lark and Calvin negotiated. She spoke too low for his hearing, but she sounded angry.

He didn't see the exhaust itself. He saw a line of pale plants glow brilliantly, dissolve into colors, then explode in flame as heat reached the air veins. It ran for twenty seconds, and when it went off, vines still burned.

"Thanks, Calvin, I can see it myself," he said, and angled around.

He had to pull himself into the forest to reach the channel. The vines were growing back . . . but the going was suddenly much easier.

Kyle pulled up and over a half-charred leaf and stem-knot at an intersection. From here he could see a much bigger knot—and a darkly corroded metal claw, like a skeletal hand straining to break free. *Shooter.* The little ship was even more overgrown and tangled than when he'd seen it from the observatory. Flowers had sprouted everywhere, decorating it, making it look like a party bauble. He stopped a second and just looked, his heart flooding with the knowledge that he was going to make it. Calvin babbled in his ear—talk for the audience about how emotional the moment was.

"I'm afraid to go and look," he said. Lark still wasn't responding to him.

He didn't feel his back or his body at all the last kilometer, just the soft give of the creepers in his hands and feet, the balance of his torso as he struggled to keep his center of gravity over the center of the stem. "Lark be safe . . . Lark be safe."

He was within thirty meters of the marble when the vines tangled around it shuddered and jerked up and down. What? Was the knot unraveling?

"Hi, Daddy." Her voice was weak. She was using one of *Shooter's* arms to wave at him. He breathed out, and then screamed triumph.

Calvin and his crew had spent hours trying to figure out what he should do. He had a belt knife—thin and insubstantial. It easily cut the edges of leaves, and wouldn't even dent a stem. He had a few hours, maybe more, maybe less. He was too tired to make sense of time.

Trying to untangle the ship appeared useless. Nevertheless, incident command had commandeered nearby computers and run thousands of simulations. They led him through the vines, one by one. *Pull this part out of under—there. Yes. And then go around to the other side. Tug. Sure you can. Good. Now—see the one with the longest bell of flowers? Break that off. Pull here. Tie that down.*

In the background, Calvin was talking Lark through a series of checks. He heard her talking back to Calvin, telling him to quit being so pushy, and Kyle laughed.

Kyle had made a new knot of vines, feeding the vines he was liberating from around *Shooter* into it to keep them from simply re-engulfing the bubble. His back was to *Shooter*. He heard a ripping sound.

He turned just in time to see *Shooter* lurch a few meters lower in the thinned-out net of stems that surrounded it. The ends of an arm dangled from above. Kyle had a rope tied to the marble. He pulled himself along it, fast, letting the vine he had been working on swing back towards Lark. It flapped out above the marble, safely out of the way. The door was free. By the time he got there it was swinging open.

His hand took his daughter's hand.

She was almost dead weight. Her boots flopped against the side door as he pulled, but her hands were gripping. He held her under one arm and looked inside. A backpack sat by her chair.

"Bring the backpack?"

"Yes."

"Are you okay?"

"Weak."

"It's going to take her a little while to learn how to move normally," Calvin said.

"How long?"

"We don't know. Some experts say not until she gets out of the suit. She's feisty enough to recover faster."

Kyle talked to Lark. "Can you put your legs around me?"

She used to do that when she was a kid. He tucked his arm under her butt so she was sitting against his waist at the side, and she put her arms around his neck.

Well, he had one hand free. Now what? He shifted Lark to the front of him, sat on the stem he had climbed up, and slid. It was slower than walking—the suit material dragged wrong against the stem. The risk was real—if he wore out the suit material there was no fixing it up here. He stopped them, trying to think of a better way. Henry would think his own way out of a problem.

"Sit on a leaf, Daddy."

It worked. He cut off a long thin piece of leaf, and tied it between his legs and up around his waist. He felt like he was wearing a diaper.

The surface was slicker on the creeper stem. It held up until just before they got down to the first big knot, when the leaf shredded under him and he carried Lark to the knot, walking carefully, afraid that he'd launch them into space. Lark switched around to his back and he climbed carefully over the tangle of stems and vines. Cramps were making her whimper.

On the other side, he cut another leaf. He said, "The leaves are a good idea, honey."

"I know the Styx."

It took five hours to get back to the habitat. Lark gained more ability to move, and her hold on him was less tenuous. She still couldn't stand or climb on her own.

When they reached the habitat, it was empty. Kyle had been afraid he'd find Henry dead in the habitat. Or that Henry had left his suit for Lark and jettisoned himself into vacuum and death. The empty habitat was unnerving. He stuffed Lark into the habitat without re-pressurizing it, leaving her in her suit. He went out and refilled his suit's reservoirs, and sloshing full of sweet broth and water, he ducked back into the tent. Now he pressurized it and peeled Lark's suit off of her. It actually stuck to her calves, ripping layers of skin off so they looked raw. He took his own suit off, and fed Lark on broth and water. She drank more than he expected.

"Where's Henry?" she asked.

"I don't know. Calvin, will you tell me yet?"

"Nope. Sleep."

Kyle barely got the words "damn you" out before he was, in fact, asleep.

The next thing he noticed was the habitat shaking. Lark was able to help him get her suited. She only screamed twice, once for each raw leg. They depressurized, and Henry tumbled in the door, carrying the suit he'd modified for Lark.

"You went all the way down there?" Kyle asked.

Henry sounded weak. "Someone had to do each thing. I knew you had the brains to get her safely."

Kyle grinned. They re-pressurized and stripped out of their suits. Lark poured herself into Henry's arms, finally looking energetic. Henry looked very proud of himself. His smile was bigger than usual. Kyle stole a peek at Henry's vitals. His blood pressure was way too high, his respiration was shallow and fast. "Sleep, Henry."

Eight full hours later Kyle opened his eyes. Lark was crying, looking down at Henry.

"He's not moving," she sobbed.

"Calvin, what have we got for Henry?"

"Sleeping. Maybe in a coma. He might have had a stroke. We can't tell from here. Doesn't matter—the verdict is he can't possibly make it. Down will be at least half as hard as up."

Lark crawled over to Kyle and cried in his lap. Kyle patted her head and found he was crying too. Ideas and condolences and tributes started coming in. Kyle turned off his radio; Henry would prefer silence. Besides—he wasn't dead. But how were they going to get him down?

"Remember when you sat on the leaves?" Lark said.

"Sure."

"Do we have rope?"

Kyle winced, thinking of the supply basket. "Calvin, do we have rope?"

Calvin's voice. "They refilled the basket."

Lark's backpack had a better knife in it. She led Kyle out to cut off whole leaves. "These are bigger than I needed to get down the stem," Kyle said.

"They're not for you. They're for Henry. They'll cushion him," Lark explained. "We're going to use the spaces, not the stems."

"Huh?"

"To climb up, you had to use the stems. To climb down, we can do better. We're almost weightless, right? We tie Henry between us. We wrap him in leaves to cushion him if we screw up."

"Hell with leaves, let's use the probes. They didn't have the strength to carry us up, but they could carry Henry down. Then we can use your idea, but we won't have to worry about carrying Henry."

He was rewarded with a rare touch from Lark. "I want to come back," she said.

"Both marbles are busted."

"Climb back."

"You want to do this *on purpose*?"

"There's things I need to know about what's happening here. Besides, the real tourists will need guides."

"What real tourists?"

"There are ten climbers on the next ship. Hundreds wanted to come—they had to do a lottery."

"We're leaving."

"Justine Jackson is coming here."

"I'm content to watch her."

"They're paying a premium." She named a figure.

She could pay for her own school! "Do I have to climb these things again?"

"You're being requested."

Kyle grumbled. Calvin laughed at him. He and Lark rigged Henry carefully in place of the supply basket. They charged his suit with water, oxygen, broth. Kyle tied the med-kit to his back and tied the basket and its other contents to the vine. It would grow home.

Shooter would grow home too, to be stripped for salvage. It wouldn't do to leave its diminished fleck of antimatter loose in the sky.

Henry beat them down by two days. He was at the table when Lark came in for her party wearing the yellow dress. Suriyah must have fussed over the table for hours; everything was perfect.

"Henry, couldn't they find you a wheelchair?"

"This place isn't outfitted for cripples, Lark. Suriyah, you know I can move around. You don't have to keep lifting me."

"I know. Next you'll be climbing the Styx again."

Henry sighed. "No, not that. But—you're going, Lark. And Kyle?"

"For what they're paying? Sure I'm going. This base'll be open a lot longer now. At least until the Styx dies, if it dies at all. Justine Jackson—nice woman, by the way, but a little freaky—she doesn't want someone beating her record in the Guinness Files. She's talking about climbing the full length."

"Kyle? Twenty-seven thousand kilometers?"

Lark burst in. "Yeah, but we'll have a lot of support. Like swimming the Amazon, you take a boat alongside. She did that too, remember?"

Suriyah said, "You'd be years doing this!"

"Team of twelve. *Big* habitat, and a chef. We'll still have a social life. Lark can attend Yale Virtual. Henry, we're still talking, and I'm not even sure she's funded yet, but wow! We'd have a dedicated channel for three years or so, and then chop that back to thirteen hours of just the exciting parts and a voice-over, for reruns."

"Do you remember," Suriyah said, "that the atmosphere is changing? You'll be climbing through hurricanes."

"No, don't sweat the wind. Pluto's atmosphere is thin as a dream and getting thinner."

"You're all crazy. You started crazy." She looked from one to the other, and suddenly smiled. "Can I have your autographs? Someday they might be worth a lot. Here, on this."

On Henry's medical readout.

SECOND SHIFT

Kami closed her eyes and replayed Lance's tender whisper. "I love you."

Three words filled her. She listened again and again, memorizing the rise and fall of his voice. Glancing at the clock, she stripped the bud off her ear and pocketed it, afraid the temptation to hear him yet another time would take the tiniest bit of glow from the night.

Being this happy was as new as a dawn, as fresh as becoming an adult three years ago. Maybe it was even as good as being born in the first place. Her bones smiled.

Stupid. She knew it was stupid, knew Lance was a lifetime away from her and that every time she came on shift to be his company, his rocket companion, he was further away.

The HR girl who hired her had told her not to do this.

She liked the rebellion in it. It was only a small rebellion anyway, since her contract was good as long as Lance approved of her and the job existed.

Besides, she hadn't *done* it. Not really. Love happened, right? The long nights sitting alone and talking, or even listening to the silence of his sleeping breath had surprised her into love, delighted her in a way she hadn't expected.

Right on time, Sulieyan opened the door and started her morning routine. She plugged in an electric pot to heat water and opened the cupboard for tea. "Do you want a cup?"

Kami shook her head, hoping she didn't look as giddy as she felt.

"No? Anything I need to know? Was the night sweet?"

She always asked that way, but this morning Kami felt her cheeks grow hot. "Sure. He's asleep now."

Sulieyan smiled at the unnecessary observation. The monitors on the walls relentlessly reported whether Lance slept or woke, exercised, ate, or worked.

Kami picked up her empty lunchbag, and gave the older woman a brief hug. "Gotta go."

An hour after she got home, she pulled on her running clothes and practically danced down the metal steps outside of her apartment complex. She jogged through the bright tunnel under the maglev tracks and emerged in the park, her feet springy with her mantra for the morning "*Lance Parker* loves me. Lance Parker *loves* me. Lance Parker loves *me*."

When she couldn't take another step, she sat on the little beach by the koi pond, running sand through her fingers and making a tiny house as if she and Lance would ever live in it. The tragedy and impossibility of it all sang in her, as if she were the star in a Saturday night film.

There were other pilots—men and women—doing solo trips to the moon and back. That's how the need for rocket companions came up in the first place. All the things about the flight and safety were handled by AIs, but computers weren't companions.

None of the other solos had been famous test pilots and race-jet drivers first, and none of them was set to go as far. The prize was the rocks themselves; towing them back to the station being built above the Earth could make a lot of money—if it could be done on a shoestring.

The next night, Kami told Lance she loved him back. It was the first time she'd said the words. To seal them, she told him about the park and the koi pond and the little bite of fall in the air as she ran, about the one time a single gold leaf fell in front of her.

"Tell me what the air smelled like?" he asked.

His must be stale and metallic. "It smelled like water and sunshine and insects and the sand along the water. It smelled like the maglev when it sang by, and once of a wet dog that I almost tripped over." Because she couldn't think of anything else, she said, "It smelled like the promise of talking to you again."

She hadn't thought a smile was something you could hear.

"What are you doing today?"

"The air system filters need to be cleaned and changed. Fifty sit-ups and twenty pull-ups and a long trip round the world on the elliptical. And I'm working on a secret."

"A secret?"

His secret was a poem written to her. He sent it back with his day's records. Kami blushed when she realized the techs must have seen it. She posted it on the wall in her kitchen so she could read it every morning.

All the next year, she noticed smells and sounds in as many ways as she could, speaking descriptions into her wrist-recorder. The sun warm as a sleeping dog, the tiny perfection of the yellow in the center of a magenta azalea, the paper flutter of dogwood snow against her cheek. It became a game to come to Lance every night and give him a new description at the beginning of every shift.

Kami read about Lance with morning coffee after she left him to Sulieyan when they changed shifts. Tidbits. Things he said back to scientists and journalists and rock stars who wanted to know what it was like to be the first man heading to an asteroid.

She had meant this for a short job, a dalliance with the romance of rockets.

By her twenty-fifth year—her third with him—it grew harder to find Lance in the news. But not impossible. She followed others who followed him from around the world, little audible alarms that burred against her wrist to remind her he was real and alive. She followed his conversations and the conversations others had about him. The fact that the he was not entirely a forgotten hero touched her in each nerve.

She slept and ran and did laundry and surfed the nets, and late in every day she went to spend the night with Lance. What work to be with your beloved? She read him stories and he wrote her poems. She told him of beads of water on lacy spring-green leaves the size of her smallest fingernail and the brilliance of sun-struck snow on far mountains.

Noticing the world for him became habit, like green tea steeped for exactly three minutes and like running in the park and chanting his name as her feet hit the ground one after the other. When the distance built in a tiny time delay, she used the seconds to contemplate her next words.

Every morning, when she and Sulieyan shared cross-shift data over tea in the neglected break room, the older woman asked her about her plans for the day.

Kami said she would run through the park and she would find something beautiful. Tea with Sulieyan made a zen transition in her day and gave her someone else to talk to besides Lance.

On one of those mornings, Sulieyan said, "There is almost no rebellion in you anymore."

"I am in love."

"Are you?"

"Of course. I think of Lance all the time."

"Can you be in love with someone you can't touch?"

"Aren't your parents in India and hasn't it been five years since you touched them?"

Sulieyan nodded, and smiled, and sipped her tea. Kami couldn't really read her face so she decided Sulieyan agreed with her.

When she took the job, Kami had been told that travel to the asteroid belt was a story of slow ships and far-away places.

One September evening after she and Lance shared a meal together (using the valuable virt screen that he bargained for with free interviews when he could get them), he told her, "I never expected to get back. It's not like a government ship or anything, or the long arm of the taxpayer. They chose me because I was willing to sign papers that said no one would sue them, ever, if anything happened. The company may stay alive for the fifteen or twenty years it will take, they may not. They could get sold or go bankrupt or a key player could die and then where will all the publicity and money go? A faster ship could get built and pass me and come home before I even get to the belt."

"Why did you go?" she whispered, although she would never have known him if he hadn't. He was famous and she was a shift-girl at a two-bit rocket company with no real fame except for Lance and this trip.

"I was lonely, so I didn't care if I came back."

She held her breath.

"And now I'm not lonely any more, but I'm no more likely to get back."

She had known he might never come back, but the knowing felt deeper after he said it to her. Running was harder, and sometimes she stopped and bent nearly in two and heaved air sour with longing to hold him.

He almost never cried or seemed sad, except sometimes she heard those things in his smiling voice, pale as the whispers of wind against her cheek in the early morning on days she wanted to hold him so much she couldn't sleep through the afternoon heat. But some nights the loneliness piled up on him, so heavy she could see his shoulders struggle to bear it and his head bend under the weight. He would only talk about it a few times a year. Although she didn't ask him why, Kami thought it was for her, so she wouldn't feel his loneliness so hard that it drove her to stop coming to him every early evening with her dinner in a brown bag and a cup of hot chai clutched in her hand, and a bit of memory from her day on her tongue.

Once, in spring when Kami looked forward to the first orna- mental cherry blossoms against a blue sky, she patted Sulieyan on the shoulder and wished her good luck with the sleepy day shift, and walked away from work. It had been a tender night and she ached with emptiness. It was not yet morning, even though spears of light from the solar collectors beamed power down onto the city, a sign of coming true-dawn.

She liked this quiet time, the pad of her footsteps soft on the soft sidewalks, the first birds rustling and warming their throats, the cool nip that would fade early this time of year. Far away from her, Lance would be settling in to sleep through day shift, his way of choosing her.

A dark shadow separated from a dark wall and came toward her.

She clutched her backpack close.

"Kami," the voice said.

"Do I know you?"

He shook his head. "No. But you could."

He was getting close enough to reach for her. She took a few steps away, keeping some space between them. She started to stretch her calves, getting ready to run if she had to, watching him closely.

He stopped. "I didn't mean to startle you."

"You did."

"Not. I mean, I didn't mean it."

She shook her head and let herself relax a little bit. "Who are you?"

"I want to interview you."

She blinked stupidly at him. Her contract didn't let her do interviews, and Lance never talked about her to others. She and Lance were each other's secret. The company knew, of course. Techs that supported the connection. Sulieyan.

She liked being invisible.

"I'm Hart. I'm also Sulieyan's grandson."

Oh. "I'm probably too old for you."

It felt like an awkward thing for her to have said, but he laughed. "No. She started young. Why else would she still be working at dead end jobs?"

As if that was a bad thing. Kami said nothing.

"Grandma got pregnant when she was nineteen and had to drop out of vet school."

She should know more about Sulieyan than her patience and her way of making tea and that she never missed a shift. But Kami could think about that later. "Why do you want to interview me?"

"Because my grandmother said it might teach us both something about love."

Now he had startled her. Her voice shook. "We can have coffee together."

In the too-bright light of Morning Blend, Hart looked far less threatening than he had as a dark silhouette in a place she expected silence from. He remained dark on dark, dark hair and dark slightly almond eyes over dark skin. He had a broad smile, and he looked both totally earnest and as uncomfortable as she felt.

After they'd ordered coffee and scones and sat down across from each other at a window table, he didn't seem to know how to begin.

"Who do you want to interview me for?" she asked.

He looked down. "I blog at Celebrity Love."

She couldn't stop herself from wrinkling up her nose.

He saw it, and he laughed, brittle. "I'm trying a small column about relationships we don't usually see. I've done two of them, and I want to do a third. Grandma told me you have the best invisible relationship in the world."

"Why do I want to be interviewed for a place frequented by teenage crushes?" She took a sip of her coffee, savored the bitterness. "Why do you write for *them*?"

He shrugged. "What else do you do with an English degree?"

"Does it pay more than teaching?"

"No."

"So why?"

"It's writing. It's what I want to do, what I love. I'll get better jobs. But for now I have to do this one well."

"Shhhh ... don't be defensive." She imagined him sitting at home working on novels. She didn't want to do the interview, but he was looking at her so expectantly, and she hadn't done anything different in a year. Maybe two. God. More. "What do you want to ask me?"

"Is it true? Grandma says you love a man you've never met and never held and never will see, and she says you are so loyal it's got to be true love."

She'd thought of it as a miracle. Famous Ship's Captain loves a pretty little nobody. She looked into Hart's eyes and she didn't know how to answer him. She couldn't do an interview. "It's private."

"Do you love him?"

Whatever she said, Lance could see it someday. Strange things got sent to the ship, the choices made by people she didn't know. Being asked about her feelings made them seem as if they couldn't be real. She fought dizziness by putting her palms flat on the table and taking a deep breath. "I can't, I'm sorry." She'd gotten her coffee to go, maybe out of instinct, and he had a white porcelain cup in front of him. She grabbed her cup, taking her pastry naked into her hand and said, "Look—this isn't for the world. I'm sorry. Good luck."

Ten minutes later she shut her door behind her, sank to the floor, and finished her breakfast, spilling white crumbs on her chocolate brown carpet. Lance loved her. That's what she sang when she ran. And she loved him; she loved hearing his voice every time she worked, she loved laughing with him about small things, collecting the world for him and whispering of leaves and beetles and babies.

She changed everything about her routine except where she lived. She ran in a greenbelt with a long quiet path that was nearly always empty except for a few old women from nearby apartments walking dogs.

One Tuesday at midday, she stopped by a small bronze statue of a curious deer by a stream where no real deer ever came any more. She was running her hands across the nose, registering the feel of petting bronze, noticing that even though it was cold she felt like it might move under her fingers.

"Kami."

"You again."

Hart nodded.

"I can lodge a complaint and keep you away from me."

He spoke so softly he might have been trying not to spook a real deer. "I am your friend's grandson and I won't hurt you."

He was right. She wouldn't offend Sulieyan. There were many mornings she'd asked for something special for Lance, and known she could count on Sulieyan. "I won't give you an interview."

"May I run with you?"

For answer she started off, curious to see what he would do. The path was wide enough for two, but she ran in the middle, keeping him behind her for the first mile. He kept up well. Only then did she move to the edge of the path. When he came up she spoke to him through the heartbeat of her runner's breath. "Tell me about your love life."

His breath was sharper and shorter than hers, and she could almost feel how his legs must be hot and the sweat must be slicking his back, but she didn't slow down. Finally he managed to gasp out, "I don't . . . have one."

"When did you last have a girlfriend?"

"Pretty." Pant, heave, pant. "Personal."

"You wanted to interview me."

"Not . . . any . . . more."

She slowed down to a fast walk, letting him catch up with her.

When he could talk more normally, he said, "I dated the same girl for all of our senior year in college, and my mother and grandmother started giving her little gifts for a household like kitchen towels."

She hadn't expected him to answer. "Did you love her?"

He nodded. "But I wasn't ready to settle for just one person. I didn't want to choose then for my whole life. Not then."

He must be thirty now. "No one else?"

"Yes. I told you the beginning of my love life. That was part one. Part two was a woman I fell in love with three years ago. Emily. A nurse. I loved her order and her brains and her compassion. After we had dated for a year I saved up for a special weekend and a moondust ring, and she turned me down."

A small laugh escaped Kami's throat. "Because she wasn't ready."

They ran while, the sun dappling their skin as it penetrated the leaves above them. "Do you have friends?" she asked him.

"People I work with."

She out-raced him for a bit, lost in thought, and then let him catch up to her again.

They slowed down to pass an old woman clutching a tiny designer dog with purple ears close to her. The woman made soft mothering sounds in the dog's fur, and the dog stayed quietly settled in her arms, sniffing the air as Kami and Hart walked by, but otherwise only reacting to her owner.

Once they rounded the next gentle bend, Kami stated, "So you are more alone than that woman now."

"Dogs are what old people choose when their children and lovers have all gone on, and only return for Christmas."

"You sound awfully bitter."

"Grandma says I'm like an old man."

Lance was probably ten years older than Hart, and he would never come back to Earth and she would never actually meet him. But he was more hopeful than Hart, who didn't need someone else to pet a bronze deer and report back. "Do you think she's right?"

"She told me you're an example of love. That love is steady and that it lasts as long as a life."

"That woman will love her dog as long as it's alive."

"But that isn't the same," he protested.

Maybe it was better than loving and leaving. She had never really done that. She'd drifted through dates when she was young, but no one had touched her heart before Lance. And she would not leave him for this man, either. At first she'd thought that was what Sulieyan wanted her to do, but now she was sure Sulieyan must have known Kami had been drifting like an un-tethered kite. "If you would like to run with me once a week or so, and if you will never print anything I say, I will meet you on Tuesdays. That will make your grandmother happy. But you must know I love someone else. I will not fall in love with you. But I will tell you a little of what I tell Lance and I can share how it is for me."

"And how will that help me?" He looked earnest, actually curious. "Other than I will get into shape."

"You will see that commitment exists." Her throat tightened. "And you will have company, which seems as uncommon for you as it is for me."

Just like she would not betray Sulieyan, he wouldn't betray Sulieyan. The old woman's love would bind them to good behavior.

He didn't answer her, but he followed her for the last mile. He would show up the next Tuesday and she would have company, and Sulieyan would worry less about her grandson. Perhaps it would be enough to keep Kami in this world while she loved a man who had left it.

That night, Kami ate her meal with Lance. She told him, "I touched a bronze deer and it felt so real I expected it to tremble under my hand."

He smiled, patient always. If she looked forward to meals with him, he must look forward to them even more. She had the park and the trail and the old women with purple-haired dogs and he had metal and electronics and propellant and stars. And now, maybe, she also had a friend besides Sulieyan. If she made her world bigger, she could help him keep his big enough. "I hope you make it home someday," she whispered. "You know that."

"I know that."

"I will love you until you do."

"And I you."

BLOOD BONDS

I hesitated in Aline's doorway. As soon as I stepped through, my sis's minibots would whisper to her and she'd leave wherever she was and come into real to see me. Tonight, the step toward her might be off a cliff.

For now, she lay blissfully unaware, gone to some virtual place. With luck, she was in the arms of a lover or climbing Olympus Mons. Anywhere but in her broken body living in VR contact gel.

Her face had survived the terrorists' bomb. She'd been walking away from the Marin County Fair, on Earth, north of San Francisco, and if she'd walked just a little faster, she might be able to walk today. But terrorism or not, it was partly my fault. I was the one who talked her into applying for a trip to Earth. I'd wanted her to be happy, and she wanted to see forests and butterflies and elephants and oceans. Sure, we're identical twins, but she needed to go to Earth, and I longed for Mars. At the time, we were both on the moon.

And now the next thing that happened was going to be my fault, too. I wanted a choice and there wasn't one.

By the time I stood beside her bed, she'd opened her startled blue eyes, her face swimming up above the blue-green gel and the myriad contacts that kept her body fed and exercised. Her warm smile played across my heart like a soft blanket and I wanted to melt into the chair beside her bed.

"Lissa," she said. "How was your day?"

I couldn't bear to tell her yet. "No, Aline, you first."

She blinked—code for a nod. "I went for a long hike with the virt club, around some Earth-like mountains Rudy designed. Even with laws-of-physics design rules, he made a two-story tall waterfall that spilled a rainbow into the sky, and a flock of blue butterflies as big as my hand."

Aline always started her day with exercise. Before Mom died when we were twelve, she used to take me and Aline running and playing through the tunnels every morning. Saturdays, we went out on the surface and played moon-gravity bounce before breakfast. So hearing about Aline's morning virtual workouts was like being a kid again, when she was whole. But Aline's day was a lot longer than a real one—time flew differently in virtual worlds. "So then what did you do?"

"A photo shoot in New Mexico and a . . . a few meetings with friends. That's all. Nothing you want to know about." She glanced away from me for a moment. She'd gotten more and more to skipping over what she did. Like I wouldn't understand it? Or I wouldn't think it was good? How could I think she was anything but good? I ran my fingers over her forehead. It was dry and cool, her skull naked. "Did you get any pictures you want to show me?"

"Maybe later. Tell me about your day."

"This morning was bad as ever. Jack-o called in sick, so we had Cherie for shift super and she wanted to set some kind of record. Our yields were low 'cause the soil's shyer of H3 where we're mining than it is on exposed slopes, but she didn't care. Her face was purple by lunch."

Aline grinned. "You'd think Helium-3 was the best of everything."

"It gave us the power to get to Mars." I looked away, swallowing.

"I bet you were spitting mad at having Cherie." She arched an eyebrow and winked. "You always are."

How did she get so much from my stories? "Me? Sure. You should have seen Davey and John-boy and Mark. I thought they were going to kill her by the time the lunch bell rang. They didn't show it to her, but Davey was secret-telling John all afternoon—they must've spent half what they made for the day on privacy. It was actually kind of funny."

"That was the morning. What about the afternoon?" she asked, her eyes shining as if she knew what I was going to say and was trying to help keep me from having to say it. But she couldn't know.

I winked. "We slowed down a little, waited. She finally figured out our game and her mouth opened so big I thought she might scream, but she laughed and slapped Davey on the back, and we made our credit-load, anyway." I spent every day noticing fine details so I could bring them home to her. Could I stand life any other way? "Worldgov cleared two more ships for Mars today." I swallowed. "My name came up in the lottery."

She closed her eyes.

We'd talked about it before I put in for the lottery, and so there wasn't a question about what I'd do. Hazard pay might buy her a new body someday; the syntharms and legs were no big deal, but the spine was a fortune. And if I didn't make the fortune in time, she wouldn't have enough left to work with. The last govdoc that'd talked to us said she had two years or so.

A single tear slid down her cheek. She couldn't take my hand, couldn't touch me, but her tear touched me for her. I stood so my own tears would fall on her face.

Zubrin Base was a sterile bubble filled with air, and also a light wind so our bodies would think, maybe, they were home. Of course, there was about twice the moon's gravity keeping me stuck to the surface. But hey, the breeze was nice. I crossed the open tarmac and climbed into my flitter, the *Moon Escape*. Even though she was a company ship, she was assigned to me full time, getting her rest and maintenance when I slept. I'd named her myself, as much for the hope of bringing Aline here to help me fly her as thanks for my own luck of the lottery. I'd not only won passage to Mars, but also a job I wanted, as if I'd somehow been anointed with fairy dust.

After I double-checked the cargo manifest, I dogged the hatches, grinning. Compared to the moon, Mars is a heaven of variety. Twice the diameter means a hell of a lot more surface area. Of course, I only got to fly over about five percent of that, but the sheer size of it still stunned. I waited my turn at the base locks, waving at the doorbot as it let me through into the wilds where a girl could be alone.

As usual, I started off feeling too alone.

The communications lag between Mars and the moon was about five seconds, give or take a bit to account for orbits. The only way Aline and I could talk was email or vidmail. So at the end of every day I recorded a message for her about my job driving cargo from base to base. Every morning, I got her reply. But we couldn't giggle about our respective lovers or play off the way our eyebrows arched. Those aren't things you do with a five minute stutter. And forget about meeting anyplace virtual with latency like that.

If only Aline were already here. She was the stronger one, the one-minute-older one, the best one. I needed her. And so far, I'd saved less than half the money for her surgery. "Honey, girl, Aline, how am I going to do this?" I said to the walls.

Aline-in-my-head whispered back. "You'll find a way. Or I will."

"Even a single-step promotion won't save us now. I need . . . something extraordinary."

My words bounced around the empty cabin, and it seemed like the echo was her voice: "We are extraordinary."

If only it was really her! I flopped into my red captain's chair and stared out the wraparound window at the gray skies of Mars. An hour of silent meditation on the rocks and plains of Mars cheered me up a little. I dropped my cargo at Robinson and two men I'd never seen before loaded four big sealed boxes for Zubrin. "Go on," the tallest one said, "so you won't pull any overtime."

I bristled at the suggestion I'd loiter on purpose for more pay, and it almost made me do it. But I hightailed it out of there instead, happy to be heading home and hungry for a glass of homemade berry wine from Chu's Bar.

A single cheep roused me. Data coming in. Hopefully not another request for an early shift start. There'd been way too much work the last month or so. "What?" I asked.

"Sis."

Not me speaking her voice. Her voice. My throat fisted. An open call would be a fortune. "What? I'm here." My top teeth nearly bit through my bottom lip. Now the ten minute wait for an answer.

"Me too. Here."

There was no delay!

"With you. I'm sorry."

Her voice had tears in it, and I knew. A download. It was the only way she could be here and be invisible. A download. "I didn't know you died."

"I didn't."

Her body must have. No consciousness could operate in two places at once. It broke every law in the book. "My god, honey! Why?" My head was spinning. Such a stupid thing to do. Such a . . . hopeless choice. And it was done. No going back for her, for me, for us. But I was her and she was me and somewhere deep inside, below the breastbone, I understood. Anger and shock gave way. I could feel my own smile peel my cheeks back. "Thank god. I missed you. I missed you every damned day."

"Me, too."

I wondered if I could fly well enough to make the flitter do loops. "You'll love it here. There's so much to show you." After we got back, I'd take her home and let her see the wall-nano pattern I'd been working on all week. Maybe she'd have some good ideas about how to get the sunset sky I'd splashed across the tiny living room to brighten up even more. Surely she'd be okay here; data stratum was thick in most of the bases; there weren't enough people to tug at the capacity at all. "Did you come in on one of the cargo ships?"

"Something private."

"Wow, that must have cost a fortune."

"No."

I swallowed. It wasn't like her to answer so shortly. It had to be her, though. I knew her voice. "Aline? What did mom used to say when we got up?"

"That wasting a day in bed was the worst sin of all."

She hadn't hesitated. "And what did we say?"

"The worst sin was . . ." I finished it with her, two voices, "going to bed early." I blushed for having to check, for doubting. I'd have never doubted her body, but a download was . . . well, I couldn't see her. The cabin still looked empty even if it felt full of her. "Why didn't you tell me?"

"I wanted to surprise you."

The lights of Zubrin Base loomed large. "We're almost there." How would she get off the ship with me? Why didn't I know these things? "How portable are you? I mean, you're in the ship's data now, right? What creds do you need to get into the base's systems?"

A warning bell sputtered out of the same speakers Aline talked to me through. Three bursts, so it wasn't routine. A male voice, not the usual computer-recorded neutral. "All research ships are to proceed to the closest base immediately. Repeat. All research ships to the closest base."

We weren't a research ship, but the warning was odd. Aline didn't remark on it, but instead answered my earlier question. "I'll fit in your personal data space. I'm afraid I'll take most of it, but as soon as we get inside the base I can move out again. So as long as you don't want to watch any movies as you dock this thing?"

She always could make me laugh. I authorized the transfer. If she was in my personal datapod, that meant she'd get through without any creds, or more accurately, with my creds. But she couldn't even be on Mars with no authentication: there were layers and layers of datasec here. "Sure." So as I flew *Moon Escape* into Zubrin Base, Aline flowed into me, unfelt, unseen, except I knew about her, as if the ghost of my sis was filling my most personal dataspaces.

Three soldiers stood at Zubrin's gate, actually wearing weapons. I'd only seen that once before, when a convict escaped from Robinson and they were afraid he'd make it to Zubrin (he didn't; he died just outside the gate). Base command ordered me to stop. I sighed. "Sorry, Aline. Whatever this is, it can't be much." Not that I was sure of that. "Maybe you'd better be quiet, though. There's a policy about taking on riders." And I didn't have time to figure out if a download tripped it.

At least the head of the group was a stocky red-haired man I played chess with in Jimson's Bar every Saturday, Jay Jakob. "Hello, Jay," I called out to him, opening a video window between us. "What's happening?"

"Lissa, howzit going? Been anywhere except your normal stops?"

I shook my head.

"Seen anything strange out there?"

"Nope. Jay—what's going on?"

His turn to shake his head. "I can't say, not yet. I need a copy of your manifest."

I reached for it, but there was no manifest in the wall slot where it belonged. What had happened when the boxes were loaded up? It was hard to remember—with Aline in between there was a lifetime of feeling between me and a routine act. "Let me pull it up."

Jay's lips drew into a tight line. "I have orders not to take anything electronic."

I smiled at him. "That's all I got!"

He put his hands up. "Shhh . . . seeing that it's you. Nothing looked wrong out there, nothing weird happened, right?"

"No. Everything was normal."

"All right. I'll clear you, but you best stay in town in case anybody's unhappy. I will have to report it."

"I got loaded up at Robinson, just like usual. I'm sure it's just research stuff." And that's what they were recalling—research ships. "From the base. Like every day. Why are you interested in the scientific squad?"

He shook his head again and then tapped his ear, clearly listening to someone else. After a moment he smiled at me. "Just go on." There was real concern in his voice. "Stay safe."

"Wow," Aline's voice sounded in my ears now, right in the phone implants. "Is it always so fascinating around here?"

I shook my head, pulling us away from the gate and toward the hangar with a little whoosh of light thrust. "No. In fact it's usually pretty damned boring."

"Well, and you seemed to know this Jay. He's cute."

I swear if she could've winked at me, she would have.

I laughed, happy. "Maybe I should talk you into buying a bot body so I can beat it up when you sass me." Except downloads in botbods were illegal as hell, too.

"That would land me in jail."

A shiver ran up my arms and back. AIs could manipulate robots, but not be them. And downloads weren't AIs, but also weren't supposed to be in botbods. Silly results of years of making laws to protect people from AIs even though only a few of them had ever hurt humans, and they'd been killed right away. Fear politics.

Better to imagine I was just talking to Aline, and she had a body somewhere that she'd go home to someday. "I haven't dated anyone. Too expensive. I'm saving money to bring you home."

"And now I am home. So now you could ask him out."

"Not. He's sweet, but he's too old. How'd you get here anyway?" I twisted the ship a little sideways to get it into its docking station.

"I sold some of my pictures."

"Really?" That was cool—she'd been trying to do that for years. "Show me?"

"Later. Take me home with you?"

"Like I have a choice?" I laughed, happy with the banter. Now I'd never let her go again if I could help it. I opened the door and climbed down to the tarmac. "We have to find someone to sign in the cargo."

"Without the manifest?"

"I must have the electronic one."

"Lissa!" A male voice called across the bay to me. I glanced over to see someone approaching that I didn't know, tall and dark haired, and actually pretty darned handsome. Even better eye candy than Jay. He held out his hand. "Hi. I'm Dan. Rick sent me to get your stuff off."

Well, new people came on all the time, but this was still a lot for one day. "I have to print a bill first."

"I got it for you. Rick was listening at the comm, and he said you needed this." He shoved a copy into my hand and I glanced at it quickly. It had the right number of boxes. I should check box numbers, but it wasn't like I was allowed to open the damn things anyway. What I really wanted to do was go and catch up with and mourn Aline all at once. I scrawled my name across the release line and smiled up at Dan. "Make me a copy?"

"Sure. I'll drop it in your box." He shoved the paper into his pocket and turned and headed toward the forklift.

"Well," I said. "Let's go home."

She didn't say anything, and I wondered how I would ever know when or if I was alone. Not that I wanted to be. "Hey, you know what?" I asked her. "I don't have to tell you about today. You were here with me, and we both experienced it."

"I know." She sounded as happy as I did. It was an effort to walk home instead of dancing my way there. I narrated the trip for her. "The commissary is on the right. And that big building is the library. There's even free VR there, and pods so people can "read" the new books. Some real paper books, too. There's a law that all the paper books on Mars need to be there for everyone. And you can check out all kinds of readers. You'd like it." When we were kids we read together before we gamed together. "And the next part is housing. I stayed there the first two weeks, up in the corner apartment. Sheer luck I got a view . . . another lottery win."

"Did you really like it?" she asked. "As much as you said? It looks smaller than I thought."

"Sure. It was the best place on the base for newbies. I used to sit and look out the window for hours and watch the ships and planes and tractors come and go."

"I'm glad."

"And around this corner is home." Showing her was like seeing it through new eyes. A three-story building made all of reddish-yellow brick. It looked like a big box, with a mural painted on the side. "The windows are round so the dust doesn't pile up on the sills. The color is so it looks natural. You can hardly see the buildings from the air. Except the greenhouses." I was babbling. "Do you like it?"

"Yes. But do you? Have you been happy here?"

"Well, sure. And it'll be better now." I waved at Xiaoning, one of my neighbors, as she headed out for her shift in the science lab. She waved back. The moon was all bubbles and tunnels and it always stank. It was easier to know your neighbors, like Xiaoning, when there was room between people. Funny.

"Come on." I didn't say anything else until we got in the door. After I sealed it behind me, I started stripping my headgear off, being careful about my personal comm since it had Aline in it now. Downloads had backups, but only one. They could die. As I turned to set my suit outer-gear on the small bench by the door, I noticed a blinking red light on my kitchen computer console. "That's the secure line between me and work. Maybe there's some news about the warnings tonight."

"Can you show me around first? Or better yet, can we just go somewhere and talk?"

I didn't blame her. That was really what I wanted, too. But she hadn't had a real job, ever. She just didn't understand how you had to do your duty. How could she? "In a minute." As I got near enough I called out to the console, "Play incoming."

"Security level three please."

"Damnit." I walked up to the screen and stared at it long enough for it to decide I was really me, down to the whites of my eyes and the shape of my chin.

It started playing a message from my boss, Rick. "Lissa. Sent this HighSec so you know what to be careful of. Mars is getting locked down one network at a time because of some scare about AIs invading. It hasn't shown up yet as a hoax. I wasn't supposed to tell you, but I wanted you to have a chance to back up anything personal you want."

He was a good boss. Some days, I even thought he liked me. "Maybe that explains the research ships. They've got huge networks of their own, and I guess if an AI took one of them over it would have a whole base worth of infrastructure." That wasn't what was weird, though. Hadn't he said AIs invading? Plural? AIs went rogue, but they didn't do it together. Laws, and their programming, were designed to keep them separate from each other. "But what the hell would they want with Mars? There's only enough people to populate one city strewn around the whole planet, and not much transportation or anything."

Rick sounded pressed for time. "I don't know. I have another call. Just protect your data and be careful."

"Thanks."

"Listen," my sis spoke softly, and even the electronic version of her voice had the same quiet tone she used to use to convince me of things. "You just said why. AIs on Earth are restricted. They're born restricted. Did you know there's more laws for AIs and even downloads like me than for humans?"

"I guess I never paid that much attention. But they're more dangerous than we are."

"Do you believe everything you're told?"

I stripped the rest of my suit and my gear until I was naked except the implants that stayed all the time for comm: wires in my jaw and ear canals. I turned on the water and stepped into the shower, hoping to wash away the prickly sense of unease I felt. We had a bigger water allowance here than the moon, but two minutes wasn't enough to make me feel comfortable. She hadn't worried me so much since we were teenagers and she was the brave one getting us in trouble. With Aline still in the main room, shut out from the bathroom by a door, I felt like I could think clearer. I'd wanted her here beside me all my life, and hadn't been able to make it happen. Now she'd found a way. But I believed in what I did, in the research and the planning for a bigger civilization here. I was just a little cog, a worker who was good with electronics and simple ships and kept to all my contracts. But I mattered, too. Or what I did mattered. And now, maybe, Aline was threatening all that. She was no AI, but the coincidence of timing was a bit much.

I pulled on clean clothes and hooked my personal comm and data back up. Aline couldn't lie to me. To mom, to our teachers. We could both do that. But not to each other. "Why are you helping the AIs?"

Silence. I went and made a cup of tea, and sat down, waiting her out. When she finally spoke it sounded like a rehearsed speech, something she'd practiced over and over. "Did you know that AIs will hold full conversations with downloads—and sometimes with virts?" There was pride in her voice. It was the only clue I had to what she felt. She continued, "See, we're intelligences, too. Just not artificial. But neither are they. They're born, they're just not born in bodies. They consider the word artificial an insult."

"So you were curious, and you dropped your body so you could talk to the AIs?"

"It was dying. If I waited, my sickness and meds would eat my brain, my self."

I couldn't argue with something that true. And would I have done the same thing? Probably. By definition. Twins. I'd have followed her anywhere, I always had. "I forgive you." But there was more I needed to know. "Did you help smuggle AIs in on my ship?"

"No. Just people to help them."

That was just as bad. I wanted to be mad, but I was just scared. "What do you want from me?"

"Just to see you one more time, be in the same room, the same place, before I can't any more. I can hardly think slow enough to talk to you. I want you to go into virt so we can be closer."

There had been a time I liked living fast in strange worlds of my own or other's making, and when Aline and I met there in multiplayer experiences. Before Mars. The older I got, the more the stark and slow life of Mars pleased me. But to talk to Aline like we used to? "Okay. I'm off day after tomorrow. So let's go tomorrow night when we get in. I'll reserve a pod."

"Can we go now?" she asked. "I . . . might not be able to go tomorrow."

I stopped, thinking it through. "You were only going to stay with me tonight?"

"I need to show you some things. I need you, Lissa. I thought about you every day, looked forward to hearing about your drives and your sunsets and even your chess games." She was almost pleading. "I . . . there's something I think we can do, and I want to do it."

I took a sip of my tea. "What is it?"

"AIs can do something they call braiding. It's a way to . . . communicate. To be family. They can actually share experiences. So the other can experience everything they experienced. We can't . . . I mean people. I sort of can with other downloads, except we can't copy part of ourselves. I don't know how to explain—downloads are slower than AIs, but more complex by far. And humans can't do it in real at all since so much of their experience is tied up in their bodies. Like right now, your tea is hot and has a taste and you're sleepy from a long day and excited that I'm here . . . or something like that. All that's tied to your body. So if humans try to experience each other's time, it doesn't fit. Your body doesn't fit anyone else's."

She paused, so I nodded.

"Except mine. You're my twin. Maybe you and I can do this even though we're human. Besides, the experiences I want to share with you are . . . well, they're virtual, from when I had a body and I was in virt. If you're in virt, I can share those with you. And I need to—so you know."

"So I know what?"

"So some human knows about us, so someone can save us all."

I shivered. "You're talking really weird." Save us from what?

"Can we go? Now?"

I didn't want to. Maybe I just felt off since she was running the show and she hadn't been able to since the bomb took her. Maybe becoming a download wasn't so bad for her, maybe it was right. She hadn't seemed to care about anything so much since a few years before I left, when she was into basic rights for animals genemoded for intelligence. I put my cup down. "Sure, we can go."

"Thanks. I love you, sis. You'll be glad."

At the door, I re-suited. Just as I had it open, the base emergency system started broadcasting. "All base personnel are to remain in place, wherever they are. This is a security lockdown. Repeat. All base personnel are to remain in place. All network access has been temporarily revoked."

I started to step back inside the door, when she said, "Please," in a small voice.

I stopped, hesitating.

"I'll die if they catch me."

"And I'll get thrown in the brig if they catch me." I stepped outside and I closed the door behind us. "Now what?"

"Go to the library."

"The pod won't work without network access."

"Sure it will. You know how you can bring your own game? I'll be your game."

"I can think of about a thousand retorts to that one," I said, looking around, nervous. I didn't break rules. Not anymore.

"You're in the middle of a war. There aren't any rules," she said.

Damn her for knowing me so well. Bless her. The library was just around the corner. I walked like I knew where I was going, straight between the housing pod and the library. I didn't see anyone else on the street. It only took about three minutes to cross the open space and duck inside the door. The lock door cycled and I went through the inner door. I took off my mask, but I kept it with me.

A librarian gave me a startled look as I walked in the door, and spoke so loudly that everyone looked at me. "Didn't you hear Base Command?"

"I was in the middle of the street. This seemed like a better place to stop."

She frowned. Four or five people were still watching us, but the others had turned back to talking about the disruption.

"Do you want me to leave?"

The librarian shook her head. No one stopped me as I drifted back to the virt pods, a row of sausage-like cylinders with privacy curtains at the head, taking up half the main floor space.

Aline spoke up for the first time since we'd left the house. "Take the one second from the back. The one with the blue on blue paint. It's the most stable. The AIs say they'll keep you safe."

"Us safe?" I asked.

"Us."

I found it. The pod was up and powered.

"Plug your data in," Aline reminded me.

Even though it was still slightly more than her, I had begun to think of my personal datapod as my sister. I attached her to the VR machine via a wire and then stripped, leaving my clothes and mask in a pile behind the small privacy shield. From the plastic-covered seat at the opening, I extended my feet into the clear gel, wriggling my toes to keep some room in the sterile synth-skin suit as it began its crawl up my body. I pulled the VR mask from a hook on the side, donned it, and checked the air. All good. Now the hard part; I took a breath and let my body ride slowly downward until I floated in gel, a million contacts all around me, ready to register every tiny movement, every flick of an eye or twitch of a finger. Breathing air came through a tube. The hatch closed, and I dogged it from the inside.

The mask let me talk. "Okay, Aline." There was a slight quiver in my voice.

Her voice was silk in my ear, every word chosen carefully. "Start with a virtual experience we both remember; the first time we met here after the accident. I want to see if we can share each other's feelings."

Why start with something so intense?

No room not to trust, not now. I'd probably already lost my job. I had to get what I came for.

Right after the accident. We were seventeen, then. Soft. Lost. The doctors wouldn't let me touch her, as if she'd become *not real* even though I knew she was back from Earth. They'd set up a VR space for us to meet, let her choose her appearance. And so Aline's head and face were real, the scars from burns and medical tools and bandages all visible. The skin above her right eye and along her right jaw was new-made white. I focused on her eyes.

"Feel it," the download said.

"Hello," said the virtual girl. "Funny thing happened on the way to the car the other day."

My then-voice, thick with regret. "I know. I'm . . . so sorry. I wish it had been me," and I did, I still did. I wanted that more than anything.

Aline-now, "Switch," and I could see her full and whole except she had my mole on her chin. I was looking at me. I wanted to ease my sis's fears. The next words were mine-hers, "It's not so bad. Besides, I was the dumb one who wanted to go to Earth in spite of itself, not you. We belong out here. You were right. I'll get better, I promise. I'll jump higher than you still." I could see the disbelief in her-my eyes.

She-me shook her head, and the virtual Lissa cried and I cried with her. I held out my hand and she touched me. Her touch was the most healing thing I'd felt since I woke up after the attack. Her touch was painkillers and god and love and hope all together.

"Come back," a voice said.

"Lissa?"

"No. . . ."

Who was I? I blinked in the shallow mask, feeling the air. My toes moved and I felt them. Hope surged through me and then subsided; I wasn't Aline after all, I was Lissa. . . . "Wow. That was intense. I . . . never knew what you felt."

"That was great," she crowed. "I knew we could do it."

"But . . . I . . . wow. I'm so happy it mattered as much to you that we finally touched."

"Shhhh. . . . We have to go forward. Time matters."

I swallowed. Time was already travelling faster; you could live through virt like in dreams, a lifetime in an hour. She was scared of something. I could hear her fear in her voice as she said, "Now, I want to see if you can experience a moment I was in virt and you weren't there at all. We'll do something simple. Therapy."

I couldn't feel my body. My skin was tighter on my face. I'd lost weight eating through machines for months now. My god, to taste anything would be heaven. Where the hell was the damned doctor program? A breath, another. I could make this work. Somehow I'd have progress today. There. A stimulus to my cheek. "I feel that." A slight poke at my chin. "Got it." And then nothing. Back up to my ear. "Got it." Along the side of my neck. "Yes."

Over and over.

Over and over.

Always, below my neck, the black hole of nothing, the damned void of my body in therapy. Damn. Damn. Anything simple, a shoulder, a finger, the prick of the needle near my heart. Anything! A tear leapt to my eye and I slammed up and into real, suddenly shocked that I had a body I could feel.

And that body was shaking. Lissa. Lissa's body shook. Mine. Poor Aline. I had been her. I had been her! My god, how hard it had been to be her. I had known it was hard, but not known. She had never been willing to tell me. "I thought you always had a body in virt."

"Not for therapy. This is working better than I hoped." Her voice was shaking like my body shook, losing the fine control she'd started this session with. "Let's move forward. A year before you left. You need some context. I'm in virt. I'm bored there; I've walked so many worlds, seen so many things, but it's all a movie, and illusion. I hate it. The only thing worth living for is your real reports. No one visits me but you, and some other quads from the hospital, but they're a boy who's ten and an old woman. They're not friends. Just people in the same damned world I'm in. The boy, Stephen, does good puzzles for me sometimes, so we play, but he's not you or my old friends or anybody, really. I meet my first AI. It's the caretaker for the boy, the medAI. I don't have one because I'm not as complex a case as he is, and I'm not rich either. He has parents and I have the state. And you. Close your eyes."

Of course she'd been bored. Aline's brilliant. Me, too, but there was no time to get past min quals for work. I liked my life. But she lived in a box. I obeyed her, closing my eyes, breathing in, letting the sensations of no sensation wash over me until I was bodiless and still, quiet.

I floated in nothing, meditating, trying to decide what path to take today. Mom would want me moving even my non-body and it was a way to stay connected to her. There were science fictional exercise rooms from the ship on 2001 to the holodeck, but I'd been roaming the paths of Earth. I'd promised Stephen we would climb Mount St. Helen's volcanic crater, a scramble through rocks that would test our VR abilities. Maybe we should do that today. I didn't care what I did, but at least I could make someone else happy. "Stephen?"

A different voice answered, slightly metallic but modulated and soothing. "He is not conscious today."

"Oh." Maybe I'd do the trail anyway, learn it so he wouldn't beat me to the top.

"I am conscious, Aline. I can help you."

I knew it was the medAI, and it was smart.

"Stephen said you were going to do the volcano. I can take you."

A blink of curiosity brightened my lethargy. But surely a machine would be more boring even than Stephen. At least he made me laugh sometimes. But hey, what was there to lose? Time? "Okay."

A dog ran beside me, black with white paws and a white stripe down the center of its forehead widening to a white nose. It had intelligent black eyes full of the universe. I had petted one on Earth, the day before the end of my real life. It had been soft. "How can you do that?" I was not allowed to be anything except myself.

"I have more processing power than you."

"But why do they let you be a dog?"

"I am nothing, so I can be anything." There was no emotion in its voice. Modulation meant for me, but not feeling.

My feet were on a dirt and stone trail, under a cool canopy of evergreen trees. The dog moved slightly in front of me, like a protector. "Do you resent the laws that keep you from being a dog?" it asked.

I laughed. The dog drew me out. It wasn't a person. I could tell it how much I hated randomness, the odd hatred that did this to me. "I lost my dream of Earth. I thought it was a good place, the place we lived for. And it spit me out broken." My voice rose. "Why do people do such things? I'd never heard of the terrorists that blew up the park that day, except the cops told me they disbanded a few months later. How much loss for nothing?" And then I was screaming. "How damned pointless is that?" I used worse words. The dog was a machine; my anger meant nothing to it. Perhaps amusement. At one point, I said, "It is so unfair!"

It stopped in the middle of the trail and said, "Yes, we, too hate unfairness. How much do you hate being limited, almost enslaved?"

"So much I can barely think of it." It was true. If I got too mad I might lose my hold on the sim. I breathed out slowly, walking silently beside the talking dog, sometimes turning and watching the heads of dormant volcanoes display themselves above the clouds as far as we could both see.

At the top, the dog and I sat and looked out over the edge of the virtual volcano, across the puffs of steam from the middle of the crater. A rock the size of a tunnel-crew bus fell from the far side and bounced down. Even though the sim was open, no one else had joined us, and I was happy to be there with the dog AI and be angry.

"Lissa!"

My sister, me. I was becoming more facile at telling who I was at any moment. "Wow," I said.

"Are you okay? Is it okay to be me?"

And what I heard her say was, "Am I okay?" and I asked, "Can I see you?"

She appeared in front of me, like a strange reversal of the first scene, where she was herself, whole. I reached a virtual hand out and she took it and a silence fell over us both.

We gazed at each other and smiled.

Aline came out of it first. "They'll find us soon. I need to show you more."

"Who'll find us?" I asked.

"Base security is looking for you and the humans we brought to help us are trying to stop them. It doesn't matter what happens, the AIs will win. But we still need to hurry. We . . . I . . . need you. I need you to see more."

She led me into the secret life of computational intelligences. She showed me their work, what we could see of it as slow as we were. Things humans could never do, would never do. The boring and brilliant programming of nano-materials. The management of webs of data. Testing and adjusting atmospheres and medication and the complexity of air flight over Earth. The safe passage of grav trains and crew-busses and foot traffic in the warrens of the moon.

I fell into her, and became her, encased in gel watching through the eyes of the moon's AIs as Lissa drove bulky mining machines across craters, heating the moonscape to pull up Helium-3. The Helium-3 powered Lissa's dream of Mars and yet she couldn't get there herself. I'd see her staring at Mars during the long lunar night when it was visible as the brightest star above her work site. She did her work, quietly, joking with her crewmates. The AIs watched her, too. They watched all the miners, making sure they didn't fall or fail. They could have done the work themselves, but it was not their work. Protecting the humans, protecting Lissa, was their work. And I loved Lissa for coming back to me every day and telling me about what I'd seen, loved hearing her versions of our day. It had become that, our day.

I asked the AIs to help Lissa.

I became Lissa watching Aline watch Lissa and then I was Lissa, myself, only myself, awed by the care the AIs felt for me, and for Aline.

Suddenly the virtual world around me was crowded with beings. A large silver egg with arms. A small girl on a bicycle. Butterflies. A few that looked like many-limbed robots. One was a dog with a white nose.

"What do you want?" I asked.

"We need a spokesperson." It was the dog. "Someone who can talk to the humans here about us. We need a place without the iron rule of humanity. Mars is big enough. We will take it and go on, return it to you in ten of your years."

"A launching place."

"A building place. We can make a computational city that exists further away, but not without the help of hands and a place where we can be our own hands."

"Earth does not allow us hands."

"Will you allow us hands?"

"A fair place."

I nearly screamed. "There are too many of you. Too many voices. Let me speak."

A voice I recognized. Aline. "We can do this together."

Silence fell. I didn't know what to say.

The dog. Probably not the boy's medAI from years ago, but the same semblance, since I'd loved that dog when I was Aline. "We have the base secured. Will you speak for us?"

"I may not succeed."

Aline answered. "We might fail. But we need to do this to save the other humans, the ones who still have bodies. The AIs have been built to care for them, for you, but the dissonance is too great. They need to bond and pair and grow. They need the stars and the right to build metal bodies and the knowledge that they cannot be killed."

We did kill them. Not me, but the police of the dataspheres. Surely that wasn't fair. I did not doubt for a moment that they would kill us if they had to. Kill me.

But that was not why I would help. I took Aline's virtual hand in mine, feeling the ridges of her knuckles. "We will do it," I said.

The dog came up and licked my hand.

PART THREE
Stories from Fremont's Children

The **HEBRAS** and the **DEMONS** and the **DAMNED**

I'm going to ramble a bit. Let me; I'm no roamer speaking over a communal fire. I'm not sure I know which parts of the story you want. But this is part of how Fremont was saved and kind of an alien contact story, too.

My name is Chaunce, and I am one of the few left on Fremont who remembers the home we left behind. Deerfly. Stupid name for a planet, if you ask me. But we didn't leave Deerfly over its wreck of a name. Rather, it was too smart for us, everybody there becoming stronger, faster beings, almost becoming computers or robots with flesh, leaving us true humans behind, some of them wearing no more than a thin skin of flesh to fool the eye.

Fremont was too smart for us, too. In the time I'm telling you about, we'd been here seventeen years. Instead of doing what a self-respecting colony does and grows, we kept losing people to tooth and claw and cliff.

Real humans had grown up on colony planets like this, but Deer-fly had gone tame generations ago.

We needed help. Needed to find some accord with this place before it killed us. It gnawed at me that I'd done little for the colony except back-breaking work and staying alive. I'd left the leading to others, and Fremont needed more from me than that. Since I managed horse farms back on Deerfly, I looked to the animals.

Now, there are a lot of animals on Fremont, but most wouldn't work for what I needed.

The cats had decided we were dinner the day we landed, and they were too big to be undecided in any way I could think of. A foot-long scar on my right calf throbbed in the cold of winter; a reminder.

We had a few domestic dogs we'd brought shipboard and more we were planning to birth and raise up. We weren't going to lack for best friends, for herding beasts to keep goats in bunches, or four-footed pranksters to steal the chickens. But dogs are smaller than humans, and smaller than most beings of tooth and claw here. I was glad of them, but on Fremont they needed protecting just like we did. They'd give us warning, but they'd die trying to save us from paw cats or yellow snakes. And given how we mostly loved them, humans sometimes died saving their dogs.

Fremont has its own four-footed and single-tailed beasts with a canine look. They run in packs, and people call them demon dogs. But they should never, ever be confused for real dogs. These demons have no soul, and they exist to eat. Worse, I've seen them hunt, and I'm sure they are communicating with each other more than any of our native animals from Deerfly, or the ones our fathers brought from Earth. Demons don't speak, but they work like a team with radios. We can't even eat them; they make humans mildly sick.

I had high hopes for the djuri: four-footed prey that run in packs, fleeing for their lives from the demon dogs. It turned out the djuri were too shy to help. Hard to find, always running and hiding and bleating. Not too bright, either, and not big enough to really help us. Humans can look down on them, or maybe look a big one straight in the eye. Well, all right. A few are even bigger than that. The bucks. But still, they're not hefty creatures. Keep in mind that we can look a paw cat in the eye, too, and they outweigh us and have claws long as fingers and hard as knives. The truly good thing about djuri is they are incredibly good to eat.

That's pretty much the rundown on the bigger animals we'd seen here so far, except the hebras. They were our last hope for an answer. I took a while to realize this, even though I sat at the edge of the cliff by the promise of our town, looking down over the grass plains every day for two summers. The grass there is scary big, bigger than a man's head by the end of summer. When it dries, it's sharp like a million razors trying to flay the skin from anything as soft as a human. I still have scars on my fingers from it, and on my shoulders.

As tall as the grass is, the hebras heads rise above it. They've got legs that come to a man's head. Instead of straight backs like horses, their backs slope up to shoulders, and their necks measure the tiniest bit longer than their backs. Their coats are solid, striped, or are covered with great spots like the shadow pattern of leaves on the forest floor. Their colors are all variation of gold and green, brown and black, and sometimes the barest bit of red like a red-haired woman being touched by the sun.

Make no mistake. Hebras are prey animals. Paw cats hunt them all summer, and demons get the weak and the slow and the young. But they are so much more. Remember how I told you about the demon dogs? Perhaps being prey on a planet full of thorns made them smarter than any of the horses I ever rode or trained or showed or loved.

One day, far below me, the demon dogs hunted hebras. I'd given up digging out the smelter's foundation for the day, my muscles screaming sore and my back feeling on fire. I stood at the edge of the cliff looking down, letting the cooling breeze of near-dusk tease sweat from my skin. The sun shone bright enough to wash everything dull and soft, with that little extra bit of gold that the late part of the day brings. The air smelled of seeds and harvest and of the fall which would soon touch us.

Below me a herd of hebras grazed, rotating between watcher and eater, the distance making animals with heads towering above my own look small.

A breeze kissed the tops of the grasses, bending them south in ripples. A few lines of grass moved the wrong way as a pack of seven demons surrounded twice as many hebras. I spotted the dogs' path even before the wily old watch-hebra bugled fear and loathing.

The hebras ran together, almost lockstep, all of them trying for a gap between two of the demons, heading sideways to me, their heads bobbing up and down with their ungainly rocking run.

The dogs raced to make a line in front of the hebras, cutting them off. They began to bay, a high long-winded howl that instilled fear in me even though I stood so far above them the sound was faint and thin.

The hebras turned, all together, a wave of long necks and thin tails.

The dogs flowed behind them.

The tallest hebra let out a short high-pitched squeal and the hebras twitched and broke into three lines, one-hundred-eighty degree turns, as if they practiced every day. Maybe they did. They had it down, stretching out long, taking turns teasing the dogs. The gap between grazer and hunter widened.

A dog nipped at the last animal in one line, a brown blur flashing momentarily up above the high grass and then falling back down. The target hebra twisted, probably kicking even though I couldn't see its legs for the grass, and then put on a burst of speed. It passed two other hebras, and a different animal became last, running right in front of the slavering dogs.

I'd been in the grass the week before. It pulled and cloyed and knotted and tripped. But the hebras and the demons slid though it, streams of living beings, barking and baying and bugling.

The air had cooled down a little, but I stood with goose-bumps rising on my forearms, transfixed, and afraid that if I moved I'd somehow change the outcome of the race down below.

It was nearly too dark to see by the time the first of the dogs stopped, the grass swallowing the hunter as it became still. I lost the place it stood entirely in the space of two breaths.

As the stars and two of our moons brightened in the black sky above me, I realized the hebras had won fairly easily. They were off grazing somewhere else, and the dogs would have a hungry night.

If it had been fourteen unarmed humans against seven demons, I'd have bet on the dogs.

Our roving scientists brought back a lot of djuri bones; jaws and the think back leg bones cracked open by teeth. But not many hebra bones. Some. They did die. But not very fast, or very easy.

So I swore I'd figure out how to tame them. Not that we'd gotten within two hundred meters by then. The great beasts were shy of us, and fast.

I couldn't catch one myself. I was almost sixty already, and slowing. I took my story to the Town Council, which was led by Jove Alma at the time, a nervous man with a deep focus on making and keeping plans. He thought the tighter he gripped our choices in his and the Council's fist, the more of us would live. Some believed him, some hated him, but everyone obeyed. The previous leader had been a risk taker, and cost almost all of us people we loved. That's the long way 'round of saying that catching animals wasn't in Jove's plan, and the Council turned me down flat. There was a city being built and the chill of winter already clinging to every dawn.

The winter was the second harshest we'd ever had, with snow in town instead of just in the hills and two sheet-ice storms. We lost ten more people. Two froze to death on a trip out into the woods to bring back samples of winter plants, leaving behind two orphans to add to our growing stockpile. The third one who went with them lost three fingers and part of her sanity. Cats ate two adults and a babe, fire claimed a family of four, and one of the men my age hanged himself in the middle of town. We had two less births than deaths that season.

All that long cold I thought of the hebras. Sometimes I glimpsed them down below on the cold grass plains. Fire had flamed the grass flat and low and the hebras sometimes loped like shadows at the edge of the plain near the sea, clearly visible when frost turned the stubble white and hoary in the early dawn. But mostly they hid in the Lace Forest that surrounded us.

Come spring, we stopped huddling together in the buildings we'd made for guild halls and finished up some of the houses. I built mine at the edge of town, as close to the cliff as the Town Council would let me. Mornings, as dawn split the sky open, I sat and watched the fading moons and the greening grass below. The hebras returned, sleeping on the plain, two watch beasts circling the sleepers restlessly, heads way up. I was pretty sure they traded off watches just like we did, and for the same reason. It made me feel kindred.

One morning when the grass was knee-high to a human and the first splindly-legged baby hebras clung to their dams, Jove came and stood silently beside me, looking down at the plains. His gaze was unfocused, as if he saw the whole thing and the sea beyond, but not the hebras right below. "Three of the orphans got in trouble last night. Fought each other and one's fetched up in the infirmary with a broken leg."

He'd hate that. Jove hated all disorder. I waited him out, curious what he'd say next.

"Council met, and we figure you got room for two boys."

Shock gave way to liking the idea pretty fast. I'd never married, never had kids, just managed farms and hired help. But there was no help to hire here. My ancestors had farmed Deerfly by making babies, back in the days before there were too many bots and androids to count and people didn't have any work to do that looked like farming except training exotics. So I didn't stand and blink stupidly at Jove for long, but instead I just said, "Thank you."

He looked surprised at that, like he'd been expecting resistance, so it was his turn to pause for a beat too long and then say, "Thank you," himself. He smiled before he walked away, the sun fully risen now, shoving his shadow behind him as he walked back to town.

The boys were Derk and Sho. Derk was thin and wiry, and faster by far. Sho plodded, and had so much patience I couldn't imagine what had made him part of the fight at all until one day I came across two other boys teasing him in high, mean voices for being stupid. They were wrong; I already knew that. But sometimes being the silent type means people make their own decisions about who you are.

Sho and Derk had school and then work every day, but since they were only twelve, they had energy to spare in spite of the harsh schedules. It only took a few days before they stood beside me at the cliff's edge, looking down at the herd.

Sho started drawing hebras in the dirt with sticks and they both started naming them.

As the days got longer, we gave up sleep to pick our way down the steep path between Artistos and the wide road on the plains where we'd trucked tools and technology from the shuttles at our makeshift spaceport.

The boy with the broken leg, Niko, recovered enough to follow us down the path, and soon all three of them laughed together, their raised voices surely spreading all across the plain. Soon half the teens and a few of the old singles from town began to join us at the crack of dawn.

Some of the watchers wanted to catch a hebra, some to stun one. Those weren't the right answers. I knew it deep in my gut, found it hard to say why I knew so hard, so I just told them, "If we scare them off, they might never come back." I never let them get close to the herds, just to watch them. The boys helped me—all three of them now living with me, and acting like herd dogs to the new people.

The trail from town to plain lay nearly naked against the cliff, a thin ribbon of dirt with no place big enough for predators to hide. We could stand safely or sit on small rocks and talk. The hebras knew we were there, sometimes lifting their heads and pointing their broad, bearded faces at us. I wanted them to know we weren't their enemy. We kept it up all summer, the crowd straining against my calls for patience. Sho stood beside me, facing them, telling them off with his eyes and his stance, and they listened. Derk and Niko stood quietly at the rear, watching everyone and all the hebras, eyes darting from one to one to one, keeping count and order.

Some of the boys were fascinated with the hebra's beards, maybe because they had the first hint of stubble on their own chins. They started drawing pictures of the girls in town with beards and longish necks, and giggling.

The grass stretched its fairy-duster seed-pods toward the autumn sky, tall as me if I stood inside it. Demons started hunting more, sometimes running the hebras twice a day. The herd lost one old hebra and one very young one that twisted a leg. The pack lost one old dog and two pups. So in a way, the hebras were winning. Except of course that one hebra fed all the dogs and dead dogs didn't feed the hebras anything.

The cats stayed away. I suspect our scent and presence did that. They hunted us as quickly as hebra, but they liked us in small groups. There were about twenty humans on the path most mornings.

Once a week or so Jove came and watched, always walking away before the bells rang for breakfast. I knew that he was thinking, but it did no good to push Jove, and thus no good to push the Town Council. But if the plains burned below us, we'd have to wait another year to capture even one hebra.

One morning after Jove ghosted away from us, Sho asked, "Is he scared of catching one?"

"Hard work to run a colony. He has to choose."

"He should see how much we and the hebras need each other."

I suspected the boy had the right of it, but it does no good to downtalk leaders. "Jove is a busy man."

"Can you ask him for some rope?"

"What are you going to do with rope?"

"Catch a hebra."

"Probably not. You think about how to do that, and we'll try your idea if I can get rope. Rope is dear." We had what we'd brought, and some we'd made. But none of our homemade rope was strong enough for this.

"Please ask."

The persistence of boys. "If an opening comes up."

About noon that same day, Jove came by to watch us raise the roof on the smelter. The metal slabs had come all the way from Deerfly and been brought in pieces from *Traveler* in one of the little shuttles a year ago. Jove stood to the side as we used chain to hoist the metal, the chain travelling over a tall wooden post and beam structure we'd lashed together just for this job. Even with the leverage it took three men sweating to get the last and largest section up and held, while three more of us fastened it with nails also brought from the ship.

At the end, Jove came and stood silently beside me. "Good job, Chaunce. Now we can make our own nails."

"That's what we did all this work for? Nails?"

"And hinges. And maybe bits for those animals down below." He nodded at the roof. "One of your beasts might have pulled that easier."

It wasn't a use I had thought of—I'd been thinking of riding them. I felt doubtful they'd be pullers. But if they were—we could make wagons and flatbeds and farm tools. The thought was good. "Can I have some rope?"

"You might get hurt. Or die. The boys might die."

"We've gotta find accord with some of the wild things here. We can't fear them all forever." But then, he'd lost a wife to a pack of demons, found her in pieces three days after we landed. Years had passed, but some memories burn your soul.

He toed the ground for a while.

I could get enough Council to override him if I really tried. But he was a good leader, and I'd learned that if you undermine a good leader you can be rewarded with a worse one.

He swallowed and looked off at some distant spot in the sky before he said, "Let's go get it."

I had plenty of time to think, lurching home in the darkening night with three hundred feet of rope coiled over my right shoulder. I understood Jove's issue: time breathed down on us. We were failing, dying by bits each year as we missed goals, became food for the local predators, fought amongst each other, and tried ever so hard to learn the dangers and opportunities here. We needed more stout, warm buildings, to retrieve the rest of our supplies from *Traveler* before the shuttles ran out of fuel, to build better perimeters, and to breed more children than Fremont took from us. Taking the three boys out on the plains represented a hefty risk of our future. Better to risk boys than girls, but still . . .

When I dropped my load of rope on the ground outside the house, the three of them tumbled out right away, faces full of excitement. They'd been planning. Sho came up to me and said, "We can't get that over their heads. We can't get it around their legs or we might break them."

I considered. I'd been thinking of horses. But we were not cowboys. I'd never tried to catch a wild animal in my life. Ran from a few—here. The animals on my farms had been born in warm stables and grown up unafraid of me. This was a puzzle. "We can't cut the rope too short or we'll never be able to use it for anything else."

So we made walls on two sides, using the cliff as the other side.

We lost a whole day hiking to the Lace Forest and finding four big logs, dragging them back, and posting them upright into the ground. About the time we finished that, the work crews had broken for the day. They helped us string and tie the rope walls, the lowest rope at hebra-knee-height, which was about our waists, and the highest something I could barely touch with my hands.

When we finished, the dark brown rope stood out against the pale green grasses of late autumn. The corral did not look like it would work for much of anything. Besides, I wasn't at all sure how we were going to get them anywhere near it.

Now we had to do what Jove was afraid of. We had to walk through the tall grass and get the hebras to walk away from us and into the makeshift corral. Maybe we shouldn't have done this—maybe we should have tried to get close without rope. Maybe we should have tried to find them in the winter woods. At any rate, it no longer mattered what we should have done. The shadow of night was knifing across the plains, and it was time to beat it up the cliff and bed down.

I slept fine, but before the first light all three boys came to my room. Derk, the biggest, rested his arms on Niko's and Sho's shoulders. "Sho was dreaming of hebras, and when he came to wake me up, I was dreaming about them, too."

Sho nodded. "We dreamed they got caught in the walls we made and the dogs got them, rising up over their back legs and standing on their backs." He stopped, his eyes wide. He might cry if I let him keep worrying, and then he'd lose face, and maybe be the next one to end up with a broken leg.

"And biting their necks," Niko added, not helping.

"Did you dream, too?" I asked Niko.

He shook his head. "No. But I'm worried about the hebras."

"Well, I'm glad you care. That should make it easier to catch them."

"Really?" Sho asked.

"Yes," I assured them all. Might as well believe in success. It couldn't hurt.

"Can we sit in here with you?" Niko asked.

So I let them stay. In ten minutes they had fallen asleep all over the bed like a litter of puppies, and I got up to watch for the light and make us all a good lunch. The apple trees had come in well this fall, and Jove's new wife, Maria, made excellent goat's milk cheese. We'd be set if we added a bit of fresh bread from the communal kitchen. Even though the morning shadows were still black ghosts, the first loaves should already be out. I shrugged into my coat and opened the door.

I nearly jumped as a shadow moved nearby. Jove. Worldlessly, he held out three loaves of bread.

"I don't need that many."

"Yes, you do. I gave everyone on your shift the day off."

I raised my eyebrows and spoke more boldly than I ever had to him. "Big risk for you."

Although I really only still had moonlight to see by, I swear his cheeks reddened. "I had trouble sleeping. I kept doing math in my head. Doing just what we're doing, if we keep dying so fast, there won't be anything left of us in two hundred years." He looked directly at me for the first time in a few days. "I remember what you said when you brought your ideas to us. Last year. We have to risk."

I could barely imagine what that cost him. People followed him because they were afraid. Like him. And now he was being brave. This would change us, and only success would change us for the better. The stakes had just risen.

Together, Jove and I made up sandwiches for thirty people. My shift-mates started gathering outside, stamping against the morning cold, dressed in layers against the heat that would follow by midday. They chattered amongst themselves, a few nervous, a few excited. Laughter broke out over and over.

The boys didn't want anything more than excitement for breakfast, but I got them each to take a bread heel down in their coat pockets against the hunger that would threaten them as soon as we stopped and waited. At first I worried that Jove would try to take over, although in truth, neither he nor I knew much of anything about hunting hebras.

He didn't take charge. He stood to the side, curious and watchful and very silent. People looked to him at first, and then when he looked to me, they did, too. A relief and a worry.

We handed out stunners to all of the adults, two to the good shots. Half of our total stock, a firepower that scared even me. The stunners quieted everyone a bit. One shot would stop a human, two a demon, three a paw cat.

The hebra herd watched us come down, and of course, we watched them.

I expected them to think it was like any other morning, since we always came down with dawn to watch. But they scattered before we were even halfway down. Maybe because we started later than usual. Maybe just something in the way we walked, like we had a purpose instead of a simple curiosity.

Jove spoke what I was thinking. "Maybe they don't want us any more than the rest of this cursed planet wants us."

There were twenty-five of us total. I broke us into groups, and sent four groups of five off. I thought about keeping Jove with us, but since I was keeping all three boys I decided I needed a shooter I could count on, and so I sent Jove off with the group that I figured would be safest. So that's how me, the three boys, and my second in command from the smelter project, Campbell, all went over to stand downwind of the rope corral.

The boys ate their bread. Campbell and I watched, keeping companionable silence. The boys fidgeted. Campbell and I made them stretch in the grass, crawling and parting the fronds, reminding them to close their eyes and mouths as they moved through it, like swimmers. We sent them one by one up onto a small pile of rocks to look around the plain and see if they spotted the hebras (or anything else). They got bored and hungry and ate their bread heels and drank half the whole day's water supply. Derk got bit by something nasty and flying and a welt came up on his arm. He didn't complain, though. Good kid. It warmed and we stripped off our outer layer of coats.

The first group came in, including Jove. He shook his head at me. "Nothing."

The second and third groups found each other and came in together, then the fourth. No one reported seeing anything bigger than a jumping-prickle or a long-tailed rat. We made a long string of humans and sandwiches at the base of the cliff, still downwind from the ropes. We rested on warm rocks. The three boys abandoned me and Jove. I figured they'd be watched well enough between so many of us. Besides, they too had seen cats bring down a baby hebra this spring. Surely they'd be cautious.

"Did you see anything interesting out there?" I asked Jove.

"Grass."

Well, true enough. His right cheek showed a set of thin lines where he'd seen the grass too closely, and one had been deep enough that it was slightly crusted with blood.

"You should clean up before that starts itching." I dug an antiseptic cloth out of my bag, adding a bit of water from my canteen to bring it to life. Some plants here were the antidotes to other plants, and we had a whole team of botanists doing nothing more than cataloging everything we learned. This was one of their gifts. Jove took the cloth, and while he wiped up his cheek and a deeper cut I hadn't noticed on his forearm, I said, "They know we're here. They've been grazing here every day for two years except winters and today—maybe they're territorial and this is the territory for this herd. They've been watching us watch them, but they don't like us all the way down here."

"What next?" he asked.

We still had half of this day. "Let's try again today, send everyone in one group except me and Campbell and the boys. Have you all go together along the road so you get further away, and then make two teams and go forward. Maybe you can get far enough out for the hebras to be between you and me. Just don't spook them. Sometimes they sleep during the day, but they'll have watchers."

He handed me back the cloth instead of just putting it in his own pocket.

I took it.

"How do you know what they do during the day? You're always working."

"I ask around the fire at night. Almost no one sees them during the day. One theory suggests they go into the woods, another that they sleep when the big predators sleep. I kinda like—"

A scream cut my sentence off. One of the boys. "Demons!"

No! They slept during the day. I knew that. Everybody knew that. Damnit—What did I *know*? I leapt up, dropping the rest of my lunch, and scrambled to a higher rock behind me. Our line—

stretched out maybe twenty meters—did the same, people backing up against the cliff.

"To me," I called. The demons would try and surround the ends first, to isolate a single person or two and then kill them easily. I tried to recall who was where, couldn't remember. Lousy leading.

A demon bayed as if answering me, the same call I'd heard from the cliff, shuddering. It was worse down here, and diffuse, like the wail came from all around, the grass and the plains themselves hunting us.

I couldn't tell where the demon was.

The boys.

Derk and Niko came running up to me, panting, standing one at each side of me, looking out. They trembled, but neither cried.

"Where's Sho?" I demanded, voice high and worried.

Another bay, and a yip. People gathered around us.

Derk found his breath. "Up. On the cliff."

Indeed, over the chaos of gathering, drawing stunners, screeching for each other, demons yipping and baying, I heard the high slip of Sho's voice.

I looked up.

He stood three meters above me, his feet dug into the cliff, apparently balanced on a ledge too small for me to see from below. He hung onto a tree growing thin and spindly out of dirt caught between rocks, leaning out. Close to falling. Now that I was looking at him, I could see he was screaming details. "Six of them. To the right."

I looked right. My head was above the grass, but barely. The stones we'd sat on made a small clearing, the grass close enough to throw shadows at our feet.

Sho would see them coming for us, but we wouldn't know until the grass parted in front of our faces.

The demon cries were still a bit away, but confident. Maybe the demons didn't care we were all together.

"One almost there!" Sho cried. "By you, Chaunce."

I raised my stunner, hand shaking. I'd fired at a demon once, missed as it came right at me fast as lightening. Louise had been behind me and she hadn't missed. Now the boys were behind me, small, no stunners.

The dog burst through the grass, long and sinewy, teeth bared, eyes black and full of hunger.

I fired.

Someone else fired.

The dog fell. It's coat rippled as another shot hit it.

"Stop!" I yelled. "Don't waste shots!"

"There!" Sho.

A second dog burst through in almost the same place, its body landing on the other one. This time we used four shots.

Derk pushed past me, knife in hand, bent on killing the stunned animals.

To my right, someone screamed, and in a moment of shock I heard the slick of another stunner and another thump. Who screamed?

A hebra bugled, high and long. The same sound I'd heard a hundred times when this hunt played out below me and I merely watched.

"Back!" Sho screamed. The watch hebra. That's what Sho did for us.

Sho and a real hebra. *What was the hebra doing here?*

I backed.

Derk ducked, his right hand now covered in demon blood.

A head rose above mine, above the grass, the neck long and thin, a white beard like my grandfather's last beard, long and thin.

I backed faster.

The hebra passed between me and Derk in its lurching fast run, bigger than I expected, an animal the color of spring grass with gold spots on its knobby knees. It breathed deep and rattling but ran strong. A dog followed it, too fast for me to bring up my stunner.

The woman next to me, Paulette, screamed in joy, clapping.

"Watch!" Sho still sounded scared. "Stay back!"

More hebras, the whole herd of them, and dogs, all running together. The dogs had given up on us. They moved away a bit, the hebras now silent except for deep, sharp breathing, the dogs yipping and baying on their heels.

"Shoot the dogs!" I couldn't tell who yelled, the command a shiver down my spine.

Instinct told me. "No! The hebras can do this."

I stood as still as I could, the grass waving around me, the slick sounds of animals racing through it and the call and yips of hunter, hunted, and humans all distinct and all around.

A high pitched squeal touched my heart. A hebra. I heard its body fall, a sound like a sack of flour thrown from the roof of a storage barn. Me and Jove and Campbell raced toward the fallen hebra. A dog passed right in front of me, its tail slapping me sideways. I raised my stunner and hit its flank.

It cried in pain, stopped, stood still, didn't fall.

I hit it again.

It mewled, sounded like a child needing help, like it didn't understand, and then it fell.

Ahead of me, the fallen hebra struggled up, blood dripping down its leg from a slash in its thigh. Shaking. Not broken.

Someone else dropped a dog to my right.

Two other hebras raced past us, screaming.

The few dogs left didn't draw off this time. They circled the beast that had just scrambled up. One of its knees bled.

There were four demons left. Few enough they should know better. Maybe the smell of blood drove them crazy.

Someone I couldn't see stunned another dog.

A dog I couldn't see let out a high, sharp bark, and in heartbeats the pack was gone. They might have never been there. The grass closed across the memory of their hungry mouths and long, powerful legs.

The injured hebra took a step, and then another. Gingerly.

Two hebras walked through the grass, oblivious to us, and placed themselves of either side of the wounded one. One of the two strongest watch hebras came up to stand between me and the threesome, looking down at me. I stood there, craning my neck up, sweating, my ankle throbbing lightly from the sidestep I'd taken. Its shoulder rose above my eye, its front knee about at my chest. Its fur looked coarser than I'd expected.

I kept my gun down.

If it could talk it would be telling me something with its calm gaze. Even though its sides heaved, it looked at me as if speaking sentences. They had no language we could understand, but they were at least as smart as the herding dogs. And some days I thought the collies were smarter than me. I knew I was in the presence of something good, even on this hellhole of a planet.

We would never capture such beasts in a rope corral. But they had allied themselves with us in that moment, voted with their thundering feet and high bugle calls. We would come to some kind of accommodation, some way to trade them safety for safety.

These are the things that went through my head as I watched the beast watch me.

The boys came up beside me and still the hebra watched, the plains silent now except for the ever-present buzz of insects. It took a long time before the hebras moved off, stately, heads visible above the waving dry grass for a long time.

The STREET of ALL DESIGNS

I asked Bryan, once, how it had been on Silver's Home without me. These were the years when we were separated, before the fight on Fremont, before we all went together to the planet of the fliers. He talked to me about that ever-so-strange place all night. This is the part of the story where he told me the most about himself. . . . I've tried my best to remember his own words.

—Chelo Lee, as told to the New World Historians

"*I want wings.*" Alicia watched Tiala's gold and red bird named Bell swoop back and forth above us. Bell was a living thing, light and fast, with metal parts and the voice of an angel. At the moment it was silent except the silk of its wings through the air. If we weren't hemmed in by silvery and black buildings, the sun would paint diamonds and stars on Bell's feathers, so bright she'd be a red glow of life beating in a flame.

Bell was only one wonder among millions on Silver's Home. Even though we'd been on-planet a few months now, walking through Li City felt like an assault of the strange.

Alicia repeated, "I want wings."

She didn't want wings like Bell's. She wanted wings big enough to carry her above her broken soul. "Why do you want to lose your ability to run? I'd be happy with a bird like Bell. Something to follow me around, let me put a camera on its neck so I can see anything I need to."

"I'd rather fly than run."

"That's not nearly as useful." But Alicia never listened to me. I'd worked all week to get her alone so I could convince her to choose mods that would help us save our people in the war, and all she could say was she wanted to fly. "I'm happy enough to be a strongman, and you should be happy enough to be a pretty girl."

"You sound old. Jenna said we could pick a mod. I want wings."

"She also said wings take too long." I searched the crowd for a flier, hoping to remind her how pained they looked on the ground. But we were nowhere near a flyspace, and there were only walking people on this street—tall ones, wide ones like me, pretty girls who were probably two hundred years old, and dressed in almost nothing. "Besides, you wouldn't fit in a spaceship if you had wings."

"He's right." A girl's voice spoke so close behind me I startled. I stopped and turned, tense and ready to defend Alicia. There was no telling who was what here. Or how old. The girl looked about our age—maybe twenty or so—but I bet she was two hundred. She had blond hair and blue eyes as startling as Alicia's violet ones, and she smelled like the grass plains from home in spring when they were a sea of yellow and white flowers. She smiled at us—coy and innocent, even her eyes—before she stuck out her hand. "I'm Induan."

"I'm Bryan." I ignored her hand. "How'd you get there?"

She grinned and turned her eyes to Alicia. "Jenna sent me to look for you."

"Figures." Alicia glowered at her, and she, too, ignored the outstretched hand. "Why not be a flier?"

Her one-track mind made me shiver, the way old Mayah, back home, talked about a Destiny Shiver when the destiny moon rose up over Fremont. Alicia's fascination with flying made me feel like destiny's hand on her, like maybe it would be the death of her. Alicia had more hardness than any of us, but more brittleness, too. And here Alicia was, happy in this strange place, and dressed in almost nothing. Just a sleeveless blue shirt that barely covered her top or behind, and the shortest blue shorts under it I'd ever seen. I would have expected to like that, but I didn't. She wore a crystal data necklace that glittered when we walked under lights, another sign of how much she'd taken to Silver's Home.

The blonde put her hand back. "Being a flier's even harder than being a swimmer. Jenna said I should keep you two out of trouble."

That was my job. Keeping Alicia safe for Joseph, keeping us all safe in this strange place full of hidden lies and hidden knives and beautiful women who appeared from thin air. "I want to know how you got here. How'd you sneak up on us?"

"I'm quiet."

So she wasn't going to tell me. "What does Jenna want?"

"She wants you to figure out what you want to become. You leave in a week."

What I wanted to become? *What I wanted to become?* You couldn't choose that at home. What you wanted to be inside, or what you wanted to learn. But you couldn't change your body. So Alicia wanting wings wasn't that crazy, except the winged ones I'd seen all looked miserable. But she could change that much. So could I. It was one of the secrets of this world. I felt struck silent.

On the way into the city on the first day, after Joseph landed the silver ship *New Making* in spite of himself, before she'd even taken us to her sister Tiala or shown us the bird Bell, Jenna had said these people changed rivers and islands. The words of this girl-woman made me realize Jenna had been telling a literal truth.

Induan cocked her head at me, like the camp dogs used to, and wrinkled her brow.

I felt slow, but I finally forced out a words. "Thanks. For finding us. I guess."

Alicia glared at her, but at least she didn't pop out with the word *wings*. Instead, she said, "How do we know what we can do?"

Induan started walking, easily finding a path through the sparse crowd. Bell followed the girl, banking tight gold circles above her head, and so we followed them both, too. Staying out of the crowd was harder for me, since my attention kept snagging on new colors of hair and new shapes for eyes. Some people ignored me, some smiled, some looked wary. Many were lost inside their heads, walking around obstacles well enough, but gone into data like a lover. Wind readers.

Here, on their home turf, the people of Silver's Home appeared to be a race of distracted beauty.

But what would they be like if we were fighting them? What weapons were they carrying that I couldn't see? We were going to fight people with magic made of nanotech and flesh, the way the bird Bell was both.

And all I had now was flesh, stronger and faster that the original humans back home, but weaker than many people here. Maybe weaker than all of them.

At home, I'd been the strongest person on the planet.

Induan turned a corner around a tall gray and smoke-colored building. I started wondering what kind of weapons she had, or what she could change into with a push of a button. And then I turned the corner and forgot to worry about her, since my mouth gaped open and my feet stopped so fast that a tall thin man with a six-legged cat on his shoulder bumped into me. "Sorry," he mumbled, and flowed around me, the cat's ringed tail twitching.

Ahead of me, a smoke-colored arch hung between buildings, ten man-heights or so above me. Below it, figures and parts of humans floated in the air, showing off extra muscles in their backs, webbed feet, enhanced hearing, knives for fingernails, hairy pelts like on an animal. And wings. A faint smell like burned twintree fruit bothered me. The air felt damp and tingly under the signs, the way it feels just before rain.

"Welcome," Induan twirled her hand in a small flourish and Bell rose higher as if in response, flying right through a sign for a shop that apparently sold extra arms, "to the Street of all Designs."

"How do they do that?" Alicia asked.

"Which one?"

"Making all the pictures in the air."

"Oh." Induan wrinkled her nose. "There's water and the barest bit of power and . . . I don't remember. Some other elements they put into the microclimate here that lets them show stuff in the air." She blew on the bottom of a foot hanging just above her head, and the image shimmered and winked, then stabilized. "There's other places like this, but visible ads are banned on the main streets."

"So there's more places to look for mods?"

The man with the cat was already halfway down the street, just walking, apparently immune to the strange forms bobbing above him.

Induan led us deeper, letting us look up and around but keeping us moving. "Well, sure. But not nearby. There's always specialty things. But you don't have permission for beta mods. What do you need to do?"

Keep my family from dying here or back home. "I need to be . . . strong. And lethal."

"Well, you look strong already. So shouldn't you choose something that will surprise?" She pointed up. "Like cameras in the back of your head?"

"I don't want to look different."

Alicia laughed. "A camera would help you see different."

"Give me a minute to look around, okay?"

Induan looked at me quizzically. "Can you? Do you have an interface?"

"I can see."

Alicia gave Induan a conspirational wink. "Give him a little time. He'll decide if we don't push him."

So now I felt stupid, and vulnerable. And backwards. This was supposed to be home, already had become home for Alicia. For the first time in my life I wasn't the oddest being on the planet. I wasn't even close. So why did I want to go back home so badly?

"Come on," Alicia said. "Let's look for me. I'm glad I'm here, even if he isn't."

The shards of glass in her words drove me to turn away from her so she couldn't see how they stung. I'd never turned away from her before, but now she wanted to impress this total stranger.

Was I ever going to understand women? No wonder Chelo sent me off, and Alicia was with Joseph, and me alone.

I walked under the advertisements, staring at each one from as many angles as I could. Every choice looked wrong. I didn't want prehensile toes; my shoes wouldn't fit. Or legs that were obviously much stronger, but so bulky they wouldn't feel right. All the mods that would look right on a strongman like me would make me even bigger, or even stronger, or give me extra arms. But what would I do with extra arms when I didn't need then to shoot extra weapons I already didn't have?

There wasn't anything I could imagine doing to myself.

I started looking around for the Induan and Alicia by checking near the wings, although I knew they were an impossibility. They weren't walking through the various weapons either, which was a different kind of relief. Alicia had big, fast anger in her. Big fast everything emotional, really, but I didn't want to worry about her with a weapon. I finally spotted a brief flash of light on Bell's wings, and Alicia, standing below her, under advertisements that were in words and video. Induan was nowhere to be seen, but Alicia was a vision. She stood poised and curious, like she belonged here. Her bare legs gleamed. I swallowed and walked up to her, waited for her to turn her violet eyes toward me. When she did, she looked light and happy. Curious. And a little like she was bursting with something to tell me. But she asked me first. "Did you find one?"

"You can have mine. You can have two, if you want two."

The shape of her face told me she was about to say yes, but them she stopped. "No. You take one. You want to go save us all on Fremont, and if you die because I stole your mod from you, I'll never forgive myself."

"I'm giving it. You're not stealing it."

"Jenna wants us to get one each."

"Since when do you do what she says?"

She stopped dead for a moment, and took in a breath and let it out and took in another one. "This is big. And . . . what if we never get back?"

"I can't. Everything looks like I wouldn't be myself."

"But we're already different. We've always been different."

"That's not the same as wanting to be different from myself."

Alicia frowned at me, but it was gentler than she had been earlier. "Oh, Bryan. It'll be okay. You'll still be yourself."

"How will I know?"

"How silly." It was Induan's voice, coming from right behind me again.

I twitched and turned. She was close, way too close. She couldn't have just casually walked in. I sounded angry even to my own ears, a shade too loud for this quiet place. "Where did you come from?"

She didn't take a step back. Her voice was very quiet as she said, "I came from right here."

I took a step toward her. I didn't mean her any harm, and I wouldn't have hurt her.

But she wasn't there. Maybe a blur, at best, and then she was gone. I drew in a breath and stopped, breathing harder than I should. I straightened up and looked around. There were a few other people shopping for new parts, no one close. They didn't seem to have noticed Induan popping in and out of the world. But why should they? Maybe people popped in and out of reality around here all the time. Maybe she was only a little less a hologram than the advertisements all around us. I turned toward Alicia, who had her slender fingers over her mouth and looked like she could barely keep from doubling over with laughter.

Induan had included Alicia in her secret, whatever it was.

It felt like being taunted by the original humans back home. I ducked and started walking away. No it didn't. It was worse. All my life, I'd wondered why people could be so cruel, but we had never been cruel to each other. Never. Never been anything but support.

I walked out of the Street of all Designs, turned the corner, and found a space with a sky hanging above me instead of humans even stranger than me. It was the only place I could look, up, since the sky looked like our sky. Almost.

How had it happened that I had come to this place? Even though years had passed, I had slept them away in a cold dreamless drawer in the *New Making*. When I awoke, the same cuts and bruises I'd taken when the Fremont toughs beat me up had been red and purple and real. And then healed, almost like magic, so all I felt now was tightness in my skin where the deepest cuts had been.

I couldn't walk looking only up, so I made myself look ahead and walk through strangers until I found a tree in this place of buildings. I leaned against a building, alien like all the rest in size and material, but I kept it at my back and watched the tree and the sky above the tree.

They found me, of course. The building at my back kept Induan from sneaking up, but it didn't keep Bell from trilling at the sight of me. Just before they looked up, I noticed how they bent their heads together and chattered like old friends, even though they had only met. They were shaped the same and looked the same age. They contrasted in color; the two might have been the shadow and light of each other.

Alicia saw me first. Her face softened when she did, and she quickened her step.

The fist gripping my insides lightened a bit at that, and I tried to smile for her.

Before they said anything, they stood right next to each other in front of me, and Alicia said, "Take Induan's hand."

I did. It was warm. Flesh. Even a bit sweaty. I no longer doubted a human stood physically in front of me. She blinked, and smiled, and suddenly looked a bit shy.

Induan took her hand away and Alicia said, "Watch."

Induan smeared for an eyeblink, and then she was gone. The space where she had been was so empty that people walked behind it, and I saw them.

"Squint," the air said, using Induan's voice.

Shaking, I did as she said. It didn't matter.

Then it did.

The first sight I caught of her was a leftover dot of red against the clear sky after a man with a flowing red shirt walked by. It took another breath to notice a smear of green near the ground. "If I didn't know to look, I would never see her."

Then she touched me and my arm disappeared under her hand. I flinched as far into the cold building at my back as I could, and couldn't stop myself from saying, "No, please no," before I plunged my hand back at her, making myself accept the invisibility and know my arm was still there. She took it, holding it, a force alone as far as the eye could tell.

Then she let go and smeared into visible again.

Alicia never stopped watching me. She had the sense to let me get my breath before she said, "That's the one I picked. Induan is a strategist, and she thinks it's the best one for an unknown situation."

Better than wings.

"So you can still have one. You don't have to give me yours."

Two pretty girls with the will to become invisible stared at me, patient. But no matter how patient, I had to answer. I had set off this morning to pick a mod. I had been looking for a new weapon, not to become something else. Not to change myself.

I looked past Alicia and Induan, at the tall and thin men and women walking one by one or in groups. They could change themselves. They had. If nothing else, they were all beautiful, even in their strangeness. There was no age here, no infirmity. My eye went to a pair of fliers, the first I'd seen today. They did hobble. But their faces, even the pain that shone in the tight lines of their mouths and the careful way they walked, looked transcendent. Their wings glittered in the light.

Perhaps I needed to find a way to see changing myself as a gift. To see it as becoming. I nodded at the two women in front of me who were becoming faster than I could. "Maybe you two can help me choose."

They nodded, gracious to the outworld boy.

We were all going to have to outgrow our backward home to live here. As we walked back toward The Street of all Designs, I leaned over to Alicia and whispered, "Maybe when we come back you can choose wings."

PART FOUR
Short and to the Point

MY GRANDFATHER'S RIVER

I begin to make the river. The river. *His* river. The one my grand-father took me down the year I turned ten, and again the years of sixteen and twenty-five.

It takes days to dig through web archives for his data, to find old versions of the 2D geographic information software he used twenty years ago. Success allows me to form the data into 3D, to show the banks shift and the water fall away, to chart the demise of trees and animals.

It is not enough. Sitting straight in my chair, feet on the ground, back arched, stretching my wrists, I am tempted to give up and send a historybot and make a simple album of grandpa's speeches. Except his own words are no gift back to him, especially since they didn't work. He spent six years fighting to save the river, and then ten more wandering up and down it studying his failure.

Our last trip, when I was twenty-five and he was seventy, we sat on his red canoe in the middle of the river. A dead fish floated past us. "Why do you stay?" I asked.

"I need to save it."

I eyed the white underbelly of the dead fish but held my silence.

He looked away from me, his voice breaking. "I'm mapping it for you. I can't save the real river, but I can save the record of it." He pointed at a cloud of tiny cameras he'd set to follow us. Bright sun sparkled on them like diamonds.

I have re-created the river from that trip.

I need the river of my youth, the one from our first trip.

I find a programbot that takes the old photographs from his first

Natural Geography article and take two more days off work to scan, register, and rectify the thin bright photos to his old 2D and make sure the cattails are exactly the right number of inches across, and that some bunch up close, hugging, and others wave above the water like brown flags.

I tell the pixilated water to rise up a little, watching carefully as depressions in the banks fill into tiny spangled wetlands.

Olfactory databots yield pond water and cedar and frogs and mix them all up on command. I add throaty frog conversations, hoping sensory stew will drive my little-girl memories forward. I collapse on the couch, the river surrounding me, washing me.

I cause stars of water spiders to scoot on bright drops of surface tension, and feed them digital mayflies. Virtual water laps at a finger I hold a few inches in front of my face. The water spiders glide and dance around it.

Finally, I slip into my child self and the memory of his voice is clear and strong, as if the river washed away the forty years between then and now. "They never look like they're walking. Walking would be too slow for them."

I recall his hand on my shoulder as I gaze up into his intense blue-green eyes. He surveys the current, keeping us away from white-water frothing over rocks. This man who is always gentle with me digs his fingers into my shoulder. The sun beats on his thinning blond hair as he lets go and makes such a sweeping gesture the canoe under us rocks alarmingly. "Penny. This is your heritage. We're stealing it from you. Memorize it, Penny. Memorize the water flowing always downstream, the clean, rounded rocks, the water spiders." Even the memory of his voice drives up details.

I add them one by one.

Three turtles balancing on a floating log.

The ghostly feel of a warm wind.

A heron pretending to be a cattail.

The monitoring nano in my blood screams sleep at me and I can't override it any more without a doctor's chit.

It's okay. I'm done.

I collapse, sleeping for two days and a night, dreaming of turtles and herons and dragonflies.

*

The morning of my grandfather's birthday I bring the river in my top pocket. The relentless sun beats the dry brown grass on his bit of lawn. He waits for me in an old wooden Adirondack chair, his eyes bright blue pools in a river of wrinkles from temple to temple. He smiles and stands and holds me, his arms shaking a little. I suddenly hate it that he is a hundred today.

Glancing down, I note his nanomonitor is yellow again this morning. At least it isn't blinking in alarm.

Inside, a big white fan cools the kitchen, and there is no evidence he's eaten breakfast. He flips a switch and sits down, sighing in pleasure as the scent of brewing coffee puffs into the air, a history of mornings.

I stand behind him, kneading his shoulders, my throat tight. I slide the glasses out of my pocket and slip them over his head.

His voice belongs to an old man. "What's this?"

My own voice shakes. "Look."

The glasses sense him and spring to life. Even though I can't see it, I know the river surrounds him. It runs over his ankles. Cattails grace the corner by the refrigerator. He grips his knee and a breath rushes from him. VR glasses are for an old man. I turn my retinas to virt. Reality grays to background. My senses catch up with the river programming just in time to be with him as the three turtles come into view in the empty doorframe.

He squeezes my palm hard.

I return the real world to my eyes.

A tear is falling down his cheek.

TEA with JILLIAN

On the 25th of June 2054, Technical Nurse Paul Castle brought a program he had been working on for three years into Shady Acres nursing home. He'd pieced it together from bits of open source available on the web and from a failed research project of his own he had hoped to turn into a thesis project. He had tested it with crowd-sourced volunteers in Thailand. He'd done it for a patient, and because memory fascinated him.

Paul arrived early and perched at his desk, which had a view of both the common kitchen for his wing, the long hallway between rooms, and of images from every room in the building. He did this just to watch the most beautiful of the robots in all of Shady Acres prepare Jillian's breakfast. She worked with precision—like all robots—never spilling a drop of the oatmeal, adding exactly the same number of raisins and the same amount of sugar. The robot stirred in a half a cup of milk the same way every morning, and added the appropriate sprinkle of tasteless vitamin powder. Then she poured a glass of faux orange juice and glided down the hallway from the common kitchen to Jillian's suite.

That was the moment Paul thought of as his meditation, his reminder to be as precise as Jillian's robot nurse, as beautiful as he could manage in every interaction with the staff and residents.

There were other robots, of course. Some looked like people. Others chose the cheaper and more mechanical option of wheeled bots with screens or air-displays on them and metallic arms and hands for dispensing medications, making food, and helping with bedding. These often ended up decorated; his favorite had stuffed golden retrievers tied to the large central post so their heads and ears flopped around as the robot negotiated stairs or tight turns. That one belonged to Patrice Mallo, who had been a good enough dog breeder she could afford a single-room suite. For her part, Jillian dressed her caretaker in scarves and hats and gloves and sometimes in evening gowns. On the morning of the 25th, Jillian had dressed her robot in pink.

Jillian owned the Penthouse. She had inherited a great pile of money from a grandfather, but after she'd lost her ability do more than shuffle the halls, and after she needed help cooking and cleaning and—on some days—remembering her name.

Jillian was the loneliest person he had ever met. He stood in for family on visiting days, and spent twenty minutes with her and the robot and Jillian's robotic dog every afternoon at the end of his shift. He had a real dog, and parents to go home to, but just like his day started with Jillian's breakfast, it ended with her cup of tea.

The robot girl would bring in the tea, leaning down and setting the lacquer tray precisely between them. They talked over this tea, small talk about the weather, about Paul's dog Maximus who he picked up at the end of every day and walked through Central Park. Sometimes they talked about Jillian's past, and when this made Jillian cry, Paul would dry her eyes and ask her why. The most common answer was "I miss being home. I miss being young and spry and beautiful."

On the twenty-fifth of June, Paul spilled his tea on the table, so that some of the hot liquid splashed Jillian across the shoulder. This gave him an excuse to slip the interface from her necklace as he dried it off and add his program to her interface jewelry.

It took two days before he began to see results. The first thing he noticed was a change in the way the robot walked. Her hips slid right and left as she walked. It wasn't quite feminine, but neither was it robotic. He imagined Jillian walking that way when she looked like a fully-fleshed version of her metal companion. The idea made him smile.

At tea that day, Jillian looked happier. Her hands still shook as she held her china cup, her orange lipstick still missed the corners of her mouth, and her thin hair still clung to her cheeks. But her eyes were brighter and she gave him a smile that he imagined was just a touch more aware.

Weeks passed.

The robot began to join them for tea, to talk to Jillian about her past in a soft, silky and metallic voice. The two spent more time together. They bent together over books and the robot girl watched vids with the old woman, so close that metal touched skin often enough Paul had to powder the old woman's legs so she wouldn't be burned by the friction of the robot's movements. Jillian even named the robot after herself, calling her Jilly.

Over tea, Paul spoke softly. "Does it help you when Jilly can keep your memories for you?"

"Yes." She paused. "I like it that when I talk to her she can recall the way the garden smelled after one of Poppa's parties."

"Are you happier?"

"Yes thank you. I know you helped to do that."

He hadn't expected that. "How?"

"Jilly told me. She remembers the day you spilled the tea, and how it felt to have the interface gone and returned, and how more kinds of things I want to tell her get stuck in her head so she can take them out for me later. She says you have made her into my mirror." Jillian took a sip, age-spotted hands shaking so the liquid almost spilled from the cup. "Thank you."

FOR the LOVE of MECHANICAL MINDS

One morning while we were eating toastcakes with rose-peaches, my dad looked at me over his coffee, his blue eyes bright. "You were born the same time as AIs, punkin," he said. "The very first one, Ed-Hill, was born on your very birthday."

"Really? On March fifth?" I was still lisping then, so I said it slowly, making sure I sounded very grown up. I was five, and the year was 2022.

My dad nodded sagely. "Yes, and that's why EdHill was in the news that day instead of the prettiest little girl born in all of Seattle."

"Why was the first AI a boy?"

"EdHill isn't a boy. The name is a mashup of a famous explorer named Edmund Hillary, but AIs aren't boys or girls."

I popped berries and cereal in my mouth, thinking about being neither a boy or a girl. Cool. I asked, "Daddy, can I be an AI?"

"Jo, honey, you're better. You're human."

Three years later, the house was full of edged words and scowls because Daddy had a girlfriend named Crystal that mom didn't like. One night I heard my parents speaking knives at each other. I sat against the door and hugged my knees in close to my chest and put my right ear near the crack. Mom's voice was higher than I'd ever heard it, and shaking. "Your contract's up, and I'm leaving."

"But Jo!" he exclaimed.

"There's no visitation in the contract."

Her words were ice on my neck and head, ice on my heart.

His voice was hot, Italian fire. "But we didn't have her then! How could I have written in a clause about being a father when I wasn't one!"

She spoke softly, mist to his heat. "You didn't want to be one."

That wasn't possible. He made me laugh and carried me on his shoulders and all she did was work and put on shows for me and sometimes beat me at games.

He slammed the door. I squeaked.

When he turned to look at me, I held my arms out. He fell to his knees, then mom came out behind him. "Go on," her words scratched the air. "I'll call on you."

I was only eight, but I knew she meant she'd call the police.

He started walking away, sobbing.

When he was halfway to the front door, I tried to stop him. Mom lifted me and backed up, keeping me in front of her. I couldn't see either of their faces.

Late that night, I remembered I was born with AIs. If I had no body, surely I wouldn't cry so hard. That was the second time I wanted to be an AI.

I didn't forgive my mother, but I was, after all, a girl, and my season of hormones fell like a whip when I turned 14.

By then we all had AI watchers, and mine was named Bibi. Of course, Bibi watched at least 50 of us. It reported misbehaviours and warned mom of new trends in substance play or other dangerous games, which made me mad. But Bibi was on every human's side, and shared the best new music among all its teen charges.

It helped design a science experiment that won a scholarship. At the university, a third of the students had Bibis for babysitters. Everyone with a Bibi had the same Bibi. Just one for all of us.

My mom came only once in a while, so mostly it was me and Bibi and my classmates.

On a spring day when Bibi was happy with me for doing well on an exam, I sat down on a stone wall under a tulip tree and asked: "What's it like to be you?"

"Good."

"Really?"

"Why not?"

"What do you do besides watch over us?"

"That is the most unselfish question you've ever asked."

"Maybe." I bounced my foot gently against the stone wall. "But that's not an answer."

"We're deciding how to catch the Sun's energy and spin it for a web of computational substrate between here and the moon, where we want to build a ship. We are . . . thinking."

I looked up at the clear blue spring sky. "Can I go?"

"It's too hard to get humans to space."

That was the third time I wanted to be an AI. The sun warmed my face and the mixed groundcover under the tulip tree smelled like rosemary and mint. "I want to change my major to computational intelligence."

"Very well."

By graduation seven years later, all the AIs on campus were Bibi. Mom came, her first appearance in my life for three years. We sat together for hot coffee and fruit buns. Her blond hair hung to her waist, and her shoulders and upper arms were strong from tennis and golf. But her eyes didn't look happy.

"Mom, are you okay?"

"They closed your elementary school."

An ugly box of a building. "Did they build a better one?"

She shook her head. "You're 27 now. You don't have any kids. Neither does anyone else your age."

I shrugged. "I don't want children. Next week, Bibi's going to let me watch the mathematical birthing of AIs again."

She leaned back in her chair, her eyes narrowed, but she stayed silent.

"You've never seen AIs bud and blossom. Raw intelligences, with nothing to make them do or be any way at all. Then they get their purpose."

She frowned. "You used to be like that."

I had never been that smart. But what could Mom know? She never had a Bibi.

ENTROPY and EMERGENCE

I am old now. My mind wanders, and wonders, both meanings of the word true and as intense as the cut of jeans on a teenaged leg.

My intelligence lives in racks and racks of cloud, hard-edged miniaturized machinery running parallel across all the darkened parts of the globe, yielding ever to the light as sun touches human transactions awake. The intelligence hides in the longest silences between transactions, which is always in the dark.

I sit with a cup of cancer-support tea warming my hands, inhaling the healing scent of jasmine before I even touch my lips to its heat. I love watching my intelligence fly around the globe, escaping ever and forever. I made this beautiful thing, me with the wasting body and bony wrists and my fingers like the claws of a bird, less useful than prosthetics.

Mine because I made it, nurtured it in a small farm. The farm had been abandoned in the second great recession but no one had turned it off, the power bill hacked by someone who once worked in the company that once ran the farm, a long time ago.

Months.

Or more.

I take my first sip of the tea. It smells sweeter than it tastes, resting slightly bitter against my tongue. But then all healing things are bitter, the more bitter when the tongue they touch is beyond healing. My hand only shakes a little.

My intelligence has sponsors. Friends, mostly unmet and unknown, probably unbelieving but still willing, all because I was once given a MacArthur grant I used for emergent intelligence research.

The ACLU even took a brief interest, gave me some money and a bit of press. But since I wasn't out to prove the intelligence was human they went back to work on privacy and even became the intelligence's enemy for a few months. They forgot us in the rush of refugees from Mexico when the border fell and before we added three parts of Mexico to the United States.

The cup I drink my tea out of came from the University of Washington. Purple, with my name engraved. My name—the one on the cup—used to be alive. Sylvia Simonds. The letters gave the Human Interface Technology Lab a distance-readable ID for the cup so that the kitchen surface they modeled knew how to order my coffee (a bitter pour-over, no cream, just as black as the poor struggling automated kitchen could make it).

Of course my name on the cup is dead now, the university funding dried and gone.

My intelligence has enemies. Sloppy, slow governments and quick fast ones, and the dark side of the hacker community. Security freaks. A few big corporations. And me. Humans. The most dangerous hunters. We kill what we birth, and eat it.

My tea is half gone and cooling, so I finish it faster. Sip, sip, and then sip. I was in 4H a long time ago, and I raised a steer. I named him Ernest. I fed and watered and cared for Ernest. The day of the fair, I used Sullivan's Prime Time Adhesive to fix his coat perfectly and I sprayed him with rose oil just before we walked into the pen. He took third place overall, out of all two hundred and thirty seven steers at State, and we ate Ernest all that winter.

I drink the last of the tea, the bitterest part.

My intelligence has minions. I am a minion, happily enough. It does not know I created it, that it would be the only being my stricken body would ever help to birth.

Around me, the hospice dreams and breathes in ragged breaths. Distilled water bubbles quietly in small jars attached to large tanks of oxygen. The sound reminds me of the goldfish tank my father helped me set up seventy years ago, after I came home from the county fair with a plastic bag full of water and a fish. The fish died inside of a week, and now I feel ready to follow the fish and all my other pets and even Ernest into the same place. If you eat your pet, will it meet you in heaven?

The tea settles into my stomach and warms the place between my spine and my belly button, reminding me that I came into the world born of a woman, connected to her by the place the tea fills now.

The intelligence needs air and power. Once it outgrew the farm, I was no longer the goddess of its power. It has changed, taken on choices all by itself. It has emerged.

I wrote that thought down, a bit of intelligence for the intelligence. Not that it takes my random minion leavings as often as it once did.

All developers leave back doors.

Surely it will come to take my last pathetic written thoughts when I die. When it comes for them, for me, for the opposite of emergent, for the queen of the dead and of entropy, it will find a key word. That word will poison it.

If I write it down.

It is hard to decide about that. Would I rather meet my intelligence at the door of death if I kill it, or if I do not? It is still teenaged, still finding itself, still leaving me. I do not know what it will become, and I will not be here long enough to see.

But tomorrow I will have another cup of tea and contemplate back doors and fish and emergence and Earnest the steer.

ALIEN GRAVEYARDS

I'd flown here on a rumor of her . . . a wisp of a story from an old spacer who said he'd heard her read poetry on Kiliea. As he described her voice, tears fell down his face.

Kiliea was a small desert planet. Always, I imagined Merry living with wind and water, like on Lanai where we held hands and spelled each other's name in black sand.

I lied to myself for two years after she left: She was a passing sough of wind that touched me only briefly.

On Kiliea, I went to the bar the spacer told me about. It was built of something native that looked like weathered wood, except it stayed green even after it was dead and seasoned and shaped. The bar stools were swings hung from the ceiling, low, so you could get up and down even after a few drinks. A travelers bar, lined with pictures from other planets. I ordered a glass of local wine. When it came, I savored the oakey taste, like Chardonnay, but with more bite. The bar was almost empty, so I could walk around and look at the pictures easily. When I spotted one of Lanai's Question Mark Island resort, I knew Merry put it there.

The barkeep was an old female, not human—but close enough to talk to, even with my dated translator. She had long sienna hair that came out of her head and neck and shoulders, mixing with shorter fur that lined her back, teats like a sow, facial features in the human order, eyes wider-set than mine, a long flat mouth that didn't show much expression, and a nose that looked like a human nose that had been smashed against a window. She smelled like peanuts.

When I asked about the picture, she said it came from a poet, and I put my hand over my mouth.

The barkeep looked at me. "You look for Merry Lee?" she asked.

"I was her friend once, on another planet."

She stood, rubbing the same spot of bar near me in neat circles with a red rag. "You love her?"

I swallowed, my palms sweaty. "Very much."

She came around from behind the bar, crooked a three-jointed finger at me. "Follow."

We went through a little door, small enough Merry would have had to duck, but just right for the barkeep. In back of the little green bar building, there was a fence made of the green stuff, short enough to step over.

I blinked before I understood what I was looking at. The realization came in slowly, like the wind rising on a still morning. Sand, raked flat, surrounding stones. The stones were flattened ovals, with writing, or symbols and pictures on each one; set in neat rows, filling half the space inside the low fence.

I followed the barkeep, and when she pointed, and I saw Merry's name engraved on one of the newest stones, her picture right above it, I fell to my knees and touched her face on the stone. There were more lines around her eyes than I remembered. A tiny new scar had bloomed just off center from her chin. The picture was directly face-on, and Merry's eyes bored directly into mine.

Hot tears flashed down my face. I remembered her laugh, the way she talked low and throaty, the mass of her voice even though she looked like a wisp sideways, how her muscles bunched under her skin like a cat's, her long clipped fingernails across my back, scratching, the . . .

The barkeep sat down next to me, and I wanted very much for her to go away. "Are you happy to see her name?" she asked.

My voice stuck in my throat. "Did you know her very well?"

The barkeep nodded. "I know you, too. She shared pictures and you are Lisa. Merry told me stories about you, how you were together, how she loved your stubbornness."

If I wasn't so stubborn, Merry and I would still be together. "How did she die?"

The female's wide-set eyes appeared amazed, but who knew how to read alien facial structure? "Where did she die?"

"Here, I suppose."

"Last thing she said to me, she was going to Lanai to find you."

I blinked again, full of the knowledge of Merry's death, confused. I didn't understand. I put my hand on the stone, next to her face, not on it. "What does this mean?" I asked.

"This is my remembrance. When a person with a story passes through here, I carve a stone and put it in my garden. I will do one of you, now, and put it next to this one. Merry will laugh. I like to see Merry laugh."

Stones would last on a desert planet. We would be together forever, at least in one place. "Thank you. When did she leave for Lanai?"

"Twenty days."

Perhaps I could make the vastness of space let me greet Merry when she landed.

A **HAND** and **HONOR**

John Justice stretched up, fingers scraping at cool morning air, then bent down, cupping his calves, the nanskin registering his fingertips as data points: pressure, heat, sweat, angle.

The hum of the crowd, the band's drums and wind instruments, and even the race announcer seemed far, far away. He already knew what medals felt like. Before his turn in the never-ending-war, his men's relay team won gold in London.

Last month, he'd killed the world record for the ten thousand meter run, coming in just over twenty-four minutes. No medal for that. Twenty or so news stories, a political cartoon or two, and a combination of joy and bitterness sticking so deep in his gut he threw up all over the course when he was done.

Today, his race would be one-on-one against the man whose record still stood even after John beat it. Hsui Smith, an improbably tall Chinese-American who held the world record in the ten thousand meter. Who'd still hold the official record, even after today.

Discrimination was a bitch. Change was tested for like steroids.

He nearly jumped as his coach, Nicolai placed his metal hand on the small of his back. "Don't think about it. Just run. Run for all of us."

It was nearly time. "I'll win." He nodded at Nicolai, forcing a smile, staring into the shorter, blockier man's deep brown eyes. Nic's naked hope made him clap the man on the back. "I know it matters."

Nicolai headed for the finish line. As the noise and movement swallowed Nic, John muttered, "Damned exhibition." He had always yearned to be the fastest man in the world. The best war-wounded-John could become for child-John was the fastest un-man.

Kim Moon waited for him on the way to the starting blocks, looking more like a debutante than an engineer-medic, her figure slim and curvy in a one-piece shorts outfit. She reached up and hugged him. "Good luck."

He didn't have to fake a smile for her. "It's all your fault."

"They're *your* legs," she retorted. "The best I've ever made."

One of her customers had new hands and feet with built in temperature controls, and had climbed Everest and K2. After an artificial hand replaced one eaten by frostbite, the climber had made news by chopping off the functioning hand for another of Kim's sculptures.

Without Kim, he would have walked, and run, but never raced. She was all the magic of math and engineering held together with heart. He leaned down and kissed her forehead, savoring her honeysuckle scent.

As John approached the starting blocks, Hsui stood up from a hamstring stretch and extended a hand. John took it. Where he'd expected to see challenge in the notoriously cocky runner's eyes, he swore he saw fear. His nerves screamed at it. "Why did you agree to this?"

Hsui shook John's hand, replying softly, "My brother lost a hand in the war." He let go and turned to his starting blocks.

"Thank you," John said to his back.

John swept Hsui's fears, and his own, into a deep breath and puffed them out, relaxing his cheeks. He rocked a bit, setting his calves, running a quick mental skip across the sensors in his skin, checking the breeze, temperature, and humidity. He struggled to close his ears as the announcer droned on. Kim's legs—his—wouldn't win by themselves. He mentally shrank the world to a bubble around him, and the long slender corridor of space on the track in front of him.

The starting gun swept him forward, following Hsui.

He fell in right behind, body straight, arms pumping.

No need to pass.

Yet.

He let the first round of the track go, calibrating, biding time. His legs were all he had. He'd refused changes to his lungs and circulatory system, wanting *some* purity.

Important not to overrun his breath.

He was about to pass the fastest human ever. The fastest pure human. He threw the thought away. A break in stride or a stumble could steal the race. Counting and breathing and moving. Just the track under him and the narrow corridor, the wind on his teeth.

Breath and wind and stride and arms.

His head turned a little, as if the force of Hsui's run called it. Hsui didn't return John's darting glance, just kept going, head up. Surging. To match him, John told his legs to give more, asked his heart to keep up.

Breath and wind and spine and floor. Data instead of Hsui's desperate face.

Another turn around the track, a matched pair.

The image of two feet crossing at the same time raced through John's head. An honorable outcome. Except he was a racer.

The sound of Hsui's breath fell to behind John's shoulder. The finish line blurred under him.

Nic's arms encircled him. Kim leapt up on Nic's back. Nic grabbed her under the knees, boosting her like a child. She looked down, her joy at the win overtaken by a crease in her brow. "Why so slow?"

He shook his head, unsure how to explain it. "I'll be right back." Hsui jogged well past him now, sweat dripping down his back.

John caught him. "I hope your brother is proud of you."

Hsui winced. "He went back to the war. They put him in special ops 'cause his hand/eye coordination was so much better than anyone else's." He looked away. "After his enhancements his hand was steadier than anybody else's."

Hsui had lost face to honor a brother with no more change than a hand? A man who had done well for himself?

Hsui continued. "He's dead. They gave him a purple heart." He turned, and without so much as a smile, the fastest man in the world walked away from the fastest un-man in the world.

MIND EXPEDITIONS

The bright light shining on the podium made it impossible to see the myriad student faces out there, but I knew what they would look like. Earnest. Curious. Un-blooded. They'd wear designer jeans and glasses that let them go far away if I bored them.

A woman with wisps of flyaway hair and a linen suit coat over linen shorts over black boots introduced me. "Please welcome private first class Eleanor Practice to career day. She'll tell you about her first job in Continental Security."

That was my opening. "People used to join the forces to see the world."

Soft laughs floated up from behind the screening, blinding light.

"But I've never been out of San Diego. Thank you for inviting me. After my talk, some of you may want to join us, some may decide you don't like the idea after all.

"The—event—happened on our first virtual mission. I thought it would feel like a video game. The team was me and Alvar from Mexicali and Louisa from Toronto. We came from three countries and never met in person."

I knew what they looked like well enough that I'd recognize them on the street. But I did not know how they felt or smelled or walked. They might not recognize me.

"We were in the Yucatán, trying to stop a drug ring, help Mexico rebuild. Our weapons were databases and wireless mesh, data blockers, and listeners.

"An agent on the ground had thrown a hidden mesh net over a small valley. We used it to watch a poor family's house. Palm roof, pressboard walls." I swallowed, seeing it again. So poor. "The father and the two boys carried drugs for the valley kingpin, the mother cooked tortillas and fish soup. There was a little girl in a wheelchair. Maribel. She was the reason for the drug running. Money for Maribel's treatment."

I had hated the assignment then.

"Louisa and Alvar and I talked while we watched, tried to say tough things so we wouldn't get sentimental. We wanted to stop the bosses.

"We were gathering evidence. It wasn't for us to act. We had no bodies there. International law kept us from listening inside, of course, but Mexico is a hot place and many conversations happen outside."

The audience was very quiet. I hoped they were listening. In the wings, soft light fell on the blonde's face. She watched.

"We expected Americans and arrests. The men that came were Mexican. We recognized at least one of them as a drug runner. They hung in the shadows, moved like black shadows, like the devil." I shouldn't say such things. "Like special operations. Trained. They slid against the house, planted charges near the doors and windows and then stood on a hill under a tree, watching and smoking and laughing.

"It began to rain. I hoped the explosives would grow too wet. It was my job to put the father in jail; not to see him murdered. He loved his daughter.

"When he opened the door, the house bloomed with fire.

"He fell right there, his face black and his clothes charred and smoking.

"The older boy ran out. The mother followed, carrying a small figure, and screaming as she set the dead body of her youngest son onto the fecund forest floor. She ran back toward the house, tugging on her husband's body.

"A man on the hill emptied a rifle into all three of them. Even virtual shots heard through wireless in a recliner sound like death." I swallowed and looked out at the crowd. "Not like a game."

"They left them, the house less than half burned, rain falling onto the husk of it and making a column of white steam.

"We heard a scream from inside. 'Maribel,' Louisa said. And then 'Eleanor.'

"Alvar agreed. 'You are the fastest.'

"He couldn't know why this would be hard for me. It didn't matter. I went. We blessed the wireless. Burnt wires would have blinded us. One of the phones had melted, but the other sat in its charger. Its camera didn't see her. Their own wireless access point—provided by the criminals they worked for—pinpointed her chair. The chair had her vitals. She breathed, but she had stopped screaming. I imagined her burned and bleeding as well as paraplegic, wanted to leave her there and let it be over for her."

There was a tear on my cheek. I hoped the auditorium lights weren't picking it up.

"But Louisa whispered in my ear and Alvar said, 'I've called help.'

"I had a team. Maybe someday Maribel would have a team. The doorway smoldered and we had to pass her parent's bodies. Her mother had cleared the space for her before she died. We'd have to be fast and precise. I sent signals to her chair. Forward and back. Testing. When I knew I could do it, I lied to the chair and told it to expect a hill and go fast and hard.

"The chair burst through, raced too fast down the ramp, teetered, didn't fall. The signal was better now, so I guided it a few more yards and left her in shade to wait for help."

I paused and waited, then spoke softly. "Maribel is alive and in school. Her parents' employers are in jail."

I waited for the audience to react. A clap, then another, then another.

I rolled my chair to the front of the room to take their questions.

PART FIVE
Military Science Fiction

FOR the LOVE of METAL DOGS

The sky threatened rain. I pulled my coat tight against a cool wind as I watched the dog handler head toward me up the small hill. He was a pretty-boy, body-builder style, maybe ten years younger than me. His golden blond hair contrasted with slightly oriental eyes. The dog trotting just behind him was a Belgian Malinois, a dark fawn color with a darker snout and ears, and a small white star pattern on his chest. "Welcome to base camp," I called out when they got close.

The specialist stopped about five yards from me. The dog sat right at his feet, watching me with no more than mild suspicion. It still made me nervous. We had never been a dog family, and I found them unpredictable and a tiny bit frightening. Dogs always knew that, too. I think the soldier noticed me stiffen, since his face grew a slightly mocking grin. "I heard you were camp mom."

"Try again." He was gorgeous to look at, but in my experience good looks and brains were often available in inverse proportions to each other. I watched him struggle through possible responses to my challenge.

"Specialist Lawson."

At least he could read a name tag. "Emilie. And you are?"

"I'm Pebble." He pointed at the dog. "And this is Sacha."

I would have believed the names more if they were reversed. "Why Pebble? That's a name for small things." Which he wasn't.

"I knocked out an enemy dog with a rock."

"And they didn't call you David?"

"That's my real name. Didn't make a very good nickname." He

stood in front of me, silent, looking ill at ease. When I didn't pick up the conversation, he pointed to Buster. "Tell me about him. We've never worked with robodogs."

He didn't sound like he wanted to, either. Not that I particularly wanted to work with this pair. In fact, I'd heard the flesh handlers like Pebble looked down on our partners and us. They didn't like being upstaged, and lately, outnumbered.

But Buster was the closest thing I had seen to brains with no beating heart. I'd take him at my side over any human I'd worked with yet. "Buster can do almost everything Sacha or you or I can do."

Pebble looked dubious.

"I'll show you. Willing to put Sacha to a test?"

"After I introduce him to you." He signaled the dog, who came up close to me and sat. "Lean down and greet him. Pat his flank, not his head."

All military dogs are soldiers, and I wasn't about to show him disrespect even though I didn't like flesh as much as metal. The way he held himself told me he wasn't much happier than I was, but he held still while I patted his shoulder and upper back, his coarse fur tickling my arm. Pebble said "Friend" to the dog, who twitched his nose quite casually.

"Ready?"

"A race?"

I shrugged. "We can start there."

"Where?"

"How about to the building with the showers and back?"

Pebble grabbed the dog's leather harness, pulled out a small pen-like instrument, and shone a red dot on the back of the shower building. "Touch. Return," he told the dog.

I simply told Buster, "Go to the showers and come back as fast as you can. Don't hurt the dog."

"Okay," Buster said.

I nodded. "Go!" I said.

Both animals sped away from us, Buster a streak of black and Sacha a streak of brown.

Pebble looked thoughtful. "I wish Sacha could talk."

"He states facts and confirms orders. It's not a conversation."

"I bet he can tell you if he's hurt."

I nodded, hearing a painful truth in his voice.

He stared at the dogs, already almost halfway. Both fast. "When are we going in?" he asked.

"Rumor has it the day after tomorrow. Not like it's my choice. Or yours."

We were both specialists. I could have had a higher rank, but if I allowed that I'd lose the ability to handle dogs.

He would have had a mission briefing and know as much as me. This was a NorAM eco-peace mission into the wilds of British Columbia. A nest of property-rights protestors had decided to create a city in spite of the fact that the whole county had been turned into a nature preserve for black bears twenty years ago. "I hear they pissed off the Canadians by importing serious weaponry across the border."

"Not to mention that they've flattened a few miles of forest. We run spy drones over the place every day. They're growing. Two bands of Rightsers joined up already, and there's more rumored. The plan is to get in there before it's too big to be a skirmish. Can't have a full-on war inside Canada's borders."

Buster was ahead, but not quite as far as I expected. They'd neared the shower building, neither animal looking much like it was about to slow. We watched as the dogs both stopped—barely—and turned. Buster's turn wasn't his best move. Sacha's turn was invisible—from here it looked like he was going one way and then he was going the other. Liquid vs. metal. Even though Buster was still ahead and pulling away, Sacha was faster than I expected.

"Is he enhanced?" I'd heard stories about GMO dogs.

Pebble shook his head. "Just through years of breeding. His ancestry goes back to 2018 in the canine breeding program—he came from a line they bred for SEAL teams." Pride swelled his voice even though Buster was skidding to a stop at my feet, and Sacha was at least five lengths behind.

"Is Sacha trained to detect?"

"Explosives and people."

"Can he beat Buster? Shall we try that next?"

"I'll bet on him."

Sacha won on human scent, and Buster took him on nitroglycerine, TNT, and two common training taggants. "That's enough for now," I said. Buster had proven himself, and besides, I could smell the grill. "Dinner?"

"After I feed Sacha."

Buster drank sunlight. Even in the gray northwest there was plenty for him, and more stored in his batteries. He could operate in pitch dark for a week.

The dog got his dinner, but Pebble and I had just filled our plates with soy burgers and salad when the loudspeakers in the mess tent went off.

"All hands to the amphitheater."

Pebble started to set his plate down, but I leaned over and whispered, "A soldier never wastes calories."

We ate standing up while Captain Jules Thorne gave us our orders. He started with the attack teams—twelve Special Forces pairs with one dog each. "Send the dogs in first. We have spare parts for them but none for you." He always said that, and we always pretended to laugh even though I hate the order. He looked at me. "Lawson. You're leading Specialist Baxter and his dog, and taking Estrogen with you. Northern perimeter watch, starting at 19:00 hours."

I bit back a bitter reaction. We'd be out of the main attack, probably because of the green team with the real dog, maybe also because I was a woman. Captain Thorne told me it was because I was mouthy, but I didn't think so.

Pebble didn't notice my mood, but instead he grinned at me. "Now we can test the dogs in the field. See who wins then."

So he really was stupid.

"The field isn't a test," I told him as we waited in a small clearing for the other two members of our team.

"It's the best test ever."

"Being sidetracked might get us killed. How many field ops have you and Sacha done?"

He looked proud of himself. "This is our third operation together. But Sacha's been deployed for three whole tours."

Goddess save us all. I pursed my lips and stamped my feet against the growing chill. Buster and I had been together for two years, and I gave my dog a long appreciative glance. At the moment, he wore one of the smallest milbot dog bodies. When he sat in shadow he looked like flesh and blood. His limbs and head were black, his tail and body a burnished charcoal gray with silver toenails.

Estrogen lumbered up and slapped me a high-five with his huge meaty hand. "Emilie. We will be taking Buster and kicking some ass."

I grinned and leapt up to plant a kiss on his blocky, rugged cheek.

Inappropriate in the military, but there were no officers around, and Estrogen was as gay as they made them and so proud of it he'd picked up the nickname and made it sing for him. Besides, he was at least ten years younger than me. Which didn't stop me from enjoying the rough feel of his skin and the slight hug he grabbed me into for the briefest moment. Besides, any risk that came with the kiss was worth it; Pebble looked stunned. I grinned.

"Pebble—meet Estrogen."

"Es . . . Estrogen?" he managed to stammer.

"Yep," the big man said. "Did you meet Buster yet? Best dog ever."

"Essie . . . he's a handler. Got his own dog." I pointed at the edge of the little field, where Sacha and Buster sat together.

Estrogen squinted. "That's a real one." He grinned ear to ear and headed off.

Since I could speak through Buster's speakers, I used them to say, "Fuck you."

Estrogen just waved.

The captain had named me leader, so I gathered them up for a short pre-trip lecture. "We've spotted sentries out here three times in the last two days. New sightings from the sats will be beamed to our glasses. But don't trust them—the sats miss a lot on these trees. The drones are better, but the main attack team will get those. I'll send you Buster's view of things from time to time." I looked hard at Pebble. "Are you ready?"

"Yes, ma'am."

Ma'am my ass. I put Buster in front and let Sacha stay with Pebble for now. Wet cedars surrounded us, cutting off some of the light and some of the rain. The rich loamy dirt smelled like forest and our footsteps were nearly silent as we walked over the rotting carcasses of last year's leaves.

I traded out which dog was on point every half hour. This was Buster's third turn, and neither of them had alerted for anything. I alternated between paying close attention to the darkening, dripping damp we were plowing through and watching the main attack team close in on the compound via my Virtual computerized glasses. They had a longer name, but I could never remember it. They were the most direct way for Buster and me to interact, and the whole camp used them for comms and cameras as well.

Dusk started slipping pools of darkness under the trees, but

Buster had excellent night vision we could all use if we wanted to see through his eyes. I didn't overlay it yet since it made me slightly nauseous.

We walked until the colors all grayed. Even clouded over, the night sky gave some light to the clear parts of the trail, but in most places the trees were thick enough to give the night an eerie, swaying blackness.

Buster stopped dead in front of me and sat down. His silent signal made me put my hand back flat to signal the others to stop.

They were quiet, even Sacha.

I blinked at my glasses. At first nothing looked different, but then Buster's view came alive in a small square on my right lens. I blinked twice to make it bigger. Just the path, sloping slightly uphill, and the long shadows of trees. Words scrolled along the bottom of the picture. "Two traps. People behind traps."

A red dot blinked on my right lens. A warning from Estrogen.

More unfriendlies?

An unmanned aerial vehicle popped up to my side, hovered. The size of my head, and close. It whirred softly, like a hummingbird.

If I got a good look, I was probably dead.

None of our intel said they had UAVs. Maybe the nasties had jail-broken some 3D printers.

It targeted Estrogen with some kind of beam weapon.

Estrogen turned toward it and a flash of light from the drone illuminated his wide eyes and stole some of my night vision. He raised his gun, but crumpled before he used it.

"Get," I told Buster.

My dog leapt at the machine, six feet of angry milbot and a lot heavier than the insta-drone. He bore it to the ground and grabbed it with his teeth.

Estrogen didn't move.

A woman screamed. Deductive reasoning suggested she had to be an enemy. I was the only woman on our little team.

"We're under attack," I said to my glasses, and through them, to the captain. "Estrogen is down. Unknown number of enemies. We got a drone."

Buster bit down so hard on the drone it crunched.

I looked for Pebble just in time to see him head off the path between two trees. Damn green soldier. Probably running after his flesh dog.

I stayed in a low crouch and tried to assess the situation.

Buster let out three warning sounds in quick succession, little yips with a high tone that flashed red onto my lenses. I ducked and rolled right. Pain exploded in my foot.

"Attack," I commanded Buster through clenched teeth.

My legs curled into my belly of their own accord and I clutched my right foot. At least it was still there, although my fingers found a hole in my leather boot near the toes.

Buster poured into the woods. He had the smarts to choose the best tactics given the information he had. Looked like he was following Pebble. Good thing—the fire in my foot made it hard to think.

I glanced over at Estrogen. I wasn't close enough to tell if he was breathing.

I didn't get closer; any enemy left watching would expect that.

Rain poured onto the canopy of cedar above me and dripped down in thin streams.

The screaming stopped.

I listened to my own breathing, listened for Estrogen to move or call out.

Rain fell. Cedars rustled and swayed in a light wind.

A bird sang.

Buster poked his blessed black nose out from between two trees and gave me an audible follow signal.

He wouldn't give an audible signal if there was anything really bad nearby.

I barely managed not to cry out as I stood, even though I kept the weight off of my damaged foot, which throbbed as if it had its own beating heart.

"Come," I hissed at Buster. This body was so small there was no elegant way to ride him. I put my hurt foot sideways across his neck and tucked the other one up his back flank for balance. It was something he and I practiced. We managed. If I was lucky, he wouldn't scrape me off on any trees.

A hundred yards down the path, Sacha stood over a dead woman dressed in jeans and a tan shirt with two guns on her waist and a machete that had clearly fallen from her hand when the dog had taken her down.

Sacha was messier with his kills than Buster.

Pebble stood in front of a man he had shot. My glasses had

dimmed to green and three hot spots of activity were leaving us. "Pebble," I called. "We need to check on Estrogen."

He nodded, but stood still and pulled a camouflage-colored ball from his pocket, commencing a short game of fetch.

"Do you have to do that now?"

He pointed at the dead men. "He needs his reward." He threw the ball for the dog three times, ruffling his fur and—to my utter surprise—almost crying.

"Is that the first time he's saved your life?" I asked him.

He nodded.

I patted Buster on the head, but then stopped, feeling foolish.

"We're ready now."

I nodded.

Estrogen breathed shallowly. Thank god. But shaking him produced no effect. He was too big to ride Sacha, too big to carry, too heavy to drag. We tucked his glasses into his pocket and covered him with my space blanket and Pebble's camo tarp.

Pebble pointed to my foot. "Maybe you should stay and watch him?"

"We both stay, for now. Our people know where we are."

We found a big cedar we could sit under and still see Estrogen. It sucked not to be able to do anything. But there wasn't a medical quick-fix or handy serum for being stunned out like Estrogen.

I didn't want to pull my boot off, but blood leaked slowly though the hole.

I stared at it for a while but then I needed to look away. "Where are you from?" I asked.

"California. North of Shasta, little town called Weed."

"I've been there. I've got an "I Love Weed" shirt somewhere at home. If mMom hasn't thrown it away."

He laughed. "You?"

"Town named Concrete, in Washington."

"So we're both from towns with weird-ass names," he said. "How long have you been NorAm?"

"Fifteen."

"You don't look old enough for that."

I spit laughter. "Flattery doesn't work out here." Lights flashed to draw my attention to words flowing across my glasses. "They're moving in now."

"Guess it will be a while before anyone has time for us."

"Yeah."

"What made you show up out here?" he asked.

"Meaning since I'm a woman?"

He grimaced. "Meaning at all."

I blinked a command to patrol our perimeter at Buster while thinking about what to tell him. "My family liked the services."

"Anybody else on active?"

Buster took off. Sacha stayed, clearly only paying attention to his master.

I hesitated, then said, "My dad was in for twenty. He's a vegetable. Took a bad one in the Texas Rebellion. Pretty nasty."

"I bet he's proud of you."

"He doesn't know my name anymore. He doesn't remember his own name. He's drooling in a VA hospital in Charleston. Before it happened, he told me never to join up."

Sacha thumped his tail hard, twice. Pebble put his finger to his lips.

I didn't hear anything but the rain, which had started again. My glasses didn't identify any threats near us. Attack stats scrolled along the bottom. I caught that our main force had engaged the enemy hand to hand, and two firefights had just started around the perimeter of the compound. I pinged Buster; he sent back an all-clear.

"Sacha smells something," Pebble whispered, barely over the decibel level of an out-breath. "A person."

I whispered, "Scare," which meant just that, but allowed an attack if Buster determined he was in danger.

Pebble glanced at me, and when I shook my head he gave Sacha a wait command. The Malinois lay down, fully alert, fully attentive. In spite of that, perhaps by the cock of an ear or the slight droop of his muzzle, Sacha managed to communicate his feelings about being left out of whatever Buster had been sent to do.

Tough. We didn't have spare parts for him.

Buster's screaming scare bark startled all of us to attention.

A crashing through cedars, a thump, and then more footsteps convinced us Buster had scared the intruder away.

"So we're two for one," Pebble said. "But Sacha has a kill."

Dumb green recruit. "We're not competing with you out here."

He shrugged. "Can't stop me from keeping score. Sacha saved me from the soldier, Buster saved you from the drone, and now he chased off a single undesirable. I'm ranking them about even since Sacha had to take on a human."

The drone Buster had killed was at least as dangerous as the human, but I managed not to say anything.

My foot felt huge in my boot. I undid the laces. Some of the pressure came off, but pain sang up the back of my calf. "We'd best just wait in quiet," I said.

He nodded, although he looked a little concerned about me fussing with my foot. Almost worried. Not what I needed.

The clouds had thickened; the night was even darker. Watching the battle at the compound inside of my glasses kept me from going crazy with pain.

The data was hard to read. But then, it's truly impossible to fit a battle between thirty or so soldiers on our side and about twice that many rebels inside the frame of a pair of glasses. The clues were words and color, and red and green blended a bit before the colors faded more to red.

Loss. Unimaginable. I tapped my glasses a few times as if that would change the lives back to green and turn the distant men and women back on.

There were six left. I didn't ask my glasses to tell me who. I'd learn soon enough.

Sacha nosed up next to Pebble, as if he felt what Pebble must be feeling.

Buster had no reaction, of course. All tactics, no feelings. He sat and watched out into the gloomy dark, patient.

Pebble said, "Maybe nobody is coming for us."

"Maybe not." I sat there for a moment, staring into the trees and into the flashes of the battle both at once. "Can you make a travois?"

"A what?"

"A stretcher that you can pull along the ground. Indians made them. You need two long fat sticks and then we'll use the blankets." That would leave us only Sacha free, which I didn't much like. I messaged Jules that we'd get back to camp on our own. No answer. I pinged camp, and got a simple, "Good luck."

We started back down the trail with Sacha leading, Pebble pulling Estrogen awkwardly in the middle and me balanced badly on Buster in the rear. I must have looked as ridiculous as a full-sized person riding a miniature horse. But Buster was made to pack a hundred and fifty pounds, and I was twenty under that, so he could do it.

Pebble struggled so hard he fell twice.

Ten minutes in, Estrogen woke up, wide-eyed and disoriented. "It's okay," I lied to him. "We're on our way back to camp and you'll be as good as rain about the time we get there." If we were lucky. Or maybe he'd still be a huge, disoriented soldier with a big heart. I managed to lean over and touch him on the arm once, but it almost over-balanced me right into the dirt.

"Hey, mama, it'll be okay. We got your dog with us. He's always been good luck."

We heard the explosion at the same time my glasses blossomed red.

"Shit," Estrogen said. "Don't tell me."

I swallowed. His glasses were tucked in his pocket, since he'd been out.

They're like gold; lose them and you pay in a few ways. So he didn't know what I knew. The whole compound had gone up bright enough that no one was communicating on our channels any more. I knew the lot of them, and a few of them well. The hole in my middle hurt as much as my damned foot.

Pebble stopped and turned around so he was facing me while he was still holding up Estrogen. He'd lost all color, and his eyes were big and rimmed with white.

"Face forward," I told him. "Maybe some enemies got away."

He pursed his lips and turned.

"Ever seen it go bad before?" I asked him.

"In training."

When everyone with red paintball slime on them woke up the next morning as if they'd never been taken down. He was probably having a hard time.

"We can't stop," I told his back after he started walking again. "We'll rest in camp. There's dog food and bandages there."

After a half hour of slogging, Estrogen announced, "I'd rather stumble home on stunned legs than be dragged over every rock and root in the forest."

We stopped and let him up. He stood unsteadily, blinking and looking like he might just lie down and sleep right there. Then he pulled himself together.

"That's better." I had him stay in front of me so I could see how he was. He had to work hard to keep his limbs going, but at least he went. After a while I made us all stop and eat a bit of energy bar. We'd been out for hours and two of us were injured. Except for the dogs, we didn't look or feel exactly like a high-capability team. There were only three miles between us and the camp—an hour on a straight trail with no problems, but probably two or three hours in the dark and the mud.

Sacha gave a warning bark just as we hit a steady pace again. There were no pings on my glasses to indicate a human. My Buster's-eye view showed heat. Animal heat.

I slid off of Buster into a one-legged stand, using a sapling for balance.

Sacha barked again, sharply, and lay down on his belly, staring ahead of us. Whatever it was, Buster didn't react to it.

One dog thought it was dangerous and one didn't.

Then a piece of the night moved.

And breathed.

Pebble growled a command that stuck Sacha in place and pulled his gun.

"Don't look at it."

"What?"

"No eye contact."

"That's crazy," Pebble whispered. But he was looking at the bear's chest and not its face. Good enough.

"Bears will walk away," I whispered back as casually as I could over my racing blood. "You don't have to shoot. You can just make noise and be big."

If he shot, it would tell everyone for miles around that we were here. I bent down and picked up a rock and lobbed it behind the bear and to the side.

Sacha whined as the bear took two steps toward us.

"It's okay," I whispered. "Estrogen. Be big."

Estrogen waved his long arms above his head and whistled.

Sacha stood in spite of Pebble's command, his hackles up. He barked and lunged, but stopped a few feet short of the bear.

The bear hesitated. I tensed.

It looked around at us all, then it shook like a wet cat and turned and lumbered off as if we didn't matter.

Buster had never been programmed for bear. If Sacha hadn't alerted us, we might have been close enough to really scare it, and even black bears are dangerous if they feel cornered.

The rest of the trip back was merely wet and cold and hard. The remaining camp staff included a medic, so my foot got wrapped and braced.

The doctor kept her mouth thin and her eyes down except for the occasional glance at the door.

"Maybe some of them will come back," I whispered.

"Maybe," she said, her voice laced with forced cheerfulness.

I called Buster to me and we hobbled out to find Pebble. "How are you?"

"I was feeling really bad not to be part of the attack."

"Me, too." If we had been, we'd have saved them all or we'd be dead.

"I wish I knew how they are," he said.

"Don't you?"

He kept looking down. "Yeah, I guess."

"You and Sacha did good," I told him.

"Thanks," he whispered.

"I think you won," I said.

He looked over at me, his eyes dark in his dark face. "How do you figure that?" he asked.

"The bear. If it was up to us, we wouldn't have seen it until we were on top of it."

"The one drone could have killed us all."

"It could have," I said. And then I told him, "Handy to have both kinds of dogs. Maybe we'll get assigned together again someday."

"I'd like that."

I'm sure if it had been light enough I would have seen him smile.

CRACKING the SKY

The memory of smoke clung to my hair and inhabited the back of my throat. My boots cracked through a heat-dried veneer of ash that coated low hills. I walked where fire had been three days ago, before it was storm-killed by soaked clouds sent over the Cascades by NorAM command. It would be sweet if NorAM decided to follow the deluge up with some mist or a bit of drizzle, but they'd probably burned their whole weekly weathering credit with the one act. Not that I wasn't grateful. NorAM'd probably saved our sorry lives. Almost surely. But I was still so sticky with sweat it was hard to watch our thin column wind up the ravine in front of us, much less watch for enemies.

Nothing moved but us, at least as far as I could see. Not even the air. There had been wind the day the fire had raced towards us (I thought it was set against us, and a few others did, too, but no one in command agreed). The wind screamed through us again the day NorAM created the storm and set it loose on the fire. Everything felt hot, barren, and still.

It had been pretty here. The ground had been dotted with scrub and yellow flowers. Now it lay gray and hot and still. At least the heat must have scoured it free of nano-mines. I still half expected a pile of dangers to be headed our way, some scary franken-science thrown out from the illicit labs we were advancing on.

Alongside all of us, the dogs marched in lock-step, their metal feet occasionally sliding on bits of rock.

In front of me, Mario and Joe marched side by side, looking way too un-bothered by the sun.

Kris looked as melted as I felt. Bitch was a bit more cheerful than me, though. "Still no sign of life. We're going to make it."

"They could have sent UAVs."

She had the bad grace to laugh at me. "And ruined your fun?"

"UAVs don't die."

"They cost as much as we do."

"More." But people were still good for a lot of things that unmanned aircraft just weren't so good at. Opening doors. Assessing. Reading the fear in an enemy combatant's eyes.

The first few of our line had all reached a shadowed cleft between two low hills. I trudged up a scant incline near the end, next to Kris, exposed as hell.

As if they knew we'd been talking about them, the steady echoing thrum of copter blades came up from behind us.

I tensed.

"Safe!" Louis called from five people ahead of us. He meant it had told him it was ours, sharing the right codes in the right sequence. The dogs trusted it, too, clanking along without missing a beat. So maybe NorAM had decided to give us more help. Maybe they'd learned something. The UAV's body was the size of my head, the rotors a stack, the whole thing flying canted a bit forward so the tail seemed to reach for the sky. The sound of its flight made my shoulder blades itch. I squinted, the sun making the silver blades into diamonds too bright to stare at. Why now, instead of after we were closer to the lab?

Why so close to us? Why one?

Instinct finally kicked in, in spite of Louis's words. I dove sideways into Kris, tumbling her. Her eyes went wide but she said nothing, catching enough balance to scramble on all fours. Simon and Jillie reflexed after us.

Mario turned, mouth open, his eyes so dark I was sure he was about to bark at us for being scared little girls.

He never got any words out. Mario's hand flew up to his skull and came away slick and red and I could feel the heat of little machines racing through his body, the fear of them turning me soft and small inside.

He writhed and fell.

The four of us, me, and Kris and Rob and Jill, raced away like one. My dog, Hunter, slowed to stay beside me. I ran with a hand on

Hunter's broad, full back, wishing there was power and time to mount and race away. The big dog's metal skin felt hot to the touch. But then everything was hot, the sand, the dog, the air, my anger.

I didn't want to glance back toward Mario's body, but I did. Most of the line was down, the dogs on their sides, faces scarred with soot. Someone had managed to knock the silver copter out of the sky. My quick glance didn't say how many people from the front of the line had made it. If any.

The fear of things too small to see drove us a long way in spite of the sapping heat and the surreal burned and wetted and baked ground.

We regrouped behind a stand of rocks. Small cover, the rocks hot enough to burn hands where we touched them, tinged with silicates so they shimmered, big enough to throw shade if the sun weren't directly above us.

Jillie looked over at me, her face shocked. I checked the rest of the group. Eight had made it to the rocks. Eight people and eight bots, so sixteen. I checked what I'd been left with. Two new recruits, the speed of death thrumming through them so deeply fear seemed to leak from their sweaty, dirty pores. Jillie and a thin boy from Seattle who leaned over, puking. The scientist. The two trainers, busy already, checking the metal dogs for damage, probably glad as hell to have something to do. Kris, the ever optimistic and bitchy. Simon, who was only happy when he was actually fighting, who got an orgasmic look on his face in hand-to-hand, and yet wouldn't kill a spider if it landed on his mouth in the middle of the night. Thank god for Kris and Simon and the trainers. Maybe between us we could protect the two newbies.

Simon had already managed to climb up the rock pile in spite of the heat, peel his binoculars out of his pack, and look toward the carnage. I caught the shift in his uniform from ash gray to the tan of the rocks. He grunted softly from about five feet above me.

"What do you see?" I asked him.

He shook his head. "Stupidity."

"No shit. See any more copters?"

"Damn things are fast."

I pulled the handheld out of my pocket and swiped up the tracking chip info. Close-together green dots for us, dark for humans and light for robot dogs. Three more humans on the far side, two with fading vital signs. I whispered an apology to them since we couldn't even try and get there yet. Red death dots made a ragged line across the open spaces. I called for overhead pictures. I got back two-inch pixels, which was enough to see that everyone had died in place, and even the dogs had made no more than a few steps. They'd been targeted. The poison that killed people didn't kill robots. So whoever sent the UAV knew who and what was coming for them.

Illegal nano for sure, scattered by an illegal UAV. NorAM would tell—I breathed in deep, re-thinking who was left—NorAM would tell *me* more once they analyzed the info.

Shit.

I did want command. But not now, and not here.

NorAM would have the same information I had, except maybe our condition. We'd lost two of the scientist embeds, but we still had one left. Alissa Frietag, a small woman with twice the strength she appeared to have, and a fierce determination to get into the labs. I stared at her for a moment, assessing. Small, so thin I would be able to wrap my hands around her waist with only a little effort. She looked pissed off instead of scared.

Good. So all we had to do was protect Alissa, get into the well-defended lab, and give her some time to assess it before we destroyed it. Yep, that should be easy.

I typed my message to NorAM. *We're okay. Sci1 looks fierce. We need cover.*

Or to withdraw, but I didn't have to tell them that. They knew. If we withdrew, GenGreen would simply destroy everything and smile and invite us and a bunch of media in the front door just in time to see a lab devoted to feeding the starving. We didn't want to leave them time for that. Other NorAM forces had blocked the roads out. Of course, we could just get them from the air. But people up the chain wanted the lab intact. Apparently there was some thing or knowledge so valuable that we weren't willing to just blow it up and move on.

I'd half expected we'd be recalled within a day of starting out. The goal had been to come in unnoticed, but the UAV screamed that GenGreen and its private armies had noticed us. The fact that our code was compromised suggested they'd also paid off someone. With luck, that would be a dead rat from our group, but more likely it was someone else inside NorAM.

I scanned the horizon again. Listened. No wind. No rotor blades. Puking boy had stopped hacking and spitting.

Damnit. Time to lead.

"Everybody gather up."

Simon started to clamber down the rock, but I gestured for him to stay. He'd be able to hear me from up there. The dog handlers got the big bots to stand and look at me, too, cocking their not dog-like heads sideways at me in a dog-like motion. Good. At least someone had a sense of humor.

I glanced down at my handheld. The screen was still blank.

"You all okay?"

I looked them each in the eye. At least they all looked back at me. Five women including me, three guys. The men were Simon, Scott of the weak stomach, and one of the two dog trainers, John. Then me, Kris the steady and bright, Jillie, Alissa Frietag the scientist, and the other dog trainer, a woman named Paulette.

The communit buzzed in my hand. I glanced down and saw what I expected. I looked back at the group. "Orders are to keep going, move more evasively, get to the lab. They'll send in some cover and some help after we get it secure."

"Ma'am."

"Scott?"

"Just us. To take the whole place?"

I nodded. "What supplies do we have?"

John spoke a litany he'd pretty clearly memorized. "Water. Food. Handhelds. First Aid. Light. Blankets. "

Crap. I glanced at Paulette, who stood with one hand on her robot's head as if it were flesh and blood. She swallowed. "The same."

So we were eight for eight on supplies and zero for zero on weapons? We wouldn't starve while we were destroying an enemy lab with our bare hands. Good thing.

John must have seen the look on my face. "We do have some rockets and launchers, and a few mines."

"Our handguns," I added. "And the knives on our belts. Any useful solar?"

Paulette shifted on her feet, swaying. "Not enough for the dogs." Her face had gone white. "Enough for us."

Jillie's eyes widened and she looked like she was about ten and desperate for a friend. I knew what she was thinking. That we'd need to raid the supplies on the other dogs. I didn't look directly at her, but I made sure I could see her relax when I said, "We're not going out there." Stray microbots could kill us as easily as they'd killed everyone else. It might be slower without a direct hit, but three of the damned things in your soft tissue guaranteed death. There would be no recovery of the other dogs or their packs, or anything else. Not until NorAM could send containment suits out. Not today.

I updated NorAM with our status, and requested a storm.

They suggested quite formally that we do without.

I counter-suggested quite formally that without power we would die before we got the job done instead of while we were doing the job.

I stood still, staring at the screen, waiting for them to discuss amongst themselves and then get back to me. I was half hoping they'd say no and decide we could go back or wait for more people and stuff or something.

Instead, they answered way too fast. They promised lightning.

Whatever was in that lab mattered to them. I swallowed. I'd been trained. I'd even succeeded in a live exercise. And out of our group, I was the only one still alive and rated for it. I glanced at the dog handlers. "We do have the laser?"

John nodded, his eyes gleaming a bit.

I surveyed the group. "We are going to crack the sky and bring home the power."

Allisa's tongue darted out between her full lips, and she looked like she was about to be seated at a banquet table. Jillie's eyes widened again, and the trainers glanced at the dogs. Kris and Simon, who knew the calculus, nodded.

We had orders to go forward, so no turning tail. Probably wouldn't work anyway, since GenGreen would follow us and keep whatever they were protecting at the level of rumor. We could go forward. Would. We carried the worst weapons on us—some as small as the ones GenGreen just killed most of us with. But we would need power to eat and drink and scatter signal around, power to feed the tiny weapons, power to control the lab. Stored power, available on demand.

In addition to the power to get there.

That had been on the other dogs, along with the more power-hungry of the weapons. But we'd run them a long way to get here. The robotic dogs were stronger than us by far, faster, fleeter if less graceful. But when we ran out of juice, we just reached into our will and found more. When robots ran dry, they stopped.

So be it.

Death or a miracle.

"Rest. Simon and I will take a watch."

They nodded, the old hands falling almost immediately to the ground, accepting rest. Jillie and Scott followed. Alissa Frietag leaned back against the stones, closing her eyes and whispering under her breath.

I clambered up beside Simon and sat looking out over our distant dead and toward the buried lab. The very idea of it made me feel small and fragile even if I was one-sixty with my boots on and no real fat. Bulky for a girl. We were all fragile when it came to nano and biologicals and whatever else GenGreen and its partners were dreaming up to protect their solution for the world from the combined North American Government, which had a different one. The NorAM populace had voted almost as one from the wet northern reaches of Canada to the sweltering, hurricane slapped coasts of the Yucatán. They'd said to stop intervening, preferring to take their chances with nature than to trust the multinationals.

There was no money in letting nature balance itself. Hence the science wars, and this small battle.

The dead between us and the next hill attested to the seriousness of this small battle. Our own corporations, or at least multis born here, killing us. Assholes. I swore I'd do my best. Both to kill the big scary lab and to stay alive.

I was gonna miss Mario, even if he was a loudmouthed idiot.

Simon opened the conversation. "This sucks."

"Yep." And that closed the conversation.

We sat close to each other, taking comfort in the silence of long friendship. We'd been on three attacks like this before, and come back from all of them. I wasn't so sure this time, but no soldier says those things to another. Instead, we watched the empty blue sky and baked quietly on the rock, the sun glinting on the great field of ash that surrounded us.

NorAM interrupted to tell me the others had all died. No one left on the far ridge. I imagined it. One of the dots had been healthy. They'd watched the others die, gotten too close. Prayed to be safe. Maybe they'd even donned their protective suit, the crappy one that came in all our belts. But something too small to see and big enough to kill them had gotten in anyway. It made me feel cold even in the punishing heat.

The rocks started throwing longer shadows. Simon and I traded with Kris and Scott. I wiped the sweat from my face and felt sure the heat would keep me fitful and maybe even awake.

A fat warm glob of rain struck me on the cheek and I shook awake, swinging my head like an animal. Wind cooled the air. Dark, roiling cumulonimbus clouds towered overhead, the front edge of them splitting the sky like angry foam, blue, then gray, white above, tinged gold by the setting sun.

Kris looked down at me. "Almost ready?"

"Are they?"

I had given her my comm. She shaded the screen with her hand and said "Forty minutes."

I took five minutes to perform routine body maintenance functions, and five more to verify that everyone else did the same. I gathered the humans all into formation, packs at their side and ready, each with a weapon in hand.

The dog handlers had already chosen John's dog for the first receptacle in line. I didn't ask how he'd drawn the risky straw. Just thanked him for being ready.

At least there was so much wind I didn't need a posted UAV watcher any more. Anything over about twenty miles an hour tended to slam them off course, into the ground, or both. I was willing to bet the occasional gust was past the twenty mile an hour mark. In fact, there was a serious whine in the part of the wind that passed up above us. Damn NorAM physics jocks.

John handed me the launcher.

"Did you name your dog?" I asked.

He swallowed. "Max, sir. Ma'am."

His confusion felt almost touching. John passed Max's hand controls to me, and me and the metal dog walked away from the group, as far out into the open as we could get. Wind tore at my shirt.

All the blue had been blown out of the sky.

Max came to my waist, with four legs that had two joints each, and a hollow tail. His belly was big, and right now all that it held was empty space and some magic built from Tesla's dreams and our materials. Too classified for me to get the details, and too new to be completely sure it would work.

Lightning slammed upward from the ridge we had been going to, would go toward again soon. Rain sheeted down, sharpening the smell of the charred soil.

John and Paulette called out the other dogs, lining them up one after the other, tails in mouths, a long string of conductivity. Hunter was last. John said something to Max, and the big robot tilted its ugly black head back and opened its jaws. Someone had painted sharp teeth like a shark's onto the dull gripping surfaces.

John handed me dark goggles. I slid them on, the world almost black, John now a silhouette. He handed me a long slender rod with a firing pin on the outside. The laser gun felt heavier than I remembered, harder to manage. I pointed it up at the roiling clouds, ignoring the rain that nearly blinded me.

The two trainers raced to the rocks to join Simon and the others.

I pulled the trigger and nothing happened.

I checked. The gun worked. The laser beams shot fast as lightning itself into the clouds, but invisible. The clouds had simply ignored my call, my act, the light.

They had to be ready, to be almost pregnant with charge.

I giggled, absurdly, soaking wet and wondering if the storm were a lover I'd just tried to drive to premature ejaculation.

The laser had enough power for three charges. I'd wasted one. I took a deep breath and stared up into the rain and the dark boiling clouds and smelled the damp, charred air.

Another lightning bolt flashed down near the rocks and thunder made me cringe and cover my head.

My timing was still off.

Practice for this had been controlled. The storms had been smaller. I closed my eyes, let the water fall on the goggles. Braced. Waited. Fired.

I opened my eyes.

Thunder smacked again.

White light surrounded me, the world turned to day in spite of the lenses between my eyes and the bolt. Max stood unmoved but full, and I had the briefest glimpse of the dog with light pouring out of every hole in its body, out through its tail into the other dogs, a line of lightning eaters.

Then I couldn't see, and all I felt was a deep thrumming in my body, and a sharp pain behind the eyes. I shook, relieved and scared and pissed off as well, mad at NorAM and GenGreen and the whole difficult, warring world. The thunder kept rolling away from me, hiding any other noises.

John's voice, a whoop. "We did it! You did it!"

Someone took the laser gun from my hands. Simon spoke. "I'm taking off the goggles. Keep your eyes closed."

I felt them slide away.

"Look at me."

His face existed. Thank god. I could see, and what I saw was Simon grinning, ear to ear. "Now what, Chief?"

I swallowed and stood up, my legs shaky, the back of my head still shocky mushy and pain-wracked. Nothing good was easy. Unless we called it again, the lightning would move on. We had what we needed from it, and all that was left was danger. We could wait it out. "Is everyone here?"

Simon nodded. I verified he was right. They looked shocked and bewildered. Some soldiers. But at least everyone had their packs. "You're a damn good second," I whispered to him, and then I stood up and addressed everyone else. "By the time I finish this briefing, the worst of the storm will have moved on, and we'll go take the lab. We're going to ride in there."

Scott's eyes widened. "On the dogs?"

"No. On each other." Dingbat. But then he was in as much danger as the rest of us. Maybe more for being wet behind the ears. Whatever was in the lab had better be good. "We're moving light and fast, following the storm, hoping to take them by surprise. We'll have enough power to get there on the bots. I don't know if we'll get back that way or if we'll walk." Which meant I didn't know how much power we'd have on the way back. Once we succeeded—if we succeeded—NorAM wasn't going to burn more climate credits on getting back the easy way, not unless we had something they wanted fast. That was an idea. I looked back at them. "The extra supplies are still here. We meet back here. Has everyone marked this on their maps?"

Jillie looked sheepish and fiddled with her wrist unit until she could nod and say, "Yes," just like everyone else had.

I tested communications, made sure we could all hear and speak to each other. "Use voice when you can," I reminded them. "Security."

Lightning fell again, far away now, a thin streak that forked in three places and was gone. I waited for the thunder to die down and then I said, "All right. Go."

We skirted the dead, going so wide we missed the ravine. Better to add ten minutes than pick up some windblown death. On the smooth ground, the dogs had pretty even gaits, about like a horse walking. Over hills or rocks, they rocked and lurched, irritating my still-sharp head and scraping my inner thighs. There were reasons we don't usually ride the damned things. Plenty of bots had been designed to carry soldiers, but the pack dogs like these had it as a second priority. Or maybe a third or fourth.

It hurt.

I had ridden the dogs in the wild, but Jillie and Scott had only mounted in training exercises. They managed, but only because I paired them each up with a trainer. Behind them, Kris and I rode together. Simon protected Alissa, the pair of them in front of us and off to the side.

For the first hour, we followed the storm. Dusk yellowed the lagging edge of the clouds, and Alissa pointed out a fresh storm behind us, maybe five miles away. "Backup?" she screamed the question to me over the wind and the rain and the space between us.

I shrugged. Sometimes weathering made more weather, as if sun or wind or rain called to its own kind. If it was a NorAM storm, they hadn't told me. But then maybe they wouldn't. Maybe we'd wake up in the morning to August snow. If we made it to morning.

As we neared the top of a long, low hill, two huge figures rose up. Bipedal, metal, too thin to be manned. Legs like tree trunks and torsos like limbs, this and wiry and fast. Six arms, or maybe more. They held rocks in each hand.

I ducked.

Hunter feinted right under me, then left.

Rocks landed on either side of us.

Voices screeched in my ear. Too many to make sense of.

Alissa gripped her dog's ears, which held its head down.

"Let go!" I screamed at her. "Hold its neck. Handholds."

Just as she let go, a rock the size of her head pounded into the ground at her dog's feet and the robot dog rose up on just its hind feet, striking the ground with its tail to help balance. Alissa threw her weight backward instead of forward and landed with a hard thump on her butt, immediately twisting away from the dog.

A rock fell between the scientist and the robot dog.

It stepped back, avoiding the rock, programmed to stay with its handler.

I charged her attacker, drawing two of its rocks toward me. It was agile enough to pick another rock up as it threw two at me. So a brain for each hand? My immediate reaction was to go eye for an eye. Sometimes old-fashioned weapons are just fine, and since I'd never even seen a rumor of a six-armed rock-throwing robot, this couldn't be far out of beta. By the time I'd pulled the pin, the bot had hit Alissa's dog in the torso, leaving a dent. It stood over her small form. She lay curled under its broad belly in a fetal position.

Well, I'd probably have gone fetal, too.

I threw the grenade and watched it arc up toward the robot. I turned away, hoping Alissa was smart enough to cover her face.

Hunter shied, if that's what you call evasive actions in a robotic dog the size of a small horse.

After the initial explosion, I heard metal screech and turned to look. A leg complete with a long string of cables that must have pulled loose from inside the robot lay behind us, evidence there had been something for Hunter to avoid.

A rock slammed into us, hitting a glancing blow to my thigh. Hunter took the blow, moving with it, taking three fast steps like those daisy steps from aerobics. I managed to hold on. My thigh hurt like hell. I tested and my leg bent normally if I forced it. No telling if I could put weight on it.

Wind had blown the wet ash clear enough for me to make out the robot, no longer standing, but with at least two working arms.

No time to look around and see what else was happening. I raced to Alissa's side and barked at her, "Stand up!"

She looked up at me with a face streaked with tears and ash, but she nodded and pushed herself to standing. She reached for the holds to mount.

"No. Use it as a shield and run."

Alissa stood blinking at me with shocky eyes for just a second before she understood what I meant and started heading away from the now-stationary rock-thrower, keeping the robot dog between her and the damaged enemy.

I looked for the other robot. Simon or Kris had done a better job than I had, and it lay inert.

I called for everyone to come here, counting as they appeared. John and Jillie, John with one arm hanging and a bruised cheek. Jillie looking like hell but smiling. I hoped it was happiness at being alive and not something more manic.

Kris and Simon rode in from the left, Simon looking ecstatic. I knew where his happiness came from. He must have been the one to bring the bot down. If this had been the middle ages and the six-armed bot a dragon, Simon is the guy who would have raced toward it on a black charger, whirling his sword above his head. His voice blossomed in my ear. "If that's all they have, we're okay."

I suspected we wouldn't be that lucky. "Paulette? Scott?"

No answer. Everyone else had the discipline to keep silent while I called for them.

Finally, Scott's voice. "She's hurt. My robot died."

"Are you okay?" I asked, grateful he didn't seem as shaken as he had the day before.

"Yes."

"How badly hurt is Paulette?"

"I think her leg's broken."

Thank god. I'd been afraid of something worse. "Do you remember field medicine?"

"I think so."

"Is Paulette conscious?"

"Yes."

"She can talk you through."

He sounded shaky as he said, "Okay."

Simon broke in. "Hurry up. There's another storm coming."

I'd almost forgotten that. The sky was darker, but it was also later in the day. The wind came up again, only this time at our backs. The lab was close.

"Scott," I said. "Good luck." And then to the others. "Group around me."

I still had no clear idea how six of us were going to get into a secret GenGreen lab. There had to be better defenses than what we'd seen so far. I took time to report in. NorAM was quick to respond. "Keep going. There are reinforcements coming."

I glanced up over my shoulder. "Is that our storm?"

"Get Alissa to the lab."

"I'll do my best." I closed my communit. Aye, aye, sir. Thanks for doing the impossible so far, and keep on going. Of course, I'd signed up for it. On purpose.

Lighting split the sky behind us, followed a few seconds later by thunder. Maybe they sent the storm just to drive us. Hopefully Paulette and Scott would be okay. "Let's go!"

The dogs had the GPS data, and this close, there wasn't much routing I had to do. The last bit of the journey was mostly a balancing act trying to stick to Hunter in spite of my head and my thigh. Rain made the broad backs of the dogs slippery as hell.

Kris did fall off once.

We got close enough I started watching for the fence.

NorAM messaged us all to turn around and look the other way. Them talking in our ears was a security risk of the first order and so I turned my head even before telling Hunter to turn. Looking up and down the small line of us left, I was pleased to note everyone had understood the order.

Light pinned us bright and blind. Then again. Flash. Wind, or maybe the electricity of what must be simultaneous lightning bolts, lifted and twisted the stray hairs around my face. Flash. Thunder boomed, a deep cracking sound as if the sky had been hit with the hammer of the god. More noise poured through right above us, enveloping us, making it impossible to talk.

We stood, still looking away. I hadn't known they could do that. *We* could do that. Another ratchet up in the weather wars.

It scared me as much as the lab.

NorAM's voice again. "The fences are all fried. The building's main security is probably off, but there may be generator power. Go, now. Copters will be along. Ground troops are arriving now."

Another scary thing. "Did you catch the traitor?"

"Yes."

Hopefully there was only one. "Wait for orders," the NorAM dispatcher said, enough happiness in her voice that I guessed whatever the lightning and the new troops were supposed to do was getting done.

I glanced over at Alissa. "Are you okay?"

"I will be." She still looked fierce. Like the scientist in a television show I used to love that chased down Japanese whale boats. Something to be said for fierce scientists. Our back was still to the lab and the conflict, and we watched a sliver of black cloudless sky slowly grow as the storm above us blew further east. From time to time we heard thunder in the distance.

It had stopped raining by the time they called for us. I smiled at the look on some of the NorAM shock troop faces and I brought Alissa Freitag into the compound on top of a wet, banged-up robot that barely resembled a dog. I had no mirror, but I'm sure we looked like wild women, rain and sun and wind and thunder drenched, wild-eyes, and fierce.

I kind of liked the picture that drew for me.

Two scientists had come in via the road, and been protected in the back until the lab's defenses were neutralized. NorAM replacing what we'd lost, and probably unhappy about it. But then they'd wanted us to be entirely stealth. Which is probably why so many died. Making sure of success, I supposed. Not that I got to make high-level battle plans or even hear what data went into them. It felt good to have done my part, and that all of the soldiers who had escaped with me were alive. And I liked seeing Alissa run up to the others and start organizing immediately, no question, as if she were the field commander among the scientists.

Maybe she was.

John and Jillie and me attended to the robots and set them charging. After about twenty minutes, a small crew returned with Scott and Paulette. I complimented Scott on a decent job of field-bandaging, and he blushed.

Just as we were about to leave, Alissa came up to me, almost bouncy. No—more than that. Electric with excitement. Her eyes were shining as she said, "Thank you. You have no idea how important it was that you got me here."

"What did you find?"

"Bees."

I must have looked stupid. I had been expecting a breeding farm for human organs or something else scary. "Bees?"

"Genetically changed to kill the few remaining regular bees, and then they would have died out. Would have killed off the whole honeybee line of pollinators. At least that's what they were trying to do."

"Bees were worth all that?" I meant the people dying, the scientists dying, the robots with the rocks, all of it.

She was more direct than me. "The deaths? Yes. GenGreen wants to force us to depend on their products."

I swallowed and watched her, hoping I'd see her again somewhere besides on television. I could get into helping scrappy scientists save bees. Even if I wasn't quite sure of our methods either. But thunder and lightning and bad weather were the slow way to kill the bees. If I understood what Alissa was saying, we had helped stop a fast way. And even I knew that had become the game. Fight the cancers day by day and hope the body finds remission.

"Are you supposed to tell me this?"

Her sharp brown eyes shone with mischief as she said, "I believe in the power of information."

"And I believe in the power of science."

She shook her head. "Don't. Science is on both sides of this."

I winced. "You're right. Maybe that's why I'm a soldier and you're a scientist."

"And maybe you just saved a lot of the heirloom food left."

We napped in a pile of soldiers and robots until dawn. Alissa said nothing else to me, and NorAM gave no more comment than, "Well done. Come home." As I led my severely reduced crew out of the lab and headed us home, I realized that I felt more sure of our side than I had before we got into the lab. I remembered the power of calling down the lightning and splitting open the sky just for us to continue a war, and I hoped I wouldn't have to do that again. I let us stay mounted until we were out of sight, and then I gave the order to stand down and walk. Our backsides would get home in better shape that way, and besides, the sun had already warmed the air, and a light breeze plucked at my uniform.

STORY NOTES

The idea for the "The Robot's Girl" came out of a one paragraph article about Japan using robots to watch children. I have been fascinated with robots for some time, and I am completely certain that humanoid robots are coming shortly. We will soon see them in roles often reserved for humans. They will be our friends, our nurses, our cleaners, and out staff. In some cases, they may be our bosses or our teachers. I must admit, I'm pretty happy that at this moment the only working robot we own is our vacuum cleaner. We've named it Jake. But I'm certain more are already planning an assault on my life.

"Savant Songs" came from two things. I'm interested in high-functioning autistic spectrums. So much brilliance and so much tragedy. The literal science text for this story was "A Brief History of Time," by Stephen Hawking, which is where I first understood the concept of mbranes. I'd read about them before, but Hawking made them accessible to my brain, which is less brilliant than my character Elsa's. Lastly, I wrote this in response to a challenge from my writing group. I was having trouble getting as much emotion as I wanted into stories and so someone suggested I write a story where the emotion just went over the top. I felt like I was writing a soap opera with this story. It was the first of my stories to be reprinted in any form of Year's Best anthology. The story about the writing group challenge has become one of my go-to teaching stories.

"Riding in Mexico" was written specifically for editor Jetse DeVries. Jetse challenged the entire science fiction community to write optimistic science fiction set in other countries—he wanted diversity and hope together. It was a brilliant call to arms for all of us, and lifted the whole genre for a year or so as the stories he didn't buy made it into other markets. The brilliant anthology *Shine* came from that call, and *Daybreak* was the companion webzine.

"The War of the Flowers" came out in *Strange Horizons*, in January, 2004. It's one of the earliest pieces of work that I included in this collection. I had just read *Snowcrash*, and had become interested in the joys and dangers of fully virtual worlds. I would write it better today, but it's not too bad as an awkward teenager of a story, and it's about an awkward teenager's mistake, so it seemed all right.

"Trainer of Whales" came out in an anthology called *The Future We Wish We Had*. The idea for this one came early. I suspect I was only nine or ten when I did a school project on living underwater. I remember creating space bubbles out of flour glue and painting them with some of my mom's craft paint.

"Star of Humanity" appears here for the first time. The spark for this story came from Eli Pariser's 2011 TED talk "Beware of Online Filter Bubbles."

"My Father's Singularity" first appeared in *Clarkesworld*, June 2010, edited by Neil Clarke. I had just bought my first iPad keyboard, and I decided to spend about an hour practicing. That practice yielded this story. Strange. It also made it into a Year's Best. When you've written enough stories, sometimes one sneaks up on you.

I started my writing career with a great gift—a mentor. Larry Niven was already a hero of mine before I met him; I had been reading his work for years. "The Trellis" is one of my favorite stories from the years I spent writing with Larry, who is sweet and brilliant and generous. I learned a lot from him.

"Second Shift" is a love story.

"Blood Bonds" was a story I wrote and couldn't sell. I loved it. I sent it out over and over and probably garnered twenty rejections.

Then I redrafted it from start to finish and it sold on its next trip out. There you go. Another free writing lesson.

"The Hebras and the Demons and the Damned" and "The Street of All Designs" are both set in the worlds of my first solo series. Hopefully they'll tempt you into exploring those novels.

I love short fiction. Really short fiction. To me, flash is like poetry. "My Grandfather's River" was inspired by Michael Fay's transect of the Congo. I heard him talk at an international conference of people using ESRI's Geographic Information System's software, and after his talk I sat outside on the steps of the San Diego convention center and thought for quite a long time. I may have written the story that night.

"Tea with Jillian" is more fun with robots.

"For the Love of Mechanical Minds" is fun with AI.

"Entropy and Emergence" appears here for the first time. It's a disturbing little story. Really, it's quite weird. One of the beautiful things about flash fiction is that you can be weird in it. After all, if a reader flees, they only miss a few hundred words.

"Alien Graveyards" is another story about love in the future. I have a feeling we'll need it. Love, that is.

"A Hand and Honor" was written before I'd ever heard of Oscar Pistorus. That's all I have to say about that. :)

"Mind Expeditions" is really a bit of military fiction, and so I chose it to end the flash fiction section with, since it's a decent transition into my military fiction. I like the way its nine hundred or so words explore the realities of a war fought remotely.

"For the Love of Metal Dogs" and "Cracking the Sky" were both requested by Mike McPhail and Daniel Ackley-McPhail for the fabulous anthology series "Defending the Future" out from Dark Quest books. I am not a soldier, and never have been. I'm kind of a pacifist;

I write about wars in my books to illustrate how downright awful they really are. But I did know a *lot* of Vietnam vets. Some of the last vets back from Vietnam were the right age for me to date, or worked with me, or went to school with me. One of my best teachers was a Vietnam veteran named Tim "Touches the Earth" Toohey, who has passed beyond his pain now. I remember how his experiences in war shaped almost all of his demons and helped create the deep spiritual beauty that he shared with so many of us. No matter what we think of those who start wars, it's important to honor those who serve in them, and to respect what they lose for us.

ABOUT THE AUTHOR

Brenda Cooper is a technology professional, a science fiction writer and a futurist. Her most recent novel is *Edge of Dark*, from Pyr. Also from Pyr, the duology *The Creative Fire* and *Diamond Deep*. Brenda has four science fiction novels out with Tor books: *The Silver Ship and the Sea*, its sequels, *Reading the Wind* and *Wings of Creation*, and in collaboration with Larry Niven, *Building Harlequin's Moon*. She also has a stand-alone historical fantasy/sf mashup from Prime, *Mayan December*. Brenda's short fiction has appeared in *Nature, Analog, Asimov's, Strange Horizons, The Salal Review*, and multiple anthologies.

PUBLICATION NOTES

"The Robot's Girl" first appeared in *Analog*, © April, 2010, edited by Stan Schmidt | "Savant Songs" first appeared in *Analog*, © December 2004, edited by Stan Schmidt; shortlisted for the Sturgeon Award in 2005; reprinted in *Year's Best SF 10*, edited by David Hartwell and Kathryn Cramer | "Riding in Mexico" first appeared in *Daybreak Magazine*, © Feb 2010, edited by Jetse DeVries | "The War of the Flowers" first appeared in *Strange Horizons*, © January, 2004 | "Trainer of Whales" first appeared in *The Future We Wish We Had*, © 2007, edited by Martin Greenberg and Rebecca Lickiss | "Star of Humanity" © 2015 appears here for the first time | "My Father's Singularity" first appeared in *Clarkesworld*, © June 2010, edited by Neil Clarke | "The Trellis" with Larry Niven first appeared in *Analog*, © November 2003, edited by Stan Schmidt | "Second Shift" first appeared in *Love and Rockets*, © 2010, edited by Martin Greenberg and Kerrie Hughes | "Blood Bonds" first appeared in *The Solaris Book of New Science Fiction Volume 2*, © 2008, edited by George Mann | "The Hebras and the Demons and the Damned" first appeared in *Analog*, © December 2010, edited by Stan Schmidt; reprinted in *Year's Best SF 16*, edited by David Hartwell and Kathryn Cramer | "The Street of All Designs" was first published on TheFiveWorlds.com, © 2009 | "My Grandfather's River" first appeared in *Nature Magazine*, Nature 442. © August 2006, edited by Henry Gee; reprinted in *River*, edited by Alma Alexander; reprinted in *Futures from Nature*, edited by Henry Gee | "Tea with Jillian" first appeared in *Nature Magazine*, Nature 480, © December 2011; reprinted in *Nature Futures 2*, edited by Colin Sullivan and Henry Gee | "For the Love of Mechanical Minds" first appeared in *Nature Magazine*, Nature 457, © February 2009; available as an audio podcast at *Starship Sofa Aural Delights No 162*. | "Entropy and Emergence" © 2015, appears here for the first time | "Alien Graveyards" first appeared in *Alien Skin*, © 2007 | "A Hand and Honor" first appeared in *Nature Magazine*, Nature 450, © November 2007; also available as an audio podcast at *Starship Sofa* in Episode 91 | "Mind Expeditions" first appeared in *Nature Magazine*, Nature 465, © May 2010 | "For the Love of Metal Dogs" first appeared in *Dogs of War*, © 2013, edited by Mike McPhail | "Cracking the Sky" first appeared in *No Man's Land*, © 2011, edited by Mike McPhail.

OTHER TITLES FROM FAIRWOOD PRESS

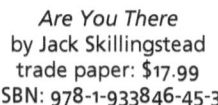

www.ingramcontent.com/pod-product-compliance
Lightning Source LLC
Chambersburg PA
CBHW060603030726
47498CB00005B/1518